To Cheri

I hope you enjoy
"The Destiny Project"!!

# THE DESTINY PROJECT

James Wharton

To Carol,

It was Destiny.

## ACKNOWLEDGEMENTS

Special thanks to Jordan Mack for her help in editing this novel. Many thanks to Carl Earl for his cover design.

"Fate, the ruler of all men, is born of past events which dictate the future. To travel through centuries and remake the past is to rule fate and command the destiny of all."

Edmund, Duke of Bramshire, 1217-1281

# PART ONE

# 1

524 A.D.  Ravenna, Italy
Seat of Power of Theodoric King of the Ostrogoths
Senate Chamber

"The Senate recognizes the Magister Officiorum of our benevolent ruler King Theodoric the Great." Anicius Boethius knew these words were his death sentence. As Boethius rose to walk to the speaker's area he reflected on how he had arrived at this point.

Born in Rome in 475, Boethius was educated in Athens and excelled as a scholar.  Because of his extensive knowledge, he was viewed with great respect by his contemporaries. King Theodoric also recognized Boethius' genius and appointed him Magister Officiorum (chief of courts) in 510 A.D.

The Roman Empire had collapsed. Conspiracies and political intrigues were rampant throughout the Ostrogoth Empire. And Boethius had made enemies. Boethius found himself caught up in the quarrel between the Church of Rome and the Church of Constantinople. Today he would defend his friend Albinus who was accused of treason for conspiring with the Byzantine ruler Justinian I. Boethius knew the charges were false, and by aligning himself with Albinus, he risked losing his position and wealth.

That morning his wife Rusticiana and his sons Symmachus and Boethius pleaded with him not to address the Senate. However Boethius considered the defense of Albinus a point of honor.

Anicius Boethius walked to the center speaker's area of the Senate floor. He spoke elegantly for over one hour. The Senators, however, were not interested in honor or the innocence of Albinus.

They were concerned only with their own survival as Theodoric had begun executing high-ranking members of his government on similar charges of treason. This was not the time to make points of honor. The Senate would sacrifice Albinus to save themselves. Boethius was not willing to do so.

Boethius concluded his defense by saying, "If Albinus is guilty of treason I too am guilty of treason, as is this entire Senate Body." Boethius walked through a now silent Senate chamber toward the door. As he passed Cassiodorous, Theodoric's trusted consul, Boethius nodded. During his speech he had noticed Cassiodorous taking notes. Boethius knew these notes would be delivered to the king.

Later that day he was arrested and brought before Theodoric.

"My old friend," said Theodoric, "you have presented me with a dilemma. While I also believe Albinus is innocent, I am under great pressure from other powerful men. Albinus shall be executed regardless of his innocence. And now you may suffer the same fate."

"I should rather die an honorable man than live as a coward," replied Boethius. "But we both know my defense of Albinus is not the real reason you have brought me here, my King. It is only a pretext for your arresting me."

Theodoric laughed for a moment but his smile quickly faded and his face took on a somber expression. "Need I remind you that as your king I do not need an excuse to bring you here," he replied sternly.

"We both know what you want, my King," Boethius answered.

"Then why do you refuse to surrender it?" King Theodoric asked.

"Because what you want does not exist," Boethius replied. "The Wheel of Destiny is merely a concept, a philosophical theory I teach my students. I simply describe history as a wheel that turns and causes the fortunes of men and empires to rise and fall. It is only one of many concepts I teach."

"You have told me that before, Boethius, but my patience is wearing thin. We both know the Wheel of Destiny is an actual device, a tool which has been used to control the destiny of men and countries. That fact is supported by ancient documents carried from the burning Library of Alexandria. And you also know that."

"I dispute those documents," replied Boethius.

"I do not believe you," Theodoric said sternly. "You are in possession of the Wheel of Destiny and I must have it today. What is your answer to your king's demand?"

"I cannot give you what does not exist, sir" replied Boethius.

"Very well, then," countered Theodoric, regaining his composure. "You shall be taken to Pavia to be imprisoned until you decide to give me what I demand. You shall be tortured each day until you comply with your king's wishes."

As Theodoric ordered, Boethius was severely tortured and suffered greatly. But he would never admit to Theodoric that a Wheel of Destiny actually existed. In final frustration, Theodoric watched as Boethius was beaten to death with clubs in 525 A.D.


In 1327 the tomb of Boethius' friend, Albinus, was unearthed and an important manuscript was discovered in the crypt. The manuscript stated the Wheel of Destiny was an actual device, just as Theodoric had believed, and it could be used to alter history. Boethius would not give the Wheel of Destiny to King Theodoric because he did not trust him and knew he would not use the device wisely.

The manuscript further stated that Boethius came into possession of the Wheel of Destiny in 520 during a visit to the town of Casinum (now Cassino, Italy). It was there he met a woman of great wealth, Ummidia Quadratilla. Boethius was astonished that she knew a great deal about him and that he was an honorable man. It was she that gave Boethius the Wheel of Destiny. She told Boethius the wheel had been created by ancient mathematicians and had been taken from the great Library of Alexandria when it burned in 48 B.C. She also told Boethius to take great caution in using the wheel and she departed.

The following day Boethius inquired of his host, the local governor Herennius Balbus, where he might find the woman. Balbus accompanied Boethius to a nearby courtyard and a majestic stone mausoleum. It was the burial site of Ummidia Quadratilla who had died over four hundred years earlier. It was then Boethius realized the power of the wheel. Ummidia Quadratilla had travelled forward in time to give Boethius the Wheel of Destiny.

Clerical scholars in the Middle Ages believed Boethius' claim that history was controlled by a Wheel of Destiny was sacrilegious and should not be interpreted literally. They burned the manuscript and continued to translate Boethius' notion of the Wheel of Destiny strictly as a philosophical theory. They stated the Albinus Manuscript had been improperly translated and never claimed there was an actual Wheel of Destiny that could somehow change history.

As time passed the Albinus Manuscript was largely forgotten. Historians assumed that if there actually was a so called Wheel of Destiny the clerical scholars were correct in concluding it would simply be an artifact which stated Boethius' philosophy of history. Its only value would lie in the additional academic information it might reveal about Boethius' teachings.

But the question that was never answered was this: if the Wheel of Destiny did exist and was merely a harmless academic teaching device, why did Boethius choose a torturous death rather than simply surrender it to Theodoric?

# 2

June 7, 1897     Pavia, Northern Italy

"Sir, please excuse me," the waiter said.

"Yes, of course. What is it Mario?"

"I am so sorry to interrupt your dinner, Dr. Walpole. But there is a man, sir, a local artist. He says it is most urgent that he see you. I told him your interest is ancient vases and sculptures and you are not looking for paintings, but he insists."

"I'm just about finished, Mario," Dr. Darius Walpole replied. "Tell the man he may join me. And, could you please bring me another glass of that excellent wine?"

"Yes sir. And sir, this man is ill kempt and unshaven. He has a bad odor."

Dr. Walpole laughed as Mario walked out of the small dining room of the River Inn, a modest but cozy hotel twenty miles from Pavia, Italy. In a few moments Mario returned with the artist who was so insistent on seeing him.

Mario was right, Walpole reflected as the man sat down. This fellow was poorly dressed and obviously spent little time on his grooming. "Thank you for agreeing to speak with me, Dr.Walpole," the man said. "Might I trouble you for a drink?"

"Certainly. It's no trouble at all," replied Walpole. "Mario, please bring a drink for this gentleman."

"Right away, Dr. Walpole," answered Mario, rolling his eyes.

"Thank you, sir. You are indeed a gentleman yourself," the man said. "My name is Ermanno Sacri. I am an artist."

Walpole extended his hand. "It's very nice to meet you, Ermanno. I understand you already know that I am…"

Mario abruptly interrupted Walpole's introduction. "I know very well who you are, Dr. Darius Walpole, curator of the Northeast Museum of Antiquity in Mecklinberg, New York. More importantly, I have something I believe will be of great interest to you."

"Mario told you I'm not interested in acquiring paintings so I presume that is not what you have in mind," Walpole replied curtly, unappreciative of the man's rudeness.

"No, I know very well what you are seeking, Dr. Walpole. But, before I say anything else, I must tell you that what I have for you does not come without, shall we say, a small fee."

"I didn't think that it would," replied Walpole. "What specifically do you have that you believe I might wish to acquire?"

"They tell me you are returning to Pavia tomorrow morning by horseback. I shall meet you along the Pavia road. There is a very large tree, the biggest one in the area. It's easy to recognize and less than one kilometer from here. I will meet you there at 8:30. This is a very dangerous business, Dr. Walpole. I would ask for your assurance that you will tell no one about our plans. You are not the only one looking for ancient objects.

Walpole nodded his head. "I shall see you tomorrow morning at 8:30." The man gulped the rest of his drink and left. Walpole was only mildly curious about what Ermanno Sacri might have for him. On his frequent acquisition trips he was often approached by men such as this. Rarely did they offer much of interest, although he had purchased some desirable pieces he recognized as coming from a known location.

Most of the time, however, these men offered items that had been removed from where they were initially found and therefore had no clear provenance. When an item is taken from its original surroundings it is difficult to develop a precise context as to how it fit into the civilization that produced the piece. It is also difficult to correctly date the object. This is probably one of those kinds of situations, Walpole assumed.

Morning came quickly, and after a light breakfast Darius

Walpole mounted his horse and began his short trip. The horse was anxious to travel and walked briskly. After several minutes Walpole saw Ermanno Sacri sitting on a dappled horse near the large tree he had described. The man was approximately fifty yards up the road and easily recognizable because of his small stature. But today, as this small man sat on his horse, he looked absolutely tiny. Walpole considered the man's small size a good thing because he was always suspicious that he might be lured into a trap in which he could be robbed or worse.

But the man appeared to be alone, and as Walpole's horse drew nearer the man was smiling and waving to him. Things seem to be okay, thought Walpole.

"Good morning, Dr. Walpole," the man said.

"Good morning, Ermanno. What do you have for me today?"

Ermanno Sacri laughed. "Dr. Walpole, surely you do not think I would be so foolish to bring the object with me. I don't trust you any more than you trust me. Besides, it is much too large to carry on my horse. We will ride together on that road over there," the man said, pointing toward the hill across the road.

"I don't see any road," replied Walpole suspiciously.

"Look closely, doctor. You will see the outline of what looks like a path around the hillside. It's an ancient Roman road, the original route to Pavia. Over the centuries many important men have travelled that road. People stopped using the road at night many years ago because of reports of ghosts. But there are also stories of treasure and valuable objects buried along the road. I searched the road often but found nothing. Then one day, totally by accident, I discovered an object partially buried in the most unlikely of places. That is what I wish to show you.

It's easier to see as we get around to the other side of the hill. Few people use it today and it's not kept in repair. There are no bridges over the streams and much of the road follows a one thousand foot cliff with a river running at its bottom. The drop-offs and the roar of the river frighten people so everyone takes the main road."

Walpole, a suspicious man by nature, had learned from hard experience not to trust men such as Ermanno Sacri. Following this man around a hill out of sight of the main road was especially foolish. "Ermanno," Walpole said, "forgive me for being cautious, but I have followed men like you before, much to my regret. I must point out to you that I carry little money with me when I travel. If your intention is to rob me, it is not worth your trouble." As Walpole spoke, he let his coat fall open so Ermanno Sacri could see the pistol stuck in his belt.

"I appreciate your caution, Doctor Walpole, but I have no interest in making my money by robbing you. On the contrary, it is you who will be greatly rewarded if you place only a little trust in me for a very short time."

Walpole paused, looked at Ermanno and smiled. "I think we understand each other," he said, spurring his horse across the road to the faint trace of the ancient route. With Ermanno leading, they followed the pathway as it snaked around high cliff faces, thick rocks and across rushing mountain streams, only some of which had small wooden bridges.

After what Walpole judged to be eight kilometers, Ermanno Sacri stopped his horse. Both men looked at the magnificent panorama of the steep mountainsides and valley below. The mountain was covered with red wildflowers and green grass and sloped steeply downward for fifty feet. It ended at the edge of the massive cliff with a thousand foot drop-off to the river below. The roar of the river sounded like a sturdy wind blowing through pine trees.

A silver-blue lake sat across the valley on the mountainside opposite from where the men sat surveying the scenery. The lake's glassy surface reflected the nearly vertical mountains like a mirror.

"This is the place, Dr. Walpole," said Ermanno.

"The view is lovely but I don't see anything else," replied Walpole.

"You will," countered Ermanno. "It's down there," he added, pointing to the imposing cliff fifty feet below the ancient trail. "Do you see the rock outcropping? It's the only one along the cliff."

"Yes, I see it," replied Walpole.

"Let's go," said Ermanno. "We must climb down to that outcropping."

"What exactly is down there?" demanded Walpole, mildly alarmed. "That's a very dangerous spot. If we lost our footing we could fall over the cliff."

"Yes we could, Dr. Walpole," Ermanno laughed. "But what I have for you is down there by that outcropping at the very edge of the cliff." He was obviously enjoying Walpole's anxiety about climbing down the steep mountainside that ended with the sheer wall of the one thousand foot cliff. "Think of it like this, Dr. Walpole," Ermanno laughed, "if you fall off the cliff you'll land in the river and get a nice bath. Then you swim out."

Walpole didn't appreciate Ermanno Sacri's humor. He looked around to make sure he hadn't been led into a trap. There was no one in sight so he climbed from his horse. Ermanno had already gotten off his horse and taken several steps down the steep slope.

"We are alone, aren't we Ermanno?" asked Walpole. As he spoke, he pulled his jacket open to remind him of the pistol stuck in his belt. "I really don't like surprises," he added.

"Like I said, you don't trust me," replied Ermanno. "I don't blame you. In times like these one must be very careful. I too have a pistol, Dr. Walpole. It's in my saddlebag. As I also told you, the black market is a dangerous place to do business."

The two men understood each other and Walpole began to carefully move down the rocky decline. In a few minutes they reached the rock outcropping and were standing less than six feet from the brink of the towering cliff. The twenty feet wide base of the rock outcropping was the only level ground. The beige colored rock extended fifteen feet outward from the side of the cliff and directly over the chasm.

"If you walk out on the rock you have a wonderful view of the river," Ermanno laughed.

But Walpole was afraid to move. "Who would be foolish enough to walk out on a narrow rock one thousand feet above the ground?" he replied. Walpole didn't like heights and he was already struggling being so near the cliff's dizzying drop-off.

"I would," laughed Ermanno. "I spent many hours sitting on that rock painting my pictures. That's how I found the ancient object I'm about to show you. Ermanno turned away from the cliff to face the side of the mountain and Dr. Walpole followed his lead.

"Alright, Ermanno, where is this artifact you wish me to see?" Walpole asked, keeping alert to reach for his gun at the first sign of trouble.

"It's right in front of you, Doctor Walpole," he said, pointing at the upward sloping ground facing them.

"There is nothing in front of me but rocks and dirt," replied Walpole crossly.

"Yes doctor; that is what I thought also. But like I said, I came to this place many times to sit here and paint the mountains and lake across the valley. I often looked right at the spot where this object is buried and never noticed it. Look more closely at the ground before you."

Walpole knelt down and closely studied the ground just eighteen inches from his face. He could see nothing but soil and small rocks. But as his eyes carefully scanned the contour of the dirt he suddenly saw a small geometric shape similar to the square corner of a stone box.

"I see it," Walpole said excitedly. "Yes, I see it. What is it, Ermanno?" he asked.

"I don't know, Dr. Walpole," Ermanno replied. "About four months ago I dug away some of the dirt and saw some tiny etching in the stone on the corner of the box."

"Well what did it say, man?" Walpole asked impatiently.

"There was only one word but that is how I know whatever this is must be very valuable." Walpole stared expectantly at the man. Ermanno smiled as he took a piece of paper from his pocket and handed it to him.

Written on the paper was the word "Boethius."

Walpole tried to control his excitement but Ermanno Sacri had transacted many deals like this one. He easily detected the anxious look on Dr. Walpole's face. "I can see you like it," he said.

"It is of passing interest, I suppose," replied Walpole, vainly attempting to disguise his excitement. "How much money will you charge for showing me this object? I usually pay twenty-five American dollars. Will that be sufficient?"

"Don't waste my time, doctor. We both know this object, whatever it might be, is very valuable."

"All right," replied Walpole," fifty dollars then?"

Becoming angry, Ermanno Sacri pursed his lips. "I told you not to waste my time, doctor. You are insulting me."

"Well how much then?" Walpole asked impatiently.

"I want one thousand American dollars, Doctor Walpole. And, I must have it today."

"You must be out of your mind. I don't have that kind of money. Besides, neither of us knows exactly what that object is. It could be worthless."

"Dr. Walpole, I'm not going to argue with you. I'm to meet with a man this afternoon if you choose not buy this object. He will have the one thousand dollars cash I require."

Walpole was certain there was something of great historical value buried just a few feet from where the two men stood. All right, I'll give you the one thousand American dollars on the condition I first dig the object up to see exactly what it is. Besides, it will take me at least one week to get the money. Do we have a deal?"

"I said I must have the money today, doctor. That is my requirement. If you can't give me the money today, I shall sell the artifact to another man this afternoon. I'm actually selling it to him for nine hundred dollars. If you can you give me nine hundred dollars today, it is yours," Ermanno followed up, thinking that asking a lower price might get Walpole to come up with the money more quickly.

"But I need to have the funds arranged," Walpole answered. "That's how the museum handles all of its transactions. As I said, it will take at least one week."

"Then our business is concluded, Dr. Walpole. I will sell the object to the other bidder this afternoon."

"As Ermanno turned to climb up the mountain, "Walpole said, "Wait, I'll get the money. Just give me four days. Don't sell this on the black market. It will get damaged or lost. It won't turn up again for years."

The man stopped and turned to face Walpole. "I care nothing about that, doctor. I only care about the money and you don't have any. Our conversation is over. I'm leaving."

"You fool!" Darius screamed. "Don't do this. Whatever this is belonged to Anicius Boethius. Its historical value is immeasurable."

Ermanno smirked. "I know. But I care nothing about history, Dr. Walpole. I wouldn't have wasted my time with you but I assumed you had money available."

Walpole panicked. If this black market thief let the object fall into the wrong hands its history would be destroyed. As Ermanno turned to climb the hill Walpole grabbed his arm and spun him round to face him. "I'm not going to let you do this. Just give me a few days to get the money."

"I told you my terms, doctor," he replied as he again moved to leave.

Reflexively, Walpole again grabbed Ermanno's arm. "Will you please give me time to get the money?" he pleaded. Ermanno, who was standing slightly higher on the mountainside, shoved Walpole causing him to stumble backward toward the thousand foot high cliff.

"Are you crazy?" he screamed. "You could have killed me."

Ermanno laughed. "See me when you have money to spend, Dr. Walpole," he said, and turned to walk away.

Without realizing what he was doing an enraged Walpole slammed his fist into the back of Ermanno's head and knocked him to the ground. Ermanno jumped up quickly and turned to face Walpole. He lunged forward clumsily but Walpole easily dodged the smaller man's outstretched arms and Ermanno stumbled past him, stopping perilously close to the cliff's edge. Ermanno momentarily regained his balance but slipped on the loose gravel and desperately struggled to find his balance. He screamed in terror as he realized he was sliding toward the nothingness a thousand feet above the raging river.

Walpole reached forward in vain as the doomed man's arms flailed wildly but he was unable to grasp his outstretched hands. The terrified Ermanno felt his body falling as he began his long plunge into eternity. Walpole listened to Ermanno's horrified screams fade as the man plummeted downward to the thundering river.

Walpole collapsed to his knees burying his face in his folded hands and sobbing. He had never killed a man before, never even been in a fistfight. He vomited on ground and was unable to raise his head. "My god, what have I done?" he cried. He threw up once more then sat shaking his head in anguish. It was fifteen minutes before he decided he must pull himself together. He was so weak he doubted he could climb the mountainside to the trail, but he slowly began to crawl upward. It was several long minutes before he reached the ancient road.

He struggled to his feet and set Ermanno's horse free. The animal ran down the narrow road in the direction from which they had come. Walpole continued on the ancient trail until it intersected the Pavia Road. As he rode he reflected on what had happened. Although Walpole didn't kill Ermanno he had started the fight. But he had only tried to stop the man, not kill him. Ermanno lost his footing when he tried to kill me, he thought.

Walpole found solace in the fact he saved an important piece of antiquity from the black market and ending up in some selfish private collector's study. In the museum's hands objects could be examined in the proper context of the time period in which they were created and more could be learned about the past. But the guilt of having caused the man's death weighed heavily upon him.

He decided not to tell the authorities about Ermanno's death. He didn't want to risk being tried in an Italian court and possibly ending up in prison. They wouldn't find Ermanno's body for days and he would have left the country by then. Walpole also knew the object would have to be smuggled out of the country. The Government Antiquities Office would never give approval to take it out of Italy.

Once he reached Pavia and the safety of his hotel room he notified the man who had helped him smuggle ancient artifacts before. They would meet at midnight six kilometers up the mountain road at a large rock spire near the artifact's location. The man and his crew would bring lanterns and wooden crates with packing materials. He assured Walpole the crew would work quickly and have the object or objects loaded on the next ship steaming for New York. Walpole would also be on board.

That night Walpole went with the smugglers to the site on the edge of the cliff. The men dug rapidly and soon uncovered a four feet square stone box. The men pulled the heavy lid to the side and Walpole gasped. In the lantern's flickering light he could clearly see a heavily inscribed solid stone wheel measuring three feet in diameter. Mathematical equations and formulas covered the artifact. Could this be the legendary Boethian Wheel, he wondered. Moving quickly, the crew carefully wrapped the circular object. Darius examined the stone box and decided to leave it until another time. He would have enough trouble smuggling the large stone wheel out of the country.

# 3

May 14, 1898    Mecklinberg, New York

It was exactly five-thirty PM and Darius Walpole's fiancée Malinda Cora Anderson was sitting in her small office in the Northeast Museum of Antiquity in Mecklinberg, New York. Walpole had arrived in Mecklinberg with the Italian artifact in July the previous year and Cora, a trained mathematician, had become obsessed with decoding the mysterious stone wheel. She requested an office at the museum in which to study it.

Walpole stuck his head into Cora's office and told her he was going to her home to pick up their dinner and bring it back to the museum. That had become their custom because Cora insisted on working late every night. Cora's sister Lydia would return to the museum with Walpole and eat with them then stay as a chaperone until Cora stopped working at nine o'clock.

Cora taught upper level mathematics at the Mecklinberg Academy for Young Women. However, she had not returned to her position there the previous fall because she was spending her time working on decoding the stone disc from Pavia. Darius had begun to think her fascination with the wheel was becoming unhealthy. Because of her obsession with the ancient object she would come to work every day and spend endless hours working on the meaning of the mathematical formulas and symbols etched into the stone artifact.

She and Walpole often discussed Boethius' philosophy that the wheel of history controls the destiny of all people, and as the wheel turns, good fortune may change to bad or conversely. Cora initially presumed the Boethius Wheel, as she now called it, was an academic declaration of Boethius' philosophy. However, as she became more deeply involved in her investigation, she had come to believe the mathematical formulas etched into the stone suggested that instead of merely being a teaching prop, the wheel was actually some sort of tool with an operational function.

This possibility fueled Cora's excitement about the ancient object. While she had come close to solving the wheel's mysteries several times, it had always been a dead end. The strange symbols inscribed in the stone were both the problem and the key to understanding the Boethius Wheel.

Walpole had quickly lost interest in the project after several weeks. He never cared for philosophy. His passion was searching for and discovering new artifacts. Besides, Cora never seemed to make any progress on deciphering the thing. During the course of his career Walpole had found other ancient artifacts where the meaning or function of the object had been lost to time. Someone else could figure these things out, he felt. He preferred the adventure of field work.

This evening Walpole and another employee walked to the main door of the museum and locked it when they left the building. Walpole then strolled the four blocks to the Anderson home. As usual, Cora's sister Lydia was looking through the living room window watching for him. When she saw him coming she picked up her waiting basket of food and came out on the porch.

"Good evening, Darius," she said. "It's a beautiful evening, isn't it?"

"Yes it is, Lydia," he replied.

This had been their usual greeting every evening for nearly a year. Walpole took the heavy basket packed with their dinner and the two of them walked back to the museum. As they walked up the front steps of the main building Walpole glanced at the large clock on the front of the courthouse across the street. It was five forty-five. As usual, Walpole's short walk had taken only fifteen minutes. He unlocked the large main door of the museum and he and Lydia stepped inside.

"We're back, Cora," Walpole called.

"Hello, sister. We're here with your dinner," Lydia yelled,

laughing.

Cora didn't answer but that wasn't unusual as she was always immersed in her work. Calling to her in a normal tone would simply not work. She would have to be nudged several times to break her concentration. As usual, Walpole and Lydia walked down the hallway to Cora's office with the nightly basket of food.

When they arrived at Cora's office, however, it was empty. A freshly made cup of hot tea was waiting, steaming on her desk. She always had hot tea with her dinner and she was ready for this evening's meal.

"She must have gone to the necessary room," said Lydia. "I shall go fetch her."

Lydia came back shortly. "She's not there, Darius."

It was then Walpole noticed several sheets of paper strewn on the floor by the table on which the stone wheel sat. "This is odd," he said. "Cora is always so organized and neat."

"Let's set the dinner out," replied Lydia. "It will get cold if we don't eat it soon."

As Lydia took the plates and utensils out of the basket, Walpole knelt down to pick the papers from the floor. These must have been written today, he thought. The three sheets were covered with mathematical formulas similar to those on the stone wheel. He didn't pay much attention to the papers because they were just scratches and jottings and Cora had produced several thousand of them in the many months she had worked attempting to decode the wheel. However, one piece of paper did catch his eye. Cora had written some notes on its reverse side.

"Darius, I have decoded the Boethius Wheel. The answer was so simple, right before me. You remember that clerical scholars claimed the Albinus Manuscript referred to a Wheel of Destiny as an abstract philosophical concept and burned it because it was sacrilegious. However, I came across the writings of a monk who was excommunicated in 1329 because he stated his superiors lied about the Albinus Manuscript. His writings say he saw the Albinus Manuscript and it claims the Boethian Wheel is a device which reveals a method for someone to move about in time and actually manipulate history! The Boethius Wheel is…….. I'm going to test my theory."

Walpole laid the paper on the desk, pondering what Cora meant.

What theory was she testing? "I wonder where she is, Lydia," he said with a worried expression.

"She'll be back soon," Lydia replied smiling. But, as she said those words her smile slowly faded. Something was very wrong here.

Malinda Cora Anderson did not return soon, nor did she return that night or the next day. Malinda Cora Anderson was never seen again.

# 4

December 21, 1937    Tammerlane's Oak Bar, Washington, DC

Dr. Elbert J. Beale, the founder and Director of the Office of
Strategic Threat Response Operations (OSTRO), sat down at his
favorite table at Tammerlane's Oak Bar in Washington, DC.
Tammerlane's, located only four blocks from the White House, was
the establishment of choice for high-level government personnel.
Anyone drinking at Tammerlane's was in charge of some military or
government agency, worked in the diplomatic corps or performed
some other high level function.

OSTRO was established by Dr. Beale in 1935 to focus on
emerging threats to the United States. Its primary mission was to
identify those threats and prioritize them according to their level of
seriousness. Initially, OSTRO issued quarterly reports which were
disseminated to specific military and government agencies dealing
with national security. From that perspective, OSTRO served in an
administrative capacity only. In theory, depending on the specific
threat, the agency most able to handle that threat would take the
appropriate action to deal with it. This had not worked well because
response authority was not assigned to any specific department or
agency. However, OSTRO soon received the authorization to
respond as well as the funding to carry out certain covert missions
itself.

Dr. Beale had come to Tammerlane's to join his friend Billy
Hargitay for a holiday drink. The two men met just two years earlier
and immediately became friends because of their military service in
World War One. Both men were in their mid-forties and had spent

their careers in government service. Billy Hargitay worked for the Office of National Security.

Beale was ordering his customary Glenfiddich on the rocks just as Billy walked through the front door. "And bring a Jamesons on the rocks too," he asked, knowing Billy's choice of drink.

"Hello, Ellie," shouted Billy as he hurried toward Beale's table. Billy is always in a rush, thought Beale.

"Hello, Billy," Beale said as he stood to shake hands. Although they saw each other every day, shaking hands seemed like the holiday thing to do. "By the way, it's your turn to buy." Beale kiddingly wanted to get that detail out of the way because they always argued about who would pay, although neither one really cared.

"So what's planned for the holidays, Ellie?" Billy asked, knowing Beale was looking forward to the time off.

"Nancy has been planning a trip up to New York for the past several months. Her favorite aunt has been asking her to come for a Christmas visit for years. The old dear is getting up in age and Nancy is afraid that if we don't make the visit this year there may not be another chance. We're driving up there the day after tomorrow."

"New York City at Christmas is always special," replied Billy. "It's all decked out. You'll enjoy it."

"We're not going to the city, Billy. We're going upstate."

"That's okay, too," said Billy. "You need to get away, Ellie."

"Why do you say that?" Beale asked with a grin.

"You're letting your job get to you. You never smile anymore. I know you have to make life and death decisions just like I do but, you've got to make them and then forget about them. Move on, as they say. You're not the fun loving guy you used to be."

"I think you're exaggerating, Billy," Beale smiled. But Billy was right in one respect. Beale had to make decisions on killing people, sometimes lots of people. But contrary to what Billy thought, he didn't mind making those decisions. In fact, he realized early on that he actually took a certain degree of pleasure in deciding to kill people.

"You know, you've taken on a dark side, Ellie," Billy continued. Although Billy was smiling, Beale knew he was serious.

What Billy didn't realize was that his friend Ellie Beale had become obsessed with destructive missions and high kill-rates. In the process, his personality had changed. Billy decided not to further pursue Beale's morbid side and dampen the holiday spirit so he quickly changed the subject. "By the way, where are you going upstate?" he asked.

"Nancy's Aunt Harriet lives in a small town called Mecklinberg. It's about a hundred or so miles north of the city. I've never been there."

"Oh, I know where Mecklinberg is," replied Billy. "I worked at the museum there one summer when I was in college. Originally I wanted to be an archeologist."

"Why did you change your mind?" asked Beale. "I always thought archeology would be an interesting field."

"There were several reasons, really. The work was too dull, too slow for me. That was the main reason, I suppose. I wanted something faster moving I guess."

"So you came to Washington to do paperwork. That's a lot more interesting," Beale laughed.

"It wasn't just the slow pace. Something else happened that dampened my interest in archeology."

"What?" asked Beale. "You've got me interested now."

Billy hesitated, pondering how he would relate his story. Beale looked at him expectantly. "It was kind of weird," Billy smiled. "Maybe you'd rather not hear it."

"You know I want to hear it," Beale laughed. "Stop stalling."

Billy smiled. "Okay, here it is. The summer I worked there a very bizarre incident happened. The curator of the museum, a man named Darius Walpole, committed suicide in the museum. It was very tragic and really quite strange. Anyway, because of that, I lost interest in archeology."

"Why did he kill himself in the museum?" interjected Beale. "That does seem weird."

"You really don't want to know, Ellie. It gets weirder."

Beale, ever the person for an interesting tale, pushed Billy to tell the full story. "Let's hear the whole thing," he demanded.

Billy looked toward Ellie Beale and chuckled. "I knew you'd be curious about this."

"Come on, let's hear it," Beale said. "I know you're dying to tell me anyway."

"All right," Billy replied. "I rarely saw Dr. Walpole. I mean, he was at the museum every day but he would arrive early and leave late at night. He was never in his office. He always worked in a little room down the hall. He was trying to analyze some ancient, wheel-like, stone artifact. At least that's what everyone said. The employees told me the thing looked like a disc but had mathematical formulas and writing etched all over it. They called it a wheel of history or destiny, something like that. I never saw it myself.

According to the people working at the museum, in the late 1890's Dr. Walpole's fiancée had worked on decoding the circular artifact for nearly a year trying to solve the mathematical formulas. One night she vanished and was never heard from again.

After that, Professor Walpole spent all of his time, in fact the next twenty years, trying to decipher this ancient object. He committed suicide on May 14, 1918. I remember that date because it was just a week after I started working there. That date was exactly twenty years to the day after his fiancée disappeared. I only worked there during the summer but I was glad to leave it behind when September rolled around and I returned to college. The place just seemed to have a pall over it after Dr. Walpole died."

"That's quite a story, Billy," replied Beale.

"I told you it would be. Anyway, it was an interesting museum. You ought to drop by for a visit if you have the time, Ellie."

"I might do that if my wife will let me get away from family visiting long enough to do anything interesting."

After a second drink, Ellie Beale and Billy Hargitay headed for home and the holidays.

# 5

December 22 & 23, 1937    Mecklinberg, New York

Dr. Elbert Beale and his wife Nancy arrived at her Aunt Harriet's late the following day. It was only three hundred and fifty miles to Mecklinberg but it had been a long, tiring drive. The roads were crowded and the weather was bad, typical for this time of year. It was nearly nine p.m. when they pulled their Ford sedan into Aunt Harriet's driveway. She was waving at them from the doorway.

"My god," Beale remarked, "she must have been standing there all day waiting for us."

Aunt Harriet's house was near the downtown area of Mecklinberg. It was a three story wooden structure with endless rows of windows and a gabled roof. A long wooden front porch was ideal for sitting out on summer nights and enjoying the enormous, ancient trees scattered about the wide yard. The decorative front door had leaded glass windows. Beale and Nancy walked into the home and open arms of Aunt Harriet.

Aunt Harriet was a large and joyful woman who wore her gray hair in a bun. Her big, flowing gray dress with a hem well below her knees was the style for women of her generation and her white shawl protected her against the winter chill. She whisked Beale and Nancy inside and insisted they have a cup of tea, which neither of them wanted. Their only desire was to go to bed. The tea, however, was a mandatory ritual they would suffer every night of their visit.

Though the home seemed freshly decorated it retained its late nineteenth century flavor. The furnishings were substantial and abundant. Several dark red, overstuffed couches were the foundation of the living room's decor. Large glass display cases highlighted the treasures generously placed throughout the massive home. The tasteful flowered wallpaper set the tone for the civility dutifully maintained by the home's owner. A glass topped coffee table held the antique floral tea service. As Beale surveyed the place Aunt Harriet chattered on. Beale and Nancy didn't have to talk, just listen. They decided the tea was actually a good idea.

Once they finished their tea, Beale and Nancy climbed the ornate, curved stairway to the second floor where they would be spending the next several nights. They were asleep within minutes.

Morning came quickly and Beale and Nancy were still sleeping at eight-thirty. Even the splendid sunshine pouring through the side window of their bedroom hadn't wakened them. However, what sounded like intentionally created noise from the first floor jostled them from their sound sleep. Aunt Harriet was informing them she was up, had been for hours, and their presence was demanded immediately.

Beale, still wearing his pajamas underneath a bulky flannel robe, went down the spiral staircase first. In a few minutes, Nancy walked into the kitchen. She was wearing a robe as she was still in her nightgown.

"It's about time you two got up," exclaimed Aunt Harriet. "Get dressed," she ordered jovially. I have some friends coming over at ten o'clock for tea and cookies. I just can't wait for you to meet them. Miss Limbers will fix you some breakfast and then you can go upstairs and get ready." Miss Limbers, a shy, quiet wisp of a woman was Aunt Harriet's maid. She immediately got to work on the mandatory bacon, eggs and toast breakfast.

At ten o'clock, Beale and Nancy walked into the side parlor. The Christmas tree was lit and the cookies and tea were waiting on the dark wooden buffet. Aunt Harriet's friends, seven of them, obviously familiar with Aunt Harriet's insistence on punctuality, also arrived at precisely ten a.m. Once everyone was seated in a circle, sipping tea and munching cookies, the female chatter commenced in earnest.

Beale was the only male in the group and found the feminine warbling boring. The only thing that vaguely tweaked his attention was the name of one of the women. It was Walpole. He knew he'd heard that name before. Then he remembered Billy Hargitay mentioned it two days earlier at Tammerlane's Oak Bar. Could she be related to the man Billy was talking about, he wondered. Everyone in town is probably related, he concluded, and didn't think further about it.

The women continued to talk and Nancy was enjoying herself, adding her own voice to the bee-like buzz. Beale secretly longed for a double scotch. Make that a triple, he ordered an imagined bartender. No libation was forthcoming, however, and he resigned himself to enduring the conversational marathon.

Beale arose from his comfortable chair to pour a second cup of tea and grab a handful of cookies. He would amuse himself by eating and hopefully fall asleep in his easy chair. That would be a blessing, he smiled. But, as he stood near the teapot, one of the women walked over to the buffet. Though Aunt Harriet had introduced everyone, Beale hadn't bothered to remember which name went with each specific face. This woman appeared to be around seventy-five years old and Beale offered to pour the tea for her. "Thank you, Dr. Beale. I don't know if you remember, but I'm Lydia Walpole."

"Thank you," Beale chuckled. "I remember your name but I couldn't associate it with your face. It's so nice to meet you once again, miss, or is it Mrs. Walpole?"

"It's Mrs. Walpole, doctor, although my husband passed away some time ago."

Beale was hesitant to ask if her husband was the museum curator who committed suicide nearly twenty years earlier. Morbid curiosity, however, moved him to probe for a connection. "Have you lived in Mecklinberg all your life?"

"Oh, yes. I was born here. My husband worked at the museum for many years, and after he died I stayed here. It's my home."

"What did your husband do at the museum?" he asked.

"He was the curator there. He loved the job but, in the end, it killed him. It's a sad story."

"I'm sorry to hear that," Beale replied. "Coincidentally, I talked to a gentleman the other day who worked at the museum the same time as your husband."

"How odd. That's quite a coincidence," she agreed.

"He only worked there for one summer. He wanted to become an archeologist but never did."

"That's a good thing. I definitely would not recommend the job to anyone. It took my husband and sister from me."

"Good lord, what happened, if you don't mind my asking?" Because Beale had talked with Billy he knew the woman's husband committed suicide and her sister had disappeared, but he wanted to hear Lydia Walpole's version because she was a firsthand witness to both events.

"No, I don't mind at all. It's a painful story, but I never hesitate to tell it if I'm asked. It's therapeutic, I suppose. To begin with, my sister Cora was engaged-to-be-married to the man who later became my husband, Darius Walpole. Late in the nineteenth century Darius brought a mysterious, ancient artifact back from Italy.

When my sister Cora saw this stone disk she became fascinated with it. She started studying it, in her spare time at first, but it quickly became her full time obsession. She quit her job as a mathematics teacher in order to study the object. The disk had mathematical formulas and writing all over it. It got to the point that it was all she did. She worked on it for a year. She even worked on Sundays and never took time off."

"That's incredible," Beale said.

"She and Darius were to be married in July of 1898. But Cora was so involved with the disk that she was completely ignoring her own wedding. That just isn't natural for a bride-to-be. Darius would come over to our house every evening just after five-thirty and he and I would walk back to the museum and bring Cora dinner. We would all sit in her office and eat together. One afternoon, Darius and I brought her dinner as we had been doing every day for nearly a year. When we got to her office she was gone. She had disappeared and we never saw her again."

"Did the police investigate?"

"Yes, of course, but they couldn't solve the mystery. You see, the day it happened, Darius left the museum with another man. Both of them saw Cora as they walked out. Darius had been gone for less than fifteen minutes. When he and I returned, everything in the office was in order. There was a cup of hot tea on her desk. She always made herself tea to have with the dinner we brought her. The only unusual thing was that some papers were lying on the floor. She was always very neat so papers strewn on the floor was a little unusual. However, the police thought that a draft could have blown them off the table."

"You don't think there could have been foul play?" Beale asked.

"Dr. Beale, except for the front door leading to Main Street, every other door was locked from the inside with a deadbolt. Darius always locked the Main Street door when he left Cora alone in the building. He had to unlock it when we returned. All the windows were also locked. The police, Darius and I checked every inch of the building, the basement and attic. No one could have taken my sister out the front door onto Main Street as there were a lot people on the street at that time of day. This is a small town. Everyone knows everyone else. If Cora had walked out herself, someone would have seen her. The police questioned everyone in the vicinity of the museum that evening. No one had seen her leave the museum nor did they see her anywhere else in town."

"That is truly a bizarre story" Beale remarked. He didn't know what else to say, but he wanted to keep the conversation going and pursue the interesting mystery. Besides, his conversation with Lydia Walpole distracted him from the din of the conversation behind them.

"Life went on as usual for several years," Lydia continued. "Darius would often drop by for dinner. He was a lost, lonely man without Cora. My father and mother never got over it either."

"What happened after that?" Beale asked.

"Eventually, Darius and I sort of fell in together. We were never deeply in love. We had a degree of affection for each other but his true love was Cora. We both knew that. One day he asked me to marry him and I said yes. I knew he could never love me like he loved Cora, but we gravitated toward each other because of what we had gone through together when we lost her."

Beale listened sympathetically and Lydia Walpole was appreciative of his interest.

"Shortly after we married he became despondent," she continued. He felt like he betrayed Cora. Even after we married he spent all his spare time studying the disk and Cora's notes. She had boxes and boxes of them. And that was so strange."

"What do you mean?" Beale asked.

"Well, I shouldn't tell you this because only my parents and I knew about Cora."

"What do you mean, Mrs. Walpole?"

"What I mean is not many people really understood Cora. She never really loved Darius or anyone else. My parents were pushing

Cora to marry Darius. In those days, that's how marriage was. You married whomever your family thought would be best for you. Cora never accepted that. She wanted to make her own choices.

There was a note to Darius on the back of one of the papers on the floor in her office. She wrote that the Boethian Wheel, as she and Darius called it, was actually a device, which allowed someone to move about to different times in the past or future. There was some kind of formula on it that was the key to being able to do so she always said. I thought it was a bunch of malarkey, but sometimes I wonder if Cora figured out the formula and used the wheel to escape to a different time where she could be herself. Oh well, enough of that nonsense."

"I don't think it is nonsense, Mrs. Walpole. I actually find it quite interesting. Can you tell me anything else?"

Lydia Walpole continued with her story.

"Darius became obsessed with that damned wheel. It got to where we seldom spoke. He would leave for the museum early in the morning and work with the wheel. He would take care of his responsibilities at the museum during the day and, like Cora, he would work late at night studying the wheel. It got to where we lived completely separate lives. This went on for a long time. Then one day, on the twentieth anniversary of her death, he killed himself in the very room from which Cora disappeared."

"That is a sad story," replied Beale. "I am so sorry you had to experience all of that."

"Well, there is nothing anyone can do about it. It's all in the past and that's where I have left it."

Beale was fascinated with what he'd heard. His curiosity about the story and the wheel greatly increased with Mrs. Walpole's account. "What ever became of the wheel?" he asked.

"After Darius killed himself, I took possession of the wheel and his and Cora's notes. The museum staff wanted to put all of this behind them and they were happy to get rid of the wheel. Besides, Darius never got official approval to remove the artifact from Italy. It was actually stolen antiquity. That was another reason they didn't want the thing."

"Do you still have it?" Beale asked.

"Yes, I have the awful thing, as well as a dozen or so boxes of Cora's and Darius' notes. Several people have asked if they could have the wheel or even buy it but I told them no. You see, in some way, and I don't know how, I'm sure that wheel had something to do with Cora's vanishing. For years I thought that as long as I had the wheel Cora might somehow return. But over time, I have accepted that she never will."

Beale realized he shouldn't have persisted with his questions, but he was intrigued with the story. "Mrs. Walpole, I know I shouldn't ask this, but do you think I might be able to see the wheel?"

"Of course, if you like. It's in the attic at my home. You're welcome to drop by any time."

"Nancy and I will only be here for a few days. When would be a good time for me to visit you?"

"Come over this afternoon if you like. I live just a few houses from here, right down the street."

"That's wonderful. Would three o'clock be all right with you?"

# 6

December 23-26, 1937     Mecklinberg, New York

Dr. Beale and Nancy, accompanied by Aunt Harriet, arrived at
Lydia Walpole's house at precisely three p.m. Not surprisingly,
Lydia had the tea ready. While Nancy and Aunt Harriet sat in the
living room, Lydia led Dr. Beale up the two flights of stairs to the
third floor.  She then led him to the far end of the hallway where
there was a doorway that opened to the attic steps. She flipped a light
switch inside the door and the lights came on in the dark room at the
top of the stairs.

As they reached the top step and walked into the attic, Beale
immediately spotted the ancient wheel lying on the floor near the
back wall. "There it is," Lydia said.

Beale followed Lydia across the room to where the wheel lay.
"How did they get that heavy thing up the stairs?" he asked.

"It only took one man," she laughed. "It was a struggle, but he
managed. I'll leave you here with the wheel, Dr. Beale, and I'll go
visit with Harriet and Nancy. You can take your time with it."

Beale spent nearly an hour studying the wheel. The words on the
ancient artifact were inscribed in Latin, however most of the
engravings were mathematical formulas and symbols. Although his
Latin was rusty, he got the general meaning of some of the
inscriptions. What looked like "rota," meaning wheel, and "historia,"
meaning history, were each written once. "Transmuto," meaning to
change, was written twice. He also recognized "Fatum," or destiny,
and "tempus," meaning time. Unable to completely translate the
Latin, he couldn't make much sense of it. Besides, if Cora Anderson

and Dr. Walpole couldn't figure it out in all the years they spent studying it, he would never decipher it in the short time he would have. On the other hand, in view of Cora's strange disappearance, she just may have deciphered the wheel's secrets, if indeed there were any.

Beale was a realist, a man not prone to conjecture or one to jump to conclusions. While he acknowledged Cora Anderson's vanishing was weird, that didn't mean she had disappeared via the Boethian Wheel, which now lay in front of him. He wondered if Cora staged her own mysterious departure to escape from a suffocating small town and the prospect of a mundane marriage.

On the other hand, Beale was intrigued that Cora Anderson, a trained mathematician, would have studied the wheel for a year. Why, he wondered. Then Darius Walpole studied the wheel for another twenty years. Both Cora and Darius Walpole obviously believed the ancient wheel had some sort of power. It comes back to Malinda Cora Anderson, he concluded. The wheel must somehow have been involved with her disappearance, but how? Obviously, Darius Walpole concluded this also. And Lydia Walpole told him the same thing earlier today at Aunt Harriet's tea.

Certainly this ancient artifact must be something very unique. There must a secret hidden in its inscriptions. Then, deciding he had left the ladies sitting alone long enough, he re-traced his steps down the three flights of stairs and into the sitting room.

"Would you have a cup of tea, Dr. Beale?" Lydia Walpole asked.

The conversation between the ladies again left Beale sitting gazing his cup of tea. In the next several minutes he thought about the story of the wheel and the mystery that surrounded it. His initial mild interest had become intrigue. As he thought further about it, he concluded the ancient wheel might hold the key to something, although he had no idea what, which might be of use to OSTRO. In what Aunt Harriet would consider a major breach of civility he suddenly blurted, "Mrs. Walpole, would you be interested in selling the wheel to me?"

The animated conversation ceased immediately as the three ladies stared directly at Beale with shocked looks on their faces. Lydia Walpole, recovering from her surprise at Beale's interjection into the solemn ritual of women's talk, replied, "Why do you want that thing?" she asked. "I'm quite sure it's worth a lot of money. Is that why you want it?"

"No, Mrs. Walpole. I would like to study it. Perhaps I could just borrow it from you for a time."

"Dr. Beale, I kept that thing all this while in the illogical hope that as long as I had it my sister would somehow return. I'm glad you're interested in the wheel and I'll tell you what I will do. You may come here any time and study it as well as the boxes of papers belonging to my husband Darius and my sister Cora. I would look forward to your visits."

"So you won't sell it to me, then?" Beale replied.

"I'm afraid not, Dr. Beale. That wheel is the only remaining connection I have that my sister, Cora. Even though I despise the thing, I could never let it out of my sight.

"Ellie," Nancy said, "it was very rude of you to interrupt our conversation to try and buy a dusty old antique from Lydia."

"You're right, Nancy. Please accept my apology, ladies," Beale replied. "I guess I was a little too excited about the old thing. Please continue and I promise not to interrupt again."

Beale wasn't sure the ancient stone wheel would be of any concrete value to OSTRO, but he had a strong hunch he should acquire the artifact. Perhaps it was intuition, but he believed there was more to the wheel than anyone knew. Malinda Cora Anderson must have figured it out. And also, someone at sometime in the distant past obviously attached a great deal of importance to it. He concluded it was in the interest of national security that he must do whatever necessary to assure OSTRO took possession of the ancient object.

In another half hour, Nancy, Aunt Harriet and Ellie Beale walked back to Aunt Harriet's house. The walk was short and the wind chilling. Beale was hoping Aunt Harriet might have a bottle of scotch in her pantry.

Once they reached the house, Nancy and Aunt Harriet sat down in the living room to visit. Beale asked if he could use Aunt Harriet's phone to make an important call. Aunt Harriet's phone was in the study and Beale shut the door behind him when he went into the room. Lydia Walpole would not sell the wheel so he would be forced steal it from her.

"Number please," the operator said.

"This is a long distance call to Washington, DC, operator," Beale replied. "Could you connect me with Harrison 4672?"

After a short pause, the operator said, "Here is your connection, sir," as ringing began at the other end of the line.

"Hello," a woman's voice answered.

"Hello Evelyn," Beale said. "There's some business here that needs your attention. Please come to Mecklinberg on December 26. Bring Chambers and Darst with you. I'll meet you downtown at seven a.m. that morning at Judy's Diner."

Evelyn Rankow was Beale's assistant. He called on her often because of her efficiency and skill handling special assignments. He worked with her a long time and she never failed to accomplish whatever mission he gave her. And there had been some nasty ones. He trusted her completely.

Beale liked Evelyn's no nonsense attitude. She was tough and wouldn't hesitate to kill. That was a necessary job requirement in the counterintelligence business. Evelyn, who was forty-eight, was not a handsome woman. Her short, graying brown hair reached just below her collar. Her face was more wrinkled than it should be, probably due to the stress of the job and long hours working outside in the elements. She was of average height, trim and athletic.

Beale had never known her to have a romantic interest and her mannish looks made him think that if she did have a special friend, it would most likely be a woman. Although she wore men's clothes when she was working assignments, she preferred tailored suits with skirts when working at headquarters. She was always friendly but didn't fraternize with anyone. Beale had drinks with her on occasion, but their relationship was strictly professional.


Beale and Nancy spent Christmas Eve and Day with Aunt Harriet and dined with her that evening. They would leave the next morning, Sunday, December 26. At nine o'clock Christmas evening Nancy and Beale told Aunt Harriet "Goodnight" and climbed the stairs to their room.

The next morning Beale suggested to Nancy that she visit with her Aunt Harriet. He wanted to take a walk and maybe have a cup of coffee someplace. As he walked into the small downtown area he saw Evelyn's car parked near Judy's Diner.

I can always rely on Evelyn, he thought. He walked into the small restaurant and over to the table where Evelyn sat with Ed Chambers and Henry Darst. "Good morning, everyone," he said. "I'm sorry to have you working during the holidays."

"That's alright, Ellie," Evelyn said. "We were bored just sitting around. What's up?"

Beale described the wheel in Lydia Walpole's attic. "She won't sell it to me so we've got to steal it," he continued. "It's best to come in the back door." I don't think they even lock their doors in this little town. It should be an easy job. There are also a dozen or more boxes of papers and notes. I want those too. I realize it's a lot to carry out of there and you'll have to make several trips. I would park the car down the street and come in late at night. If you're quiet and don't use flashlights until you're inside the house, it should go smoothly."

Evelyn nodded. "It's just an old lady with an unlocked door. It sounds pretty easy."

"There's just one thing, Evelyn," Beale said.

"What's that?" asked Evelyn, with a knowing look in her eye.

Beale nodded at Evelyn. "We'll kill the old lady," she said.

"She knows I want the wheel. If you don't kill her she'll figure I was behind the theft. Make it look like an accident." Evelyn smiled. "We'll take care of it, Ellie."

When Beale got back to Aunt Harriet's breakfast was ready. Less than an hour later he and Nancy were driving out of Mecklinberg and headed for Washington.

Late that night Evelyn and the two men arrived on the back porch of Lydia Walpole's house. They were dressed in black and wore black scarves to cover their faces. The porch was wide and there were six chairs lined up to face the back yard. There were three windows overlooking the porch. Evelyn remembered Beale said the back door would probably not be locked. People in small towns didn't find it necessary to lock their doors as there was virtually no crime. However, when she turned the handle, the door wouldn't budge. It was bolted and there was no way to jimmy a dead-bolt lock.

Evelyn quickly removed her right glove and reached for the knife in her pocket. The knife worked well on window locks because people often neglected to completely close the brass slider part. If the slider was not closed all the way she could slip the knife blade between the space where the upper and lower sections of the wood-framed window overlapped. She could then press the blade against the slider of the lock and push it to the unlock position. That way she could avoid breaking the glass and waking the old lady or the neighbors.

They were in luck. The old lady hadn't closed the flat lock completely. The three intruders quietly climbed through the window and walked from the kitchen into the living room and began creeping up the large staircase leading to the second floor. Evelyn had pulled the scarf from her face. It wouldn't matter if Lydia Walpole saw her since they were going to kill her anyway.

When they reached the top of the stairs on the second floor it was so dark Evelyn had to turn on her flashlight. She wasn't sure which room Lydia Walpole slept in and hoped the old woman would not wake. They would steal the wheel and boxes of notes first and kill the old lady after they loaded the stolen items the car. That way, if the woman happened to make a commotion, they could quickly make their escape. They continued up the staircase to the third floor then moved quietly down the hallway toward the closed door at the opposite end. Behind this door was the staircase to the attic.

So far, there had been no problems. Once they reached the top of the attic stairs she shined the light to the far wall and immediately spotted the wheel and large boxes of notes. They walked across the attic and Henry Darst knelt down to pick up the wheel. Although it was heavy Darst managed to get if off the floor and into his arms. Ed Chambers picked up a large box of notes.

Evelyn, carrying a second box of notes, held the flashlight in her mouth as she led the two men back across the attic. In less than a minute, they had taken the items down the stairs and through the kitchen to the back porch.

They went back inside the home to retrieve the remaining boxes of notes. Following their same path they quickly climbed the stairs to the third floor and then the attic. The twine-bound boxes were large and heavy and each person could carry only one. Darst picked up the first one. "It's as heavy as the wheel," he said. After a half dozen additional trips to the attic they had all but one box of notes stacked on the back porch. Evelyn knew it would be a struggle getting the heavy load to the car. She decided to have Ed Chambers fetch the car and pull it into the driveway even though it would increase their chances of being seen. "Keep the lights off, Ed," she told him. "Henry and I will go get the last box."

Once in the attic, Darst picked up the last box of notes and Evelyn double-checked to make sure they hadn't left anything behind. Then she led the way down the steps and closed the attic door behind Darst. They walked down the hallway to the main stairway leading down to the second floor and stopped to listen. "Lydia Walpole slept through the whole thing," Evelyn whispered.

They carefully made their way to the second floor, first floor, and finally the kitchen. "We made it," Evelyn said.

Suddenly, the kitchen light flashed on temporarily blinding them. Lydia Walpole stood pointing at them. "Dr. Beale sent you people to burglarize my home, didn't he," she said calmly.

"It's too bad you woke up, Mrs. Walpole," replied Evelyn. Darst had set the large box on the floor and moved next to Evelyn.

"Get out of my house, you thieves. I'm going to call the police," Lydia Walpole said, as she began walking from the kitchen toward the study and the telephone.

Evelyn nodded and Henry Darst moved quickly, seizing the old woman from behind.

"What are you doing?" the shocked woman gasped. Those were her last words and Darst clutched the old woman's head with both hands and snapped her neck. She slumped in his arms, and without speaking, he dragged her lifeless body to the foot of the stairs leading to the second floor. Laying the dead woman on the carpet, he lifted her right leg to place it on the bottom step, thus positioning her body to make it appear she had fallen down the steps.

Evelyn pushed the switch to shut off the kitchen light and picked up the box sitting on the kitchen floor. As she carried it out the back door to the porch she saw the car parked next to the house. Chambers had pushed in the clutch and shut off the engine fifty yards up the street and coasted the car noiselessly into Lydia Walpole's driveway.

The wheel and boxes filled the trunk and the back seat of the car forcing Evelyn and the two men to share the front seat. "We'll drive all night to Washington and take all this to OSTRO headquarters," said Evelyn.

# PART TWO

# 7

April 9, Present Time     St. Louis, Missouri

"Teacher broke my nose," screamed the hysterical fourth grader to the school nurse. Blood streamed over his lips and dripped onto his shirt. "She tried to kill me," he wailed. "I want my mommy."

As Catherine "Kate" Darron pulled her six year old Honda into #87, her assigned parking space at Sun Lakes Apartments, she was reflecting on the events of the day. It had started badly with legendary fourth grade demon Bernard Mangole cursing and screaming like a banshee as he ran wildly around the classroom. Although Kate knew she had done everything possible to get Bernard under control, he would have none of it. In desperation, she threatened to send Bernard to the principal's office, but even that didn't register with him.

Seemingly reinvigorated by the negative attention, he screamed a fresh stream of expletives as he ran past Kate's desk. As he rounded the back of the room on his fifth lap, he slapped Susan Tyler on the back of her head nearly knocking the small girl from her desk. Then he slapped two other children on his way to the front of the room. All three children immediately began to cry, adding to the anxiety of the other students already upset by Bernard Mangole's insanity.

As he ran crazily toward Kate she reached out to stop him but Bernard sidestepped and ran into her desk nose first. Instantly, a crimson nasal torrent splashed onto his shirt, the floor and everything near him. To make matters worse, though little Bernard didn't fear reprimands or being sent to see the principal, he was terrified by the sight of his own blood. When the bright red deluge began, it was immediately followed by his screams causing several other students to cry.

As she held a paper towel to Bernard's nose, she glanced at the other children and saw they were horrified by the scene. "Teacher hurt Bernard," their accusatory eyes said. It suddenly occurred to Kate that she now had an even bigger problem. Oh my god, she thought to herself. She had inadvertently injured this child. All she was trying to do was stop him from distracting the class.

"Class, open your math books and do the set of problems on page seventy-two," Kate directed the students as she walked from the room with the injured Bernard.

The rest of the day had gone even worse. The principal, Mr. Edgerton, had to notify Bernard's mother of the incident. The school nurse had to write a report. Kate also had to write a report. Mr. Edgerton reprimanded her and put her on notice. She could be suspended or lose her job, he informed her in his sanctimonious, patronizing mewl.

What a class guy, she thought. I told him it was an accident and I would never harm a child. He sides with the child and parent explaining that I am a new teacher with only four years experience and he will see that I get counseling in how to better control a classroom. Even though she knew in her heart that Bernard Mangole was totally uncontrollable and did not belong in a classroom, she still felt she somehow failed to do her job. I did everything I could to control the monster, she reassured herself. But the guilt wouldn't go away.

Kate stepped out of her car, shaking her head in disbelief at everything that happened. She struggled to balance her pile of "squirk," which was her acronym for schoolwork and all the rest of her daily baggage. The squirk pile was a conglomeration of lesson plans, assignments to be graded and so on. As she walked toward her apartment the perilously balanced heap was in her left hand and the strap of her purse hung over her left shoulder. The cell phone in her right hand was against her ear and she was talking to a boyfriend she no longer cared about. It was Friday night and he "couldn't make it" because he had to work late. That meant he found someone else or he too had lost interest in their relationship which had never existed in the first place.

"Okay, maybe some other time," she said, as she clicked off her phone. "What an idiot," she mumbled to herself. "He called at six o'clock to tell me he couldn't meet me at seven."

It was going to be another Friday night alone in her apartment. She could call some friends. It wasn't that she didn't have friends. She had some really great friends but they always ended up at a bar someplace with the "standard fixture guys" coming over to their table looking for some "action."

Standard fixture guys, her group of girlfriends theorized, were male bimbos hired by bars at what couldn't possibly be more than $1.00 per hour, free beer and all the sex they could score with whichever desperate females were drunk or horny enough to cave in. They would approach women, launch into their act and pretend they were the proverbial rocket scientist, CEO of a new start-up company, lawyer, etc. Oh yeah, and the other thing about them was their hair. They all had a spiky, oily patch of hair resembling an abandoned garden on some distant planet with its untended alien plants grown wildly out of control, lying in wait to eat random visitors from earth. Yeah, she thought, that's a good description.

She remembered a night several weeks ago when the "girl group," as she and her friends referred to themselves, had the displeasure of a random "SFG" (standard fixture guy) inviting himself to sit down at their table and interrupt their conversation. The only thing she remembered from that boring discussion was that he said he spent half an hour getting his hair just right.

The normally reserved girl group just couldn't handle that one and immediately burst into uncontrollable laughter, literally driving the poor guy from the table. His hair pile looked like a bird's nest constructed by some deranged miniature vulture who had a one-night stand with an extremely out of sorts crow. "All's well that ends well," she smiled to herself.

Kate considered herself an attractive woman at five feet eight inches, light brown hair and hazel eyes. Though she was twenty-eight years old she had never seemed to come across the right guy. She often thought she would have to get a handle on that problem, but never did. For whatever reason, it wasn't at the top of her agenda and she found herself drifting from one short-term dating partner to another.

Carefully balancing the squirk pile, she managed to unlock the door of the main building and climb the stairs to her second floor apartment. The squirk pile was teetering dangerously now. She got the key into the lock and pushed her apartment door open at exactly the same moment the ten-inch high squirk pile decided it could no longer keep its balance and dove from her arm to scatter in a thousand directions as it hit the floor.

"Darn, I almost made it," she said to herself. She threw her purse on the coffee table and collapsed on the sofa. She would pick up her demolished squirk pile later. What a day it had been. Martini time, she thought, as she walked to the cupboard and reached for the bottle of Bombay Sapphire gin. She filled her silver metal shaker half full of ice and poured in a larger than usual amount of gin because of her especially bad day. She pushed the lid topped by the little red vested bartender onto the shaker. Then she shook the concoction vigorously for a minute and a half and poured the gray, syrupy mixture through the strainer into the stem glass. "The perfect terminally dry martini," she complimented herself, as she brought the glass to her lips.

Her cell phone rang. "Hey Kate, it's me again. Great news, I don't have to work late after all. I'll meet you at seven."

"Oh, I'm sorry, Norm. I've made other arrangements for this evening."

"Aw wait a minute, Kate. I'm sorry for that earlier call, but you know how work is. I'm an important guy around here. The place would grind to a halt without me. Come on now, forgive me. I'll see you in fifteen minutes."

"Norm, I'd love to but you know what, I've got something much more important to do. I've got to clean the mildew out of my bath tub and somehow I find the mildew more attractive than you."

"Oh, that hurts, very deeply. Come on now. You know you want to see me. You know you love my jokes. I'm a real funny guy."

"No you're not. I told you I'm busy."

"Well, how about next week?"

"Let me check my calendar. No, I'm busy then too," she said, obviously without looking at her calendar. "And also the week after. Actually, I have no openings ever for the rest of my life." She clicked off the cell phone and took a long sip of her martini.

It was almost six-thirty when she sat down in the easy chair by the large window facing the grassy common area between her building and the apartment building directly opposite. She sat staring through the window at the park-like area sipping her martini for ten minutes or so.

Some crackers and cheese might be nice, she thought, taking the final gulp of gin from the glass. There has to be a better way, she thought, as she got up to refresh her drink and put some crackers and cheese on a small plate. I'm basically happy, content, I suppose. But, I'm bored. I'm tired of all the nonsense a teacher goes through. But after Mr. Edgerton meets with the school superintendent and tells him how incorrigible I am, I'm going to lose my job anyway. I'll be unemployed Monday morning. "That should be fun," she muttered to herself.

I love to teach, she thought, continuing to sort out the disastrous morning and her life in general. And I love children. I want them to learn. But how can I teach when kids like Bernard Mangole literally take over the class? The principal is afraid of the parents and law suits and blames the control issue on the teacher. Some children just can't be controlled and need to be out of the class. The hell with the child psychology hocus-pocus, she concluded.

Kate was thinking Bernard Mangole would remain in class to terrorize some other teacher after she was fired on Monday. She had almost reached the point of not caring about it any more, however, she needed the income to support herself. Her apartment rent alone consumed almost thirty-six percent of her paycheck. She still owed $1867 on her car. She couldn't afford to not have a job.

She took the first sip of her second martini. That tastes better than the first martini, she thought. She wondered how that was possible because the only ingredient in her martini was gin. Technically, it wasn't a martini without the vermouth, but that's how she liked it and that's what she called it.

Although it was still light outside, the sun was moving downward in the sky and the lights of the other apartments were beginning to come on. Okay, think about the positives, she reflected. The martini is a good one. Kate always drank Bombay Sapphire. That was her rule. The martini is not the most important thing, but it's a start. Or maybe the martini is the most important thing, she countered her own thought. The two drinks were starting to have that soothing, relaxing effect, as she liked to refer to a slight buzz.

Back to the other positives, she had a nice apartment. It wasn't cheap, but it was worth the higher rent. She didn't have a romantic interest. The guy she just hung up on had never come close to being a romantic interest. Wait a minute, that's not a positive, or is it, she wondered. Yeah, she decided. Having no romantic interest is a positive. She had a little bit of savings. If they fired her on Monday, she could last three, maybe four months in her apartment. Well, there's a positive. While there weren't a lot of strong positives, she was happy.

The crackers and cheese would be dinner. When she finished the second martini she would move back to her couch and read, then drift off to sleep until the sun came though her dining room window on Saturday morning.

Suddenly, there was a knock on her front door. Who in the world could that be, she wondered, as she got up and walked across the room. She assumed it was someone from another apartment in the building because only they had a key to the main entrance.

Kate opened the door and found herself facing a smiling, nattily attired woman in her late forties. The woman's face was full and weathered, the deep wrinkles between her sunken eyes and around her mouth signaling worldly sophistication and hard won wisdom. Her gray-flecked brown hair was arranged in a bun at the back of her head and she was wearing a crisp, dark blue suit and a white blouse with wide collars. The skirt extended several inches below her knees. While her outfit was attractive, even elegant, it was hopelessly out of date making the woman appear as if she stepped out of an early 1940's movie. Her pearl necklace must have cost a fortune, Kate guessed, not to mention the bracelet on her right wrist. Kate's first impression was that the woman was intimidating. Her sincere smile, however, eased Kate's apprehension.

"Miss Darron," the woman said, "I'm sorry to bother you this evening. I do hope you'll forgive me," she added, staring at the clutter of squirk papers scattered on the floor behind Kate.

"Of course," Kate replied. "What can I do for you?"

"I'm afraid I have some bad news," the woman replied. "I accidentally bumped into your car and caused some damage. Of course, I'll pay for whatever it costs to repair. I'm sorry to ruin your evening."

"Oh, you're not ruining my evening," Kate replied. "Someone has already beaten you to it," she added laughing.

"Oh, I'm so happy you're not upset," the woman said. "It's none of my business, but who ruined your evening, dear?"

"Oh, this guy cancelled a date tonight. Frankly, I'm just as happy he did. But please," Kate added smiling, "don't worry about the car," while actually thinking that someone bumping into her car was the perfect ending to a horrible day. "We'll exchange the usual information and let the insurance companies figure it out. Do you have your insurance card with you?"

"Oh darn it," the woman said. "Isn't that absent-minded of me? I left my purse in my apartment. Look Kate, since your plans were cancelled for the evening, why don't you come over to my apartment and we can exchange insurance information and you can have dinner with me."

"Oh, I couldn't impose," replied Kate, thinking she just wanted this day to end.

"You won't be imposing, dear. I promise. When was the last time you had a good home cooked meal?"

"All right," Kate said, after initially hesitating and remembering the crackers and cheese on the coffee table. "That sounds great."

"I'm in the building directly across from yours. My apartment is number twelve," the woman said. "We'll see you there in say, thirty minutes." Then she turned and walked away.

Kate's cell phone rang again. She walked over to the coffee table to pick it up. It was Norm or whatever his name was. She clicked the power button shutting the phone off for the night.

# 8

April 9, Present Time    St. Louis, Missouri

Kate was still wearing the slacks and blouse she wore to work that day and decided she was too tired to change clothes. She took a last gulp of her martini and picked up her squirk pile strewn on the floor by the apartment door. She liked to stay organized. Life was simpler that way. It was embarrassing when the woman saw the mess on the floor when Kate spoke with her.

As she walked over to the door, for some reason she stopped to look back into her apartment. It's a nice place, she thought. I'll miss it if I get fired and have to move. She pulled the door open and walked into the hallway and the door swung closed behind her.

Kate knew the woman's #12 first floor apartment was located across the courtyard just below and to the right of her own because all the units in the complex were designed alike. As Kate walked out of the front exit of her own building and stood facing the courtyard she began to wonder about the woman. How did she know my name?

As she walked her thoughts switched back to the events of the day and that mousy little principal. How did he get that job and who would marry a jerk like that? There ought to be a law, she reflected, but how does one legislate against stupidity? Too profound a question, she decided, as she stepped up on the porch and reached toward the doorbell at the entrance to the woman's building. But she hesitated, suddenly remembering she hadn't looked at the damage to her car. I should do that before I see the woman, she thought. She turned and stepped off the porch and walked toward her car, which sat in the parking lot fifty yards away.

Once she reached the car she carefully inspected it. There were one or two tiny dents in the left rear panel but they'd been there a long time. Kate couldn't see any other damage. She carefully walked around the car again. There was absolutely no damage. Puzzled, Kate re-traced her steps to the main door of the woman's apartment building. She pushed the doorbell for #12. In a few moments she saw the woman smiling at her through the glass of the door.

"Come in, Kate," she said, as she held the door open. "You're very punctual. I like that in a person."

"It's one of my faults," laughed Kate, as they began walking down the hallway. Kate wondered about this oddly dressed woman who invited her to dinner when they hadn't even known each other less than an hour before. The woman was strange, mysterious, Kate thought.

"Here we are," the woman said, as she stopped at the apartment with #12 on the door. She opened the door for Kate and followed her inside.

"You have a gorgeous place," Kate remarked, admiring the tastefully furnished living room. While the room was filled with Craftsman style furniture that was always in vogue, it was appointed in a more modern style that contrasted noticeably with the clothes the woman wore. Kate had seen old movies with women dressed as this woman, but she had never seen anyone in person attired in such ancient fashion.

Two facing couches, deep red and adorned with gold floral patterns, were the center-piece of the room. The drapes, also a deep crimson, were tied back with gold rope. The lamps had large full bases and towering shades. They were museum quality, Kate presumed. Carefully placed vases held fresh flowers. "It's wonderful," Kate said.

"Thank you dear. I'm so happy you like it."

"What are those pictures?" asked Kate, as she noticed a long row of nicely framed photographs hanging on the wall above the couch.

"Oh those are photographs of some old friends," the woman answered.

"They're all black and white pictures," Kate remarked, noticing there were no color ones.

52

"Dinner is nearly ready, Kate," the woman replied, not addressing the question. Let's sit at the table and have a glass of wine."

Kate wanted to tell the woman she couldn't find any damage on her car, but hadn't yet had the opportunity. She walked toward the dining room, which was actually part of the living room. The only thing that made it a dining room was the chandelier above the table located in front of a large picture window facing the common grassy area between the apartment buildings.

Kate marveled at the beautifully set table with its stunning dinnerware, exquisite silverware, and the two large lighted candles atop elegant silver candle-holders. The table was set for two people.

"Thank you for going to so much trouble........," Kate remarked. It was then she realized her hostess had never mentioned her name.

"Oh, it's no trouble. I fix a formal dinner every night. It's the best time of day, don't you think?"

After pouring the wine the woman put on an apron and went into the kitchen. She returned shortly with two plates of grilled salmon, setting one before Kate and one at her own place at the end of the table. As she took off her apron and prepared to sit down, she smiled and said, "So tell me about yourself, Kate. Do you still shoot? Didn't you reach the state championship when you were in high school?"

Stunned, Kate hesitated then replied. "How did you know I was a competitive shooter? And, how did you know my name? And, what's your name?"

"Oh, I'm sorry dear. I didn't mean to be rude. I'll tell you all about that later. It's a long story," she laughed.

Why is this woman dodging my questions? Kate wondered. And why does she want to know more about me? It seemed like an odd request from someone she'd just met and who was herself very odd. However, Kate felt comfortable with the older woman and realized they probably didn't have a lot in common. There wasn't much else to talk about, Kate decided, so she might as well answer her questions. Then she remembered she'd seen no damage on her car.

"Oh, I almost forgot to tell you. I couldn't see where you bumped into my car."

"Well, I didn't think it was noticeable, however, I felt so guilty about backing into it, I thought I better tell you," the woman replied.

Kate briefly reflected on that explanation and decided to forget about the car. She began to answer the questions the woman asked.

"I've lived in St. Louis all my life. My father and mother also live here. His name is Terry and hers is Maryanne. Like me, they lived here all their lives."

"Oh, how nice that is for you."

"Yes, it really is," replied Kate.

"My grandparents on my mother's side live in St. Louis also." Kate added, taking a small sip of wine. "I don't shoot anymore. I quit shooting after the state championships because I lost interest. I never really cared for guns."

"Kate, what I understand is that you were quite proficient with both a pistol and rifle. And you won first place in both categories at the state championships."

Kate shrugged, not wanting to pursue that particular matter.

"You were so good you might have made it all the way to the Olympics. Isn't that true?" the woman continued.

"I don't think so," Kate replied. "You have to be extremely dedicated to compete at that level. I just didn't care about it enough to put in the time and effort. And like I said, I really don't care for guns."

"How is it you started shooting, then?" the woman asked.

"My parents both wanted a boy, but got me instead. Dad's obsession was hunting deer. I couldn't stand shooting animals. He made me shoot a deer once and it made me ill and depressed me for weeks. I never shot another animal of any kind. In an effort to please him I took up shooting as a sport. It kind of got out of control when I started winning matches."

"You really went into competitive shooting to please your father then. Is that right?"

"Yes, I guess so," answered Kate, becoming more puzzled as to why the woman continued with her questions.

"But then you quit shooting after you won at the state competition and did nothing for a year. Wasn't that a rebellion against your father?"

"Excuse me," replied Kate. "I don't even know you but you seem to have an uncanny amount of information about me? What's going on here?" Kate asked, mildly alarmed.

"One more question, dear," the woman persisted. "I know you had a close relationship with your Uncle Stew. He taught you to fly an airplane. Do you still fly?"

"How do you know that?" Kate asked more forcefully. "You seem to know everything about me and I find that very upsetting. In fact, I find it spooky."

"I apologize, Kate," the woman laughed disarmingly. I really have a logical explanation. I promise. I'll tell you all about it after dinner. But you were a competitive shooter and you have flown an airplane. Is that not correct?"

"Yes," Kate said, shaking her head in amazement. But I only flew an airplane a couple of times. I never got my pilot's license."

The woman hadn't answered any of Kate's questions but her manner and tone were calming. Kate was puzzled how this perfect stranger seemed to know so many details of her life. Kate asked her several more times how she knew so much about her. But while the dinner progressed nicely, the older woman continued to sidestep Kate's questions. And although Kate had initially felt uncomfortable talking with the woman, she now felt relaxed. It must be the wine, she thought.

But it was now Kate who decided to ask some questions. "Why did you ask me to come to dinner tonight? I mean, I'm glad you did but you've never even met me."

"But I do know you, Kate," she replied. "And I asked you here because I needed to see you in person."

"What do you mean?" Kate asked. "Why do you need to see me in person?"

The woman smiled. "Would you like some more wine, Kate?"

"No, thank you," Kate replied. "I've had more than enough wine this evening."

"But, you only drank half your glass," the woman laughed.

"I'm afraid I had two drinks earlier this evening," Kate answered. "I'm past my limit."

After saying she didn't want more wine, Kate took another sip of her Chardonnay. She was again becoming uncomfortable, sensing there was more to this dinner than just a neighborly visit. Her hostess was looking across the table gently smiling. Kate smiled back, trying to figure out whom the woman was and what it was she wanted.

"Kate, you asked about the pictures on the wall. Would you like to see them?"

"Yes, I'd love to," Kate replied, although she didn't really care about the pictures. However, she felt awkward sitting talking with someone about whom she knew nothing. Besides, her face was warm from the wine and she needed to stand up and walk around.

"Why don't you go into the living room and take a look at the pictures while I clear the table? I'll join you in a few minutes."

"Can I help you with anything?" Kate offered.

"No, that's all right. I'll be finished shortly."

Kate got up from her chair and walked across the room to the row of pictures near the red, flowered couch. Gazing at the photographs she again noted that every picture was black and white and remembered the woman never responded to her observing that fact when she first arrived at her apartment. She didn't know much about airplanes, but found it striking that all the photos were of old, propeller driven military type aircraft. There was not one jet engine airplane in the entire group.

The pictures were obviously taken during World War II nearly seventy years ago. Amazingly, they were in such good condition they appeared to have been taken only recently. What was also curious, every picture was of women in flight suits standing near airplanes. There wasn't a man in any photo. The women must be pilots, Kate thought, as she sat down on the couch beneath the pictures.

The older woman came into the room and sat down on the couch across from Kate and the row of photographs. Kate again began to feel uneasy and looked around the room, and then at the woman gazing back at her. She noticed the lace edge of a slip showing below the hem of her dress, something rarely seen anymore. She's dressed like she's living in 1940, Kate thought once again. I must be in some sort of time-warp, she silently chuckled.

"Is everything alright, Kate?" the woman asked.

"Yes, of course," replied Kate. "You know, I love your clothes," she added, hoping the woman would mention where she bought them. Where on earth could she buy those things? Kate wondered. No store would stock outdated women's clothes.

"I'm glad you like them, Kate," she replied. "What do you think of my pictures? They're very unusual, wouldn't you agree?"

"They're wonderful," Kate said, wondering why she didn't talk more about her wardrobe after she was given a compliment. Most women would have jumped at the opportunity to talk about their clothes after a flattering remark.

"Are the women in the photographs all pilots?" Kate asked, although the answer to the question was obvious. However, she was looking for an explanation. Why were these old pictures hanging on the woman's apartment wall? One would have expected more personal photographs of family and friends, but there were no other pictures in the room. These photographs were obviously taken at a military location in the distant past. That these pictures were the only ones being displayed by the mysterious woman was also strange.

"Yes, every woman in the photographs is a pilot," the woman answered. "The pictures were taken during World War II."

"I guessed that one right," Kate said. "But, I didn't know women were flying airplanes in World War II."

"There were quite a few women flying planes during the war, Kate. That's the real low down. Most people don't know that." The woman then stood up from the couch and walked toward Kate and the row of photographs. "I'm in some of those pictures," she said. Kate rose to again view the photos. "See if you recognize me," the woman said, pointing to the third picture in the first row.

Kate definitely saw the resemblance. "Yes, it is you!" she exclaimed, not understanding why she was so excited about recognizing the woman. But Kate suddenly stepped back, perplexed. "But, how can that be you?" she asked in a puzzled voice. "These pictures are over seventy years old."

"Maybe it's my grandmother in the photo," the woman replied laughing.

Kate smiled, accepting the woman was joking. Her humor seemed bizarre and out of place however.

"Did you see this one?" the woman asked, pointing at another picture.

Kate looked toward the photo at which the woman pointed, moving closer to the wall to see it more clearly.

She looked back at the woman. "Is this a joke?" Kate gasped in alarm. Her voice shaking, Kate asked, "Who are you?"

"I'm sorry that particular photograph upset you, Kate," she replied. "In answer to your question, my name is Evelyn Rankow."

Kate again looked closely at the picture. Anxiety surged through her body and her knees began to weaken. The woman in the black and white photograph staring back at her across the decades was

Kate Darron herself, wearing a flight suit and kneeling in front of a B-17 bomber.

# 9

April 9, Present Time    St. Louis, Missouri

"Think of me as the fairy godmother of death, Kate, come to deliver the unfortunate news that you shall be dead in less than half an hour," Evelyn said.

Astonished and trembling, Kate sat down on the crimson couch and looked up at Evelyn Rankow standing next to her.

"Yes, it's really you in the photograph Kate. And, it is me in the other picture, not my grandmother."

"What the hell are you talking about?" demanded an astonished Kate Darron. She was struggling to regain her composure and feign a brave front. "That picture is seventy years old and was obviously altered. Who are you, Evelyn? Why are you playing games with me?"

Evelyn turned and walked to a table across the living room and pulled something from the drawer. As she walked back across the room, she said, "The photo was not altered, Kate. It is you in the picture. Perhaps this will help explain things," she added, handing a newspaper to Kate.

Kate looked at the paper and noticed it was dated April 10. "This is tomorrow's newspaper," she said. "How did you get this? They don't deliver the paper until morning." As she glanced down the front page she saw her own picture and the heading above an article. "Local teacher Catherine Darron killed in car accident."

"I'm getting out of here!" Kate exclaimed as she stood up.

"I'm afraid not, Kate," Evelyn replied.

"Try and stop me," Kate said, and turned to run to the apartment door.

"Running is useless, my Dear," countered Evelyn, as Kate pulled the door open.

Two stern looking men stood blocking the doorway. The unsmiling man with coal black hair, wide lapel and double breasted dark suit moved through the doorway, easily pushing Kate back inside the apartment. The second man also came into the apartment and positioned himself in front of the door. Both men were muscular and intimidating; neither was one to be fooled with.

Kate, forcing herself to remain calm, challenged Evelyn Rankow. "You can't keep me here forever. I'll escape sooner or later."

"Sit down, Miss Darron," Evelyn ordered forcefully, abruptly changing her tone. "I shall do the talking as you have very little time left." She turned to the larger of the two men. "Henry, please bring some wine from the table." Unsmiling, somber Henry Darst walked to the dining room table, poured the wine and returned with two glasses of Chardonnay.

"I prefer civility, Miss Darron, don't you? A toast to life," Evelyn said, lifting her glass. As she couldn't escape, Kate concluded her best strategy was to cooperate with the intimidating Evelyn Rankow. She would bide her time and make her move. Kate took a long gulp from the glass.

"Are you kidnapping me, Evelyn?" Kate asked, although she couldn't imagine why. Her family was not wealthy and Kate had no money herself.

"It is good wine, Kate," is it not?" Evelyn asked, avoiding Kate's question. "Henry is a connoisseur, you know." The woman took another drink. Kate followed her lead and took another long gulp, wondering if she was trying to find courage in the alcohol.

"I'm sorry. I forgot to introduce Henry Darst and Ed Chambers, Kate. They're my two goons, although I say that affectionately."

Kate noticed Evelyn had used the terms "low down" and "goons," expressions from an earlier era. Kate heard these terms in old movies from the 1940's. This was further unsettling. "Who are you, Evelyn, and what do you want from me?" Kate asked, ignoring Evelyn's introduction of the two men.

"The reason I asked you so many questions," Evelyn said, "is because I had to be absolutely certain it was you, Kate. That's why I asked you about your experience with guns and flying airplanes. To answer your other question, I would prefer to say that I'm here to offer you a proposition, however you really have no choice in the matter."

Kate, increasingly fearful of Evelyn Rankow, listened. As Evelyn sat on the couch facing her, Kate again noticed the woman's dated clothes. The men's double breasted suits and wide ties were also a style from a bygone era. While Kate thought Evelyn's clothes were eccentric, the men's equally out of date wardrobes added to the mystery of the visitors. Something quite eerie was happening and Kate was becoming more frightened with each passing second.

"How can I be in a picture taken seventy years ago? How can you have tomorrow's newspaper which hasn't even been printed yet?" Kate asked fearfully.

"Kate, what I'm going to tell you will sound preposterous, but I will try to explain in the short time we have. You will die in that car accident. That is your destiny."

"What?" Kate gasped, her voice shaking. "Who are you people? Are you crazy?" Kate asked, unable believe what she was hearing.

"Henry, Ed and I live in the year 1939 and work for the government agency OSTRO. That acronym stands for the Office of Strategic Threat Response Operations. OSTRO came into possession of an ancient device that allows us to travel in time. Because World War II shall begin in two years, OSTRO created the Destiny Project."

Kate found Evelyn's story incredible, but seeing herself in a seventy year old picture and in a yet unprinted newspaper article announcing her death imparted frightening credibility to the woman's words.

"What does that have to do with me?" a frightened Kate asked.

"When the war starts, the United States will need many pilots and other people with critical skills such as those who know how to use guns. That's where the Destiny Project comes in. Because we are able to travel in time, we go into the future and bring people with certain critical skills back to 1939. You are one of those people because you know how to fly an airplane and handle a gun. OSTRO will use you for covert missions behind enemy lines."

"But what about my life here?" a still unbelieving Kate angrily asked. "If what you say is true, you're kidnapping me and robbing me of my life."

"That's the beautiful thing about the Destiny Project," answered Evelyn. "Kate, we're actually giving you your life. We only kidnap people from the future who either have died or are going to die. We travel in time to the minutes before those people are going to die and take them with us. They avoid their destiny, which is death. That is what we mean by the Destiny Project. We change people's destinies. We give them life when they would otherwise have died. Don't you see how wonderful this is for you Kate?" You are going to live, not die in that car accident."

"You are playing God," Kate snapped.

"And you're going to die in that car accident in less than twenty minutes just as it says in that newspaper you're holding, countered an irritated Evelyn Rankow. We're taking you back to 1939 and saving your life. You should be grateful."

"Just how am I going to die in a car accident when I'm sitting here talking with you?" Kate replied crossly.

Evelyn Rankow smiled. "That's precisely the point, Kate. Although your destiny is to die in the automobile accident, my curious profession allows me to adjust peoples' destinies. I'm here to make sure you aren't killed in the car accident," she replied. "Can't you understand this? Why must I repeat myself?"

Nearly speechless, Kate blurted, "This just isn't right. It's too bizarre, too crazy. I'm not going with you, Evelyn."

"Oh you're coming with us, all right," Evelyn said smiling. Evelyn gulped the last of her wine and set her glass on the coffee table.

Kate began to feel dizzy and struggled to focus her eyes. Her vision was blurring and her eyes grew heavy. She tried to stand but fell backward onto the couch. "You drugged me," she moaned, as the wine glass slipped from her hand and fell to the floor. She felt herself falling toward the glass coffee table as powerful hands gripped her shoulders.

# PART THREE

# 10

May 11 1939    Ebbers Field

Acton, Maryland (33 miles from Washington)

Kate groaned, reluctantly waking to nasty throbbing in her head. Her eyes instinctively refused to open to the blinding light until she cupped her left hand to her forehead to shield them from the brightness. Raising her shoulders, she leaned to her right and propped herself on her arm. She struggled to focus her eyes as she stared at the faded green walls surrounding her narrow cot in the tiny room. There were no windows, only an open transom above a painted white door.

The room was spinning like a drunken top and she knew the stubborn dizziness would be slow to pass. She shook her head to whisk aside the cobwebs and chase the pain. It made her more alert, but the aching in her head was unrelenting.

She sat up and swung her legs right to get her feet to the floor. Drawing a deep breath, Kate reached her left hand to the brown metal footboard and steadied herself as she cautiously rose to stand. She paused briefly before shakily walking to the white door.

She grasped the round doorknob and turned it, but the door was locked. "Naturally," she mumbled, as she leaned against the dull green wall and tried to recall the events of the night before. She remembered the mysterious Evelyn Rankow and two men and being afraid. They must have drugged me, she concluded. And here I am, wherever here is.

Kate suddenly remembered her cell phone and reached into her pocket to pull it out. She smiled as the reassuring light appeared when she flipped it open and turned it on. "Damn!" she exclaimed when "No Service" flashed on the screen.

Kate pounded twice on the door, abruptly stopping because the noise hurt her head. "Let me out!" she yelled weakly. "Open the door!"

Surprisingly, the lock clicked and a soldier in a khaki Army uniform slowly pushed the door open. "Good morning, ma'am," he greeted her.

"Good morning," Kate replied. "Where am I?" she asked.

"Please, ma'am, come with me," the soldier answered.

Kate followed the soldier down a bleak, narrow corridor painted the same faded green as her room. Dark brown ceiling fans rotated stirring the warm air. Kate noticed there was no air conditioning. In a few moments the man stopped and opened another white painted door and motioned to Kate to go into the room.

"Good morning, Kate," smiled Evelyn Rankow sitting behind a large wooden desk on the other side of what apparently was an office. Kate noticed several wooden chairs scattered about as well as an antique looking typewriter sitting on a small table. An ancient looking black telephone and a green blotter-style desk pad sat on the desk. Nobody uses wooden chairs and desk pads anymore, Kate thought.

Two brown ceiling fans twirled lazily recirculating the air drifting in from two open windows on Evelyn's left. The hardwood floor was worn and the spaces between the wood were black from old dirt and wax. Kate noticed the floor squeak under her weight. The large, plain calendar hanging on the wall showed the month of May and the year 1939. It was then that Kate became shaken.

"I said good morning, Kate," Evelyn repeated.

Kate didn't return the greeting. "Where have you taken me, Evelyn?" Kate asked tersely. She tried to disguise her fear but the distress in her voice was noticeable even to her.

"I find your hostility boring, Kate," replied Evelyn. "After all, you're alive only because I brought you here."

"Brought me where?" Kate asked, glaring at the woman.

"I've brought you to this lovely little air base in Acton, Maryland. You could show a little gratitude, you know," Evelyn added with a sarcastic smile.

"What do you want with me?" Kate persisted. "I'm sure you didn't bring me to this place just to keep me alive."

"All right," Evelyn replied curtly. "We'll cut to the chase if that's the way you want it."

"All I want is for you to leave me alone and let me go back to my apartment," Kate replied in a shaky voice.

"Your apartment doesn't exist, Miss Darron," a male's deep voice abruptly answered from behind.

She hadn't seen the man sitting in back of her in the right corner of the room. As she spun round she saw that he too was dressed in the odd, dated wardrobe of an earlier time. He wore a wide blue tie and a double-breasted gray suit.

"Who are you?" Kate asked, in a defiant tone. "What do you mean my apartment doesn't exist?"

"My name is Dr. Elbert Beale," the man answered authoritatively. "I am in charge of the top secret government agency called the Office of Strategic Threat Response Operations, OSTRO for short. But I'm sure Miss Rankow told you that. Miss Rankow works for me, Miss Darron, as do you beginning today. I'll get right to the point and you will keep quiet and listen. Do you understand?"

Kate nodded, realizing she had no choice and was talking to a dangerous man. The intimidating Evelyn Rankow was not nearly as frightening as this man Beale. Abruptly, Kate pulled out her cell phone, quickly flipped it open and pushed #1. The cell phone direct dialed "911" and the GPS would pinpoint Kate's location. But as Kate looked at the phone's screen she saw "No Service" flashing.

Dr. Beale and Evelyn Rankow watched Kate calmly.

"We don't have cell phones in 1939, Kate," Evelyn said.

"If you're finished," Dr. Beale said, "I'll answer your question." Kate looked over at Dr. Beale, trying to control her surging anxiety.

"Miss Darron, your apartment doesn't exist because it will not be constructed for another seventy years."

"What are you talking about?" Kate gasped. "I've lived in my apartment for four years."

"I told you to be quiet and listen," Beale said assertively. "We have not only brought you to a different place, Miss Darron; we have also brought you to a different time. Today is May 11, 1939."

Kate was shocked, unable to accept what Beale said. She felt tears welling and she struggled to maintain her self-control. But she was also furious and screamed. "You people are crazy! This is preposterous. It's some kind of practical joke."

"Miss Darron, I have neither the time nor patience to indulge or coddle you. You have landed in the middle of a highly secret government operation critical to our national security. You are to play a central role in this operation. As Miss Rankow surely told you, this country is going to enter what will be known as World War II in the very near future. As Miss Rankow also told you, the Office of Strategic Threat Response Operations has discovered a way to move forward or backward through time. I don't expect you to understand that. I'm not sure we understand it entirely ourselves. In your case, we moved forward to your time in order to procure your special talents."

"But, why do you want me? I'm only a school teacher. I have nothing to offer you."

"Oh, but you do, Miss Darron. You and others like you whom we brought here have a great deal to offer. You, Miss Darron, are quite handy with firearms, a champion markswoman. You have also flown an airplane, though you will need much more training for the mission you will undertake. Those are two talents you possess. But most importantly," Dr. Beale smiled, "your greatest talent is that you are anonymous, though I suppose that's more circumstance than talent," he chuckled.

"What do you mean by that?" asked Kate, her fear rising.

"What that means, Miss Darron, is that in the year 1939 no one is aware that you exist. Officially, there is no Kate Darron."

"I don't understand," replied Kate.

"Basically, Miss Darron, you weren't born yet."

"I was born in my own time," Kate countered, if I really am in the year 1939. I still don't believe any of this." Kate was trying not to panic as she spoke, but it was difficult.

"You may have been born in your own time, Miss Darron, but that hardly matters," Beale countered.

"And why is that?" asked Kate, an anxious expression on her face.

"Because, Miss Darron, you no longer exist in your own time either. You were killed in a car wreck, just as Evelyn said would happen."

"I don't believe you," Kate replied. "How can I be dead and be here too?"

"We staged your death in the car accident that you were supposed to be in, Miss Darron," Beale replied. "There was a dead body at the scene, but it wasn't yours."

"You mean my parents and friends think I'm dead?" Kate asked bitterly.

"I'm afraid so," Dr. Beale replied.

"You bastards!" Kate screamed. "That will kill my mother. What's the point of your insanity?"

"Don't talk to me in that tone of voice, Miss Darron," Beale snarled angrily. "I can have you killed with a snap of my fingers. That would be such a shame because Evelyn has gone to so much trouble to get you here. You best remember you are quite expendable. There are thousands of women available to us simply by travelling to their time and bringing them back to 1939. We can take our pick. Remember that. You can easily be replaced."

Kate glared at Beale, but wisely chose not to argue further. She now grasped exactly what he was telling her. Dr. Beale and OSTRO had complete control of her life and existence.

"What do you and your sick agency gain from doing this?" Kate asked.

"Do you not see the brilliance of our plan, Miss Darron?" Beale asked. "As I said, officially, you don't exist in 1939 or in the year from which we took you. You are not yet born, but you are already dead. And that is your main value to us. Also remember that.

Because we don't have to account for you, no one will come looking for you or the others if you or they are killed. That gives us an unlimited source of manpower, rather womanpower, for our highest risk missions. That makes things very convenient for OSTRO because we can use you and others like you in any way we wish. But it is also very fortuitous for you, Miss Darron. You are alive because of OSTRO. Had we not brought you back in time you would be dead. It's a win-win situation, don't you think?"

Staring at Dr. Beale, Kate shuddered, no longer doubting the reality of her situation. OSTRO was intent and without scruples. "So you will use me on a mission where I am certain to die?" asked Kate.

"Like all things in life your good fortune at not being killed in your own time comes with a price. Yes, Miss Darron, you have a high probability of being killed, as unfortunate as that is for you. On the brighter side, assuming you survive your particular mission, we reward you by letting you go free in our present time so you can build a new life for yourself. You can live happily ever after," Beale quipped, laughing once again. "That's fair enough, don't you think?"

Kate didn't answer.

"The bottom line," Dr. Beale said, "is you can either cooperate with us or we shall make other arrangements."

Kate knew what Dr. Beale meant by "other arrangements."

Dr. Beale continued. "In order to protect the security of the program, should you attempt to escape we will track you down and kill you. I believe I've covered all the bases, Miss Darron? Do you have any other questions?"

"Just one," replied Kate. "It sounds like there are only women in the program. Why is that?"

"You see, Miss Darron, the Destiny Project is also an experiment. If we are successful in this first phase of the project in which you and other women are participating, we can expand the program to include men but in much greater numbers. That is our ultimate goal."

"So you're using women as guinea pigs to see if your experiment works," replied Kate.

Beale laughed. "I suppose you could say that, Miss Darron. The point is that there is a terrible war coming and our country will be fighting for its very survival. OSTRO will do whatever is necessary to make sure the United States is victorious. You also need to remember these two things. First, only our country's survival matters; our individual fates are unimportant. Second, if you're successful with your mission, you will be rewarded with freedom. If you cooperate and don't gum up the works, things could turn out well for you."

"I guess I have no choice," Kate replied.

Dr. Beale smiled. "You don't, Miss Darron. But I believe you will do well. You see, this conversation we just had was actually an interview. If I didn't approve of you, we would send you back to your own time to die in your car accident. But I like your defiance and willingness to fight. You'll need every bit of that toughness for the mission we are planning for you and your partner."

"Who's my partner?" asked Kate.

"I'll introduce you to her," Evelyn said. "From now on, you'll report to me, Kate. You probably won't see Dr. Beale again."

The only good news of the day, Kate silently told herself.

# 11

May 11, 1939    Ebbers Field

Dr. Beale left the office and Evelyn Rankow made a brief phone call. She hung up and told Kate they would be leaving immediately to meet her partner. The two women walked down the hallway past the room Kate had earlier occupied and continued to the door at the end of the corridor. Kate followed Evelyn through the door onto a small porch.

"There she is," Evelyn said as she raised her hand to wave to a woman standing next to an old airplane fifty yards away.

A light breeze tossed Kate's hair and the drone of airplane engines murmured from across the field as she followed Evelyn toward the woman and the ancient aircraft. Kate couldn't see any planes other than the one toward which they were walking, but its propeller wasn't turning. "Those airplanes you hear are being repaired in the hangars over there," Evelyn said, pointing to the buildings at the far side of the airfield.

As they approached the woman, Kate noticed she appeared to be about the same height and age as her, had short, blond hair and an athletic build. She was a bit masculine looking in the leather flight jacket she was wearing, but definitely attractive. The stately manner in which the woman stood, exuded self-confidence and leadership. She also looked as if she didn't take life too seriously. We'll see, thought Kate-

Apprehensive, Kate pondered her situation. She was here against her will and in the hands of brutal, driven people. While she didn't care for Evelyn, she loathed Dr. Beale. She feared them both. That either of them could snuff out her life at the snap of a finger worried her. Whose side is she on, Kate wondered as she stared at the woman standing near the airplane. Is she one of them or is she like me, kidnapped from some other place and time?

Kate and Evelyn walked onto the grass airfield to where the woman stood.

"Hi, I'm Bebe Beardsley," the woman smiled, extending her hand in an easy, friendly manner.

"I'm Kate Darron. It's nice to meet you."

"Are you ready to go?" Bebe asked.

"Go where?" Kate asked warily.

Bebe looked at Evelyn. "I didn't tell her about that part of the program, Bebe. That's your job," Evelyn said.

"I'm training you to be a pilot, Kate. If you pass, you and I will be partners."

Kate looked at Evelyn in alarm. "I've only flown a plane three or four times in my life, Evelyn."

"Well, you're going to fly in earnest now," Evelyn replied with a menacing smile.

"Shake a leg, Kate," Bebe said, turning to walk over to what Kate thought was an antique airplane. The aircraft was painted dark blue and appeared new, but Kate figured it had to be a hundred years old. That was a bit of an exaggeration since the airplane wasn't invented until 1903, thirty-six years earlier.

"We're not flying in that thing, are we?" Kate asked nervously. "It's old!" I don't believe this is happening, Kate thought. This has got to be a bad dream. It's impossible.

Bebe climbed into the plane and looked at Kate and laughed, not sarcastically, but in a sincere, reassuring way. "It's only twenty-one years old, Kate. It's a 1918 Curtiss JN-4 'Jenny.' The technology is old but it's a good airplane. You'll like it," she said. "I promise."

Bebe's voice and manner put Kate at ease. I like her already, she thought.

"Come on, get in Kate," Bebe said as she started the engine.

Kate hesitated, still trying to sort out all that happened. What's going on, she asked herself as she looked around the wide expanse of the air field. This whole thing is impossible to comprehend.

"Hurry up, Kate. Climb aboard," Bebe yelled impatiently over the gasping bumble of the engine.

The wind-blast from the plane's propeller whipped Kate's hair and her short sleeve white blouse slapped against her body. She held her hand just above her eyes to deflect the propeller's gusts.

"Kate," Bebe yelled again, laughing. "Will you get in before this old bird runs out of gas?"

Kate cautiously climbed aboard into the front seat. For some reason she felt confident and safe with Bebe in control. The "Jenny" was an open cockpit plane, which meant no canopy. The pilot and passenger sat in separate, tandem seats or cockpits facing directly into the wind. The plane was flimsy looking and was made out of wood and fabric, its tail sitting on a skid instead of a wheel. There were two wings, one above and one below the fuselage in which the cockpits were installed. From the back seat, Bebe handed Kate a leather pilot hat and a pair of goggles, then opened the throttle and the plane rolled forward slowly increasing its speed. In a few moments the plane lifted off the grass field and was slowly gaining altitude. The wind scrambled Kate's hair sticking out from under the hat but the strong breeze felt good on her face.

Kate turned around to look at Bebe sitting in the cockpit behind her. "Where are we?" she yelled.

"In an airplane at three hundred feet," Bebe laughed. "Concentrate on your flying lesson, Kate. We've got a lot of work to do."

I shouldn't be here, a bewildered Kate thought to herself as her anxiety returned. I'm not a pilot. Why am I in this antique airplane?

The plane was climbing higher as Bebe yelled it would take about ten minutes for the airplane to reach two thousand feet. Its top speed was seventy-five miles per hour in level flight, but slower in a climb. They soon reached two thousand feet and Kate was looking over the side of the open cockpit at the ground below. She had never seen the ground from an open cockpit and it was scary. It seemed so far away.

But Kate was now focusing on flying in the airplane. It seemed so natural. Though still nervous, she suddenly had a feeling that she belonged up here peacefully flying through the blue sky.

"How're you doing up front?" Bebe yelled. Kate could barely hear her because of the engine's noise.

Kate turned and, surprising herself, gave a "thumbs up."

"Good," Bebe yelled. "I was worried about you back there on the ground. You looked like a little lost puppy."

"I'm good! I feel great," Kate said loudly, again surprising herself at her reaction in view of all that had happened.

"That's good, Kate, 'cause you got the airplane," Bebe abruptly shouted.

"What do you mean?" Kate screamed, realizing exactly what Bebe meant. "Don't even think about me driving this thing!" Kate yelled.

"You don't drive an airplane, Kate," Bebe yelled laughing. "You fly it. I don't have the controls, Kate, you do!"

With neither woman holding the control wheel, the Jenny began to turn toward the left and slowly lose altitude. The plane was actually "steering" itself because the propeller's air blast was stronger against the left side of the airplane than the right. This created a tendency for the plane to always veer slightly to the left.

"Give it some right rudder, Kate. Push the pedal with your right foot but keep the plane level. You're losing altitude. Pull the nose up with the control wheel and turn it so you line us up on the hill straight ahead."

Kate grabbed the control wheel and pressed the rudder with her right foot and pulled back slightly. I should be afraid, she thought, but somehow I'm not. The airplane turned back to the right, but swung too far causing it to be lined up toward the right side of the hill. The nose dropped slightly and the airplane was again losing altitude. Kate was trying to remember what her Uncle Stew told her the three or four times she'd gone flying with him.

"You gave it too much right rudder, Kate," Bebe yelled. "And you let the nose go down so we lost altitude. Pull the control wheel back and let's climb. Take your foot off the rudder controls and it will drift back to the left and then lightly press right rudder to hold it in line with the hill."

Kate was trying to maneuver the plane as Bebe directed.

"Pull the wheel back a little more," Bebe shouted. "Yeah, that's it. No, you let it drift left too much. Don't be afraid to control the airplane," she yelled.

Kate could see Bebe had little tolerance for mistakes, however, Kate knew very little about flying an airplane. Uncle Stew only let her "fly" the plane when he was in it and holding the yoke. What am

I doing here she wondered.

"Okay, let go of the controls, Bebe shouted. "I've got the airplane. Hold on, this is going to be scary."

Kate wasn't looking forward to whatever was going to happen. In fact, if she realized what she was about to experience before she got into the plane, she would have run the other direction while they were still on the ground.

Suddenly, the plane lurched over on its side in a steep left bank and began to "slip" or fall inward, rapidly losing altitude. In seconds the airplane began to "spin" wildly around to its left, pinning Kate to the back of her seat. She couldn't move her arms or any other part of her body. The fields and trees below were spinning crazily and the wind roared like a monster seashell as it rushed past Kate's head.

"Oh my god," she screamed. "I'm gonna' die."

"We're in a spin, Kate," Bebe shouted. "It doesn't get any worse than this."

Kate heard Bebe yelling to explain something, but it made no sense to her. "In a spin, the ailerons and elevators don't respond because the air flows at them from the side instead of from directly in front of them," she heard her say. "The ailerons and elevators are the flight control surfaces, but aren't any help in recovering from a spin. You gotta' apply hard rudder in the opposite direction of the spin to correct the out of control situation. Got it?" Bebe laughed.

"No!" Kate screamed back, becoming panicked. "I don't know what the hell you're talking about!"

Bebe laughed again.

Inexplicably, Kate felt a surge of confidence, some inner force welling up inside of her. She couldn't understand why, but she was no longer afraid and accepted the situation she was in.

"How do we fix it?" she screamed.

"Press the right rudder hard. Put both your feet on it. You'll feel the control return to the ailerons and elevators."

What was actually happening was Bebe had already made the correction, so when Kate pushed down on the right rudder it was already pushed in as far as it would go and the airplane was in the process of righting itself. However the ploy worked and Kate assumed it was she who pulled the airplane out of the spin.

Her confidence increased dramatically, and as she felt the flight controls gradually beginning to respond, she took charge and began flying the airplane. This was exactly what Bebe wanted and she knew that Kate was the person for the mission that was to come.

Bebe had directed Kate to bring the airplane to a lower altitude and they were now flying at three hundred feet. As she was steering the plane in the general direction of the grass airfield they passed over a small town. Kate looked down and saw cars and people going about their daily routines. She noticed all the vehicles were "old cars." There were even a few horse drawn wagons moving through the town.

Kate noticed only one concrete road, and though it was narrow, cars passing each other indicated it had two lanes. Other than this main road, all other roads were made of brown dirt. There were no four lane roads or expressways. There were no large metal power line poles. There were only dark brown wooden telephone poles and what Kate thought must be wires for electricity also strung on them.

If Kate had any doubt about whether she was actually in the year 1939 the Main Street scene in the town below removed it.

To be sure, Kate looked back and asked Bebe, "What's the date today?" she yelled.

"It's May 11, Kate," Bebe answered.

"No, I mean, what year is it?" Kate replied.

"What?" Bebe laughed. "What do you mean what year is it?" she yelled, shaking her head.

"Yeah!" Kate yelled back. "What year is it?"

"It's 1939, Kate," as you well know. What a silly question? I think you need a beer."

Kate, still trying to sort out her situation, shook her head in mild exasperation. It didn't matter that she couldn't understand or accept the bizarre circumstances in which she found herself. The fact was she was in the year 1939 in Acton, Maryland and World War Two was going to start in Europe in less than four months. "Yeah, I do need a beer," she yelled.

As the airplane approached the airfield Bebe took the controls. In minutes, she brought the plane over the field and set it down on the grassy runway. The airplane bounced along toward the east perimeter of the field. As the plane rolled Kate saw Evelyn Rankow standing by a car at the edge of the airfield. Bebe taxied the plane to a point about fifty feet from where Evelyn stood, braked and shut off the engine. Kate climbed out of the Jenny, and when she stepped onto the grass field, her legs felt wobbly. It must be the excitement of flying in the plane, she thought.

Bebe climbed down from the rear seat and walked over to Kate and smiled. "That was a great job, Kate," she said, pulling her leather cap off her head.

Kate smiled back. She really liked this woman, Bebe Beardsley.

"Come on," Bebe said, "let's go see Evelyn," and she turned to walk toward her.

"We're back, Evelyn," Bebe said smiling.

"How did she do, Bebe?" Evelyn asked.

"She did great! I want her flying with me," Bebe replied.

Kate felt good about what Bebe said and suddenly found herself smiling also.

"It's nice to have you in the program, Kate," Evelyn Rankow said. "You'll enjoy flying with Bebe. She's the best pilot in the world."

Bebe laughed. "I think Evelyn exaggerates things a bit," she said, "but not much."

"I'm looking forward to working with you, Kate," Evelyn said. Then she turned and walked toward the black Ford sedan.

"What's with that woman?" Kate asked.

Bebe laughed. "She's a strange one for sure."

Evelyn's car pulled forward and quickly picked up speed then soon disappeared down the dirt road leaving small swirls of tan dust dancing across the green grass field.

"Come on, Kate," Bebe smiled. "Let's get that beer I promised you."

Kate followed Bebe to a black Ford coupe parked on the dirt road, watching her closely as they walked. She noticed earlier that Bebe wore no make-up and wondered why. Bebe's short blond hair tossed in the wind, making her appear efficient and organized, Kate thought. It was obvious Bebe was a take-charge person and in control of things. From the short flight, Kate could see Bebe was precise, detail oriented and optimistic. They climbed into the car and Kate searched for the seat belts.

"What are looking for?" Bebe asked.

"Seat belts," Kate said.

"There aren't any seat belts," Bebe laughed. "Seat belts are only in airplanes."

Kate frowned. "It really is 1939," she said.

"Don't worry about it, Kate," Bebe replied. "I had the same trouble accepting I was in a different time when I got here. I didn't understand it either. All I can say is that you have to adjust because there's nothing else you can do. You can't escape and if you told anyone what happened to you, they'd lock you up in a mental institution."

Kate smiled at Bebe. Unlike Bebe, Kate was favored make-up and bright lipstick. And she wasn't nearly as self-confident as Bebe. Kate had never been in a bad situation and wasn't sure how to handle one. Also unlike Bebe, Kate was a generalist, didn't like details and was fatalistic.

"They told me you were coming, Kate," Bebe said. "I'm glad you're here. Since I'll be your flight instructor we'll be spending a lot of time together and I know we'll be friends."

Kate was still bewildered by what had happened to her, but she realized she had no choice but to accept the situation because she was in a life and death game. She had to change her priorities fast if she was going to survive. It was no longer about trying to figure out her predicament and how to get back to her own time. It was now about staying alive. She knew she had to do well and please Evelyn Rankow and Dr. Elbert Beale.

"We'll be great friends, Bebe. I'm looking forward to working with you," Kate added, feeling she could trust this woman completely.

"I have a lot of questions I'd like to ask you, Bebe."

"I know, Kate," she said. "We can talk when we get to the bar."

The two women drove to Acton, a small town in which the main attraction was a minor Revolutionary War site where an insignificant battle had occurred nearly two hundred years earlier. Actually, the battle was not so much itself remembered, but rather what occurred later as a consequence of the fight. While there were only a half dozen deaths of the British and American soldiers who fought there, during the course of the brief battle a stray bullet went through a window of a nearby farmhouse and killed a woman named Annie Jepison.

That event would not have been memorable except for the fact that Annie Jepison was thought by the local population to be a werewolf. This rumor was based entirely on Annie's scraggly appearance. She was a gruesome looking woman with unkempt hair, long fingernails, and prominent eyeteeth. Poor grooming was the primary culprit responsible for her looks.

Every time a farm animal was killed or disappeared, the townspeople blamed it on Annie. In truth, there was some livestock theft and there were packs of wild dogs in the area that would attack farm animals. But, it was more interesting to blame Annie.

However, after she was killed, the disappearances of animals increased. Even a child or two came up missing. The people blamed it all on "Werewolf Annie." Anyway, that was the story on the sign in front of the Acton Inn, which was not an inn at all, but an old tavern which itself had been around for over one hundred years.

The Acton Inn was a re-fitted log structure with streaked whitewash covering the outside walls while a poorly shingled roof tried its best to protect customers from the elements. It had a thickly varnished wood entrance door and the usual lights in the windows advertising beer and billiards. On this particular day, there weren't many people inside the aged building.

As Kate and Bebe walked through the door, the smell of cigarette smoke and stale beer greeted them. A sparse number of customers, the usual bar flies, were sitting at the main bar. The bar was a dark, heavy wood structure with a worn red leather armrest running its full length on top and a brass foot rail extending across the bottom. The bar flies and regulars sitting on the stools glanced in the direction of the women as they walked to the back of the darkened room to find a table. "What's your story, morning glory?" one of the men called.

Bebe and Kate sat down in the corner and ordered a couple of drinks. "We're going to be flying all kinds of airplanes, Kate. I'm sorry about this old bucket today, but that's all that was available. It's actually a pretty good plane though."

"I liked it," said Kate.

Bebe continued. "You already know we're working for OSTRO. Their function is to launch secret missions to neutralize threats to the country. The thing is these missions are always extremely dangerous. That's where we come in. We have to do the neutralizing, or destroying, I should say. They know the war's coming Kate. That's why our work is so critical."

In a few minutes the bartender brought their drinks over to the table. Even though it was a ratty place, Bebe came here often because she liked the atmosphere. Kate was used to a more upscale watering hole but the martini she started to sip was just right, not that straight, cold gin could ever be a problem.

In a few minutes, another round of drinks arrived, though neither Bebe nor Kate had ordered them. "These drinks are from the gentleman at the end of the bar," said the bartender, as he pointed toward a thick-framed man wearing a black leather jacket and a baseball hat. The man looked over and waved at the two women, his piano keyboard-like dentures flaring in a wide smile.

"Tell him 'thanks' but we'll buy our own drinks," replied Bebe.

"Ma'am, that's Frank Caperra. You better take the drinks and let it be."

"I said we'll buy our own drinks," reiterated Bebe.

The bartender picked up the drinks and went back to the bar. He said something to Frank Caperra who then looked over at the two women but didn't flash a smile this time. He got up and walked toward their table.

Although Bebe saw him coming, she continued discussing the working situation in which the two women would be involved.

As usual, Kate thought, there's some guy interrupting the conversation of women. Now it was this big lug, Frank Caperra, or whoever he was.

"Ladies, I bought you drinks," he said, as he pulled up a chair next to Bebe. "You hurt my feelings when you didn't drink them."

"We're only having one drink," replied Bebe. "Thanks anyway, but we have to leave soon."

"Well, just one more won't hurt anything," the lout replied, as the bartender arrived at the table with three drinks.

"I said we had to leave," replied Bebe as she stood up. "Come on, Kate, let's go."

Caperra also stood up. "I bought you dames drinks and you're going to drink them," he snarled. It was obvious he had drunk too much himself. The bartender set the three drinks down on the table.

"Now sit down and join me in one little drink here."

Bebe threw a dollar on the table for the bartender and said, "We're leaving."

Caperra grabbed Bebe's right arm and pushed her backwards toward her chair. "Sit the hell down," he ordered.

It happened faster than Kate could believe. Caperra, holding his testicles, slumped to his knees with his face twisted in a painful grimace. He gasped for air with his mouth open wide and trying to speak. He was bending slightly forward when Bebe's right foot came up a second time and slammed directly into the center of his face. The precise blow broke Caperra's nose with a dull, sickening crunch, causing his heavy body to hurl backwards and crash to the floor. Blood gushed down his left cheek onto the worn linoleum.

Bebe picked up the glass of straight whiskey and poured it into Caperra's face. He screamed in agony as the alcohol splashed onto the torn flesh around his nose. She let the heavy glass drop from her hand, striking Caperra on his forehead causing him to lurch. He reached his hand to feel for damage.

Now that's how to handle these guys, Kate thought. I really like this woman, Bebe Beardsley. Kate found herself attracted to this strong willed, no-nonsense female aviator. Bebe was a perfectionist in the cockpit, did not tolerate being pushed around and was extremely sure of herself. Kate liked those qualities in a woman. However, Bebe's strong personality also made Kate more aware of her own shortcomings. She vowed to get a handle on her self-confidence issue and not let anyone push her around ever again.

The two women walked across the barroom toward the exit. "See you next time, Oscar," she said as she waved at the bartender.

Oscar, not believing what just happened, waved back feebly.

The two women got into the car and drove away and Bebe continued to brief Kate on what was happening. "What was I saying?" Bebe asked. "Oh yeah, OSTRO conducts top secret combat operations. These operations are against specific high value targets. Germany has a lot of secret weapons projects under development. OSTRO will identify those projects that pose the greatest danger to this country and destroy them. At least, that's the intent of the agency. And that's what you and I are going to do eventually."

"You mean we're going to be flying combat missions?" Kate asked in disbelief.

"You and me both," laughed Bebe. "They'll be dangerous missions with little chance of success. Won't that be fun?" she asked wryly. "But, I'm going to train you first and you'll be just as good a pilot as me when we're finished. My plan is for you to be my co-pilot so we'll be flying those missions together."

"But why are women performing these dangerous missions?" asked Kate.

Bebe thought for a moment and then looked over at Kate. "There's a shortage of male pilots, Kate. OSTRO uses women like us because we're an unlimited supply and expendable."

"That's exactly what Dr. Beale said," Kate replied. "So they kidnapped you too, Bebe? I guess I wasn't one hundred percent sure."

"Yeah, Kate, they did, just before my fiancée and I were to be killed in an airplane crash in 1947. They took me and let him fly to his death."

"That's a really sad story, Bebe," replied Kate. "What was your fiancée's name?"

Bebe smiled. "His name was Francis Hopkins. We hadn't known each other long but he was a really great guy and we loved each other very much. OSTRO saved me because I was a pilot and they needed me. Francis owned a hardware store. They didn't need him so they let him die."

"Dr. Beale and Evelyn Rankow are terrible people," replied Kate.

"If I ever get the chance, I'll kill them both for letting Francis die," Bebe said bitterly.

# 12

August 6, 1941    Long Beach California

The last two years with Bebe were the happiest times of Kate's life. The two women had become inseparable. Bebe spent enormous amounts of time training Kate and both women were exceptionally accomplished pilots. The bond, which formed between them early on, had grown into a much deeper friendship.

They flew as pilot and co-pilot in large airplanes or in the same group when flying single engine aircraft. It seemed like 1939 was only yesterday, but it was now 1941. Both Bebe and Kate accumulated fifteen hundred hours of flying time in the two-year period. The world was moving quickly too. Germany invaded Poland in 1939 and World War II had begun in Europe.

Kate and Bebe had flown to the Lockheed factory in Long Beach, California to pick up a B-17 to deliver to Chanute Field in Rantoul, Illinois. That evening, as they sat together at a table in a nearly empty restaurant in Long Beach, Kate decided to ask Bebe about something that had been bothering her. "Bebe, we've been working together for over two years. We've dated a lot of men as we ferried airplanes back and forth across the country. But neither of us has had a serious romance. Is that because we never stayed in one town long enough to date the same man more than two or three times? Or is there another reason?"

"Yeah," said Bebe. "That's one of the hazards of this job, other than possibly getting killed when they send us on the 'doomsday mission' they have in mind for us. Is that what you're getting at?"

she added, her tone hinting she knew Kate had something else on her mind.

"You know what I'm talking about, Bebe," Kate replied. "Is the reason neither of us has gotten close to any man is because you and I have become too close?"

Bebe momentarily looked away and stared out the restaurant's front window, then slowly turned to Kate and looked into her eyes. Bebe's face had saddened and a tear was slowly making its way down her left cheek. She was about to say something, Kate thought, but hesitated, looked down at the table, and put her fingers around the stem of her wine glass.

"Bebe," Kate said, "we don't have to talk about this now. I'm sorry I brought it up."

Bebe looked toward Kate, nodded reassuringly, and in a voice just above whisper said, "It's all right, Kate." She took an easy sip of wine, slowly put the glass down on the white tablecloth and smiled. "Kate, do you remember when we first met in 1939 and I told you about OSTRO kidnapping me and letting my fiancée Francis Hopkins be killed in an airplane accident?"

"Of course," said Kate. "How could I not remember such a tragic thing?"

"I never told you about Francis and me and how his death happened, but I think it's time I did."

Kate leaned forward, knowing how devastating this event was for Bebe. She also remembered the nights in the last two years when Bebe woke up screaming from frightening nightmares. She couldn't let go of Francis' horrible death at the hands of OSTRO. And Kate would never forget what Bebe told her in 1939. "If I ever get the chance, I'll kill Dr. Elbert Beale and Evelyn Rankow."

Bebe took a sip of wine and signaled the waitress to bring another round. "I don't know if I ever told you, I'm from Omaha, Kate. I worked for a little outfit called Osterman's Flying Service that was located about eight miles out of town. It was owned by a rough, but loveable old girl named Nancy Osterman. We carried some mail and did a little crop dusting and repair work. Occasionally we did charter flights and gave flying lessons. I loved that job. Nancy owned half dozen small airplanes and we were busy all the time. She had just bought a 1947 Piper Super Cruiser for the crop dusting work. I loved that airplane. It was so much fun to fly. Nancy was great to work for and life was good.

In those days I raced airplanes. Nancy had also raced airplanes and done pretty well at it. She became my mentor and sponsored me. I raced more and more until, eventually, it was taking most of my time. But, I was making a lot of money on the race circuit for myself and Nancy .

That's how I met Francis. He loved airplanes and came to some of the races. There was a big race in Omaha in 1946 and I was getting my plane ready to fly. Francis walked up to me and started talking, asking me about the airplane and so on. I had to make some final adjustments on the plane and told him to leave me alone because I was busy. He got this hurt expression on his face, sort of like a little puppy might do. I said, 'Look, come back after the race and I'll give you a ride. But, I gotta' work now. Okay?'

'Yeah,' he said. 'I'm sorry. I didn't mean to be a pest, but I like the look of your airplane.' As he walked away, he stopped and turned around. 'I like the way you look too.' It was so simple and sweet, I never forgot his saying that."

"That's a wonderful story," Kate said. "Tell me more."

"We started dating and pretty soon we fell in love. Francis was busy starting up his business, a small hardware store, and I was racing airplanes for Nancy. Francis asked me to marry him in late 1947. We didn't want a big wedding so we planned to get married in Las Vegas. We booked a flight leaving Omaha two weeks later on a Saturday afternoon."

"That really sounds romantic," said Kate. "It sounds like you were both very happy."

"We were," said Bebe, lifting her glass to take a sip of wine. "We were ecstatic."

"What happened next?" Kate asked.

"One of our airplanes needed an engine overhaul and our shop was backed up. Whenever our shop got overloaded Nancy sent the work we couldn't handle out to Grand Island, about one hundred and twenty-five miles west of Omaha. Nancy had a friend there who was a really good aircraft mechanic. We could have gotten the work done without leaving Omaha if we wanted," laughed Bebe, "but Nancy always sent the work out to this guy who worked out of his barn.

We always thought he was an old boyfriend or something. It was silly to send the work over one hundred miles away when it could be done right there in Omaha. Besides," Bebe laughed again, "none of us could picture gruff old Nancy ever having a romance. Anyway, that's where she wanted the work to go. So on Friday, the day before our flight to Las Vegas, Nancy asked me to fly the airplane over to Grand Island. I didn't think anything of it. It was a routine flight."

"How were you going to get back?" asked Kate. "That engine overhaul would take longer than one day."

"Nancy's mechanic friend was going to let me use his truck to drive back to Omaha. I figured I'd be back Friday afternoon in time to pack for our trip to Las Vegas the next day. Anyway, I flew the airplane to Grand Island and got there around one-thirty that afternoon. As planned, I dropped off the airplane and at around two-fifteen and started driving the truck back to Omaha on Highway 30."

Bebe held the wine glass near her face, momentarily pondering it. "Good wine, Kate," she smiled, then continued. "I drove for about half an hour and stopped at this little cafe in the middle of nowhere to have lunch. I'd eaten there a couple of times before and the food was good. You know how I am about my favorite eating and drinking places, Kate," laughed Bebe.

"Yeah, you do seem to get in a rut when you like a particular restaurant, or worse, some off the wall bar," Kate laughed. It was an intentional tease to lessen Bebe's anxiety as she related the painful details of her fiancée's death.

"You should talk, Miss Bombay Sapphire terminally dry martini girl," Bebe kidded back laughing.

"You forgot it has to be accessorized with two stuffed blue cheese olives on the side," Kate said, smiling.

"I didn't forget," Bebe laughed. "It was just too much to say. I always feel sorry for the poor waitress when you drag her through your laborious martini building ritual. 'It's simple, yet complex. All I want is straight gin, very cold. Don't let the stuffed olives touch the glass. Tell the bartender to not even think about vermouth when he walks by the bottle. We'll pretend it's a martini.' Then you quote the poor woman statistics of the percentage of bartenders who screw your drink up. That would be about 99% if memory serves."

"Alright, you win," Kate laughed. "I didn't mean to get you off track."

"That's okay," said Bebe. "It's always tough when I think about that day, but it's comforting to be able to talk to you about it."

"I'm really glad you feel that way," smiled Kate. "And I'm happy you feel comfortable sharing that part of your life with me. Anyway, you were in the little cafe having lunch. What happened next?"

"I had my lunch," Bebe continued, "and then went out to the truck to drive the rest of the way to Omaha. But the truck wouldn't start. I knew it had plenty of gas so I opened the hood to check the engine. I couldn't believe it. The distributor cap was gone. The wires were just hanging there. Who steals a distributor cap? I should have known then something funny was going on."

"I would have missed it too," said Kate, trying to comfort her. "Besides, you had a lot on your mind. You were going to get married the next day. I know you're a detail-oriented person, but that causes you to be too hard on yourself. Ease up, Bebe. You can't control everything."

"I suppose not," Bebe replied. "Anyway, as I stood there looking into the engine compartment, a woman came up behind me and asked if I was having car trouble. It was Evelyn Rankow. Of course, I didn't know who she was then. She was travelling to Omaha, she said, and I was welcome to ride with her. She just wanted to grab a quick bite to eat before we left. I told her I appreciated it and went back inside the cafe with her. I figured I'd call Nancy's friend when we got back to Omaha and he could come and pick up his truck at the diner.

She insisted I have a cup of coffee with her, which I did. We left the cafe about ten minutes later. I got into Evelyn's car and we drove out of the parking lot and headed east on Highway 30. That's all I remember. The next thing I knew I was at Ebbers Field and it was 1939. It shocked the hell out of me just like it did you, Kate. I argued with Evelyn and Dr. Beale and told them I'd never cooperate with them. They said if I ever wanted to see Francis alive again I had to do what they said. They also threatened to kill my parents if I didn't do what they told me. Like you, I had no choice."

"They take total control of your life, Bebe." Kate agreed. "You have no choice but to do exactly what they say."

"That's how I figured it," replied Bebe. "What I didn't know was they left a message for Francis telling him my plans changed and I'd fly my plane to Las Vegas and meet him there Saturday afternoon. Bebe began to cry softly and wiped her eyes with a napkin. Francis got on the airplane to Las Vegas the next day and it crashed on takeoff. Everyone on board was killed."

Shaking her head in shared anger, Kate felt tears in her own eyes as she put her hand on Bebe's.

"I didn't find out about Francis until later," Bebe said. "Evelyn told me right out of the blue one day. 'It was destiny that you and Francis Hopkins were to be on board the plane when it crashed,' she said. 'Consider yourself lucky that OSTRO changed your destiny."

"I can't believe they are so barbaric," Kate said. "They have incredible power."

Bebe smiled wistfully, recalling happier times. "I know," she said. Her thoughts abruptly turned to the present. "Anyway, there you have it," she said.

"Thank you for confiding in me, Bebe," Kate replied. "I'm really sorry they put you through all of that and Francis died. What they did was horrible."

"Yes," Bebe said with bitterness in her voice. Her face darkened and her expression became severe, hateful. "It was unconscionable. OSTRO will do anything it needs to do to accomplish their missions, no matter what the cost. I'm going to kill Dr. Beale and Evelyn Rankow, Kate. It's only a matter of when. But, I guess I already told you that."

Kate empathized with Bebe's hatred of Dr. Beale and Evelyn Rankow, likening it to OSTRO's faking her own death and the pain her mother and father must have felt when they heard she had been killed. She looked at Bebe and smiled understandingly.

Bebe raised her right hand, and putting it on the back of Kate's neck, pulled her close. She leaned forward and put her face next to Kate's, their cheeks touching. She turned and kissed Kate lightly on her cheek. "Kate, I can't stop hating them for what they did. I'm obsessed with stopping them from controlling people's lives. The only way to do that is to kill them. And my mind is also focused on surviving the mission they're going to give us. There's too much going on in my head right now and most of it isn't good."

"I understand," replied Kate. "I really do." She touched Bebe's hand and said, "I'm with you all the way on this, Bebe. Somehow we'll survive the mission and stop OSTRO. I don't know how, but together we'll do it."

Bebe smiled at Kate. "I know," she replied.

Abruptly changing the subject, Bebe said, "A couple of days ago I overheard Dr. Beale talking with Evelyn about the Destiny Project. What they said was top secret and I didn't tell you about it because there was always someone else around who might hear us."

"What did they say?" asked Kate.

Bebe looked around the deserted restaurant and moved her head closer to Kate and whispered. "They said the United States will be in the war before the end of the year. While many of the newspapers are also saying that, the fact that Beale said it means it will happen for sure. But here's the important part. The Germans use a secret device called the Enigma machine to code all their messages. The British figured out the secret code and were able to find out many of the German's secrets."

"Does that mean what I think it means?" Kate asked apprehensively.

"You guessed it," Bebe answered. "Dr. Beale told Evelyn that OSTRO has now identified all the top secret German sites where their projects are located. Until now, they didn't know where the most important sites were. You and I are going to be dropping bombs on one of those sites before long."

"So our mission is coming soon," said Kate.

"No doubt about it," Bebe replied. "But, there's something else. OSTRO has been conducting other missions and their success rate has not been good. So far, they carried out sixteen missions. Only one of them was successful. In all the other missions the OSTRO agents were killed or captured by the Germans and executed. Dr. Beale told us the missions would be dangerous, but the odds of getting out alive are a lot worse than he said."

"That's gruesome," replied Kate. "It's like we've been condemned to death."

"You're right, Kate. Do the math. One mission out of sixteen is just a little better than a five percent survival rate. When they send us out, it's virtually guaranteed we'll be killed. That's the other reason I didn't tell you what I heard."

"Bebe," Kate said, "why don't we escape? Let's run away."

"Kate, they'd find us in twenty-four hours. Several women already tried to escape. One of them was killed. Two others were brought back but disappeared. OSTRO is powerful and ruthless. We both know that. They play for keeps and we need to be very careful. Our lives are at stake."

"Then we need to escape, Bebe," Kate insisted. "At least we should try."

"We need to do more than try, Kate. If we try and don't succeed they'll kill us, just as I said. Trying is not an option. If we're going to plan an escape, it has to be foolproof."

"Then let's go for it, Bebe."

"We started when I met you two years ago, Kate. Why do you think I trained you so thoroughly? You were part of the plan when you climbed into that old Jenny at Ebbers Field."

"Well, what are we waiting for?"

"We need a mission, Kate. We need to have a mission so we'll be killed."

"We'll get one of those, Bebe, and we will be killed. And that's the part that bothers me," Kate laughed, although she cringed at the thought.

"I'm not too crazy about that part myself," replied Bebe. "But that's exactly the point. They expect us to die so we will, or at least we'll make them think we did."

"What do you mean?" Kate asked, although it was beginning to dawn on her what Bebe was saying.

"I mean we fly the mission, get the job done and then crash the plane. We just make it a point not to get killed in the process. That's a pretty simple plan, don't you think?" Bebe laughed.

Kate found herself laughing too. "The situation is so hopeless we might as well enjoy it." Both of them were laughing so hard they ordered another drink.

"We're gonna' make it," Bebe said. "You know, I purposely waited until someone I could trust came along before I thought about an escape. I also needed someone really good with an airplane. Two people working together have a much better chance to pull it off than one person alone."

"What about the rest of the crew?" Kate asked. "How do we deal with them?"

"If we make it back to friendly territory, we tell them there's something wrong with the engines and they have to bail out. If the plane is so shot up it goes down behind enemy lines, everyone will have to bail out anyway. Either way, you and I will stay with the plane as long as we can to get away from the rest of the crew. They'll think we either died when we bailed out or went down with the plane."

"I think that sounds like a good plan, Bebe, but I don't like our chances for survival."

"Kate, we have no choice. They'll kill us if we don't fly the mission because we would no longer be of any use to them. What else can they do with us? You know they aren't going to send us back to where we came from so we can tell everyone what they're doing here. Yeah, we have a good chance of getting killed if we fly the mission, but that's our only way out. We're not in a good spot here. But, most importantly, we take care of each other, no matter what. Agreed?"

"Definitely," replied Kate. "Your plan is dangerous but it's all we've got."

# 13

August 18, 1941    Chanute Field, Rantoul, Illinois

Working for OSTRO, Bebe and Kate had been using false names when they ferried airplanes from aircraft factories to military bases in the United States. Like many other women pilots, they were flying for the Women's Flying Training Detachment (WFTD) and the Women's Auxiliary Ferrying Squadron (WAFS). Also like these women, they were not in the military, but worked for them.

Unlike the other women pilots, however, they were working undercover for the government, which was the reason for using fictitious names. Kate and Bebe had been flying only B-17 bombers for the past year. Both Kate and Bebe knew there was a specific reason for their getting so many flying hours in this airplane. They had to become highly proficient in the B-17 because that's what they were to fly on whichever mission they were ultimately assigned. They knew that mission would be coming soon.

Evelyn Rankow actually told them they would fly their mission in a B-17 that was being specially modified. Apparently there was a soft spot in her heart. She seemed to want to give Bebe and Kate every chance possible to fly the B-17, probably thinking the more experience they had with the airplane the greater their odds for survival. That led Bebe and Kate to guess their mission was being delayed for the development of some kind of special bomb, which did not yet exist. Evelyn ordered Kate and Bebe not to speak to anyone about this mission. Kate and Bebe both laughed when they left Evelyn's office. They had no idea what the mission entailed so how could they talk to anyone about it?

Kate and Bebe had never flown a B-17 with a full crew. In combat operation, the B-17 carried a crew of ten. The pilot and co-pilot flew the plane. There was also a navigator, bombardier, flight engineer, radio operator, ball turret gunner, left waist gunner, right waist gunner, and tail gunner. But on the flights Bebe and Kate flew, there was just the pilot, co-pilot, navigator and flight engineer.

It was late afternoon and Kate and Bebe had just landed a B-17. They were taxiing the big bomber on the ramp at Chanute Field in north central Illinois. Bebe pulled the four-engine plane up to its parking spot as directed by the flag-man signaling them. As the crew climbed out the hatch door in the forward portion of the belly of the airplane, a corporal raced across the concrete ramp. "Colonel Andrews wants to see you immediately," he informed Bebe and Kate.

The two women reported directly to the colonel's office, and after they entered, the corporal who accompanied them closed the door. Both women thought this was unusual because their duties were confined to flying planes from one point to another and they did nothing which would require closed door discussion. As they sat down, however, Evelyn Rankow walked into the colonel's office.

"Hello, Bebe," Evelyn said. Then she looked toward Kate. "Kate," she smiled.

Colonel Andrews spoke. "Ladies, I'm told that you are two of the best B-17 pilots we've got. Is that really so?"

"No Colonel Andrews, it's not," replied Bebe. "We are the two best B-17 pilots you've got."

The colonel laughed. "That's exactly what I hoped you'd say. The reason I asked to see you is because I heard you were good, maybe even the best, he winked.

Bebe and Kate thought that whether the colonel did or did not really believe that statement he was intentionally flattering them. Both women knew it was a man's world out there on the flight line. "But," they concluded, "he must at least consider us pretty good B-17 pilots, and that's a nice feeling."

The colonel continued. "Evelyn is here today to work with me on some details of your upcoming mission. It's been so long since anyone has mentioned it, you've probably forgotten about it." Of course, Kate and Bebe hadn't. "But, the wheels have been grinding forward. OSTRO wanted me to rate your flying skills, which I've already done. All your checkout pilots have been exceptionally complimentary in their ratings of both of you.

We've gotten preliminary information about your assignment. We knew it would be dangerous like all bombing missions. And it goes without saying we figured your mission objective would be more heavily defended than routine bombing targets. However, the Germans have further beefed up their defense systems of your particular target because of its high priority. The Luftwaffe (German Air Force) has doubled the number of fighter aircraft in the area because they suspect this particular facility will be attacked."

Kate saw Evelyn glare at Colonel Andrews. He mentioned the target was in Germany and she must have thought he was saying too much. But Kate and Bebe had heard numerous rumors and they already knew the target would be in Germany. While that news was hardly a surprise, Evelyn Rankow left nothing to chance. Every scrap of intelligence could be useful to someone. Kate glanced at Evelyn Rankow again. The perturbed look remained on her face.

"Just a moment, Colonel," Evelyn cut in. She looked directly at Bebe and Kate. "Your briefing includes extremely sensitive information of the highest secrecy level. You can never repeat what you hear today. Do you understand that completely?"

Bebe and Kate nodded apprehensively, wondering what they'd gotten involved in.

"You are being sent to an ultra-secret air base known as Station 121 located near Bannickbourn, England. Officially, Station 121 doesn't exist. In that respect it's similar to you and Kate, Bebe," Evelyn smiled. Neither woman appreciated her humor. "As you know," Evelyn continued, "the United States has not officially entered the war in Europe. However, OSTRO thinks we will be in the war within the next year. That's why OSTRO has been flying B-17 missions out of Station 121 for the last seven months. We have targeted the German's secret weapons development sites. Again, no one must ever know we have begun combat operations against Germany. You may continue, Colonel," Evelyn said.

"Besides upgrading extensive Luftwaffe fighter plane coverage, the Germans have also beefed up anti-aircraft gun emplacements," the colonel continued. The result is what was originally considered a dangerous objective has now become exceptionally high risk. The odds are not in your favor.

However, the very survival of the United States depends on your succeeding on this mission. This target absolutely must be destroyed no matter what the cost. We don't want to throw away your lives on a mission that has little chance of success, however, the necessity of undertaking this assignment no matter what the cost is obvious. I'm just sorry it has to be you."

"You mean you'd rather have us get killed on a mission that has little chance to succeed rather than one that will most likely fail," replied Bebe sarcastically. Kate kicked Bebe's foot, reminding her to ease up and the colonel was only doing his job.

The colonel didn't take Bebe's comment lightly. "Frankly," he said, "we'd prefer you survived to fight another day, as the saying goes. However, the success of this mission is absolutely critical. Unfortunately, the German defenses are so formidable that getting through the flak and Luftwaffe fighters will come down to dumb luck more than flying skill. Any comments?"

"I think I can speak for both of us, Colonel Andrews," replied Bebe. "We want to fly that mission. The only question is how soon we start."

The colonel looked at Kate and Bebe, a serious expression on his face. "You will start tomorrow morning. Report to me at 0600 hours and we'll get you ready for take-off at 0800. I'll see you then. Good evening."


On the following day at 0500 hours Kate and Bebe were awakened by a jangling alarm clock. They packed their bags and were ready to travel as they left the women's barracks and headed for the mess hall to grab a light breakfast. It was a beautiful fall day. Most of the leaves had already dropped but the bright sunlight and brisk air would make for good flying.

They walked into Colonel Andrews's office at precisely 0600. "Good morning, Colonel."

"Good morning, Bebe, Kate. Please have a chair. I'll be right back."

A few moments later Colonel Andrews returned with three other officers. As the men entered the room, the colonel closed his office door behind them. "Gentlemen, this is Bebe and Kate. They will be your pilots on the LX-1."

The two women stood to shake hands and greet the three men. Kate and Bebe noticed the astonished looks on the men's faces. They were obviously shocked they would be flying with women pilots on a B-17 bomber.

"Ladies, this is your crew. Captain Brumfeld is the navigator on this flight." Normally a lieutenant, not a captain, would be doing this job, but as Kate and Bebe would later find out, Captain Brumfeld would accompany them on their mission. "Lieutenant Miller is the flight engineer." Bebe and Kate knew that the flight engineer's job was normally filled by an enlisted man. The presence of an officer handling that responsibility was just another indication of the importance of the airplane and the upcoming mission. "Lieutenant Costigan is the radio operator. Okay, if everyone will take a seat we'll begin a short briefing and then get you on your way."

The colonel continued. "You'll be flying in a specially modified B-17 bomber today. It's called the LX-1." The colonel didn't say how the airplane was modified, knowing they would see the changes themselves when they boarded the plane. Their destination was airfield Station 121, Bannickbourn, England.

The airplane was being pulled out of the hangar as they spoke. Colonel Andrews handed Kate the flight plan and said they would be going to Platt Field, New York. From there, they would fly directly to Station 121 at Bannickbourn, England, although there were several re-fueling stops along the way. There would be a long over water portion of the flight. Theirs would be the only B-17 making the trip. The colonel asked if there were any questions. There was only one. Kate asked the colonel why the B-17 was designated as the LX-1. The colonel declined to answer that question. He then reminded the five-crew members that every aspect of this operation was Top Secret. Absolutely nothing concerning the operation, not even the fact that they were involved in a secret mission, could be discussed with anyone or even themselves. It was designed to be the most secret operation of the war.

Colonel Andrews, followed by Bebe, Kate and the three men walked out of his office and through the front door of the headquarters building. There were two cars waiting to take them to the airplane. The plane was parked on a remote part of the ramp, well away from the rest of the normal daily activities and congestion in the main area of the air base.

Bebe and Kate rode with Colonel Andrews in his car. As they drove in the direction of the big four engine plane they noticed the plane was painted completely black with no markings. Most of the B-17's were unpainted and silver, gray, or a combination camouflage of lighter color on the bottom and darker color on top. Also, B-17's normally had markings such as bright colored tail numbers for easy identification when grouping for bombing missions. There was also nose art, a row of bomb decals for missions flown and so on. But there were no insignias on this one.

Bebe and Kate got out of Colonel Andrews' car and looked at the airplane. B-17's normally carried up to thirteen machine guns, which were positioned throughout the plane. This plane was stripped of most of its defensive gun positions. There was the typical clear nose cone for the bombardier, Norden Bomb Sight and two fifty-caliber machine guns. There was also a navigator's machine gun and tail gunner's compartment with two fifty-caliber machine guns, but, that was all. The two machine gun turret behind the flight deck was not installed. The two machine gun ball turret pod in the planes belly aft of the wings was missing. The left and right waist gun bays were not installed. That meant that half of the defensive machine guns were not on this plane. They were planning to send them on the mission with only half the guns and half a crew. Bebe shuddered. "This is going to be much more dangerous than I thought," she said.

The second car carrying the rest of the crew pulled up next to the mysterious airplane. The five-person crew got out of the two cars and retrieved their luggage from the vehicles' trunks. Colonel Andrews told the three men to board the plane but he wanted to have a further word with Kate and Bebe.

The three men threw their bags through the forward belly door, which was located just underneath the plane's cockpit. They each pulled themselves upward into the plane's belly and found their respective seats and got ready for the long ride to the East Coast where they would spend the night.

"Okay ladies, here's the situation. As you know we don't use women in combat, however, we're obviously breaking that rule. I've seen a lot of outstanding B-17 pilots but the mortality rate for bomber crews is high. A lot of good pilots are dead. It had nothing to do with their flying ability. The German anti-aircraft defenses fill the sky with flak and bullets and the Luftwaffe keeps lots of fighters flying and they've taken their toll.

Since you agreed to fly this nasty mission, I've asked for an exception to policy and requested you both be activated as second lieutenants. That would make you both military pilots. This is my way of honoring you," he concluded.

"You noticed we've taken half the machine guns off the plane and it has no identification markings. When you climb into that B-17 over there you will notice the bomb bay has also been heavily modified. That plane is designed to carry a different type of bomb which I can't describe to you at this time. That's mainly because I don't know what it is myself. I'm only telling you that because you and the others will figure it out pretty fast anyway. But, you are not to discuss this modification with anyone under any circumstances. And, as Evelyn said, neither you nor the crew may discuss this secret mission with anyone at any time.

There is one last thing. I don't think I did a very good job emphasizing the danger involved and the terrible odds of succeeding on this mission. I feel badly about that."

"We said we would go on this mission Colonel Andrews," Kate said. "We know the odds. Let's get moving." Kate and Bebe realized that Colonel Andrews didn't know they had no choice about flying the dangerous mission. Although he knew OSTRO's role, he was not aware of OSTRO's method of kidnapping people from another time and forcing them to go on high-risk missions with little hope of surviving.

"I admire you two. You've got guts. Good luck and Godspeed."

"Thank you, sir. Do I salute you now or wait for my commission?" Bebe laughed.

"Let's wait until you officially receive your commission which you should get before you fly the mission."

"Thank you colonel and goodbye," Kate said. Neither of them cared about getting a commission and becoming an officer. All they wanted was to survive and escape from OSTRO.

"I'm not really sure you should be thanking me ladies. I just hope you realize what you're getting into and I hope you come through it okay."

Kate and Bebe saluted Colonel Andrews anyway and turned to

walk toward the B-17. The crew was working through their pre-flight checklists. Kate and Bebe carefully went through the checklist on the exterior of the airplane and once it was completed, they both climbed into the plane.

Bebe was now in the command pilot's seat and she and Kate completed their pre-flight checklists. Bebe began starting the four engines, each one in succession. Everything looked good and she started the engine run up process. Kate called the tower, got clearance and released the brakes and Bebe pulled the big plane out on the taxi strip to head for the active runway. Bebe stopped the B-17 just short of the take-off end of the runway.

Kate radioed the tower and got clearance to enter the active runway and Bebe slowly moved the airplane onto the runway to position it for take-off. Kate set the brakes. Bebe pushed the throttle forward and the roaring engines sounded fine and looked good on the gauges.

"Okay, let's go," Bebe said.

Kate released the airplane's brakes and the ominous looking black B-17 rolled forward. It moved slowly at first, but because of the light load, gained speed quickly. As the B-17 reached take-off speed of about ninety miles per hour Bebe pulled the nose up slightly and then pulled it back further as the airplane's wheels left the ground and they became airborne. "Platt Field, here we come," said Kate.

Of the five crew people, only Bebe, Kate and Captain Brumfeld were to actually go on the secret mission. The other two crew members were en route to Station 121-Bannickbourn to fly with the 91st Bomb Group. Neither Bebe nor Kate had any idea who else was to be assigned to fly the mission, but with the number of guns aboard cut in half, that meant that at least four crewmen would be eliminated. They would be flying the mission with a crew of only five or six people. With fewer defensive machine guns, the chances of getting shot out of the sky increased dramatically. That would make the flight even more terrifying.

Bebe and Kate had never flown combat missions, but they had gone through intense training several months earlier. They would get additional combat flying training at Station 121-Bannickbourn on actual missions. Up to now, the worst thing they had flown through was rough thunderstorms. Rather, they had flown around rough thunderstorms. Nobody flies through a thunderstorm. But they had both experienced heavy turbulence and unnerving flying conditions.

Combat flying however, was a lot different, and they both understood that harsh reality. It was a totally different dynamic comprised of brutal fear and risk of serious injury or horrific death. The plane could be blown out of the sky, roll over into a dive, or go into a flat spin from which there was no recovery. However, Kate and Bebe knew they were ready for whatever came their way. They were both outstanding pilots and the B-17 was an iconic airplane which could withstand incredible damage and still stay in the air.

The long flight to Platt Field went without incident, or nearly so. When they had flown to within one hundred miles of Platt Field they began picking up some turbulence. Kate was flying the plane when she saw the lightning flashes directly ahead of them. She figured it would get a little bumpier and they would get some rain. Platt Field confirmed that a storm was brewing, however they should be able to land before it broke out.

They nearly made it. They got within thirty miles of the field and the turbulence got much heavier. The lightning had been flashing steadily and the wind had grown stronger. Just before getting into the landing pattern, they picked up a few drops of rain and then heavy chop. The rain drops turned into a shower as they began their downwind approach. As Kate turned left into their cross wind leg, the clouds let loose with a squalling wall of water. The bumpy ride continued as she turned the B-17 into the final approach for their landing. As she positioned the airplane to line up with the runway, heavy crosswinds from the northwest (left side) were pushing the airplane hard to the right. Strong northwest winds continued buffeting the plane and Kate applied aggressive left rudder. The plane maintained perfect alignment with the runway. Kate angled the plane left into the wind thirty degrees to maintain the necessary approach path to the runway.

As the B-17 continued to descend with its nose crabbing hard left into the heavy wind the ride got much bumpier. The airplane pitched up and jumped around harshly in the turbulent crosswinds, but Kate held her course. Finally, the plane landed with a gentle thump as she set it down perfectly. It was a great landing under incredibly bad conditions and poor visibility. It was approximately eight p.m. Eastern time.

The crew went to a nearby restaurant and drank a few beers and had dinner. They talked about the coming war. They knew the United States would soon be involved but no one knew how that would come about. Bebe bought a last round for everyone and they got a taxi and headed back to the base to turn in early. Tomorrow would be the first leg of their long ride to Bannickbourn, England. The crew was wondering what the future would bring and if they'd be alive at the end of the war.

# 14

August 19, 1941          Platt Field, New York

The one hour time difference between Illinois and New York made 0500 hours much too early for Bebe, Kate and the crew. But they got up, quickly finished their breakfasts and were soon walking out to their airplane parked beside a large hanger. What seemed like millions of shining water drops from last night's rain sparkled on the black airplane's wings and fuselage. It reminded Kate of the stars in the Milky Way. They climbed inside the cold, damp B-17. It had no heating system but the crew could put on their heavy flight coats or plug in their high altitude heated flight coveralls if it got too uncomfortable.

Bebe and Kate went through their checklists and the plane was soon ready for take-off. The big plane lumbered to the end of the runway, got its clearance and started rolling forward. They would make an overnight re-fueling stop at Goose Bay Labrador. In less than an hour the dawn was in full swing and the plane was passing above the eastern shore of the United States heading over the Atlantic Ocean. They were flying one hundred and sixty miles per hour at eight thousand feet. At this altitude, they didn't have to wear their oxygen masks and it also was warmer than flying at higher levels. The weather was good and the winds favorable, a nice change from the thunderstorm the night before.

Bebe decided to take a break and let Kate do the flying for a few hours. It should be an easy flight. She would stretch her legs and take over for Kate later. There wasn't much room to walk around in the B-17. Like the exterior, the interior of the plane was all business. Every inch of the airplane served some function and there was no wasted space.

Bebe climbed out of her seat on the left side of the cockpit, stepped back and climbed down from the flight deck into the nose section of the plane. She would visit with Captain Brumfeld to see what kind of guy he was. Lieutenant Miller, the flight engineer, was sitting aft of the cockpit in the radio compartment talking with Lieutenant Costigan, the radio operator. That left the bombardier's seat at the front of the plane's nose cone unoccupied.

Captain Brumfeld had the best seat in the house. He sat in the glass nose cone with his seat located just below and forward of the flight deck (cockpit). This gave him the best view as well as the most space making it a considerably more comfortable ride for him. Bebe sat down in the bombardier's seat and asked Captain Brumfeld how he was doing.

"I'm fine," he said. "That was a pretty remarkable landing Kate made last night. You two are great pilots, and I've ridden with the best of them."

"Yeah, Kate made a fabulous landing," Bebe agreed. In an uncharacteristic boastful comment she added, "I trained Kate, but she would have been good no matter who trained her."

"I understand we'll be working together in England," Brumfeld said. Both Captain Brumfeld and Bebe knew they were not to discuss the mission so they purposely avoided any specific references to it in their conversation.

They talked for the better part of an hour. Most of Captain Brumfeld's conversation was about the different bases at which he'd been stationed, both overseas and in the continental United States. For her part, Bebe had been ferrying airplanes for two years. She spent a lot of time traveling to and from Seattle where Boeing was manufacturing B-17's. In fact, in 1942 she happened to be at the plant picking up an airplane when President Franklin Roosevelt came through on a tour.

She had long ago lost count of the number of airplanes, particularly B-17's, she and Kate had ferried from Boeing's Seattle plant and other locations around the country. Sometimes she flew them to debarkation bases on the east coast. Anyway, she and Kate each had over a thousand hours in B-17's. She told Captain

Brumfeld the two of them had performed every maneuver in the B-17's operating manual as they ferried the planes around the country. They both knew the airplane inside and out. It was easy to fly and very forgiving.

As Bebe got up to leave Captain Brumfield said "I'll look forward to working with you, Bebe."

For some reason, maybe the way he spoke or the way he said he'd look forward to working with her, his words and manner rubbed Bebe the wrong way. There was something about Brumfeld that just didn't feel right. That impression would stick with Bebe.

She decided to go back to the cockpit and ducked her head low as she exited the nose cone section leaving Captain Brumfeld alone to enjoy the ride. He mentioned his first name was Maxwell although he preferred to be called Max. He was an interesting enough guy, pleasant and polite. There was just something about him that Bebe found unsettling. I shouldn't do that, she thought to herself. I shouldn't judge people on first impressions. She remembered Kate always admonished herself for doing exactly the same thing. He's probably just an odd guy, she concluded.

Before stepping up to the cockpit, she walked back into the fuselage to check with Lieutenant Miller in the radio compartment. Bebe balanced herself with the metal pole hand-grips as she stepped onto the narrow catwalk crossing the cavernous bomb bay. She stopped for a moment and stared into the dark crevasse beneath her. The metal canyon would soon be filled with powerful bombs. The Army had gone to a lot of trouble and expense to modify this airplane and they wouldn't take a badly needed B-17 bomber out of combat service unless there was a very good reason. The mission we're gonna' fly must be as important as they told us, she thought.

She wondered exactly what the Army had cooked up. Things had moved so quickly she never thought about what the mission might entail. That it would be complicated and dangerous was a given. She knew B-17 bomb bays were designed to handle standard five hundred pound bombs at a six thousand pound load, but with external racks, the bomb load could be increased to eighteen thousand pounds.

She thought about the possibility of some new bomb. This airplane could carry a lot of weight. The main challenge was fitting all the weight into the airplane. The standard bomb bay, though large, was not huge. However, what it held could cause massive destruction. The bomb bay on this airplane was designed to hold something much bigger and heavier, some type of super bomb or bombs.

Bebe shook her head as she turned to take the final steps to the radio compartment. Other than the little bit of exercise and that she was able to stretch her legs, the trip to see Lieutenant Miller was unnecessary. He was sleeping soundly, his head resting against a jacket he was using as a pillow. Lieutenant Costigan was stretched out on the floor, also sleeping. There was no point in waking them.

She stood in the radio compartment for a moment and walked back into the tail section of the plane. It was dark and spooky. The B-17, like all airplanes, was a long metal tube. Most of the compartments were located at the front part of the plane. The bomb bay and radio compartment were located between the wings toward the front of the plane. The two waist gunners' positions were aft of the wings on either side of the airplane. The remainder of the fuselage was open space until the rearward or tail portion of the plane. On this airplane however, there were no waist gunners' windows.

The airplane's tail wheel retracted into the rear fuselage area and the tail gunner crawled around it to reach his compartment with its two fifty caliber machine guns. This isn't first class, Bebe smiled as she looked at the small fixture with the tube extending out of the rear of the plane. This tube allowed men to take care of urgent personal needs, but there was no accommodation for women.

She climbed into her seat and strapped in. "Why don't you take a break, Kate? I'll fly it for a while."

"Thanks, Bebe, I'll do that." Kate climbed out of her seat and out of the cockpit.

Bebe had never flown over the open ocean out of sight of land. The only scenery was the deep blue water and the bright blue sky but it was moving and invigorating. There wasn't a single cloud in the blue infinity filling the B-17's windshield.

They arrived at Goose Bay, Labrador in what seemed to be a short time because the experience of flying over the ocean had been new and interesting. The next morning they took off for the long over-water flight to Bannickbourn, England. Bebe and Kate continued to trade off flying duties, allowing them to sleep and stay refreshed in the cramped quarters.

Kate was flying the plane when they sighted the English coast. She had never been to England and the dark, moonless night didn't seem like a fitting welcome. It was another hour before they landed at Bannickbourn. The five tired people climbed out of the B-17 and were looking forward to a comfortable bed.

Oddly, a Colonel Slater met them on the ramp. Bebe thought it unusual an officer of that high a rank would be the one to the meet them, particularly this late at night. Colonel Slater directed the three men to the officers' quarters and they immediately climbed onto a waiting truck and headed in that direction. Then he asked Bebe and Kate to come to his office for a de-briefing. The colonel's driver opened the back door of his car and they got in, while the colonel climbed into the front seat.

What does he want with a debriefing, they wondered. It was a routine flight and it was long. That was all there was to it. But they knew there had to be more to the meeting than a meaningless de-briefing.

Kate and Bebe followed the colonel toward his office, and when they entered, he closed the door behind them. He poured himself a cup of coffee from the pot on a table next to his desk, pointedly not offering any to the women.

The colonel was a short and balding, a pot-bellied, unhappy little man. This was definitely not going to be a pleasant conversation, Kate thought to herself. It was now Kate who was scolding herself for jumping to conclusions about people. I shouldn't do that, she reminded herself. Bebe was having precisely the same thoughts.

The colonel was the first to speak. "Let's get something straight right off the bat, ladies. They tell me they're going to make you two second lieutenants and that you're pretty good pilots. Well I don't agree with that. We're in a real war here where people are shooting at each other. These guys back in the states are saddling me with a couple of females who screwed some headquarters type yoyos to get their commissions and blaze some trails for the rest of womankind. I don't have the time or patience for that."

Maybe I should pre-judge people after all, Kate thought to herself.

The colonel continued. "Ladies, you're tying up a badly needed airplane to prove something to somebody and it pisses me off. I'm going to be watching you very closely. You play grab-ass with any of the men risking their lives so people like you can have the freedom to pull this kind of stunt you're pulling, I'll kick your little asses all the way down to the end of runway 142. You understand my position on this whole thing?"

While Bebe and Kate were startled, they weren't completely shocked. They had run into some of the macho routine and crummy women jokes while they were ferrying airplanes. But this guy was a real crumb, a woman hater who was going to make it his job to make their lives miserable.

"I see clearly where we stand, colonel," replied Bebe. "Is that all?"

"No, that's not all. Women should be back on the home front. You have no business being here. You make any mistakes, just one, and I'm running your asses off this base. By the way, if you say anything to anyone about this conversation, I'll say it never happened. So don't bother complaining. I know everybody in the IG's Office (Inspector General). Do you have any questions about that?"

"I have just one comment, colonel," replied Kate."

"What is it and make it quick?"

"I didn't screw anybody to get here and I could care less about being a second lieutenant. I was told to volunteer for this job and I did. I have a job to do and I intend to do it to the best of my ability. If you give Bebe and me any more grief or ever threaten us again, I'll kick you in your balls so hard you'll end up with a second set of tonsils. Get off our backs, you dumb son of a bitch. By the way, if you complain about what I just said, I'll deny I ever said it and say you're just sore because I wouldn't cooperate when you made a pass at me."

Colonel Slater was not used to being talked to like that, particularly by a woman. He tried to sputter a reply but Kate reached across his desk and turned his full coffee cup upside down dumping the contents all over his papers. Kate turned and walked over and opened the door and Bebe followed and slammed it hard behind them. Bebe was a good teacher. Kate realized her self-confidence issue had been resolved.

With no help from Colonel Slater, Bebe and Kate managed to find a room where they could sleep. There was a detachment of nurses quartered in a small building near the runway. It turned out to be a comfortable place to stay.

# 15

February 12, 1942    91st Bomb Group, Bannickbourn Air Base,
England

On December 7, 1941 the Japanese attacked the United States
Naval Base at Pearl Harbor. On December 8, the United States
declared war on Japan. World War II had officially begun for the
United States. Everyone knew this day was coming because war had
been raging in Europe since September of 1939. It was in
anticipation of the United States going to war that Bebe and Kate
had been sent to England.

It was now February 12, 1942. Since they arrived at
Bannickbourn in late August of 1941, Bebe and Kate had continued
flying, including some combat missions. They reported to
Lieutenant-colonel Edwin McKilleps.

Station 121-Bannickbourn was a small air base, a wide expanse of
runways and grassy area with weathered, gray wood buildings and
hangers built in a rectangular grouping parallel to the airfield. Things
were lean here. There was no time for painting buildings. Besides,
painted buildings would make better targets for German airplanes.

Today Kate and Bebe were to have what they assumed was yet
another of the many up-date meetings with Colonel McKilleps. Their
mission had been scheduled but then postponed several times
because higher headquarters decided to change the date of the strike.
Bebe and Kate knew that each day headquarters delayed the
Germans would have that much more time to develop whatever
weapons they were creating.

Bebe and Kate walked into the Spartan-like building where Colonel McKilleps held the update meetings. There were three or four offices, a few long tables and chairs and a couple of desks. A young corporal named Roosevelt sat behind a desk just inside the entrance to the building.

"Good morning, ma'ams," he said, not sure how to address two women at once.

"You're new here, aren't you? Kate asked.

"Yes ma'am, I am. I'm Corporal Roosevelt, ma'am. No relation to the president, but everybody always asks me that."

"My name is Kate Darron and this is Bebe Beardsley. We're looking for Colonel McKilleps."

Colonel MeKilleps overheard the conversation and came out of his office and walked over to Kate and Bebe. "Good morning, girls," he said. "Come into my office."

Kate and Bebe followed Colonel McKilleps into his sparsely furnished large office and after they entered he closed the door.

"I'm going to brief you on what's happening," he said. "I think we've got a definite 'go' this time."

"You mean this is really it?" asked Bebe.

"This is it. I can't tell you anything else because that's all I've heard. As you know, this is the most important mission of the war. No one will ever know that, however. That's how secret the mission is and will forever remain. I know we've been through all this before, but I have to cover everything again. Bebe, you're the leader of this mission. Kate, you're second in command. As you know, it will involve only one plane, the one you flew here back in August.

As you're well aware, the plane was modified significantly. However, there have been further modifications of which you aren't aware. The main reason for the postponements of your mission was not that headquarters couldn't decide on a date to strike. The real reason was that there was a delay in the completion a new, more powerful type of bomb you will be dropping on the Germans."

"What kind of bomb is it?" asked Bebe.

"That's the part I can't tell you," said Colonel McKilleps. "All I know is that it's far more destructive than a standard five hundred pound bomb."

"Colonel, I assumed if they were giving us a new bomb to drop it would be more powerful than the bombs we have now. How will we know at what altitude to fly so we don't get blown up ourselves when the bomb explodes?"

"The engineers have it all figured out, Bebe. Everything will be the same except you'll fly a few thousand feet higher."

"Colonel McKilleps, our lives are on the line here. Has anyone dropped this bomb from an airplane? How do I know the engineers' calculations are correct?"

Kate smiled as Bebe persisted. That's just like Bebe, she thought. She wants the exact details. But Kate's amusement was tempered by the fact she knew Bebe was right. Once in the airplane and over the target, they were on their own. They both knew OSTRO didn't care if they lived or died. Now they wondered if the military was concerned about them. That wasn't a pleasant thought. The mission was dangerous and the odds for survival poor. Now there was added uncertainty about the magnitude of the bomb's explosive force. Kate thought about that as Bebe continued to question Colonel McKilleps regarding the size of the bomb's explosive range. The airplane could be blown up by the bomb they themselves dropped.

It had happened before. Airplanes flying too low when they dropped their bombs had been destroyed in the explosion of their own bombs.

Colonel McKilleps, annoyed with Bebe's persistent questions, concluded the conversation brusquely. "Yes, Bebe, your plane will be carrying a very lethal weapon, in fact several of them. The bombs are heavier than the five hundred pound bombs, but they are specially designed to fit into the modified bomb bay. That's all the information I have at this time."

"When do we start the mission, Colonel?" asked Kate.

"Once again, Kate, I can't really say. It will depend on when the special bombs arrive here. But, I'm thinking it will be in a few weeks. While we're waiting we'll do several more combat flights to practice the bombing runs and maneuvering the plane once the bombs are dropped. The other jobs on the airplane are pretty standard stuff however your entire crew will get a final dose of retraining with respect to the new weapon.

I'll be doing some of your training myself. You know your navigator, Max Brumfeld, but you haven't met your bombardier Lieutenant Frank Spinella. They will also get some mission specific instructions and training. Colonel McKilleps got up and walked over and opened the door and told Corporal Roosevelt to find Lieutenant Spinella.

"He's standing by sir. He's over at the mess hall." Corporal Roosevelt rushed out of the office to fetch the lieutenant.

"We'll meet with your crew and do some training today. Do you have any questions?"

"Colonel," Bebe replied, "you talked about the pilot, co-pilot, navigator and bombardier. Half the guns are removed from this plane. It looks like we at least have a tail gunner."

"You do. Johnny Bradford is his name. He's the best we've got and he loves his job. I don't know why anybody would love a job where they're getting shot at all the time. But he shoots back and he's had half a dozen confirmed kills."

"Then all we've got are the guns in the nose cone and the tail," Bebe said. She already knew that but wanted to make sure Colonel McKilleps was aware she didn't like not having the additional machine guns aboard the plane.

"Bebe, we had to lighten the plane up as much as we could. You know that. That was done for speed and maneuverability. You'll need to fly out of there fast when you deliver the bombs and you'll need all the speed you can get. That's the main reason for stripping the weapons off your plane."

"What about a flight engineer and radio operator?" Kate asked.

Colonel McKilleps stared at Kate with a "we've eliminated them too kind of look." Kate, as I said, the crew is composed of you and Bebe, the navigator, Captain Brumfeld, bombardier, Lt. Spinella, and the tail gunner, Johnny Bradford. It will be a five-person crew. That's it. Like I said, you can't afford the extra weight."

"Colonel, we're going on a very dangerous mission with half the guns and half the crew we're supposed to have. This sounds like a suicide mission to me," replied Bebe with an angry look on her face.

Colonel McKilleps looked at Bebe and Kate. "Look girls, you knew it was going to be dangerous. You also know what OSTRO expects you to do. We took these measures because you've got to fly in at low level to avoid radar and then climb out fast before you drop the bombs. You have to bank hard and climb once you drop the bombs. It's a surprise strike and a fast get-away. Any extra weight, man or machine, will just slow you down and reduce your chances for survival. Unfortunately, it's extremely dangerous and the odds of your making it back couldn't be much worse. I'm sorry about that, but you knew what the deal was."

Bebe and Kate nodded their heads. "We got it," said Bebe.

"Okay, we'll meet with your crew and do some flying. As we've been doing, we'll take one of our own B-17's from the line. We're not taking yours out of the hanger until its time to go on the mission. They're doing the final checks now to make sure it's mission ready. Once the special bombs get here, we're gonna' go."

There was a knock on the door and it opened slightly as Corporal Roosevelt stuck his head in. "Lieutenant Spinella is here, Colonel."

Lieutenant Frank Spinella walked in the door with a big smile across his face. "Good morning, colonel," Spinella said as he saluted.

"Good morning, Lieutenant. Have a seat."

"Lieutenant Frank Spinella, this is Bebe Beardsley and Kate Darron. They will be your pilot and co-pilot on the assignment I discussed with you yesterday."

Spinella's smile faded as he turned to greet the woman who was the aircraft commander. "Good morning, ma'am," a bewildered Frank Spinella replied weakly. He was taken off guard by the idea of flying with a female pilot.

"Good morning, Lieutenant," Bebe replied.

Reflecting his obvious concern Lieutenant Spinella asked, "Have you been flying for quite a while, ma'am?"

Bebe understood Spinella's apprehension, especially since this mission was going to require considerable flying skills. "Well Lieutenant, my daddy gave me my first lesson in a Piper Cub just last year. I think I'm ready for the big ones now, as soon as Colonel McKillips shows me how to fly them. Our co-pilot Kate hasn't been flying as long as me, but she's really good just the same."

Spinella was horrified. Colonel McKilleps was laughing. Then Spinella realized questioning Bebe's flying abilities was out of line and he started laughing also.

"I'm sorry ma'am," Spinella apologized. "It's just that I've never flown with a woman."

"Don't worry about it, Frank. We'll get along fine. I'll do my best to keep us all alive. Remember, I want to stay alive too."

That reassurance calmed Spinella.

"Okay," Colonel Mckillips interjected, "let's go fly."

Bebe took the left seat and Kate sat in the co-pilot's seat. Colonel McKilleps positioned himself on a jury-rigged jump seat behind the two. It was crowded but he wanted to watch their performance closely. McKilleps checked before they left the ground and there were no reports of enemy aircraft in the area. However, he had a tail gunner as well as one waist gunner from another crew come along with them just as a precaution (Johnny Bradford, the tail gunner for the actual mission had not arrived at the base yet.) Captain Brumfeld and Lieutenant Spinella took their respective duty locations in the nose cone of the B-17.

They were in the air shortly and Colonel McKilleps directed Bebe to head the plane out to a remote area to get away from the heavy traffic at the base. They spent about an hour doing standard maneuvers and both women handled the aircraft skillfully.

"Bebe, pull a one hundred and eighty-degree turn to the right, Colonel McKilleps ordered."

Bebe immediately turned the wheel hard while pulling back the yoke to maintain altitude. She held it for one hundred and eighty degrees and the plane was now flying in exactly the opposite direction as Colonel McKilleps ordered.

"Kate, are you that good?" he asked. "Bebe, give Kate the airplane. Kate, do a one hundred and eighty degree left turn on my command."

Kate nodded.

"Now!" the colonel shouted.

Kate immediately executed the one eighty perfectly, holding her altitude precisely.

"Both McKilleps and Lieutenant Spinella were amazed. Brumfeld, having flown with both women before, already knew how skilled they were.

Colonel McKilleps had complete confidence in the women. He was impressed they volunteered for the most dangerous of missions. While he realized Kate and Bebe worked for OSTRO, he was unaware they didn't volunteer for the mission and actually had no choice.

Suddenly, the terrifying sound of ripping metal screeched through the B-17 as a deadly barrage of machine gun fire ripped the fuselage aft of the bomb bay. The waist gunner spun round, his pulverized chest and stomach spewing blood and tissue. He was dead before his body hit the floor. Colonel McKilleps cursed and looked through the cockpit windows but saw nothing. "We got at least one German fighter on our tail," he screamed. "Kate, put in a mayday call for fighter assistance."

As Kate put out the fighter assistance call, Bebe yelled into the intercom, "Tail gunner, you have a fix on enemy aircraft?"

As he tried to answer she heard a second burst of machine gun fire smash through the tail section. The tail gunner managed a brief burst of return gunfire then abruptly went silent.
"Tail gunner, tail gunner!" she yelled, but there was no response.

Heavy strafing tore through the B-17's left wing and engine number one burst into flame. From the right side, larger shells from a second German fighter blew the propeller off engine number three. Bebe was struggling now, fighting to keep the B-17 in the air. "There are two of them, colonel," she yelled.

Colonel McKilleps raced back through the bomb bay to man the waist gunner's machine guns. He frantically searched for the German fighters but could see nothing. He ran toward the front of the plane to try and spot them from the top turret gunner's position. "My god, half the tail is shot away," he gasped.

Then he saw two ME 109's coming in from the left rear for another pass. The two German fighters must have sneaked into the area hoping to catch unsuspecting British or American airplanes by surprise. They had done just that. They knew they killed the tail gunner, leaving the B-17 un-defended in its rear section. They also knew they had taken out the waist gunner. No defensive fire was coming from the B-17 and now it was simply target practice for the German ME 109's. Neither Brumfeld's nor Spinella's guns in the nose cone were of any use as long as the attacking German fighters stayed to the rear of the B-17.

Another storm of machine gun bullets riddled the fuselage and wings. Colonel McKilleps was now firing the left waist machine gun at one of the German fighters but it sped by the ailing B-17 leaving a hundred sunlight filled bullet holes in the mid-section of the airplane. Brumfeld and Spinella were staying put in the nose cone hoping to get a shot at the German fighters. Besides, they would never be able to move the tail gunner's body out of the rear turret in time to do any good.

In response to Kate's call for fighter assistance, a flight of four British Spitfires was racing toward the burning B-17. The German fighters saw them coming and both airplanes turned hard, doing their best to escape the oncoming British fighters. Because of their high closing speed, the Spitfires quickly engaged the ME-109's.

While Colonel McKilleps was anxious to see if the British planes caught the enemy fighters, his number one concern was that the B-17 keep flying. Bebe had already turned the plane on a heading toward the base. The fire extinguisher slowed the fire in engine number one but it was still burning. Luckily, number three engine, minus the propeller, wasn't burning. The airplane was pitching and yawing. The shot up tail section was aggravating the already difficult control problems and Bebe suspected the ailerons were also badly damaged. The airplane was losing some altitude but generally holding steady.

Although this wasn't their first time flying in combat, their airplane had never been hit by enemy fire before. However, Bebe and Kate remained completely calm. That two of their crew had been killed bothered them, but they realized casualties were unavoidable and it would happen again.

Engine number two began running rough but was still operating. The base was in sight and she was carefully nudging the airplane to the right to line up with the runway. She knew she would only have one shot at making the landing.

Colonel McKilleps intended to take over but Bebe and Kate were already doing exactly what was supposed to be done. The airplane was rumbling through the sky at a higher than normal altitude when this close to the base, however, Bebe didn't want to chance dropping too low because she knew the plane was unable to regain altitude. It had been continually descending as Bebe nursed the plane from the area of the fighter attack toward the base. Kate had radioed the mayday to base so the fire trucks would be waiting for them.

Colonel McKilleps was amazed Bebe had been able to keep the plane in the air. He had considered ordering the crew to bail out. Lieutenant Spinella couldn't believe it either. This plane should be on the ground burning and we should have bailed out, he thought to himself.

"Drop the landing gear," Bebe directed Kate.

Kate tried to lower the landing gear, but couldn't get it to go down. "The hydraulic lines must be damaged, Bebe," she said.

"Go for the emergency hand crank," Bebe yelled. Kate immediately went for the crank, but couldn't get the wheels to drop into landing position.

"The landing gear must be shot up," yelled Kate.

The plane was getting close to the runway now. "Brace yourselves," Bebe ordered. "We're going in wheels up and on our belly."

The big airplane was quickly closing in on the runway and Bebe lessened the pressure on the yoke and let the bullet riddled B-17 gently settle on the concrete. The two remaining engines shut down as the propellers struck the ground and the plane slid down the runway for a perfect landing. Colonel McKillips, Captain Brumfeld and Lieutenant Spinella followed by Kate and Bebe scrambled to get to the door at the right rear of the plane. Engine number two was burning and they had to get out fast in case the plane exploded.

The fire crew was on the scene and quickly doused the flames. As Kate, Bebe and the rest of the crew stood on the grass watching the firemen work, Colonel McKillips said he would buy the beer and everyone headed to the bar. Captain Brumfeld seemed badly shaken by the experience, but everyone else had stayed calm. The beer was good and tomorrow would be another day.

## 16

February 13, 1942    Bannickbourn Air Base, England

The following morning Lieutenant-colonel McKilleps, Bebe and Kate were in Colonel Slater's office explaining how they had nearly totaled a badly needed B-17 and lost two men. Colonel Slater listened carefully to Colonel McKillep's briefing. He hadn't gone out with a full crew because the Germans had not been operating in the area. He conceded that was a mistake. Surprisingly, Colonel Slater said he was satisfied with the explanation, although Kate and Bebe were sure he would have more to say to Colonel McKilleps later.

"You didn't bail out," Colonel Slater remarked.

"Colonel, this woman did a fantastic job bringing the aircraft back home. We stayed with the plane because of her flying skill. So we still have a B-17. It does need a little work, however."

"Don't worry about it," Colonel Slater said. I know the importance of your mission and that you had to check out your crew and provide final training."

"I didn't actually need to do much training. Beardsley and Darron are up to speed on every aspect of B-17 operation. They fly better than most pilots I've flown with," replied Colonel McKilleps.

"Are they the best B-17 pilots you've flown with?" asked Colonel Slater.

Colonel McKilleps paused for a moment to think about that one. "They might just be the best B-17 pilots I've ever flown with," he said, winking at Bebe and Kate.

Colonel Slater looked like he was having a hard time with that one, but he was very impressed that Bebe and Kate landed the badly damaged airplane.

In a gesture that Bebe and Kate would never forget, he said, "Miss Beardsley and Miss Darron, I made some inappropriate comments to you in this office when you first arrived at this base. I was wrong. I want to apologize for those comments right now. I was out of line and I'm sorry."

Stunned, Kate looked at Colonel Slater and said, "Forget about it, Colonel. Thank you for your apology. I said some inappropriate things also. I would like to apologize for those comments."

"There is no need to, Darron. Thank you for the job you and Beardsley did yesterday. Things could have been a lot worse if you and Beardsley hadn't been cool under fire. By the way, may I call you Bebe and Kate?"

"Sure," Bebe smiled.

After a final compliment, Colonel Slater dismissed Colonel McKilleps, Bebe and Kate. His final comment to Kate was, "I'm glad I'm not going to get a second set of tonsils."

Bebe and Kate laughed as did Colonel Slater. Colonel McKilleps didn't know what they were laughing about.


In the following weeks, Colonel McKilleps had the navigator Captain Brumfeld and the bombardier Lieutenant Frank Spinella fly with combat groups flying bombing missions over Germany. Colonel McKilleps didn't want to risk losing Bebe or Kate and he kept them close to home doing routine ferrying runs between bases around England. He did send them out on a half dozen low risk missions to they would gain further combat familiarity.

On an overcast Sunday afternoon one of the combat groups was returning from a bombing run. It hadn't been a critical target but the group ran into heavy ground fire and unusually high Luftwaffe fighter resistance. Three of the twenty four planes didn't come back. The bombardier Frank Spinella was on one of those three planes.

Colonel McKilleps called a meeting for Bebe, Kate and their crew for Monday morning. They had all heard the news about Frank Spinella. Bebe and Kate, Captain Brumfeld, and tail gunner Johnny

Bradford walked into the colonel's office and met their new bombardier, Lieutenant Naston Geyerson, a slightly built, dignified, Ivy League type gentleman sitting in one of the chairs. Colonel McKilleps introduced Naston Geyerson to the group.

Colonel McKilleps explained that Lieutenant Geyerson had just arrived at the base from Bassingbourn, one of the other bomber bases in England. Another back-up bombardier was in the hospital with a shrapnel wound from a flak burst. I was out of back-up bombardiers and Nasty volunteered."

"What did you call him, Colonel?" asked Kate.

"Nasty. His nickname is "Nasty," replied McKilleps.

"They call me "Nasty Guy," actually," interjected Lieutenant Geyerson. "You know, Naston Geyerson and Nasty Guy. Get it?"

"Yeah, I get it," replied Kate. "Does that nickname have anything to do with your skill as a bombardier, I wonder?"

"As a matter of fact, it does," Nasty Guy" replied. "I can hit an ant's behind from twenty thousand feet."

"Actually," said Colonel McKilleps, "he's also accurate in what he's telling you. He's got one of the highest success rates of any bombardier in Europe. The other good news is the special bombs arrived late yesterday. The mission is scheduled for Friday, March 6. We'll go over some final details today and tomorrow morning. You guys can have Wednesday off to go have fun. But don't get too drunk. Thursday afternoon you get a briefing on the target and that will be the final one. You take off early Friday morning."

The rest of the meeting was routine to the point of boring. Bebe, Kate and their crew were already aware of everything Colonel McKilleps was telling them. The early morning take-off on Friday had been selected because the weather would be clear. They were to fly to the target in Germany at the extremely low altitude of three hundred feet. The hope was that they would avoid detection by the German fighters in the early morning hours.

Once they were within ten minutes of the target they would begin a steep climb to an altitude of eight thousand feet or as near as they could climb to that level. Normally it took thirty-seven minutes for a B-17 to climb to twenty thousand feet. On this mission they would climb to a much lower altitude, but because of the heavier weight of the special bombs, Bebe and Kate both knew ten minutes was well short of the climbing time needed to reach eight thousand feet.

They're telling us something they know is impossible, the women realized. Why?

Colonel McKilleps continued talking. The reason for this maneuver was to counter the highly effective German ground defenses and the large number of Luftwaffe fighter planes protecting the area. They would have to do the best they could under the high risk circumstances. Once the bombs dropped, they were on their own to escape out of German airspace.

Everyone thought the plan was more wishful thinking than sound tactical bombing procedure. "They're nuts," Bebe whispered to Kate. "It doesn't even qualify as a crap shoot. It's suicide. We'll make our own flight plan, Kate."

In fact, that was exactly what Colonel McKilleps wanted them to do. The pilots would be the masters of their own fate. With the German defenses as strong as they were, there was just no good way to approach the target without getting blown out of the sky. Colonel McKilleps' flight plan specified coming in at a low altitude to avoid radar but German ground spotters would detect the plane long before it got close to the target.

The last thing Colonel McKilleps said was that if the target wasn't absolutely critical to the outcome of the war this mission would have never have been set up. The odds of successful completion, even reaching the target, were slim. What he didn't say was the odds for survival were probably zero.

On Tuesday afternoon Bebe and Kate went back to their room in the nurse's quarters. They had officially become Second Lieutenants earlier that day and Colonel McKilleps gave them their gold bars.

Bebe felt continuing discomfort with Captain Brumfeld. She mentioned it to Kate several times, but while Kate didn't especially care for Brumfeld, she didn't sense danger with him. Bebe, on the other hand, couldn't get rid of a feeling that something was not right about him. She couldn't put her finger on exactly what the problem was; she just didn't trust him. She hoped she could forget about it because she and Kate were taking a much-needed day off.

On Wednesday morning they left the base and headed for a quaint little English Inn in Brattlesbury, a small town thirty miles from the airfield. They decided they would spend the night there as the briefing the next day didn't start until five p.m. They were now driving across the beautiful English countryside in a borrowed jeep. Neither Bebe nor Kate ever heard of Hadrian's Wall, but there it was before them stretching into the countryside on their right and left.

Kate was wondering about the history of the wall when Bebe spotted a roadside historical plaque. Bebe stopped the jeep so they could read the sign. The wall was built in approximately 122 A.D. to address military issues the Romans were having in wars two thousand years ago in this same location.

Kate and Bebe walked along the wall imagining the people who stood guard there so many years before, maybe fighting or maybe charging tolls to travelers. As they walked, they wondered if they would be alive in two days. It weighed heavily on them.

They walked without talking. After they'd gone a few hundred yards, Bebe reached for Kate's hand. They stopped to look at the lush, gentle valley rolling below them on the other side of the wall. Bebe was standing to the left of Kate and she stepped behind her and put her right arm around her neck. Kate moved her hand up to Bebe's arm. They stood close to each other looking into the valley.

"I hope we come through this alive, Bebe," Kate whispered.

"Somehow, we will," Bebe said. "I know we will."


Bebe and Kate enjoyed some of the best cooking they ever encountered at the Three Bells Inn. The drinks were also delightful. It had been a nice day and evening. Bebe and Kate knew this might be the last dinner they would ever have together. They didn't really think they were going to die, but they knew they would be exposed to incredible danger and there was a high probability they could be killed.

The room they shared was warm and cozy and decorated in the English country style. There were two single feather beds with light blue covers. The thick wood furniture was substantial and reassuring. They both agreed it was the most comfortable room either of them could remember.

Morning came too quickly. Breakfast was fabulous and they lingered, having more coffee than usual. They didn't want to leave the place and wished they could stay forever, but it would soon be time to go back to the base.

Several minutes later, Bebe and Kate rose from the table and walked to the stairs leading to their room on the second floor. They packed their clothes and were ready to depart.

"I'm really going to miss this place," remarked Bebe, as she opened the door to the hallway. "Can we come back here some day?"

Kate smiled, "We'll plan on it." Even as Kate said the words, she knew in her heart the dangerous mission they would begin just hours from now might make a return trip to the quaint inn impossible.

As they got into their jeep and drove away from the Three Bells Inn on the road leading to Hadrian's Wall, Bebe and Kate wondered if they would ever pass this way again. Even though the base was nearly an hour's drive, it seemed like they were pulling up to the sentry at the gate in just minutes. They went to their quarters to pack the few things they would take with them on the mission.

The final briefing for their mission was to start in less than two hours. After the briefing, they would return to their room and sleep until midnight. Although they didn't yet know the exact time for mission departure, it would be early morning.

Kate looked at Bebe. "It looks like this is the chance we've been waiting for," she said. "If we can make it to the target site and get the bombs off okay, we can make our escape from OSTRO on the return trip just like we planned."

"I'm counting on it," replied Bebe. "Are you scared?"

Kate looked directly at Bebe. "Yes."

"Me too," Bebe said, "but, we're gonna' make it, Kate. I promise."

At exactly five p.m. on Thursday Lieutenant-colonel McKilleps walked into the building where his office and briefing room were located. The five-person crew was in the room seated around his rectangular table. Bebe and Kate sat across from each other and near Colonel McKilleps at the end of the table. Next to Kate sat the bombardier Lieutenant Naston Geyerson and next to him the navigator Captain Max Brumfeld. On the opposite side of the table next to Bebe was the tail gunner Sergeant Johnny Bradford. It was a five person crew which was going to man a ten person crew airplane.

Colonel McKilleps walked into the conference room and closed the door. "Good evening," he began. "I'll make this short. Everything that I say and everything you do is absolutely top secret, now and in the future. No one must ever know what is said here tonight or what happens on this mission. I'm giving you a statement to sign in which you promise that you shall never reveal any information regarding this entire event. Please sign this and give it back to me immediately." As he said it, he gave each of them a document.

"Captain Brumfeld, just before take-off, I shall give you and Lieutenant Beardsley the sealed envelopes with the coordinates of the target. You shall assemble at the aircraft at 0130 hours. Take-off time is precisely 0300 hours. Time to target is just over two hours. I cannot emphasize enough the importance of what you are going to accomplish. Failure is absolutely unacceptable." Colonel McKilleps paused to look at the five people he was sending into harm's way.

"You are going to strike a nuclear facility. If you are not familiar with the term, there is a new kind of weapon called an atom bomb. The Germans have that bomb. The facility where they produce this bomb is at a location called Lorgenberg. It's your job to destroy this facility. Again, you are never to speak about any of this. It's permanently top secret."

He paused and looked directly at the crew. There are six bombs installed in your bomb bay. As I've already told you, these are a new type of bomb and are much heavier and larger in size than the standard five hundred pound bombs presently used. Also, the intensity and magnitude of their explosion is much greater than a five hundred pounder. These bombs will all be dropped on a single, relatively small target, a building complex. Accuracy is imperative. You will not get a second chance. In fact without a lot of luck, you won't even get a first chance."

"Colonel McKilleps," interrupted Bebe, "you told us the engineers calculated we should be flying at eight thousand feet when the bombs are dropped. If we fly in at less than five hundred feet to avoid radar, we can't get to that altitude in the ten minutes you allow us in the mission flight plan." She asked the question even though she knew Colonel McKilleps was well aware of that situation. Bebe knew she was going to modify the flight plan, but she wanted McKilleps' blessing. She wanted him to tell her it's okay to deviate from the planned course and altitudes.

Colonel McKilleps paused and looked down for a moment. He walked over to the door and opened it to look outside and make sure no one was listening. Then he walked back to the head of the table and spoke softly, almost whispering. "I shouldn't be telling you this, but you're right," he said. "And everyone sitting at this table knows you're right. You can't climb to eight thousand feet in ten minutes, especially with that heavy bomb load.

All I can say, Bebe, is you're the commander of the aircraft so you need to do everything you can to keep yourself and your crew alive. Assuming you make it past the German defenses and get close to the target, climb high and dump those bombs. That's all headquarters cares about. Do what you think you have to do, not what the flight plan calls for. All that matters is that you get to the coordinates of the target and drop your bombs. I don't give a damn what you do along the way."

Bebe nodded. This was a strange briefing, she thought. It was not standard procedure. Colonel McKilleps just told the crew that all headquarters wants is the target destroyed. Although he didn't say it, it seemed like he cared about the crew. If Bebe followed the flight plan, when the powerful bombs detonated they would not only destroy the target but blow their own B-17 out of the sky. It was obvious that headquarters not only assumed they wouldn't reach the target but, if they did, they'd never be able to fly out without getting shot down.

Kate was having the same thoughts. She looked at Bebe, her lips silently saying, "The jerks."

"As I said, the building complex is a secret Nazi laboratory where they are producing atom bombs," Colonel McKilleps continued. "To give you an idea of the destructive power of this type of weapon, if they should drop an atom bomb on London or New York City the loss of life would be incalculable. The explosion and fire radius would exceed five miles. That is why Lorgenberg must be destroyed. The bombs you have on your airplane will be dropped together and they are set to detonate at exactly one hundred feet above the building complex. As nearly as we can tell, there is nothing target worthy beneath the ground. The explosion these bombs create will destroy everything in the immediate target area and create a massive fire storm which will engulf whatever is left."

Colonel McKilleps continued with the flight plan, knowing Bebe would fly her own flight plan as they approached the target. "You will fly to within ten minutes of the target area at three to five hundred feet above the ground. It will be tricky. Captain Brumfeld has the conversion chart for various check points along the trip and he will read you your above ground altitude as the terrain varies in height. As it will be dark, the black airplane has less chance of being sighted by enemy spotters. When the bombs have been released, you must immediately turn away from the explosion just as we have practiced many times.

Colonel McKilleps continued. "We refer to your airplane as the LX-1 however that designation has nothing to do with the plane. Rather it's the type of bombs you shall be carrying. The LX-1 bomb has been in development for over five years. Its explosive power is incredible, overwhelming. I cannot tell you what the bomb is made of because I don't know myself. Nasty, when you are a half hour away from the target area you will arm the bombs. Bebe, whatever altitude you have reached when you are two minutes from target time, you are to level off and turn the plane over to the bombardier. Remember, you better be high or you'll blow yourselves out of the sky."

Kate and Bebe already planned on staying high and getting to that altitude in plenty of time before the bombs fell.

"Once the bombs are away, Bebe," Colonel McKilleps said, "you immediately take control of the plane. Remember, the nose of the plane will pitch up violently so don't let the plane stall. Immediately turn hard right in a ninety-degree turn. In less than twenty seconds the bombs will detonate and the force of the explosions will send a shock wave that will severely buffet the plane. With a little luck this thing will come off without a hitch. Are there any questions?"

The crew was silent, sitting stone faced and apprehensive.

"All right crew, we shall re-assemble at the aircraft at exactly 0130 hours."

As the crew got up to leave the room, Bebe motioned to Kate to stay behind.

"Colonel McKilleps, may I have a word with you," Bebe asked.

"Yes, of course," he said.

Bebe walked over and closed the door to his office. "Colonel," she said, "I'm sorry I waited until the last moment to tell you this, but I've had a bad feeling about Captain Brumfeld since the day I met him. Has he been checked out thoroughly?"

"You mean about his proficiency as a navigator?" he replied. "He's one of the best."

"I wasn't worried about his ability to perform his job," Bebe replied. "Frankly, sir, I don't trust Captain Brumfeld. I have a really bad feeling about the guy."

"Bebe, if you're talking from a standpoint of security, Brumfeld's got a top secret clearance. Don't worry about him. He'll do a great job for you and bring you back safe. McKilleps looked down briefly when he said that because he knew the odds against their surviving the mission.

"I'm afraid I still have the same concern, Colonel," Bebe replied. "I'm sorry, but I can't shake my bad feeling about Brumfeld."

"Look, Bebe," Colonel McKilleps said firmly, "you can't let your personal feelings about Max Brumfeld interfere with this mission. You've got to get your airplane to the target area and drop your bombs. Brumfeld will do his job. You do yours. Any questions?" he asked brusquely, concluding the conversation.

"No Sir," Bebe said.

"Good luck, Bebe," he replied, extending his hand. "You too, Kate," he added, as he shook her hand.

# 17

March 6, 1942     Lorgenberg Nuclear Facility, Germany

Kate and Bebe went back to their room and set their alarm for one a.m. Neither of them slept well but it seemed like they'd just gotten into bed when the alarm went off six hours later. They strapped on their pistols and headed for the black B-17 and its lethal cargo.

When they arrived at the hanger the B-17 was sitting on the ramp and the crew was waiting in front of the airplane for Colonel McKilleps to arrive. It was 0110. Bebe went underneath the plane's belly to climb into the plane through the escape hatch beneath the cockpit. As Kate watched Bebe hoist her legs up and pull herself through the small opening, she felt a chill and the hair raised on the back of her neck. She felt a deep foreboding about the mission.

Once Bebe was inside the B-17, she quickly went into the cockpit in front of the narrow passageway leading to the bomb bay and aft section of the airplane. She unbuckled her pistol holster and put it on the floor on the left side of her seat.

As Kate went through her pre-flight check of the outside of the aircraft, she remembered the day of her first flying lesson with Bebe almost three years earlier. The time had gone so quickly.

Bebe climbed back out of the B-17 twenty minutes later and joined Kate and the small crew on the ramp. At 0130 the colonel pulled his jeep up beside the assembled group standing on the right side of the airplane by engine number four. The colonel got out of his jeep and shook each crew-member's hand while saying, "I know you will succeed. Good Luck and Godspeed."

Kate, Bebe and the crew quickly boarded the airplane. The colonel drove his jeep over by the hangar and got out to stand and watch them get the airplane ready to go. Bebe completed her systems check as the crew worked through their individual checklist routines. Kate had already walked around the airplane to check the exterior and also the runway area to make sure no equipment or debris was around which might damage the plane as it moved away from its parking spot.

Captain Brumfeld came up the steps into the cockpit. "We're on our way to Germany" he said, holding his sheet with the coordinates. "Everything okay?" he asked. Kate nodded and gave a thumbs-up. Captain Brumfeld went back below into the nose cone.

After the pre-flight checklists were completed Bebe and Kate began starting the engines one at a time. As each engine rumbled to life they checked their instruments closely to make sure there were no abnormal readings on the gauges. By the time they completed the engine run-up, the time was 0230. Kate released the airplane's brakes and the heavily loaded bomber rolled forward. The entire crew was in the front end of the plane in the nose cone or the cockpit. As they waved goodbye, Colonel McKilleps lit a cigarette, wondering if he would ever see any of them again.

Bebe taxied the plane down the ramp and headed for the take-off point on the active runway. In a few minutes they were there, lined the plane up for take-off and went through the final engine run-ups. It was now 0238 hours and they were ready to go.

Kate called the tower for clearance as Bebe pushed the throttle forward.

"Alright Kate, let's go," she said.

Kate released the brakes and the big bomber began its take-off roll. Bebe gave it full throttle immediately because they would need more distance to get the loaded bomber off the ground. After what seemed like a long take-off time the nose began to rise and the plane groaned, slowly lifting into the air.

Bebe's voice came over the intercom to remind the crew to keep all lights off because it would be difficult to fly at the low altitude at night unless she could clearly see what was in front of her. Lights would also help the enemy spot the plane. There was some moonlight and that helped, however, she was watching her altimeter closely. Captain Brumfeld continuously called off true altitude numbers as the plane flew toward the hostile territory of Nazi Germany. Kate had her eyes glued on the nearly invisible horizon out the front window of the cockpit. Because of the darkness it was difficult to see where the night sky ended and the ground began.

Kate Darron sat tense and alert in her co-pilot's seat as the B-17 roared through the black pre-dawn of what would be a deadly and destructive day. Their black B-17 was carrying them to an appointment with fate. Kate's thought about the tough, driven woman sitting next to her. Bebe was daring and methodical, completely focused on what must be done today.

Kate, trained and mentored by this powerful woman, now shared her characteristics. She had honed her flying skills to the point she was nearly as proficient as Bebe. There was no question they would perform well today. The only question was whether the German's ground defenses and fighter pilots would blow them out of the sky. Neither Bebe nor Kate had ever heard of Lorgenberg. It was someplace in Germany and they were going to destroy it and kill a lot of people. They had never been there, and in all likelihood, would never come back. The whole thing is so strange and barbaric, Kate thought to herself.

Shortly after take-off Johnny Bradford crawled through the back of the plane's belly to take his place at the tail gunner's position. Tail gunners and ball turret gunners were always chosen for their small size. They had to be small in order to fit into their cramped enclosures. In order to get to his tail gunner's station he had to go through a bulkhead door, squeeze around the retracted tail wheel and climb into the claustrophobic tail gunner's compartment. Even with his tinier size, Johnny always found it an awkward maneuver. But he was now in position and ready with his machine guns.

Captain Brumfeld and Lieutenant Geyerson were also manning their machine guns at the navigator's and bombardier's positions in the plane's nose cone. There were ghostly flashes of moonlight from behind the black clouds and occasional flickers of light from the farm houses below. Lights of small villages began to appear. Bebe steered the B-17 away from these lights, keeping the airplane in the safety of the cloud shadows and away from eyes and ears that could detect them.

There was no sound or sign of life inside the dark airplane. Only the dim glow of instrument lights and monotonous rumble of the engines gave evidence of their existence. Kate wished there was some chatter on the intercom but they had to maintain radio silence. Tension was an unwelcome intruder. It pierced their consciousness as the twenty-six ton growling, black metallic monster plunged forward through the night sky. Kate looked through the cockpit window into the blackness and wondered what their fate would be.

Bebe strained to see through the darkness to focus on the nearly non-existent horizon, her only external visual cue to the airplane's attitude. She also kept her eye on the attitude indicator to keep the airplane's nose level. "Five hundred feet," Brumfeld yelled, continuing to call out the plane's altitude to Kate. Without the intercom, it was hard to hear his voice. Kate double checked her altimeter. Because they were flying dangerously low Bebe wanted Brumfeld monitoring and confirming the plane's altitude.

Except for the engines everything was eerily quiet. But the quiet ended abruptly as four flak bursts buffeted the plane. Luck was with the German gunners. They had multiple hits on the B-17 and Kate heard the wind whistling through shrapnel holes in the airplane's belly. There were more flak bursts and the airplane shuddered and yawed to the right as explosions lighted the night sky. Bebe struggled to maintain altitude and level flight as the booming flak and bright orange lines of anti-aircraft tracer bullets pierced the blackness.

The airplane was hit again as enemy fire drilled a streak of holes in the airplane's fuselage. So far the engines and wings hadn't taken serious hits. Strikes on either could bring the plane down. The plane's fuel tanks were located in the wings and if they were hit, fuel would leak. If one or more engines were knocked out, the plane would not be able to hold altitude and would travel more slowly, making it an easier target for the Germans.

A burst of tracer fire ripped through the waist gunner area directly behind Kate and scattered a dozen holes in the plane's fuselage. The plane rolled to the right and its nose dropped toward the blackness of the earth and the deadly torrents of gunfire pouring from German guns. Bebe pulled the plane's nose up, but not before the airplane dropped two hundred feet.

Bebe abruptly turned the airplane hard left and pushed the throttles forward to maximum power and put the plane into a climb. She abandoned the low altitude flight plan in order to get the plane further above the flak and anti-aircraft fire and make it a more difficult target. If she stayed at her planned altitude, the B-17 would be destroyed before it ever reached its target. She kept the airplane climbing until it reached nine thousand feet. Also, by flying further away from the cities they would encounter less flak and the danger of German fighter planes. It would extend the flight time to the target however.

Captain Brumfeld worked feverishly to plot a new course. It was obvious they would never make it to the target if they stayed on their initial heading. Bebe and Kate figured the only reason they hadn't encountered more German fighter planes was because the Germans must have assumed their single airplane was not on a bombing mission. Or maybe the Germans ignored them because it was still early morning and they wanted to sleep. Neither of those reasons was likely. The reality was they had just been lucky up to the time of this attack. But Kate had a feeling their luck was running out.

Oddly, the time passed quickly and they were soon half an hour from the target area. They were supposed to drop their bombs from eight thousand feet, but Bebe had climbed to twelve thousand, still fretting that if they were too low when the bombs exploded over the target their airplane would be destroyed by the blast. She also had a feeling the engineers recommended the lower altitude to insure greater bombing accuracy and disregarded the safety of the airplane and crew. That's all well and good, Bebe thought, unless you're a member of the crew.

She would drop the bombs from twelve thousand feet. It would give them fifty percent more altitude when the bombs detonated and more time to fly away from the blast because it would take longer for the bombs to fall to their target. As they were maintaining radio silence, Bebe told Kate to go below and tell Nasty Geyerson and Captain Brumfeld about the change in altitude. Neither man would object because they too were concerned about how powerful the bombs' explosions would be.

They were now eight minutes to target. Nasty Geyerson was concentrating on the Norden bomb sight. The time was drawing near for him to prove the bombardier's prowess he boasted of in Colonel McKilleps's office.

Dawn was beginning to break when Kate suddenly pointed ahead. She had spotted the shadowy profile of the Lorgenberg complex in the day's first light. As Kate counted eight buildings a chill went down her spine. The compound's shimmering lights seemed to welcome the approaching bomber, imparting a surreal appearance to the scene.

Although she and Bebe had discussed it many times before, the time was at hand when they would kill hundreds of human beings. It was a thought that had always haunted Kate, but the act of doing so was always in the future. But the future and the murder of hundreds of people was now minutes away. It sickened her. They were actually going to kill people. She remembered the time she shot the deer and the guilt she felt for weeks. But these were human beings in the dark buildings on the horizon. They had families they loved and who loved them. In minutes they would all be dead. Kate struggled to control her emotions. We have no choice, she told herself, but the agonizing guilt only grew. She wondered if Bebe felt the same way.

Kate turned her head toward Bebe who was barely visible in the pale light. She reached over and touched Bebe, but instantly drew back her hand when she felt a warm wetness on Bebe's right shoulder. Kate looked down at her fingers. In the dim light she saw black splotches of blood on her fingertips. "How bad is it?" asked Kate.

"It hurts. We're five minutes from target. I'm okay and I've got the airplane, Bebe said."

"Let me take it, Bebe!" Kate exclaimed.

"I've got it, Kate," Bebe replied sharply.

"Right on course," yelled Captain Brumfeld on the intercom. "Our target is just ahead."

'What the hell is he doing?" Bebe shouted. "He broke radio silence. He just announced to the Nazis that we're here. Call down and tell him to shut up, Kate."

Kate jumped up from her seat and looked down into the nose cone. "Brumfeld, we're on radio silence," she yelled. He nodded he understood, an embarrassed look on his face. Kate climbed back into her seat and strapped in.

"Look at it, Kate," Bebe said calmly, as she pointed at the complex of buildings directly ahead.

"Big operation," Kate shouted. Numerous cars and trucks were parked around the buildings and smoke was pouring from tall smoke stacks. The compound was brightly lighted.

Suddenly, a cannon shell roared through the bottom of the fuselage behind the cockpit and continued through the roof, leaving two ragged holes of howling wind. Deadly streaks of anti-aircraft tracers sailed gracefully past the aircraft. In seconds, the tracers' arcs shifted and riddled the B-17's wings, fuselage and tail section. Engine four sputtered then stopped completely as fire broke out in the nacelle. Kate quickly hit the fire extinguisher and feathered the propeller to reduce the drag.

"We're here," Bebe called into the intercom, no longer concerned about radio silence. "Nasty," Bebe yelled to the bombardier," we're three minutes out. You have the plane." There was no answer. "Nasty!" Bebe screamed into the intercom once more. Again there was no answer.

Suddenly there was a rush of wind as the door opened in the back of the fuselage. Kate looked back to see Captain Brumfeld standing by the door and aiming his pistol toward the cockpit.

"Duck, Bebe!" Kate screamed. Both women quickly bent down in their seats and moved their heads toward the walls of the fuselage. Brumfeld fired his gun four times and then stepped through the doorway. The shots missed and slammed into the instrument cluster in front of them.

"Brumfeld parachuted out," Kate yelled.

"Kate, see why Nasty won't respond," Bebe shouted anxiously. "If he can't drop the bombs, you've gotta' do it." The urgency in Bebe's voice signaled she figured something bad had happened.

Kate quickly climbed out of her seat and moved from the cockpit down to the bombardier's compartment in the nose cone. Kate expected to find the worst and she did. Nasty Geyerson was slumped in his seat, his throat cut. The Norden bombsight was smashed. "Damn," she gasped.

"He's dead," Kate yelled into the intercom. "The bombsight is destroyed. "I'll drop the bombs manually, Bebe."

Flak bursts filled the sky and the plane buffeted and rolled. If Brumfeld hadn't damaged the Norden bombsight it would adjust for the turbulence. However, with the bombsight damaged, Kate would have to do her best to release the bombs when the airplane was flying smoothly. But continuous ground fire mercilessly pounded the plane. If the bombs were to be accurate, Kate would have to get very lucky.

They were less than one minute away from target. The big plane lurched as flak exploded nearby. Shrapnel and bullets ripped through the bottom of the fuselage and blew holes in the roof above top turret gunner's position. The plane was honeycombed with window-like holes that let in the morning light and whistled as wind blew through them.

"Bebe, get ready," Kate yelled into the intercom.

"Set," yelled Bebe.

"Just a few seconds…………..Bombs away" Kate said calmly.

When the bombs dropped from the bomb bay the airplane's nose lurched up sharply. Bebe quickly brought it back to level flight and immediately steered the aircraft into a hard ninety-degree right turn in order to get away from the bombs' detonation. They were at twelve thousand feet, four thousand feet higher than specified in the mission plan. Kate climbed back into the cockpit.

The big airplane, slow to complete turns under the best of conditions, now lumbered even more slowly with only three engines operating. The B-17 was just half way through the right turn when the dull gray of dawn instantly turned to brilliant orange as the six powerful bombs exploded in consecutive bursts above the Nazi atom bomb complex.

The shock waves of the explosions hit the plane in seconds, crashing against its fuselage and pitching the plane violently upward. The nose of the plane abruptly dropped wildly and the B-17 was plunging in a nearly vertical dive toward the earth. Bebe instantly jammed the throttles forward to full power. She and Kate pulled the yokes hard to try and bring the nose up and take the plane out of the fatal dive.

Out of the corner of her eye, Kate could see the altimeter's needles spinning backwards as the plane dropped. In what seemed like hours, but were only seconds, the women could felt the flight control surfaces becoming functional as the airplane recovered from the dive. If they had dropped the bombs at eight thousand feet as directed, the shock waves of the explosions would have blown the plane out of the sky, just as Bebe thought.

But now they were headed home. They had to gain back some altitude, and if they could get through the flak and whatever else the Germans might throw at them, they would get back alive.

But as they retraced their flight path, the outbound flak began in earnest. Number three engine suddenly exploded and burst into fire. Bebe was struggling hard to control the plane and Kate hit the fire extinguisher and quickly feathered the propeller. Two engines were gone. Kate heard Bebe curse. The plane was crabbing hard to the right as both right engines were out of operation. She was fighting to hold heavy left rudder to counter the two left engines trying to pull the left wing ahead of the right wing which would cause a loss of control of the airplane. The flak was constant and growing heavier. It was now daylight and the anti-aircraft defenses could see what they were shooting at.

A massive explosion rocked the airplane, ripping a jagged hole in the aircraft's floor just aft of the cockpit. Kate glanced behind to check the damage and saw large metal strips of the airplane's underbelly had been ripped upward and across the nose cone's exit.

The airplane rocked back and forth and shuddered violently. The vibration of the plane resembled a car driving over a washer-board dirt road with regular intervals of successive bumping bouncing the driver and rattling teeth.

Kate immediately saw the problem. Engine number one was also down and the B-17 was rapidly losing altitude. The airplane was shot to pieces and struggling to stay in the air with only one engine operating. They weren't going to make it back.

"Get out now, Kate!" yelled Bebe. "Tell Bradford to jump!"

Kate yelled into the intercom, "Johnny, bail out! Bail out now."

"Johnny, get out! Do you hear me? Get out!" Kate screamed.

"I can't move," the wounded tail gunner moaned. "I'm hit and bleeding all over the place. I can't make it."

"Bebe, he can't get out. Try to bring it in," Kate yelled.

"Kate, we're going down! Get out. I don't want you to die," Bebe screamed. "I'll land somewhere down there."

The plane was dropping toward what would otherwise have been a beautiful pine forest. But, the tall trees below meant certain death if the airplane crashed into them. Kate's brain was racing. She looked at Bebe hoping she would give some command, some direction. But Bebe slumped forward, barely conscious. Kate reflexively grabbed the yoke.

"I'm not going to leave you Bebe," Kate screamed. "We've got to live! We can do this."

Bebe mumbled, "Get out Kate. You can make it. I'll hold it

steady. Go!"

"No," Kate screamed, tears filling her eyes. "I'll never leave you! Never!"

Kate looked out the cockpit's windows. The dark green pine trees rushing toward them covered the ground as far as she could see. There was no clearing. The plane would crash into the trees and be torn to shreds.

"Kate, why are you doing this?" Bebe mumbled. "You can still make it."

But it was too late, even if Kate wanted to bail out. The B-17 was only a few hundred feet above the treetops and there was no time for a parachute to open, even if she did make it out the airplane's door. The plane was dropping fast and escape was impossible.

As the tops of the pine trees raced beneath them, Kate screamed, "I love you, Bebe."

Nearly unconscious, Bebe murmured, "I love you too Kate!"

Kate heard loud scratching against the bottom of the fuselage as the airplane skimmed across the roof of the forest clipping off tree tops in its path. She was pulling the yoke with every ounce of strength, trying desperately to keep the plane in the air and praying for a clearing. Suddenly, there was a thunderous crashing sound, a bright flash and deafening boom.

# PART FOUR

# 18

April 11, Present Time    St Louis, Mo.

A loud banging in the parking lot awakened Kate Darron. It was a beautiful Saturday morning and the sunrise was happening just for her. She had slept soundly and felt good. As she looked out the bedroom window of her apartment she saw someone who was moving into or out of Sun Lakes and who was also the source of the noise. She could see her old car and it looked reassuring, although a little tired. Her dinner with the woman the night before had been pleasant, although she must have had too much wine because she didn't remember walking home. If she drank too much, she rationalized that it must have been because of that little devil Bernard Mangole.

The woman had been an elegant and charming hostess. "What was her name, anyway?" Kate decided she would go buy a nice flower arrangement and take it over to the woman's apartment. She was also trying to remember what they talked about at dinner, but was drawing a complete blank. She remembered the woman inviting her to dinner and getting ready to go to her apartment. "But, what had they talked about?" That was the strangest thing. She remembered very little about the dinner other than arriving at the woman's apartment building and then walking down the hall with her.

But she also remembered being inside the woman's apartment and the rich furnishings. And she had some wine, Chardonnay, she thought. And they talked, but about what? It must have been a powerful Chardonnay because I can't remember anything, she thought. Oh well, she would remember later. Right now she was going to get a shower, have breakfast, and go buy some flowers for her hostess of the previous evening. She felt she should repay the woman for the nice dinner and she wanted to find out her name. This is ridiculous that I can't remember her name, she thought to herself.

On her way to the flower shop, Kate noticed a church parking lot filled with cars. It must be a wedding Kate thought to herself. It's Saturday.

Kate remembered the woman had a large number of vases filled with fresh flowers. She would get her something very nice. But when she got to the flower shop it was closed. Kate looked at her watch. It was nearly eleven o'clock. She checked the store hours posted on the door. "Open at eight a.m. every day. Closed Sunday." That was odd, Kate thought. She got back in her car and drove to the supermarket. She picked out a large, expensive arrangement and a vase to go with it. As she swiped her credit card she gasped, "These are expensive. I hope she likes them."

That was when Kate noticed the date of the receipt. It read April 11. "It's Saturday, April tenth", Kate mumbled. However, as she walked toward the supermarket exit, she noticed the thick newspapers on the racks. Those look like Sunday papers, she thought. She walked over and looked at them. The newspapers were dated, April 11, Sunday. Kate was shocked. How long did I sleep, she wondered.

In just a few minutes Kate was back in the apartment building's parking lot and stepping out of her car with her bouquet of flowers. She was still perplexed how she could have lost a day. It was supposed to be Saturday, yet it was Sunday. She had dinner with the woman just last night, which would have been Friday. But, today is Sunday, she puzzled. I hope she's home this morning, she thought.

Kate walked up to the front door of the building and looked at the apartment numbers with an individual doorbell next to each one. Unlike the night before, she knew the number of the apartment. "Twelve," she said to herself. Kate pushed the doorbell.

There was no answer. She pushed it again. "Yes, who's there?" a voice responded.

"It's me, Kate. I'm here to see you. I hope this isn't a bad time."

There was a hesitation. "No, I guess it's not a bad time," a perplexed voice answered. "I'll be down to let you in. Who is this again?"

"It's Kate, Catherine Darron from across the courtyard." This doesn't sound like the woman I met last night, Kate thought. Her voice sounds different and she doesn't seem to recognize me. Maybe the person answering the intercom is someone visiting her.

Kate also thought it strange the woman didn't press the button in her apartment which would unlock the main door where Kate stood waiting. Kate could see someone inside coming toward her.

The door opened and a nice looking but slightly overweight black woman leaned out the door and said, "May I help you?"

"No thank you, Ma'am. I'm waiting for my friend in apartment number twelve. She should be here in a minute."

"Dear, I am in apartment number twelve. That's where I live."

"That can't be," replied Kate. "I was just here last night and I had dinner with my friend in apartment number twelve."

"That can't be right dear. You must have been in another building. Did you say your name is Kate?"

"Yes, my name is Kate. I was in apartment number twelve last night with my friend. Wait a minute," said Kate, remembering today was Sunday and not Saturday. "I mean I had dinner on Friday night, the night before last."

"Kate, I've lived in apartment number twelve for the last four years. Whether you think you ate here last night or Friday night, you must have the wrong apartment. Do you want to come in walk down the hall? You may be able to figure out the right apartment from an inside look."

A perplexed Kate followed the woman into the apartment building and down the hallway. Everything looked exactly the same as it did last night, rather Friday night. The woman stopped at the fourth door on the left, apartment number twelve. This was the same door she walked through the night she had dinner here.

"This is it," said Kate .

"Honey, this can't be it. You couldn't have been here last night or Friday night. These buildings all look alike you know. You're mistaken, dear. By the way, my name is Norma Sykes."

"It's nice to meet you, Norma" replied Kate. "My name is Catherine Darron. I live right across the courtyard in that apartment on the second floor. Last night, I had dinner with my friend in what you're telling me is your apartment."

Norma Sykes, although suspicious of Kate's mental state earlier, concluded that she was just confused. Anyhow, she decided to invite Kate inside, if for no other reason than to help her straighten out her confusion and find her friend.

"Kate , you're not on drugs or anything, are you?

"No, absolutely not," replied Kate.

"Well, then come on in, dear. Welcome to apartment number twelve."

Kate followed the woman as she walked into the apartment. "Does this place look like where you ate last night or whenever, Kate?"

"Yes," Kate said. "This is absolutely the same place I had dinner. I remember the beautiful red couches and drapes. It's all the same. Norma, I had dinner right here in your apartment."

"Kate, I was here all night. I never go out. You couldn't have had dinner here because….," Norma paused in mid-sentence. "Wait a minute, Kate," she said, sitting down. Norma sat on a red couch and stared at the floor. "Kate, sit down for a minute."

As Kate sat down on the red couch across from her, Norma said, "It's true I was here but something strange happened. I didn't remember that until just now."

"What happened?" asked Kate.

"On Saturday morning I woke up with all my clothes on. That's what happened," Norma replied with a puzzled look on her face.

Kate smiled. "You mean you normally wake up naked?"

"No, I wake up with my pajamas on. I never go to bed without putting on my pajamas. But, Saturday morning I woke up fully dressed, like I came home from work and went right to bed. And, I don't remember having dinner Friday night. That's really weird. Kate, are you absolutely sure this is the apartment in which you had dinner last night or Friday night? Norma asked. "You're sure about that?"

"Of course, Norma," Kate replied. "Your decorating style is unique. I'm absolutely certain this is where I was. There's got to be an explanation. I'm not crazy."

"Maybe this apartment was the one," replied Norma. "And, I'm not crazy either."

"What do you mean, Norma?"

"Like I said, when I woke up Friday morning I was fully dressed. And, I don't remember going to bed. Now, that is crazy. But, there was something else."

"What?" asked Kate.

"Well, I live here alone and hardly ever have visitors. When I walked down my hallway Saturday morning, I noticed the toilet in the hall bathroom had the seat up, like a man had used it."

"Maybe you left it up after you cleaned it or something," said Kate.

"Kate, I always keep the lid down. Besides that, in usual man fashion, there were spots on the toilet where a man tinkled, if you know what I mean. Kate, someone was in this apartment Friday night. And you say you were here too. Who else was here?"

"Norma, I told you a woman invited me to have dinner with her. She and I were the only ones here. At least I think it was just her and me, but now I'm not sure. All I know is that I was here and had dinner with a woman. Oh, wait a minute, when I woke up this morning I thought it was Saturday. Norma, either I slept through or somehow lost a day. Saturday never happened for me."

"Why did the woman invite you here? What did you talk about?"

"I don't remember," said Kate, exasperated.

"Are we both crazy?" Norma asked.

"Wait a minute," replied Kate, as she stood up. She turned around and looked closely at the wall behind the couch. "Did you have pictures hanging on this wall, Norma?"

"No, I never did."

"Well, how did these little holes get into the wall then?"

Norma got up and walked over to where Kate stood. "Where'd those holes come from? I never put them there."

"Maybe they were put there by the last tenant," Kate said.

"I painted that wall myself," replied Norma. "I filled in every hole before I painted the wall. I'm very careful about that. Look Kate!" Norma exclaimed, pointing to the top of the couch against the wall.

Kate looked where Norma was pointing. Directly below the nail holes were several little grains of sawdust on the back of the couch. Someone had pulled nails out of the wall and the tiny flakes of sawdust from the small holes had fallen onto the couch.

There was someone in the apartment Friday night, Norma concluded. "This is getting spooky," she said.

Kate gave the flowers to Norma and the two women talked a while longer but came to no conclusion. They were both convinced that someone besides Norma was in the apartment on Friday night. Kate thought it was a middle-aged woman and Norma swore it was a man. "Maybe they were both right," they decided. They said they would talk again soon and Kate walked back to her apartment.

Unable to figure anything out about Friday night, Kate spent the rest of the day running errands. She was tired and went to bed early. She knew she would be meeting with Mr. Edgerton and Bernard Mangole's parents in the morning and that she would probably be fired. For some reason, it didn't bother her like she thought it would. She was surprised she was no longer worried about it. "I'm going to beat them to the punch," she said. "I'm going to quit."

# 19

April 12, Present Time    St. Louis, Missouri

On Friday night Kate was worried that she would be in trouble for injuring Bernard Mangole. She was dreading Monday morning and facing the principal Mr. Edgerton, Bernard's parents, and the probability of being fired. She didn't intend to harm the child. She was only trying to stop him from disrupting the class or harming other students.

However, on Sunday night she decided that she would quit on Monday morning. That was very much out of character for Kate, but strangely, her attitude had completely changed and she felt supremely self-confident. That put a whole new perspective on the situation.

Now that it was Monday morning, she was on her way to work with the intention of resigning the thankless job. Trying to teach a group of relatively great kids while one maniac was allowed to disrupt the class is not how she wanted to spend the rest of her working years. While she loved teaching, the lack of backing by Mr. Edgerton and the constant threat of being fired was too much grief to put up with. She pulled her aging Honda into a space in the school parking lot.

When she arrived at her classroom there was a substitute teacher in her chair. Oh well, she thought, who cares? I'm going to quit anyway.

As she suspected, Mr. Edgerton wanted to see her right away. He had instructed the substitute teacher to tell her come to his office immediately. The hell with him, she thought. I'll collect my things first. In a few minutes she had taken all of her personal possessions from her desk and hauled the box of items out to her car. She wouldn't have to come back to her room when she quit.

She closed her car door and began walking up the sidewalk leading to the principal's office. She thought she had seen Bernard Mangole's parents arrive in a Mercedes when she passed the door on her way to the office. She didn't intend to spend any time with them. They want her fired but they wouldn't get the satisfaction. She would have already resigned by the time they came inside the office.

She walked down the hallway to Mr. Edgerton's outer office. "He wants to see me," she said to his assistant.

Margaret, the constantly distressed looking secretary, said "Yes, Ms. Darron."

I've known her for four years. Couldn't she call me Kate?

Margaret emerged from Mr. Edgerton's office and motioned to Kate. "He'll see you now!" she said. The tone of her voice was that of someone telling her she had arrived for some exciting event. She's taking pleasure in this, Kate thought.

"Thank you, Margaret," Kate said, shaking her head in disgust. Kate entered Mr. Edgerton's office and he asked her to sit down in front of his desk.

"Miss Darron, we need to pick up where we left off Friday. Mr. and Mrs. Mangole are here this morning and they're very upset. We'll need to meet with them and decide what needs to be done to satisfy them regarding Bernard's injury."

"What do you mean his injury?" Kate asked. "Other than his bloody nose, I didn't know there was an injury."

"There's no physical injury, Miss Darron. Mr. and Mrs. Mangole took Bernard to the Emergency Room Friday night on the advice of their attorney. He checked out fine physically, but, according to Bernard's psychiatrist, the child suffered quite a bit of emotional trauma and is seriously injured in that regard."

"You've got to be kidding me," replied Kate .

"I'm quite serious, Miss Darron. Mr. and Mrs. Mangole have agreed to talk with you and if you will promise to apologize to Bernard in front of your class, they will let the whole matter drop. Of course, Superintendent Lochmaund and I will need to consider a course of action with you. It will probably amount to nothing more than a reprimand placed on your record.

Anyway, I trust this is satisfactory to you and that we can move on from here." With that, Mr. Edgerton pushed his intercom button and said, "Margaret, have Mr. and Mrs. Mangole come in please."

Kate was flabbergasted at the idiocy she'd just heard. Then Mr. and Mrs. Mangole came in. After exchanging greetings and sitting down, Mr. Edgerton outlined what he had just told Kate. Kate was fuming. She fully intended to quit, but hadn't spoken yet. She was curious as to how far the stupidity would go.

Mr. Mangole spoke. "Miss Darron, Bernard absolutely loves you as his teacher. I'm just sorry you had this little misunderstanding with him. We never have any problem with him at home. We asked Bernard, 'If Miss Darron would apologize for hurting you, would you forgive her?' And do you know what? He said he would. He's a great kid, isn't he?"

Mr. Edgerton, smiling, spoke next. "Miss Darron, we can settle this whole thing now and move on."

Mrs. Mangole then spoke. "Miss Darron, I have several child rearing books I would be happy to lend you. They are just amazing."

Kate was about to explode. She definitely could not, would not put up with this idiocy any longer.

Mr. Mangole then said, "Well, I think that we have resolved this matter. We're very happy that Miss Darron is willing to admit her mistake and apologize to Bernard."

Then Mr. Edgerton spoke. Well we are certainly satisfied also Mr. and Mrs. Mangole. Don't you agree Miss Darron?"

Mr. Edgerton and Mr. and Mrs. Mangole turned their heads toward Kate.

"Mr. Edgerton, I mean Fred, you don't mind if I call you Fred, do you." No, I'm absolutely not satisfied. As for Bernard, Mr. and Mrs. Mangold, I seriously doubt he's not a problem at home because he's an absolute shit in class. And as for your books on child rearing, Mrs. Mangold, you can shove them up your behind. I resign effective immediately. Fred. I became a teacher to teach, not to put up with the likes of you three jerks and your idiotic child."

With that, Kate walked out Fred's door. She would never teach a class again.

Although Kate needed the paycheck she had enough money to last for three or four months. Knowing she would quit her job, she had decided that when she returned to her apartment she would immediately clean the place out. She would throw away everything she didn't need and then look for another job. That way she would be ready to move if she found a position out of state.

When she got back to her apartment she changed her clothes and started going through the place to decide what she could get rid of. Except for her clothes, she actually had everything already pared down to just the essentials. Her clothes were another matter, however. She could probably get rid of a whole lot of clothes. She opened up both doors of her closet and began the task of throwing things out.

She went through the blouses first, throwing a dozen or more on the floor. Those are going to the Goodwill Store, she thought to herself. As she went through each item of clothing she checked the pockets. Smiling, she shook her head, amused that she always checked pockets in case she might have stuffed a crumpled up one hundred dollar bill into one of them.

Then she began going through her slacks, all of which were neatly hung on hangers. She started from her right and was working her way toward the left closet wall. She had checked out every pocket on nearly every pair of slacks she owned and was down to the last five or six pairs.

That was when she saw the last item in the line of slacks. But it wasn't a pair of slacks; it looked like a heavy dark shirt or a masculine type jacket. She didn't recognize whatever it was. She moved the half dozen pairs of slacks to her right so she could see this odd piece of clothing hanging in her closet. It was a pair of coveralls. "Where did these come from?" she wondered.

She lifted the hanger with the coveralls out of the closet. As she looked more closely, she realized she was not holding a pair of coveralls. It looked like some kind of flight suit. She'd seen them in the movies, but where had this pair come from? The flight suit was filthy and had dirt and oil all over it. There was a tear in the left leg near the knee. Then she noticed several dark red blotches on the chest area and the legs. It looked like dried blood. "My god!" she exclaimed. "How did these things get here? Is someone playing some kind of morbid joke on me?"

No one had ever stayed at her apartment. The only one who would have clothes in her apartment was her. What in the world is going on? She put her hand in the front right pocket of the flight suit to begin her search. She wasn't expecting to find a one hundred dollar bill, but wanted to get some clue as to where this flight suit or whatever it was came from. Who owned this thing?

There was nothing in the right front pocket. No, there was nothing in the left front pocket either. Kate suddenly gasped as she glimpsed the name-tag sewn above the left chest pocket of the dark flight suit. It was Darron.

Her anxiety building, Kate checked the back right pocket and then the left. There was nothing in either of them, or was there? She almost missed it, but her hand felt a small scrap of torn, folded paper in the left rear pocket.

She tossed the flight suit on the floor and unfolded the small piece of paper. There was something written on it and she looked closely to read the writing. "Oh my god," she cried in shock, as she read the words out loud. "Please Kate, come back to me. Lorgenberg, Germany, March 6, 1942, B-17 crash site. Bebe."

Aghast, Kate stepped back and slumped to her bed. An inkling of fear, a foreboding, began to stir inside her. What is this note all about? Is the note written to me? And why? Where did the flight suit come from? Is that blood on the suit? She stared at the crumpled flight suit lying on the floor. She was afraid to touch it, but felt she must.

Trembling, she stood up and slipped off her skirt. She hesitated, gazing at the disheveled flight suit. It lay in a heap chest side up, the name-tag Darron seeming to call out to her. She cautiously reached for the suit and picked it up. Taking a deep breath, she lowered the suit and stepped into it. She pulled it up over her blouse, put her arms into the sleeves and zipped it up. It fit perfectly. Fear again welled up inside her. "What is going on?" she mumbled, her voice breaking.

It was then Kate noticed a faint odor of oil. She looked down at the black streak on the right leg of the suit. She touched the dark smudge and looked at her hand. There was a smoky stain on her finger. She slowly raised her finger to her nose. It smelled of oil. The dirt and oil seemed fresh, as if the flight suit had just been worn. She felt a chill along her spine and quickly took off the outfit and threw it to the floor. What was happening was unbelievable and eerie. She put on her skirt and sat down on the bed.

She looked at the note again. How can this note be for me? It's dated March 6, 1942. That was decades before I was born.

But there was something tender and haunting about the words scrawled on the torn paper. "Please Kate, come back to me. Bebe." Who is Bebe? There is something very wrong here, something unexplainable. Even though the apartment temperature was seventy-three degrees, she felt cold. Kate walked across her bedroom to the dresser and found a sweater. She always felt more secure when she was warm. She walked back across the room to where the battered flight suit lay on the floor.

Kate sat down on the bed and stared at the suit, her distress growing. She wished she was not alone. She looked at her watch and it was eleven forty-five. Her best friend Steffy would be at work. It was Monday morning and Steffy, a buyer for a department store chain, would be busy. Kate decided to call her anyway. She had to talk to somebody.

Kate had known Steffy Thornton since they were in grade school. They had gone to college together. That Steffy was a smart, attractive brunette with long hair and brown eyes enabled her to skip a few rungs on the corporate ladder and she rapidly rose to an executive position. Her eyes, though serious looking, hid her impulsive nature which sometimes got her into trouble. Whenever that happened, which was every time she switched boyfriends, she relied on Kate to help her through the turmoil.

But now, Kate needed Steffy, and hoped she would answer her phone.

"What, Kate?" Steffy answered. "It's Monday morning and I'm swamped."

"Steph, I have a big problem. I need your help," Kate said.

"You want me to drop by after work, Kate?" Steffy asked.

"I want you to come to my apartment right now, Steph."

Kate had never called her for help before. "This sounds serious," Steffy said.

"You won't believe it," Kate answered. "Can you come now?"

"I'm on my way," Steffy said. She was going to add, "and you'll have to take me out to dinner for screwing up my day," but the tone in Kate's voice was tense. Steffy knew Kate must have a serious problem.

Half an hour later Kate heard the doorbell and pressed the intercom. "Come on up Steffy. The door's open."

"What's going on, Kate? Steffy asked as she walked into the apartment a few moments later. You didn't sound so good. I was worried."

"I quit my job this morning," Kate replied.

Steffy was visibly shocked. "Kate, that's not like you," she said. "You never do anything that dramatic without thinking about it for weeks."

"I know," replied Kate, "but that's not why I called you. I wouldn't have asked you to rush over here if that's all that happened."

Steffy's face reflected her anxiety as she looked at Kate. "Quitting a job is a big decision," she said, "but you don't seem at all worried about it. If that's not why you called, you must have something really big on your mind. So, what's going on? Did someone die or something?"

"Sit down Steffy," Kate said, gesturing toward the couch. Kate sat down in a chair across from Steffy. "First of all, I surprised myself when I quit my job this morning. I mean, I just made the decision without even thinking about it. I just walked into the principal's office and quit. I've never done anything like that."

"Yeah," Steffy laughed. "You would have called me Saturday to meet for martinis to talk to me about it. By the way, you were going to call me Saturday but you never did. I left you a couple of voice mails but you never called back. I figured you went over to your parents or something."

"That's another thing, Steffy," said Kate. "I don't know where Saturday went. I mean it never happened for me."

"What are you talking about?" asked Steffy, puzzled.

"I remember Friday night. A woman in the apartment building across the grassy area asked me to come to dinner. The next thing I knew it was Sunday morning and I was in my apartment."

"What?" laughed Steffy? "Maybe the woman was some kind of pervert or something," she added, still laughing.

"It's not funny Steph," said Kate, with a somber expression.

Steffy was taken aback at Kate's response. It was obvious Kate was very concerned about something, but Steffy wasn't sure what. "Kate," she said, "you're telling me a day in your life never happened. Seriously, are you're sure you weren't drugged, or something?"

Kate thought for a moment. "Of course not, Steph," she said. "Wait a minute," Kate continued. "It seems like something happened but...." She thought for another moment. "No, I guess not. I don't remember much about the dinner," she concluded.

'This is really bizarre," Steffy said.

"It gets worse," replied Kate. "I went over to the woman's apartment yesterday to thank her for inviting me to dinner Friday."

"Didn't that refresh your memory?" Steffy asked.

"That is where it begins to get really weird," Kate answered. Kate related her conversation with Norma Sykes, the current resident in Apartment 12.

"Kate, you're telling me some very outlandish stuff," said Steffy.

"That's why I called you, Steph. But, the craziest part is what I'm going to show you next."

Steffy had become very serious. "Kate, I've never heard anything so strange in my life. You're making me very nervous. Actually, I find it scary, but go on.

"After I quit my job this morning," Kate continued, "I decided the first thing I should do is clean out my apartment because I figured I would have to move when I found another job. So, I started going through my closet and that's when I called you."

"I hope you didn't call me here on my busiest day of the week to help you clean out your closet," Steffy said unbelievingly.

"Come into the bedroom with me, Steph. There's something I want to show you."

As they walked into the bedroom, Steffy saw the piles of clothes by the door. "You really are cleaning the place out. What are those things?" she asked, shocked at the sight of two pistols on Kate's dresser. "I knew you were a competitive shooter, but those two guns look like serious business."

"The larger pistol is a Glock 19," Kate replied. "It's a semiautomatic with a 33 round clip. The small gun is a .38, a five shot Smith and Wesson Chief's Special. It's an older gun my father gave me. It's more of an accessory, something to get the bad guy's attention. The Glock handles the really bad guys with attention deficit."

"I wear a size thirty-eight bra," laughed Steffy.

Kate laughed. "I'd rather carry my thirty-eight on my right hip than hanging from my chest."

"Good points," Steffy replied, "no pun intended."

Kate smiled. "The guns aren't what I wanted to show you, Steffy. Here's the reason I called you." Kate picked the tattered flight suit from the floor and held it up for Steffy to see. "I found this hanging in my closet this morning. What do you make of it?"

"It looks like a flight suit, a very dirty one at that," Steffy replied.

"Thanks for confirming that fact, Steph. You're a big help," smiled Kate.

"Funny," replied Steffy. But her smile quickly faded. "Those spots look like blood."

"I think they are blood," Kate said.

"Did you murder somebody, Kate?" Steffy laughed.

"Come on, Steffy. This isn't funny. I've never seen this thing before. I have no idea where it came from."

Steffy looked closely at the flight suit. "It looks like a man's outfit, but the name tag says Darron."

"It's exactly my size," said Kate. "I tried the thing on and it fits perfectly. But, there's one more thing."

"Does this never end, Kate?" Steffy asked. "What is it?"

"This note was in the left rear pocket," Kate said, handing Steffy the piece of torn paper with the message. Steffy carefully read the note. "Please Kate, come back to me. Bebe. Lorgenberg, Germany, March 6, 1942, B-17 crash site. " Steffy studied the piece of paper for several minutes and then looked up. "Kate, you aren't playing some kind of joke on me, are you?" But, Steffy knew no game was being played here. Kate wasn't like that.

"I wish it was a joke," Kate replied. "It's the strangest thing I've ever experienced and scary as hell."

"I know," Steffy replied. "What's spooky is that it's so real. If you look closely, you can see the note was written with a fountain pen, not a ballpoint. They used fountain pens in 1942. Let's google Lorgenberg, Germany."

"I'm ahead of you, Steph. I went to Google and Bing. There's nothing on the internet about anyplace called Lorgenberg."

"Kate, I don't know what to say. Why don't I go back to work and talk to a friend of mine who is in the Air Force Reserve. Maybe she would have an idea of how to approach this."

"Okay, Steph. If you find out anything call me right away. This thing is really freaking me out."

"Will do. Have glass of wine and relax. I'll talk to you later today or tomorrow."

Though she had trouble falling asleep the night before, Kate was up early Tuesday morning. She had to get started with her job search and also wanted to take a load of clothes over to the Goodwill Store. She would donate slacks and blouses and half a dozen bags of miscellaneous junk. She hung the flight suit in the closet and put the mysterious note in her dresser drawer.

But she couldn't get them out of her mind. Who wrote the note? Was it really meant for her? How did the note and flight suit end up in her closet? She racked her brain wondering if any of her friends could be playing some sort of not so funny joke on her. She decided there was no way anyone she knew would concoct such a prank. Even if they had, that couldn't explain how she lost one day of her life. Then there was Norma Sykes' apartment. What about that? No, there was too much that was unexplainable, she decided.

Kate wondered if Steffy talked to her friend, and if so, did she have any information? She walked into the kitchen and started a small pot of coffee. As it was brewing, she sat down at her computer to check her e-mail.

There was an e-mail from Steffy forwarding one from her friend Lieutenant Janie Belski. It was sent an hour ago at 8:30. "Steffy, I couldn't find anything on Lorgenberg however, a few minutes after my search, I received a notification of job openings on the Federal Personnel site. One of the Intelligence Services needs people. You mentioned that Kate was looking for a job so I attached an application and contact information if Kate is interested. I have no idea what these jobs entail. Tell Kate 'good luck' with whatever she decides to do. Sorry I couldn't help you on Lorgenberg."

Kate clicked on the attachment. She never thought about a career in the Intelligence area, but jobs were hard to come by these days. Maybe I should put in an application to see if anything comes of it.

First I need a cup of coffee, she decided, and headed for the kitchen. She quickly returned to the computer to fill out the application. I'll shoot this in and then get serious about my job search.

She had no experience which would qualify for a job in Intelligence, but it was a wild shot. In less than half an hour, she had forwarded the application to the contact person, a man named Jack Farley. She then promptly forgot about it because it was a wild goose chase and she needed to look for a real job.

Kate skimmed through her other e-mails. It was now 10:15. As she got up to get ready for the day ahead, her computer dinged and an e-mail appeared. It was from Jack Farley. "Miss Darron, we are most interested in talking with you regarding the position for which you applied. How soon would you be available to come to Washington for an interview?"

"What!" Kate exclaimed. "I've got a teaching degree and four years teaching experience. How can an Intelligence Agency be interested in me?" She picked up her phone and called Steffy."

"Hi Kate," Steffy answered. "I was just going to call you. What's going on today?"

"I got the e-mail you forwarded from Janie Belski."

"Good, Steffy said. You might as well apply for the job. It doesn't hurt to give it a try."

"That's why I called," replied Kate. "I applied for it right after I got your e-mail. They e-mailed me back ten minutes later. They want me to come to Washington for an interview. This is really crazy. Why would they want me? I'm a school teacher."

"Who knows?" Steffy laughed. "Go for it."

"You think so?" replied Kate.

"That's why you called, isn't it Kate?"

"Yeah, it is. You really think I should go see them?"

"Kate, it's hard to find a job right now. Besides, while you're in Washington you can look around for other jobs and sight see. I'd do the interview if I were you."

"Okay, Steph. If it turns out bad, I'll blame you," Kate chuckled. She hung up the phone and clicked Reply. "Dear Mr. Farley, I would be available to come to Washington at any time that is convenient for you." She clicked Send.

Kate got up and went into the bathroom to take a shower and put on make-up. Just as she turned on the water, the phone rang. It's

Steffy, she thought. Naked, she turned off the shower and ran into the bedroom to answer the phone. "Hello, Steffy," she said, without checking the caller I.D.

"Hello, Miss Darron," a man's voice replied. "This is Jack Farley."

Kate, caught completely off guard, was taken aback. "Hello, Mr. Farley," she answered, her voice reflecting surprise.

"Miss Darron, I appreciate your getting back with me so quickly," he said. "How long have been looking for a job, if you don't mind my asking?"

He must think I'm desperate to find a job, Kate thought. "I've only been out of work since yesterday, Mr. Farley. I actually applied for this job as a lark, not thinking I would ever be considered for it. I have no experience in the intelligence area and I'm really not that anxious to find a job immediately. The job you have is the first thing that came along," she said. "I just applied for it because a friend mailed me the application and suggested I apply. I doubt I'm qualified for the job."

"I've never met anyone quite so honest," laughed Jack Farley. "But why don't you let us decide on your qualifications, Miss Darron? You said you could you come to Washington any time. Could you be on an afternoon flight leaving Lambert Field in two hours?"

Kate was shocked. "Mr. Farley, how long has this job been open?" Kate replied. This is surreal, she thought. I can't believe they're so anxious to talk to me.

"The job has been open for a while. You see, we're looking for a particular type of person for this job and we think you may be the one we're looking for."

Kate thought for a moment then said, "If I pack right now I can make the flight. I'm only twenty minutes from the airport."

"Good," replied Farley. "I e-mailed a boarding pass to you already. Just print it and you can go directly to the gate without a check-in. I'll have a car waiting for you at baggage pick-up at Dulles. The driver will also pick you up at your hotel and bring you over to the office for an eight o'clock interview tomorrow morning. We'll cover all your expenses. Just keep the receipts. Sound okay?"

"Alright, Mr. Farley," said Kate, reeling from the fast moving events. "I'll see you tomorrow." Kate rushed to pack and easily made the 12:30 flight.

Kate called Steffy to let her know all that happened but got her voice mail. When she boarded the plane she tried to call her again, but no luck. She left a voice mail. "I'm on my way to Washington, Steffy."

# 20

Sept 16, Present Time     OSTRO-Washington, DC

It had been five months since Kate Darron applied for the job with the Intelligence Services. For reasons of which she was not aware, her application had been funneled to the ultra secret spy agency OSTRO (Office of Specific Threat Response Operations). Kate had spent the entire five months in training that consisted of intense study and the analysis of the threats to this country and other countries vital to United States' national interests. There was also a great deal of physical conditioning and self-defense training. Today was the first day she would work in the office.

OSTRO was so secret not even Congress knew about it. Very few people in OSTRO were even aware where their agency's funding came from. Kate still hadn't adjusted to the intense secrecy under which OSTRO operated. When Jack Farley hired her, she began training the following day. They needed her right away, he said, so badly that she wouldn't need to return to St. Louis to move out of her apartment. The agency would take care of that for her. Because of the generous salary offer, nearly double her teacher's pay, Kate took the job. She kept in touch with Steffy and her parents by phone and e-mail.

As Kate walked into her small office she noticed an envelope taped to the top of her desk. She pulled open the sealed flap and took out the note. "Please see me this morning." It was signed "D." D. stood for Dan Scoggins, the agency's boss. He had never asked to see her before. She made it a point to see D. right away.

It wasn't a big facility and only one hundred and sixty-two people worked there. D.'s office was hidden in the very back of the building and was large compared to the offices of the rest of the staff. Kate walked through the office complex and around the corner to the door labeled "Dan Scoggins." As Kate prepared to knock, she heard a voice say "Come on in." Apparently D. had a camera focused on his office door so he could see who was coming and going.

Kate entered the storied office where so many counter-terrorism strikes and other covert operations had been planned. "Good morning Mr. Scoggins," she greeted him.

Scoggins was a fit man at one time in his career, but he'd been at a desk for many years and his belly was too big for the waistline on his pants. Hanging over his belt, it looked like it was about to fall off of his body at any moment. It had to be uncomfortable wearing pants from high school when you were sixty years old, Kate thought. Scoggins was a kindly looking grandfatherly type with a grayish, receding hairline and a nice smile. But Kate had gotten the word. Don't mistake him for a teddy bear. He was all business and intensely results oriented. He would not hesitate to plan a bloody attack that would make even the most hardened of soldiers squeamish.

"Good morning Darron," he said. "Have a seat. You want a cup of coffee?"

Kate assumed he was trying to put her at ease, even though she was not intimidated by this man with the dangerous reputation. "Are you finding the job to your satisfaction?" he began.

"Yes, it's been fine Mr. Scoggins. The people are all great to work with."

"Good. That's nice to know," he replied, with noticeable insincerity. "I've never met you. Farley has been keeping you under wraps for some reason. Anyway, a problem has come up and someone mentioned your name for this particular job. Darron, do you know anything about history and archeology?"

"I know a little bit about those subjects, probably more than the average person. I've always been interested in both fields."

"That's good," Scoggins said, without explaining why he asked the question. "Do you like it here in Washington?"

"I don't care for Washington, really. I like to be out doing things and Washington is too claustrophobic. The walls of the city always seem to be closing in on me."

"I guessed that about you. So I take it you'd like to do a little field work?"

"I'd love to. When do I leave and where do I go?"

"Not quite yet. You'll need to stay in Washington a while longer to do some archaeological training with the Smithsonian. But it won't be for long. We need to get you out in the field very quickly. What we really need is your pilot's skill. You seem to have more flying experience than anyone in OSTRO. I also see from your application you've flown quite a few different types of airplanes."

Shocked, Kate answered, "No, I've never flown a plane in my life, Mr. Scoggins. Where did you get that information?"

An equally astonished Dan Scoggins sat back in his squeaky wooden chair, the old type that no one used anymore. Everyone else had gone to those black plastic, webbed, depressing looking wheeled chairs. Scoggins' chair was a big brown wooden throne with a cushion on the seat. There weren't many of these kinds of guys around anymore, but he was still hanging in there. Scoggins sat speechless, looking very dismayed.

"What do you mean by that Darron? On your application you stated you were an experienced pilot and flew all kinds of airplanes. What gives here?"

"I never wrote on my application that I was a pilot? Other than going up with my uncle a few times, I've never flown a plane in my life."

"You're scaring me, Darron. You say you don't know how to fly an airplane but it says right here on your application you've got over three thousand hours of flying time in multiple aircraft types. You lied on your application in order to get the job."

Kate knew she couldn't have written that on the application. "I never put anything like that on my application," she said. "I didn't even care about the job that much when I applied so why on earth would I lie? Besides, all you have to do is check with the F.A.A. to see I have a pilot's license. That's not really something someone can lie about."

"Well apparently you didn't feel that way when you filled out the application."

"Can I see that application, Mr. Scoggins?"

An upset Dan Scoggins tossed the file across his desk to Kate.

She picked it up and looked at page three which Scoggins had folded back. It was just as Scoggins said. In her own hand-writing was a list of airplanes she stated she had flown. There were over forty planes listed, and not that she realized it, but they included every type of World War Two bomber and fighter type aircraft. It looked like the list stopped there because there was no more space on the form.

Kate tossed the file back across Scoggins' desk. As he looked at it more closely, he said, "I don't know why Farley didn't catch this Darron. Now that I study this, all these airplanes you said you flew are from the 1940's. And nobody has flown this many different types of aircraft no matter what the year. I'm going to kick Farley's tail about this. I'm also going to kick my own tail for being so stupid.

I look over most of these applications myself, but I must have missed yours. None of these planes have flown in years, unless you count antique air shows. This is really cute Darron. I'm not at all happy about this. We hire agents based on specific skills which the agency needs to balance out its field force capabilities. Farley must have hired you because you said you were an experienced pilot. Your lying on this application has caused me and the agency a big problem."

But now it was Kate that was upset. "Mr. Scoggins, I didn't lie. I don't know why I wrote I could fly all those airplanes on my application. I don't know one of those airplanes from the other."

"But, you do admit this is your hand-writing on the application. And you do admit that this is your signature at the bottom of page six," Scoggins said.

"Yes, it is my writing and my signature but I don't remember filling out that part of the application. There must some mistake."

"There is, Darron. And you made it. I had high hopes for you. I'm going to talk with Farley on this and get it straightened out. I intended to give you an assignment today however your falsifying your application changes all that. It's our fault here also. In fact, it's really ninety-nine percent our fault. We check all this stuff out six different ways to Tucumcari. It's impossible we didn't catch this.

I'm going to suspend you temporarily until we get this resolved. Farley won't be back in the office for several days. He and I will talk then. This is a very serious matter. It's not only the huge amount of money we've spent training you, but it comes down to your basic honesty and reliability. We have to be able to trust our own people."

"Mr. Scoggins, I'm the most honest person you'll ever meet. How my application came to have all the wrong information on it confounds me. Maybe I'm losing my mind or something. It is my hand-writing but I don't remember writing it."

"Darron, get out of town for the weekend and come back and see me Monday morning?" Scoggins replied. "We'll see what we're going to do about this whole thing after I talk to Farley."

"Mr. Scoggins, I don't know what happened here. But, I don't really care for the job that much and you obviously can't trust me and will never be able to. Why don't we forget this ever happened and I'll resign?"

Scoggins thought for a moment. He could have her prosecuted on several federal charges but the agency was too busy to fool with something that trivial. Besides, it was agency policy to maintain a low profile. Having an employee put on trial would mean publicity, the one thing the agency didn't want. "Okay Darron, clean out your desk. Have a nice life."

Kate was distressed as she returned to her desk to get her belongings. I'm not doing real well on my job performance lately, she thought. Then she wondered how she could have claimed she was a pilot on her application? Where would she ever have gotten that list of airplanes? She didn't know a Cessna from a Chevrolet. She decided to go back to her apartment and pack a suitcase. She would take Scoggin's advice and get out of town for the weekend, maybe go home to St. Louis for a few days. She picked up her cell phone and called Steffy. "How would you like a house guest this weekend?" Kate asked.

# 21

Sept 16, Present Time     St Louis, Mo.

On her way to the airport Kate thought about her situation. Once again she was out of a job. Then her thoughts turned to filling out the job application five months ago. OSTRO had e-mailed the application to her. It couldn't be filled out or submitted on line. The application specifically had to be filled out in the candidate's handwriting, signed and faxed. She did so that same day. The original copy of the application had to be submitted in person if the candidate was called to Washington for an interview.

This is absolutely astounding, she thought. She couldn't remember falsifying the application by writing a list of airplanes she'd never flown. What would be the point of lying on a job application when they could easily check out the details with a couple of clicks on the computer? She had no pilot license. Certainly the federal government would catch that instantly.

For some reason, Kate suddenly thought about the flight suit and the note she found in the closet of her old apartment five months before. She still had both of them. Then she started thinking about Jack Farley hiring her so quickly. She didn't have any specific qualifications for an Intelligence job. It had all happened so fast. At the time it was surprising, but now it seemed bizarre. She wondered how she could have come up with a list of airplanes she'd never heard of to list on the job application. She wasn't even serious about the job when she applied for it. This whole thing was absurd.

When Kate boarded the plane she called Steffy again. Steffy

sensed that something was wrong when Kate called her earlier. "What's going on, Kate?" she asked.

"Things have been happening too fast since I took this job. They flew me to Washington and gave me the job the day after I applied. That was really weird. But now, I had to resign or they would fire me." Kate told Steffy the whole story about the job application and the list of airplanes she had never flown.

"That is really weird," said Steffy. "Just take it easy, Kate."

"Easy for you to say," replied Kate. "You haven't been fired from two jobs in the last six months."

"Yeah, I know, but there's obviously something going on here. We'll talk when you get to St. Louis."

"Okay Steph. We're about to take off now. Thanks for not chewing my head off for doing such a poor job of staying in touch with you. I'm surprised you didn't fire me too. I'll see you tonight."

Kate hadn't called her parents to tell them she was coming into town. She would do that when the plane landed.

Kate's airplane arrived at six-fifteen, and as she walked from the gate, she saw Steffy waving. The two women ran toward each other, hugged and headed for Steffy's car.

"Thanks for meeting me, Steph."

"No problem," Steffy said. "Come on, I'll buy you dinner."

They caught up on each other's lives at the restaurant. Steffy's love life was still a disaster. Kate didn't have time for a social life while she was in training. Steffy got a big raise two weeks ago. "I didn't tell you because I know you government types don't make that kind of money," she laughed.

"You mean former government types," replied Kate.

"Kate," Steffy said, becoming serious, "I found out something but I didn't tell you because I knew you were focused on your new job. Besides, I thought your phone might be bugged."

"What do you mean? Why would my phone be bugged, Steffy? My job wasn't important. I was in training the whole time. Nobody cares about me."

"Let me tell you what I found out," Steffy continued. "After you left for Washington, I did some more checking on Lorgenberg. Once again, I found absolutely nothing on Lorgenberg itself. So I took a different approach. You remember my friend Janie Belski, the Air Force Lieutenant who told you about the job. Anyway, Janie helped me research B-17 bombers that crashed in Germany on March 6, 1942, the date on that note you had."

"What did you find out?" Kate asked.

Three B-17's crashed in Germany on that date." Steffy replied. "Janie got the names of the crewmen on two of the airplanes. In one of the planes, three men were killed. The rest of crewmen in those two planes parachuted to safety. They were all men in the two crews. No one in either crew was named Kate, obviously, or Bebe. And no one in either crew had a name for which Bebe would be a logical nickname."

"What about the third plane?" Kate asked.

"That's where it gets interesting," Steffy said. "There's no listing of the crew names. I mean there's nothing."

"Well that could be some kind of administrative thing," Kate replied. "Maybe they didn't have the names available when they listed the other information."

"I don't think so," replied Steffy. "Kate, there's no town named Lorgenberg. The crew names on that third airplane are not on the Army Air Force's official record. On your job application you gave a long list of World War Two airplanes you said you flew. Maybe we need to connect some dots here. I think all the weird things going on with your job have something to do with that flight suit and note you found in your closet?"

"How could they?" Kate asked. "That B-17 crashed over seventy years ago. How could that have anything to do with me?"

"I don't know. I just think that somehow they're connected," replied Steffy. "Why don't we go to Germany and check out where that third airplane crashed and see if we can find out anything."

"Steffy, you're crazy. I'm not going to Germany. I have to find a job."

"No you don't. You can move in with me until you find another job. Besides, I know you're really curious about the flight suit and the note. Admit it. You want to go find out what's going on."

That's true, Kate thought to herself. "Alright, let's go find out where that third airplane crashed."

# 22

Sept 20, Present Time      Washington, DC

It was seven forty-five Monday morning and Dan Scoggins had summoned Jack Farley to his office to discuss Catherine Darron. Farley was a pot-bellied man of seventy-eight years who could have retired when he was sixty. However, he had dedicated his entire life to OSTRO, never married and had nothing else. Farley was the link to the agency's early history. He knew all of OSTRO secrets, and there were some very dark ones.

He was also the personnel manager, or as close to one as the agency had. His job was to hire prospective agents and scrutinize personnel matters. He took his responsibility for personnel hiring decisions very seriously. He had a sixth sense about who would or would not fit into the surreptitious culture of OSTRO.

Farley was short, balding and maintained a perpetual quizzical expression. When speaking, he would peep over red-framed glasses perched half way down his nose. Sparse patches of white hair clung to each side of his head like bleached saddlebags. He was known for his habitually too large wild colored shirts and clashing ties routinely displaying spots of that day's breakfast.

His benign grandfatherly appearance concealed his manipulative, ruthless nature. Farley's facade of benevolence mirrored the deception that defined OSTRO. Jack Farley was OSTRO and OSTRO was Jack Farley. Both Farley and OSTRO presented themselves as operatives carrying on those necessary but unpleasant covert activities within established humanitarian norms. In truth,

Jack Farley and OSTRO were the most deadly of operators, executing their missions with total disregard of the human toll or collateral destruction.

Jack Farley had long ago concluded that one could not have a conscience and work in this business. The main qualification for selection as a leader in OSTRO's management hierarchy was the ability to operate without scruples or moral constraint. Farley had been crucial to the success of countless missions because he operated under this philosophy. He always figured out some unique and often merciless way to accomplish especially complex operations.

Farley was hired by OSTRO in 1964 and his job was to organize and retain the records of all missions and operations. He knew many of the original people who worked at OSTRO. Over time Jack Farley became involved with every facet of the agency and eventually was responsible for obtaining budget approval for the agency's operations.

Because of Farley's influence with the other intelligence agencies, he could access unlimited monies with which OSTRO funded covert operations. Farley's uncompassionate planning skills and his careful selection of the right people assured a high success rate for the agency's secret missions.

Dan Scoggins knew Jack Farley well. He respected his knowledge and knew that if Farley hired someone there must have been good reason for his decision. However, Catherine Darron was a mystery. Scoggins figured Farley must be losing his touch when he let Kate Darron convince him she was a pilot. Why didn't Farley check to see that she actually had a pilot's license? That Darron was a schoolteacher with no specialized skills applicable to intelligence work greatly upset him.

Her employment application listed over forty types of aircraft she supposedly had flown. Ninety nine percent of them had been retired from service. There was no way she could ever have flown these airplanes because they were no longer in operation when she would have gotten her pilot's license.

The more he thought about it, the more upset he got. The North Africa mission specifically required the pilot skills Kate Darron claimed she had. Scoggins wanted answers. Why did Farley hire this woman? As Scoggins sat with his third cup of coffee he heard Farley's familiar knock on his office door. "Come on in Jack," he called.

Farley opened the door and walked into the office and headed straight to the coffee pot without even acknowledging Dan Scoggins' presence.

"Good morning to you, too Jack," Scoggins greeted him in a mock sarcastic tone.

"Hey, Dan," responded Farley, in his typically distracted greeting. He had important things on his mind and didn't want to take time to talk with Scoggins.

Dan Scoggins was used to that greeting. He knew Farley had more important things to do than talk to him, but he had to get to the bottom of this Catherine Darron thing. It had thrown the agency's mission agenda off kilter. He confronted Farley immediately as the latter was pouring powdered cream into his coffee already loaded with sugar.

"Jack, the agency invested a lot of money in Catherine Darron with payroll and training expense. I just found out last Thursday she lied on her employment application. She stated on her application she'd flown a variety of airplanes, but when I talked to her, she admitted she'd never flown in her life. What's going on here Jack? Didn't you check all that stuff out?"

Jack Farley laughed. "I was wondering when you'd catch that little oversight of mine, Dan. If you paid more attention to what I'm doing you wouldn't be caught off guard in matters like this."

Farley was right. Scoggins essentially ignored his activities whether it was hiring personnel or working on secret operations because of Farley's expertise and history with the agency. Scoggins considered him to be on cruise control and do whatever he thought needed to be done.

"Did you say little oversight?" Scoggins responded. "That little oversight has cost the agency a quarter of a million dollars in training expenses for Kate Darron."

"Okay Dan, settle down and I'll tell you why I hired her." Seeing he had Scoggins rattled, Farley decided to chide him just a little more. It was the sort of game he enjoyed and he clearly had Scoggins riled.

"Actually Dan, I hired her on a hunch."

Scoggins could see that Farley was playing with him and he didn't take the bait. "Alright Jack, tell me what's going on and stop with your little games. I have a lot riding on this one, especially that North Africa thing which you yourself are working on."

"Seriously, Dan, I did hire her on a hunch. I thought I'd let you train her first and then I'd check into my hunch, but I'm pretty sure I'm right."

If it had been anyone other than Farley telling him this, Scoggins would have bitten their heads off. But Farley's hunches were uncannily accurate. "Will you please tell me what the hell you're talking about, Jack?"

"Alright Dan, but you look so pretty when you're mad, you know, your red face and all," he laughed.

"Cut it out, Jack. Get to the point."

"Okay, okay. I guess a guy can't have any fun around here. Anyway, you remember Dr. Elbert Beale, the man who started the agency back in the 1930's. "

"Yeah, I remember. You've talked about him several times."

"Do you remember I mentioned an ultra secret project back in World War Two called the Destiny Project?"

"I don't know. I think I remember you mentioned it once, but you were drinking at the time and I sort of forgot about it."

"Oh yeah, it was the Christmas party. God, I still have a hangover. Loose lips sink ships, as the saying goes. I had the good sense to shut up after I started yapping about it."

"What's that got to do with Catherine Darron, Jack?"

"You have to know about the Destiny Project to understand why I hired Catherine Darron. You see, they're both directly related to the North African operation."

"You really have me wondering now," Scoggins replied, perplexed why a long ago project had anything to do with what was going on today. "But give me the short version," he added, knowing Farley had a tendency to get off track and recount sometimes irrelevant details.

Jack Farley smiled. "In 1937 Dr. Beale came into possession of an ancient artifact, a three foot diameter wheel-like object made of stone. It had an incredibly interesting history."

"Just a moment," said Scoggins, and he got on the intercom and told his secretary to hold his phone calls and appointments.

"Thank you, Dan. Anyway, the item Beale acquired dated back fifteen hundred years."

"Yeah," said Scoggins.

"The object had Latin inscriptions and mathematical formulas carved into it and Dr. Beale hired a Dr. Horst Lange to decode the thing. Lange translated the Latin, and it took a while, but he finally figured out the mathematics and discovered the function of the wheel. That's the part you'll find most interesting."

"I'm on the edge of my chair," Scoggins replied sardonically.

"You will be on the edge of your chair when I tell you what Dr. Lange discovered." Scoggins abruptly became more serious.

"Dan, the Boethian Wheel, as it is called, described a type of inter-dimensional transference process. It revealed a method to cross dimensions into other time periods in the past or future. In other words, it was a kind of time machine," exclaimed Farley.

"You've got to be kidding me. A time machine?" laughed Scoggins.

"Not exactly, Dan. I said a kind of time machine. An actual time machine implies a mechanical apparatus, a vehicle with which to go backward or forward in time."

"Yeah, I've seen them in the movies," Scoggins smiled.

"That's not what the Boethian Wheel is, Dan. Like I said, the Boethian Wheel details a method to implement an inter-dimensional transference process. There's a big difference."

"I'm sure I don't know what it is," said Scoggins.

"The distinction is that time machines are the stuff of science fiction, Dan. You and I know they don't exist. If they did, our agency would have one."

"So, what's the secret?" asked Scoggins. "How did it work?"

"I've got to give you some background first, Dan," Farley replied.

"Nothing's ever easy with you, is it Jack?" Scoggins sighed.

Farley smiled. "Be patient Dan." Scoggins nodded.

Farley continued. Ancient scholars, as well as Einstein, believed that the past, present and future exist simultaneously and that all events that have ever happened, are happening now, or will happen, are actually occurring at the same time. They never accepted the idea of a past, present and future. They believed time is omnipresent. In other words, all time is happening at the same moment, but in different dimensions."

"Really," Scoggins interjected. Jack Farley could see the mention of Einstein's name had gotten his attention.

"The Boethian Wheel explains the practical application of this theory. In other words, it tells us how to travel to any point in time, more correctly stated as the time-space continuum. But let me finish. The mathematical symbols and Latin script carved into the stone wheel provide a formulaic philosophical prescription to achieve an elevated degree of metaphysical consciousness, a total awareness of one's being and his or her position in space and time, which is the Universe. When a person has achieved this level of consciousness, he or she can pass through billions of dimensions to any specific place or time they wish."

"That's a lot of big words," Scoggins said. "Tell me what it all means in simple terms."

"In simple terms, Dan, the Boethian Wheel explains how a person can access unused compartments of their own brain to induce a mental state by which they can cross dimensions into other periods of time."

"That's incredible," Scoggins said. "You really think this thing worked, don't you Jack."

"I can prove it did," Farley said. That's why I hired Kate Darron. She is our link to OSTRO's past, Dr. Beale and the Destiny Project."

# 23

Sept 20, Present Time      Washington, DC

"Tell me more about this Destiny Project, Jack," Scoggins said.

"Got you interested, huh, Dan," Farley said. "Here's the rest of it. Once Dr. Lange de-coded the Boethian Wheel, OSTRO could travel in time. During the war, the Nazis had a large number of secret weapons projects. OSTRO needed to conduct aerial missions to destroy these operations. But there was a tremendous shortage of pilots in the country. You probably remember they recruited women to ferry military airplanes from factories to the military bases."

"Yeah, I know about that," said Scoggins.

"OSTRO needed pilots also, but they had to be pilots who could be sent on high risk missions. Because of the dangerous nature of the missions, OSTRO knew the great majority of the pilots would be killed. They didn't want to sacrifice badly needed men pilots so that's when they came up with the idea of using women."

Scoggins listened intently. "That sounds like Japanese kamikaze pilots who crashed their airplanes into ships. Congress would never buy off on something like that. And they would never approve sacrificing women any more than they would men. I don't get it."

"OSTRO knew that, Jack. They also knew they couldn't go out and recruit ordinary citizens even if they could find people crazy enough to volunteer for these assignments. That's where the Destiny Project came in. Dr. Beale and Dr. Lange came up with the idea of using the Boethian Wheel to travel to the future and kidnap women with specific critical skills. They would initially target female pilots and women trained to use guns."

"That's unbelievable," Scoggins said.

"OSTRO had to experiment to see if the idea would work, but they needed pilots quickly because the Nazis had so many secret projects underway. They decided to experiment with women first. If the idea worked with women, once they got the operation into gear, they could expand the program to include men, scientists, doctors, and so on."

"Wouldn't the women they kidnapped from the future be missed?" Scoggins asked.

"Yes," replied Farley, "but here is the genius of the Destiny Project. OSTRO would only kidnap women who were going to die anyway, those who were going to be killed in accidents or somehow die prematurely. These women would be kidnapped in the last moments of their life."

"That's brilliant," Scoggins said, shaking his head.

Farley continued. "Technically, the women kidnapped would be dead in their own time and non-existent in 1937 or whatever year they were transferred to. No one would miss them when they were killed on OSTRO's suicide missions because they didn't exist. That's the beauty of the Destiny Project."

"How did they identify women to kidnap?" asked Scoggins.

"All OSTRO had to do was read random newspapers in a future time and see who was killed a few days earlier. Then, OSTRO agents transferred to the time just before a woman was to die and kidnap her. They would transport that woman back to the late 1930's and train her as a pilot and she would be sent on a mission to destroy one of the Nazi's top secret facilities. These women were completely expendable."

Scoggins sat transfixed listening to Farley. "This is getting good."

"The Destiny Project was so named because it altered the women's destiny. Instead of dying an early death in their own time, they would die in the 1940's on an OSTRO mission. There was no accountability for their lives. That way, OSTRO could lose as many women as they wanted on their missions. If they got lucky and didn't die on a mission, they could live their lives out in the earlier time to which they had been transported. So there was something of an upside to the scheme."

"I can't believe the government ever went along with anything like that, especially back in those days." Scoggins said.

"Dan, the government never knew," Farley replied.

Scoggins shook his head and thought for a moment, still trying to digest what Farley had told him. "You're telling me Beale and Lange really did travel to other times, go backward and forward in time? I mean, I'm still having trouble believing all this."

"That's exactly what I'm telling you, Dan. They kidnapped at least twenty women for the Destiny Project experiment. I'm sure of that."

Amazed, Scoggins shook his head.

"But there's something else," Farley said. Dr. Beal and Dr. Lange couldn't control what became of these women. They sort of got lost in time so to speak. Some disappeared. Some flew their missions and were killed. The strange thing is that none of their bodies were ever recovered. Beale and Lange never found out where most of the women ultimately ended up. There could be some of them walking around today."

"My god," said Scoggins.

"Eventually, the Destiny Project was scrapped."

"But why," Scoggins asked. "It's a magnificent program."

"There were several reasons," Farley said. One reason was that OSTRO couldn't control it. It became a liability because if Congress found out what was going on, they'd put OSTRO out of business."

"What's the other reason?" Scoggins asked.

"Good question, Dan," replied Farley. "And that's where the real problem begins. You see, Dr. Horst Lange suddenly disappeared. He just vanished. Dr. Beale suspected that Lange travelled into another time with the intent of enriching himself. That's another reason Dr. Beale shut down the Destiny Project. There was now a rogue scientist on the loose somewhere in time. Dr. Beale was terrified of what Dr. Lange might do with his power to move around in time. He was distraught that Dr. Lange might use the Boethian Wheel for destructive purposes. His greatest fear was that Dr. Lange would use the power of the Boethian Wheel against the United States. At the end, Dr. Beale destroyed all the records of the Destiny Project and committed suicide."

"Dr. Lange must be long dead by now, Jack," Scoggins said. "So what's the connection with Catherine Darron?"

"The Destiny Project, Catherine Darron and the North African problem intersect. That's also where my hunch comes in."

"But I thought the Destiny Project scheme only worked a few times and was scrapped," Scoggins interrupted. "I don't understand."

"That's what I thought until about a year ago when that North African problem came up. Dan, you've seen pictures of Patrice Betaine, the warlord causing our problems there."

"You're telling me, Scoggins interjected. "How'd that guy get hold of those nuclear weapons he's threatening to sell to the rest of the world?"

"Did you ever look closely at Patrice Betaine's picture, Dan?" Farley continued.

"Yeah, I've seen his ugly face a hundred times," Scoggins answered impatiently. "So what?"

"Is this the man?" asked Farley, handing Dan Scoggins an 8 ½ by 11-inch photo.

"That's the SOB," said Scoggins.

"You're sure about that," asked Farley.

"I'm positive," replied Scoggins, glancing back at the picture. "That's Patrice Betaine."

Scoggins looked at Farley, a puzzled expression on his face. "What's your point, Jack?" Scoggins knew that when Jack Farley focused on the details as he was now doing, something big would follow.

"Like I said, Dr. Horst Lange disappeared."

"Yeah," replied Scoggins. "You told me that already."

"I know," Farley replied. "You're sure the picture I just showed you is Patrice Betaine?" Farley asked.

Scoggins looked at the picture again, then back at Farley, an apprehensive look on his face. Of course that's Patrice Betaine." Scoggins again looked at Jack Farley, unsure of the point he was trying to make.

"You're right, Dan. The man in that picture is Patrice Betaine, the nuclear arms dealer."

"So what's your point, Jack?"

"My point is that picture was taken was taken in 1948, nineteen years before Patrice Betaine was born. The name of the man in the picture is not Patrice Betaine. His name is Dr. Horst Lange."

"You're saying Patrice Betaine and Dr. Horst Lange are the same person?"

"That's exactly right," Farley calmly replied. "As I said, when Dr. Lange disappeared, Dr. Beale figured that he travelled to another time. And here he is, Dan. The son of a gun landed right in our lap and we have to deal with him."

"I'm still trying to get a handle on this whole thing," replied Scoggins. "Let me understand this. When Dr. Lange disappeared in 1948, he went to North Africa in our present time."

"God only knows where he might have gone," replied Farley, "but we've got him here with us now."

Scoggins nodded. "How did you find out about this, Jack?" asked Scoggins.

"It wasn't that hard," Farley laughed. "I had the computer run a face recognition program."

"You mean you had your secretary Della run the program. You can barely do e-mails, Jack," Scoggins replied with a grunt. Farley laughed.

"But, how did you find out about the Destiny Project?" Scoggins asked.

"I actually started working on it in my spare time about six years ago when I first told you about it. It was hard to get any information because, like I said, Dr. Beale had destroyed most of the Destiny Project records."

"But you found out enough to keep you curious," Scoggins said.

Farley smiled. "I found out a little bit. Della and I went back into the archives and pulled out every scrap of information we could find, but it wasn't much. It seems the Germans had a facility called Lorgenberg that was constructing atomic bombs. However, the Lorgenberg facility was masquerading as a mental institution with fifteen hundred patients.

President Roosevelt wouldn't approve a military strike on the off chance it really was a mental hospital. However, OSTRO decided Lorgenberg had to be bombed immediately, regardless of what the president said. They put together a strike plan using a single airplane, an unmarked B-17 bomber. The president was never told about it. I'm probably the only one in the country who knows the United States was behind the Lorgenberg bombing."

"You're amazing, Jack," Scoggins said, "but where does Catherine Darron enter the picture?"

"Since OSTRO carried out the mission, I concluded the pilot or pilots had to be women. Here's where you owe me a raise, Dan," laughed Farley. "I loaded a blind, one-word link 'Lorgenberg' on the internet. Anyone who searched for Lorgenberg wouldn't find it, but, their e-mail would come to my site. In six years I only got one hit. It was an Air Force Reserve lieutenant. A friend had asked her to find out what Lorgenberg was all about. That's when I connected with Catherine Darron. I put a phony job opening out there and sent it to her. She responded and now you know the rest of the story as they say."

"What are you telling me?" Scoggins asked.

Jack Farley looked Dan Scoggins in the eye. "I believe Catherine Darron was a pilot on the airplane that flew on the Lorgenberg mission in World War Two? That was the hunch I talked about, Dan."

"You don't know this for sure but you spent a quarter million dollars training her?"

Farley laughed. "I'm afraid so, Dan. I also don't know who the other pilot was. Then there's the question of what happened on that mission? The crew managed to drop their bombs but they were all killed when the B-17 was shot down."

"Then how could Darron be alive, Jack?" Scoggins asked. "Where are you going with this?"

"I'm not certain about Catherine Darron, but I do know this. There were approximately ten nuclear weapons manufactured at the Lorgenberg facility," Farley continued. "Those ten nukes disappeared shortly before Lorgenberg was bombed and were never recovered."

"Where did the nukes go? Who took possession of them? Scoggins asked.

"That's the other part of my hunch. I'm wondering if Patrice Betaine's nukes are the ten German nukes that disappeared back in 1942."

"I see what you're getting at," said Scoggins.

"My hunch is that he got all ten of them in 1942, went forward in time, and is now using the German nukes as models to manufacture nuclear weapons for Third World countries. That's why we have to destroy that North African facility and kill Dr. Horst Lange in the process."

"I get it," said Scoggins. "Patrice Betaine and Dr. Horst Lange are the same man and we gotta blow him and his bombs up. Simple enough, but, why do you need Catherine Darron? You don't know if she's the person who flew that mission."

"I said it was only a hunch. I'm playing it out now, but to answer your question, we need Darron for the same reason they needed her back in World War Two. She is the only link to finding the other pilot and validating the time travel methodology detailed on the Boethian Wheel. If the wheel actually works, we can send people backward or forward in time. There's no limit to what we can do with that thing."

"You mean we still have the Boethian Wheel?" Scoggins asked.

Farley smiled. "Only I know where it is, Jack," he said. Scoggins laughed.

We can also use Darron and the other pilot to carry out the North African mission," Farley added. "We'll arrange for them both to die and become anonymous, just as the Destiny Project did back in World War Two. That way, nobody will miss them if they get killed on the mission. And we will make sure they get killed on the mission. That way, nobody knows anything about it except you and me."

"That's a fabulous plan, Jack. I'm really glad I kept you around here!"

"That's the other thing about using Catherine Darron and her fellow pilot, if we can find her. We'll put them into an old B-17 and use them to blow up Patrice Betaine and his bomb factory. No one will ever figure the United States did the bombing. Who would use an old B-17 to carry out a military mission today? And who would use two women? It will look like some Third World country did the bombing and we can plant information that implicates one of our enemy Third World countries."

"So you hired Catherine Darron because you think she is one of the twenty women that Horst Lange and Elbert Beale pulled back to 1938. That explains her employment application and the list of forty plus airplanes which stopped being flown before she was born."

"That's right," Farley replied. "The time transference process might have caused her brain to suppress her memories from that time. Then something must have triggered her memory when she filled out the application and listed the airplanes she flew. She probably didn't even realize she wrote them down."

178

"I think you're really on to something, Jack," Scoggins said.

Farley smiled. "Darron is a work in progress. If she can remember what happened when she and the other pilot flew the mission in World War Two, we might find out if Dr. Horst Lange aka Patrice Betaine is in possession of those German nukes. Catherine Darron is a valuable resource, Dan, even though we'll eventually kill her," he laughed.

"That's brilliant, Jack," Scoggins said, but I'm afraid I screwed us up. I forced Catherine Darron to resign last Thursday."

"What?" Farley said. "You fired her?"

Scoggins shook his head sheepishly. "I'm afraid I did."

"We've got to get her back, Dan

# 24

Sept 21, Present Time     Bad Steffen, Germany

Their flights were long, but uneventful and Kate and Steffy landed in Berlin and secured a rental car. The crash site where they were headed was approximately one hundred and twenty miles from Berlin and located outside the small town of Bad Steffen. Kate and Steffy spent the night in Berlin where Kate abandoned her standard martini and drank some German beer.

They left early the following morning and began a pleasant drive through the German countryside. Kate was enjoying the trip and Steffy's company so much she almost forgot why they'd come. Then she remembered the name, Bebe. That was an odd name for a man she thought, even if it was a nickname.

Several hours later they reached the town of Bad Steffen. Steffy's travel agent had reserved a room at a small inn, and when they arrived, a pleasant, older gentleman greeted them at the front door. The inn was cozy and inviting. They walked into the lobby and registered. Their second floor room was almost too comfortable. Steffy jokingly suggested they spend their whole trip in the inn and just order room service. "Let's have lunch," Kate laughed, and the two friends headed out the door.

The innkeeper's chatty wife Helene led Kate and Steffy to a table in the dining room. As they were the only customers, the talkative woman sat down to visit. Initially the conversation centered on small talk, but eventually Kate asked the woman if she knew where the B-17 bomber had crashed during World War Two. The woman's expression suddenly became serious.

"That was so long ago," she said. "Yes, I know where the airplane crashed. It was in the forest north of town. I went there only one time when I was young. It was very sad. The subject of that airplane used to come up at times when I was growing up. Nothing of much interest ever happens in our little town and the American airplane crashing in the forest was the most exciting thing to ever occur here. People talked about it for years after the war. I remember the stories. I'm too old to take you there, but I know someone who would be glad to show you where it is. "It was so sad," the woman again said.

"Why do you say that, Helene?" asked Kate.

"It was sad because those young people died. There were four people on the plane when it crashed."

"Did any of the crew members bail out before the crash?" asked Kate.

"None of the crew bailed out," she said. "I know that for a fact. My mother and father owned the inn originally. During the war there was a Luftwaffe air base near here. Some of the Luftwaffe pilots would come to our inn and stay when they were on leave. One of them told my father that Luftwaffe fighter planes were chasing the bomber as it was going down. He said that he knew that no one bailed out of the plane because they didn't see any parachutes."

"You said there were four people on the airplane?" Kate asked.

"Yes. That was also something very strange."

"In what way was it strange?" asked Kate.

"The two pilots of the airplane were women," she replied.

Steffy gasped when she heard that information. "But they didn't let women fly combat missions in World War Two. The military just started letting women fly combat missions a few years ago."

"I'm telling you what my mother told me," the woman said.

"Please, continue," said Kate.

"When the plane crashed, some people from town went out to see if they could help. They brought the four crewmembers back to town. I think they were all dead, but I don't remember. Nobody talks about it much anymore and my memory is not so good."

"Do you know their names?" asked Kate, realizing it was doubtful the woman did.

"Oh no, I have no idea of their names. It happened before I was born and I have forgotten many of the stories about the airplane."

"Would there be any record of their names in town?" Kate asked.

The woman thought for a moment. "Possibly," she said. "The undertaker might have that information."

Kate asked the woman if the undertaker who handled the bodies was still alive.

"Oh no, he is dead long ago. Nearly all the people who were adults during the War have passed. However, his assistant Ludwig is alive. He is a very old man now but he still has his wits about him. The man who will show you the crash site can take you to see Ludwig. When would you like to go see the airplane?"

"Could he possibly take us there after lunch?" Kate replied.

"I will ask him," the woman said, as a waiter brought Kate and Steffy their lunch. She rose from her chair. "I'll call him now."

It didn't take long for Kate and Steffy to eat, and just as they were finishing, a young man with blond hair and blue eyes walked into the dining room and over to their table.

"Hello, my name is Klaus. I am here to take you to see the old airplane."

"We're ready to go," Steffy said excitedly.

Kate laughed. "You're really worked-up about this thing, Steffy."

"I am," she replied. "Come on. Let's get this adventure started."

Kate asked Klaus how much his services would cost and he said the Inn would add a small amount to their bill. "I do not charge a great deal," he smiled, as the two women and their guide walked out of the dining room.

"Steffy, I need to run up to the room and get my backpack with the note and flight suit. I want to bring it along to see if the undertaker can identify it."

"That's a good idea," Steffy said.

Kate returned shortly and the two women and Klaus walked out of the inn and over to the small rental car. Steffy decided she would drive and they began their trip into the pine forest north of Bad Steffen.

"These pine trees are huge!" Steffy exclaimed, as she drove the car north on the main road. They had travelled for about ten minutes when Klaus, sitting in the back seat, pointed ahead and said, "Turn left onto that country road."

"Country road" was Klaus' description for an unpaved, rough road. As the car slowly bounced along the bumpy path Kate noticed the speedometer indicated approximately 30 kilometers (20 miles) per hour. "It is only six kilometers ahead," said Klaus, realizing the ride might be too uncomfortable for the two American tourists.

Steffy laughed. "We'll manage, Klaus."

As the car rolled along the dirt road Kate, who had initially been as excited as Steffy, was becoming apprehensive. I wonder what we're going to find there, she worried. She began to have an eerie feeling that she had been to this place before.

"Steffy, stop the car," Kate said abruptly.

"What's wrong, Kate" Steffy replied, a startled look on her face.

"Please, pull over right here," snapped Kate. Steffy slowed the car to a stop and Kate opened the door and got out.

"What's up, Kate?" Steffy asked, as she walked around the front of the car to where Kate stood. "Is everything alright, Miss?" Klaus said, as he climbed from the back seat.

"I need to get some air," Kate replied. "I'm feeling a little queasy, that's all." Kate looked at the massive pine forest surrounding them. The trees were beautiful, but claustrophobic. Kate was anxious and breathing more heavily than normal.

"What the hell is wrong, Kate?" Steffy asked.

"Don't Steph," Kate replied, as she slowly walked a dozen or so paces down the road in front of the car. She folded her arms and shivered then looked back and asked, "Are you cold?"

"No, not at all," Steffy answered. Klaus stood at the side of the road near the car and stared.

"I can't do this," Kate said. "I can't go there. Let's go back now," she said, in an agitated voice.

"Kate, for god's sake, what are you talking about?" Steffy replied, shocked.

"I don't want to go there, Steffy. I've got a really bad feeling about this place. It's like something bad happened here."

"Kate," Steffy said firmly, "we've come thousands of miles to find out what did happen here. We're not even two miles away and you want to go home. You're talking crazy. There's nothing in these woods but a wrecked airplane. Now, come on, Kate. Get it together and let's get going. I'm really excited about this."

Kate stood in the middle of the dirt road, staring at Steffy and Klaus.

"How far is the airplane, Klaus?" she asked.

"It's only two or three kilometers," he replied.

Kate turned and looked in the direction they had been driving. The sienna colored road narrowed in the distance, easing into a gentle left curve and disappearing behind the trees. She suddenly spun around and looked toward Steffy and Klaus. "After the curve!" she exclaimed. "It's after the curve."

"Yes, miss," Klaus agreed. "The airplane is in the forest after we drive around the curve."

Kate glanced back at the road and the far curve as it angled into the woods. "Alright, let's go," she said, walking back to the car.

Steffy started the car and they began driving once again. Kate stared through the treetops toward the blue sky. Dark green branches arced overhead at spots where the road narrowed. As the car passed through the shadows, Kate's anxiety increased.

"Stop here," said Klaus, pointing to the left. Steffy eased the car to the left side of the road and parked. Klaus, Steffy and Kate stepped out of the car, pausing to look at the large pine trees. Klaus motioned for the women to follow as he walked into the high grass between the road and the woods. Kate stood in the road to the right of the car, continuing to stare at the tall trees. She didn't understand why she was trembling. She slowly began walking into the grass toward the trees.

Once the small group entered into the trees there was no longer grass, only the damp, pine needle floor of the forest. The walking was easier. Every thirty or forty feet, there was a fallen black tree trunk to climb over or a branch to duck under. The towering pine trees were the largest Kate had ever seen. The two women and their guide had walked for eight or ten minutes when Klaus yelled, "Here it is."

Kate, who was lagging behind, watched Steffy disappear behind the trees as she moved toward where Klaus stood. Kate couldn't see anything through the trees but she began moving faster as she got closer to the sound of Steffy's and Klaus' voices. Suddenly, she was there.

Kate couldn't tell it was an airplane at first. The large black fuselage was lying on the ground broken into two pieces and resting on its side. The aircraft's tail was missing. Moss covered sections of the fuselage and its entire area was pockmarked by a bullet holes, large, small, jagged and circular. "Those holes were made by bullets and shrapnel," Klaus said, pointing out the obvious.

It was amazing. It seemed like every inch of the plane had been damaged by gunfire. The plane had gone through hell before it went down. One of the wings, the left one, had fallen across the fuselage, its engines no longer attached. It was peppered with bullet holes. The right wing was lying on the forest floor about fifty feet away. It too was badly damaged by bullets and shrapnel and the engines were missing.

"You can look inside," said Klaus.

Kate was breathing rapidly and trembling and her knees felt weak. Something about the forest and this place with the crashed airplane was causing her great anxiety. Kate leaned back against a tree, her eyes focused on the demolished aircraft.

"Kate," Steffy yelled, "come look inside this thing."

Kate straightened her body, took a deep breath and walked towards the dark twisted remains of the airplane. "You look pale, Kate," Steffy said. "Are you all right?"

"Yeah, I'm fine, Steph," she replied. As she walked up to the fuselage, Kate looked around. She saw what looked like an engine lying in the forest twenty yards away. The forest was so dense she couldn't see anything else. Kate bent over to look inside the gaping hole where the rear half of the fuselage had broken off.

Though it was dark inside the aircraft, she could see the cockpit area. There was nothing inside it. The instruments, pilot seats, everything had been taken for other uses or souvenirs. The once proud B-17 was reduced to a stripped down, broken hulk.

Steffy had moved away from the airplane and was looking around, for what, she had no idea. Behind the aircraft was a long dead tree with its upper half broken off. Obviously in the plane's fatal flight path, Steffy wondered if the tree was hit by the B-17 just before it crashed. Would the tree still be here after all this time?

Klaus was very polite as he continued to point out obvious details. The airplane landed on its side. The crash was in 1942. Thank you, Klaus," Steffy said, looking toward Kate and rolling her eyes with a "give me a break" expression.

A feeling of foreboding surged within Kate as she stared at the airplane. Slowly, vague memories stirred within her mind. Suddenly, she recoiled in horror. Gasping for breath, Kate exclaimed, "I've seen this airplane before!"

"Are you alright, Kate?" Steffy asked. "Here, sit down by this rock." Steffy held Kate's hand as she knelt down and sat on the ground with her back against the rock. "Is that better?"

"Yes, it's fine, Steph. Thanks." Kate rested her head against the rock and closed her eyes. The name Bebe kept repeating in her brain. Bebe. Bebe. Who is Bebe, she wondered.

As Steffy knelt, she noticed some letters etched into the rock twelve inches from Kate's head. "Look, Kate," she said. "Something is carved on the rock." Kate turned her head to watch Steffy scrape away the moss covering half a dozen symbols. They could see the letters clearly now. "Kate. OK, B B."

Kate slumped forward but Steffy caught her so her head wouldn't hit the forest floor. Kate could feel Klaus and Steffy pull her back up by her shoulders and place her against the rock. Steffy opened her plastic bottle and splashed some water in Kate's face.

"Kate, are you okay?" she asked.

Kate opened her eyes and tried to clear her head. "Steph, do you see the note? Do you see it?"

"Yes, I see it, Kate. I see it right in front of me."

Kate began to cry softly. "Who is Bebe? Who is he?"

They stayed at the crash site for another fifteen minutes. Kate kept looking at the note which was carved into the rock so long ago. Finally, Klaus suggested they leave. "It looks like rain is coming," he said. "It is a good time to go. We shall see Ludwig."

# 25

Sept 21, Present Time     Bad Steffen, Germany

Twenty minutes later the small car pulled into town and stopped in front of the local undertaking establishment. It was actually a house with the undertaking portion on the first level and the living quarters on the second floor. Klaus led the way up the steps to the porch and knocked on the door. In a few moments a genial, older man in his mid eighties answered. Smiling as if he had known the women forever, he invited them in. Although he spoke English, when he greeted Klaus he spoke German.

"My name is Ludwig," he said. "Helene from the Inn called and told me you were coming. How may I be of service to you ladies?"

"I'm Kate and this is Steffy, Kate said, noticing Ludwig was closely watching her. His gaze made her feel awkward and uncomfortable.

Kate explained they had come to see the B-17 that crashed during World War Two. Ludwig listened carefully to what Kate was saying. Kate told him Helene mentioned he might have taken care of the bodies from the crash.

"I was a young boy then, only an apprentice. I remember there were four bodies, two men and two women. One woman survived the crash but died a few days after they brought her into town."

"Do you remember their names?" asked Kate.

"Yes, of course I do," replied the old man. "I mean I can look up the names in our records," he laughed. "I don't remember what I had for breakfast this morning, let alone names from seventy years ago. Oh, and I also have pictures of the deceased if you care to see them.

We keep a file on everyone we take care of here."

"Yes, I would like very much to see the pictures," replied Kate.

She thought it was odd that Ludwig had continued staring at her throughout the conversation. He motioned for them to follow him down into his basement funeral parlor. "I pulled the records out when Helene called me," he said. "I wanted to be ready for you." Klaus, obviously uncomfortable in the funeral home, told Kate and Steffy he would wait for them in the car and he walked out the front door. The old man laughed. "He's always been like that. Some people don't like to think about death."

"I keep all my records down here," Ludwig said, as he switched on more lights. He walked over to the three file cabinets in the corner of the room. On the top of one of the cabinets were several files. He reached for these and brought them over to the table near Kate and Steffy.

"Here are the files," he said, "one for each person." He put the four folders on the table and opened the one on top. "The first page in each file is a photo, a headshot," Ludwig told them. "This file is a sergeant by the name of John Bradford." The man's face was so badly damaged that he would not have been recognizable even by someone who knew him." Kate and Steffy turned away when they saw the dead man's mangled face.

Ludwig closed the file, put it aside, and picked up the next. "This one is a lieutenant named Naston Geyerson," Ludwig said.

"His throat has been cut," Kate said abruptly, as Ludwig reached to open the folder.

Ludwig paused, his face paled. "How do you know that, madam?" he asked in a cracking voice. "My god, Kate, what are you saying?" asked Steffy, a distressed look on her face.

Ludwig was shaking his head from side to side. "How did you know Madam?" he asked again, as he opened the folder to reveal Naston Geyerson's face and the jagged cut across his neck.

Kate, even more alarmed, replied "I don't know," as she gazed at the dead man.

"Kate, you're freaking me out," said Steffy fearfully. "How the hell did you know his throat was cut?"

Kate looked at Steffy, then Ludwig. She couldn't believe what was happening in this tiny undertaking parlor in a place she'd never been. Or had she? "What is the name on the next folder?" she asked.

Ludwig picked up the folder and handed it to Kate. Neatly printed on the tab of the folder was the name, Catherine Darron. Steffy gasped in horror and collapsed on a chair, terrified by what she was witnessing.

Kate's hands were shaking as she fumbled to open the file. "Oh my god!" she cried, as she looked at the dead woman in the photograph. She was staring at a picture of herself taken on the day she died, March 6, 1942.

Confused and frightened, Kate looked toward Steffy. But Steffy, who was usually adept at handling difficult situations, was no help. She sat motionless, her hand over her mouth and breathing heavily, a blank stare on her face.

Ludwig turned to the next page in the file and there was a full-length photograph of Kate dressed in a flight suit. Though frightened, Kate pulled herself together and took the flight suit from her backpack and laid it out on the table. The blood spots and oil stains on the suit matched the photograph exactly.

"Oh my god!" Kate exclaimed. "Steffy, the flight suit is the same one in the picture," she said in a panicked voice. But there was no response from Steffy, who sat motionless in the chair.

"Steffy!" Kate snapped angrily. "It was your idea to come all this way. Don't fall apart on me now. Get up and look at this picture. It's me."

"I already figured that out, Kate. That's why I'm about to faint," Steffy replied, not moving from her chair.

Suddenly, Kate remembered the other decade's old photograph of herself standing in front of a B-17. "It was in Evelyn Rankow's apartment," she mumbled, "but it wasn't Evelyn's Rankow's apartment. It was Norma Sykes' apartment."

"Kate, you're talking to yourself," said Steffy, trying to regain her composure. Kate looked at Steffy, then Ludwig.

"You knew, didn't you," she said to Ludwig. "That's why you were looking at me so closely."

"Yes, Madam," he said. "I knew." Like I said, I pulled the files after Helene called me. I recognized your face from the picture in the file the moment I opened the door."

"Do you remember what happened after the plane crashed?" Kate asked.

"Yes, of course, madam. That is an easy question. After the plane crashed in the forest, the bodies of the crew were brought to the funeral home. As I said, one of the women was still alive but she died after a few days. The two men on the airplane are buried in the cemetery here."

"What about the women?" Kate asked.

"There are two graves for the women, but their bodies are not buried there."

"Why not?" asked Steffy, in a weak voice.

Ludwig paused before answering. Then he said, "It was very strange, mysterious. The women's bodies disappeared shortly after they died. Only those of us at the funeral home and the police chief knew about this and he told us to keep it secret. He was afraid it would start a panic about dead people walking around town at night or something. You know how those rumors start in a superstitious place like the German countryside."

Steffy nodded, but was uncharacteristically silent. She had never seen anything like this nor could she even imagine it. Finally she spoke. "Who is the woman in the other folder, Ludwig?" The old man picked up the file and read the name. Her name is Brittany Beardsley," he said, and handed the file to Kate. "She is the one who survived for several days."

Kate opened the file and looked at the picture. "Oh god!" she exclaimed. "I remember. I remember now." But, her expression quickly changed to one of sorrow. "Bebe," Kate cried. As she gazed at the picture, tears came to her eyes. "No, Bebe," she blurted. "No. You can't be dead."

Realizing how important this woman was to Kate, Steffy rose from her chair to look at the photograph. She thought for a moment, then said, "Maybe Bebe's not dead, Kate. I mean, you're alive. Couldn't whatever happened to you also have happened to Bebe? It only makes sense. Think about it."

"You're right," said Kate, considering that possibility. "Maybe Bebe is alive."

"She must be," smiled Steffy. It suddenly occurred to Steffy that Bebe Beardsley may have been more to Kate than just a friend. "Were you in love with Bebe Beardsley, Kate?"

"I loved her," Kate replied, tears welling in her eyes. "It's all beginning to come back. I think we cared deeply for each other, but I don't know if we were in love. I don't understand how I couldn't know. The memories are returning, but they are coming in unrelated pieces. I remember when I first met Bebe and some of our time together. How could it have ended so horribly in a plane crash in this faraway place?"

Steffy stood silently, unable to answer Kate's question. Everything was so confusing, so frightening. How could her best friend Kate have lived before either of them was even born?

"Where is Bebe now?" Kate asked, tears rolling down her cheeks.

"I don't know," replied the old man. She asked him about the note carved into the rock, "Kate O K, B B."

"I remember seeing letters etched into the rock," Ludwig said, "but I have no idea what they mean."

Struggling to regain her composure Kate asked, "Ludwig, where is the town called Lorgenberg?"

Ludwig thought for a moment. "There is no town by that name madam."

"But, there must be. I keep hearing the name Lorgenberg and it must be the name of a town."

"Madam," Ludwig replied, I know of no town by that name."

"Are you sure," Kate pressed him.

Ludwig stared downward, trying to recall the name Lorgenberg. Then he looked up at Kate. "I believe I recall that during World War Two there was a secret Nazi facility north of here. It was thought the Nazis were making some kind of powerful bomb at that place. It might have been called Lorgenberg. The airplane that crashed in the forest bombed that facility and destroyed it."

"Kate," said Steffy, "Lorgenberg might have been the name of the mission to destroy the Nazi facility. I've seen enough movies to know that. That would mean that Lorgenberg is here."

"If Lorgenberg is here, Bebe must be here," replied Kate. "Bebe is here! I know she's here!" Kate exclaimed. "We have to find her."

"Kate," Steffy interrupted, "if Bebe is here she would be ninety years old."

"No she won't, Steffy. Somehow, I know she won't. She's been waiting for me. She's here. I know it."

"May I see the file?" Steffy asked. Ludwig handed her the brown folder and Steffy looked through it. "Kate," she said, "Brittany Beardsley's military identification card is in here. It says her hometown is Omaha, Nebraska. Do you remember anything else that might help us find her?"

Kate thought for a long while. The memories were becoming clearer. "Steffy, I remember one time Bebe told me she was from the year 1947. I don't know why I thought of that now. Bebe must have lived in Omaha in 1947. Then, like me, she ended up in World War Two. Does that make sense?"

"It makes no sense whatsoever," replied Steffy, "but that's exactly what happened."

# 26

September 21, Present Time    Bad Steffen, Germany

On the drive back to the inn, Kate remembered more of what she and Bebe had been through. There were things she couldn't recall, lots of missing parts. She couldn't understand how she managed to blank out the memories of that time. However Steffy, who still struggling to recover from the unnerving events at the funeral home, had some ideas.

"Kate, what happened to you and Bebe speaks of some kind of outside influence," she said.

"Are you suggesting some supernatural intervention, Steph?"

"No," replied Steffy, "although, that would be interesting. But, I think it's got something to do with that super secret agency you work for. Somehow, I think they're involved. Remember the day you got the job? That was way too weird, Kate. You didn't have any special expertise, but they wanted to interview you right away. Then they hired you so quickly they wouldn't even let you come back to St. Louis to move. That's really strange. I mean, you're a smart girl but there are lots of smart girls out there. No, this whole thing with your agency is just too bizarre."

"What do you think happened?" asked Kate.

"I think that you were somehow taken from the present time and transported back to the 1940's, or maybe earlier. Why they chose you is a mystery, however, because you're just a schoolteacher. You do have expertise with a pistol and rifle from your competition days but that can't be it. There's got to be more to it."

"It sounds like a bad movie," Kate replied, but I agree. A lot of people know how to use a gun. Wait a minute," Kate said abruptly. "The apartment. I remember the apartment. A woman named Evelyn Rankow asked me to come to her apartment for dinner. She mentioned an agency called OSTRO. I think she drugged me because the next thing I knew I was back in 1939. I remember it clearly now."

"What else?" asked Steffy, in an excited voice.

"Steffy," said Kate, "OSTRO is the agency I worked for until last week. I never told you the name of the agency because it is so secret they won't even let us tell anyone who we work for."

Kate and Steffy arrived at the Inn and went upstairs to their room to freshen up and get ready for dinner. Kate wanted to put on more dressy clothes for dinner, but Steffy decided not to change her outfit. "Kate, why don't I go downstairs and get us a table while you change? I'll have a drink while I'm waiting for you."

"Okay Steffy, I'll be along soon," Kate smiled, as Steffy opened the room door.

Fifteen minutes later Kate came downstairs and walked into the dining room. Only half the tables were occupied, but as Kate glanced around the room, she couldn't see Steffy. Maybe Steffy's in the bar, she thought, as she turned to walk out of the dining room. Kate walked into the small bar across the lobby from the dining room. There were only a few customers, but she couldn't see Steffy.

"May I join you for a drink, Miss Darron?" said a familiar voice behind her.

Kate quickly turned to face the owner of that voice. "Mr. Farley!" Kate exclaimed, shocked.

"Hello Kate," he said. "Why don't we sit at this table."

"Of course," replied Kate. "I'm surprised to see you here, "Mr. Farley," she said, off balance at his sudden appearance on the scene. Regaining her composure, she said, "Please excuse me for a moment. I'm looking for my friend Steffy and I want to check the dining room again to see if she's there."

"That won't be necessary," Jack Farley replied.

"Why?" Kate asked, a puzzled look on her face.

"Because Steffy's not in the dining room Kate," he replied. "In fact, she's not in the hotel."

"What are you talking about, Mr. Farley?" Kate replied

apprehensively.

"We need to get down to business, Miss Darron," Farley said, abruptly changing the subject and his tone. "First of all, you're not fired. That unfortunate event was a misunderstanding by Mr. Scoggins. He tends to overreact now and again."

"He said I was fired," responded Kate. "There was no mistake about that."

"Kate," Farley said, "first of all, I want to apologize for Dan Scoggins' actions. If you can forgive Mister Scoggins for his impulsiveness, we'd like to put this little matter behind us. We want you to come back and work for the agency. I hope that is agreeable to you?"

"No, it's really not, Mr. Farley. I'm happy Mr. Scoggins fired me. I don't want to work for OSTRO. I want OSTRO out of my life. Now, let's get back to Steffy. What did you say about Steffy?"

"I said she's not in the hotel so don't bother looking for her."

"What have you done to Steffy?" Kate asked, a feeling of alarm coming over her.

"Do you remember Evelyn Rankow Kate? Steffy is with her. If you wish to see her alive again, you will do exactly as I say. Is that clear?" Farley asked in a suddenly ominous tone.

"I thought Evelyn would be dead by now," responded Kate.

"So, you do remember what happened to you," Farley said.

"The pieces are slowly coming together. How could I not remember dear, sweet Evelyn?" Kate replied sarcastically.

"That's fine," Farley said with a smile. "And yes, Evelyn is very much alive. She's a survivor. I came across her some time ago and we became, shall we say, very close friends."

"You're sleeping with a murderer, Mr. Farley," Kate said bitterly. "Evelyn is the perfect partner for you."

"She is perfect in many ways," Farley replied with a sinister smirk.

"Mr. Farley, I told you I don't want to work for the agency any longer," Kate said, attempting to end the conversation. "Too many strange things have happened to me since I got involved with it. You better release Steffy immediately or I'll go to the police."

"Don't be ridiculous, Kate," said Jack Farley, a look of amusement on his face. I could care less if you go to the police. I could also care less about killing Steffy to teach you a lesson. So I think you better reconsider. You either agree to do what I tell you or your friend Steffy will be dead in less than a minute."

"Can't you people leave me alone?" said Kate, her voice rising.

Jack Farley's face assumed a menacing expression and was flushed with anger. "What do you mean leave you alone? You were technically dead, Miss Darron, and you don't even know it. OSTRO gave you back your life."

"What are you talking about, Mr. Farley? Kate said angrily.

"It's very simple, Miss Darron," he replied. "You don't seem to remember that on the day you were to die in a car accident Evelyn Rankow brought you back in time and thereby saved your life. If it weren't for OSTRO you'd be dead. Is that so hard to understand?"

"Mr. Farley," Kate replied, "let me alone or I shall go to the authorities at the very highest level."

"You're being ridiculous," Farley responded, an amused look on his face. "We are the authorities at the very highest level. You are working for OSTRO, Miss Darron. You have no choice. You owe OSTRO your life. OSTRO owns you and we will do with you what we wish. Will you cooperate or shall I make the phone call that will end Steffy's life?"

"You bastard!" Kate said.

Farley smiled. "That's the spirit, Kate. I knew you'd see things my way. Also, Miss Darron, if you try to escape or cause any inconvenient problems, OSTRO will kill Steffy. You would also do well to remember that I can destroy you before you take your next sip of wine. I can fix it so you never existed. So be a good girl and do what you are told."

"Ludwig the undertaker knows about your little tricks," Kate replied. "He will tell the world about OSTRO."

"Yes, he would if he were alive. But poor Ludwig is dead, Kate. I'm afraid your little visit to him this afternoon caused a minor stir. OSTRO doesn't like publicity. Ludwig was a victim of your curiosity. Of course, the newspaper will say he died of natural causes."

Kate was horrified. "You killed that innocent old man?" Kate said angrily.

"Keep your voice down, Miss Darron. Our business must remain secret."

"So I am an indentured servant for OSTRO," Kate said. "Do I

ever get my freedom?"

"That's much better," Jack Farley replied. "Dan Scoggins and I need an extremely urgent mission carried out. If you and your former partner Brittany Beardsley successfully complete the operation, we shall release you both. Your debt will be paid."

"Why do you need Bebe Beardsley and me to go on this mission? Certainly, you have many people more skilled than us."

"That's true, Miss Darron. However, as in World War Two, we are using you as a precaution in case the operation fails. If that happens, we must be able to say we know nothing about it. Miss Beardsley is anonymous, a person from the past who was killed long ago. No one will miss her. No one will miss you either. You see, we've fulfilled your destiny of being killed in a car wreck. Several days ago, we staged the accident in which you were killed. We simply substituted another woman's body. It was a bad wreck, Miss Darron. It required a closed coffin funeral. Like I said, you're already dead. Your family has accepted that. Your mother didn't take it well, I'm sorry to say."

"Damn you!" an infuriated Kate shouted

"That's the second time you've spoken harshly to me, Miss Darron. You're beginning to annoy me. That is not a wise move."

Kate glared at Farley as he spoke. "There is one other reason you and Miss Beardsley are required for this mission. You both know how to fly a B-17 better than anyone alive. All the World War Two pilots are old or have died. There are only a few B-17's left and no one flying those has had the combat experience you and Beardsley have. You're also an expert markswoman. During your training, we spent a great deal of time and money upgrading those shooting skills and teaching you to handle every type of weapon. We need those skills for this mission."

"Not to change the subject, Mr. Farley," Kate interrupted, "but how did you find me?"

Jack Farley described the baiting process he used with the keyword Lorgenberg planted on the Internet. "I didn't know for sure if you or any other women who participated in the Destiny Project were still alive," he added.

"What did you call it?" asked Kate.

"The Destiny Project," Farley replied. "I still wasn't sure about you when you responded to our employment advertisement, but when the movers came to your apartment, one of our people found your World War Two flight suit in your closet. We still don't know how it got there. Obviously you didn't know what it was or where it came from. I was pretty sure who you were at that point, but I had to be positive. That's why I hired you. And finally, you and I both know who you really are, Miss Darron.

OSTRO's old mission files were destroyed in a fire and we didn't know the name of the other pilot on the airplane until we followed you here. The undertaker told us Beardsley's name and that she was from Omaha. He also said you mentioned the year 1947. That's when we learned where and in what year to find her. You unwittingly helped us sort it all out. Actually, I started working on this over six years ago but I didn't get serious about re-instituting the Destiny Project until a bad situation recently arose. Believe it or not, this situation is related to the original Destiny Project."

"What do you mean, Mr. Farley?" Kate asked.

"Miss Darron," Farley whispered, "you and Miss Beardsley bombed the Lorgenberg complex during World War Two. It was a secret Nazi compound which was building atomic bombs."

"The Nazis were making nuclear weapons there?" asked Kate.

"Yes," Farley replied. "You apparently don't remember all of the details, Miss Darron," Farley said.

"At first, I didn't remember anything about that time, but each day I'm remembering more. Now that you mention the atom bombs, I do remember them," Kate replied. "But why are you coming back seventy years later and re-examining this mission? What's the point of all of this?"

"I'm getting to that, Miss Darron. Your mission was to destroy the facility and the nuclear bombs stored there. You and Miss Beardsley did that. Unfortunately, there were complications which are now creating a huge problem for the United States," Farley whispered. "That is of the utmost secrecy and I can't tell you anymore at this time."

"But why are you involving me in all of this? I'm just a school teacher from St. Louis."

"You are a school teacher who is also an extremely skilled B-17 pilot, Miss Darron. On top of that, you are a world-class marksman, or should I say markswoman. We need Brittany Beardsley because she is also a skilled B-17 pilot. And as I mentioned, you two are anonymous. No one will miss you if you are killed on the mission we have in mind. Of course, I'm sure that won't happen"

"Apparently we were killed on the Lorgenberg mission, Mr. Farley. I'm afraid I'm not as confident as you about surviving another potentially fatal mission."

"Don't worry, Miss Darron. This mission will be much less risky than the Lorgenberg mission."

"I don't believe you, Mr. Farley, but, if I help you, I want you to guarantee that if we're successful on this mission, I will never have to do anything else for OSTRO. I'm finished with OSTRO forever. Is that a deal?"

"If you and Beardsley do what we ask, we'll give you your freedom and you shall never hear from OSTRO again. I promise you."

"Where is Miss Beardsley?" Kate asked.

"We're tracking her down now," Farley replied. "We've got better search tools than we had six years ago. Well actually, the undertaker told us where to find her just before he died today," Farley laughed.

"What's the next step, Mr. Farley?" Kate asked. "What do you want me to do?"

"We want you to come to Washington, Miss Darron. We'll brief you and Beardsley when you arrive."

"I obviously have no choice, Mr. Farley."

"I'm afraid not, Miss Darron."

"Am I free to return to Washington on my own?" Kate asked.

"Of course," Farley said. "You're not being arrested. Besides, you're aware of the consequences if you don't show up or decide not to cooperate."

"I'll see you in Dan Scoggins' office at eight a.m. September 24, Miss Darron. That gives you the 22nd and 23rd to travel. That should be plenty of time. We have to get the operation underway as quickly as possible. When you arrive in Washington, you'll see Miss Beardsley at your hotel. Here are your airplane tickets," Farley concluded, as he got up from his chair. "Have a nice dinner."

As Jack Farley walked out of the bar, Steffy walked in. "Who was that guy, Kate?' she asked.

"Where have you been Steffy?" Kate replied, wondering why Steffy didn't mention Evelyn Rankow or being abducted.

"You won't believe this," Steffy replied, "but when I left our room, some older woman passed me as I was walking down the hall. The next thing I remember is walking into the bar just now. I don't remember coming down the steps. That's really weird."

"That's strange," Kate said. "You must be getting old," she laughed, purposely changing the subject. "Why don't we have a martini and talk about something fun?"

"Cut it out, Kate," Steffy said in a serious tone. "What the hell's going on here? Did that woman do something to me?"

Seeing she could not put her off, Kate told Steffy what happened with Farley and that she had been momentarily kidnapped by Evelyn Rankow.

"That's really scary," Steffy said. "I didn't think things like that really happened or guys like Jack Farley actually existed. I mean you only see things like that in the movies."

"I wish it were a movie," Kate said. "Unfortunately, it's all very real. Steffy, don't ever breathe a word of what I just told you to anyone. I've never been more serious about anything in my life. Do you understand?"

"Yes, I understand, Kate. I'll never say anything about it. I don't mean to ask a stupid question, but what are you going to do?"

"Obviously, I've got to do what OSTRO tells me. If I don't, you and everyone else I care about will be in danger. They won't hesitate to kill me either. Somehow, I'm going to get out from under OSTRO's grip. I remember talking to Bebe about that. I think we had a plan but I can't remember what we were going to do. Maybe she'll think of something."

"Kate, what is your relationship with Bebe? Is she your friend or something more than that?"

"I don't remember," Kate replied. "I really don't," she added, looking directly at Steffy. "I remember her clearly now, but there's so much I just can't recall. But I think it's definitely time for another martini," Kate smiled.

"Good idea," Steffy said.

# 27

September 22-24, Present Time     Washington, DC

The following day, September 22, Kate and Steffy drove back to Berlin. Their flight would leave on the 23rd, and with connections, Kate would arrive in Washington on September 24. They had dinner that night but neither Kate nor Steffy felt like celebrating. OSTRO cast a long shadow over their lives and they knew that once they parted, it would be a long time before they would see each other again.

Though lengthy, the flight the following day seemed to pass quickly. When they arrived in New York, Kate boarded a plane for the short flight to Washington and Steffy headed for St. Louis.

As she travelled by cab toward the hotel, Kate wondered what would happen when she got there. She was excited but nervous about seeing Bebe. A half hour later, the cab pulled up to the front entrance of the hotel. Kate walked into the lobby and over to the registration desk. As the clerk handed her the room key, she asked if Brittany Beardsley had checked in.

"Yes ma'am, she is checked in."

"Thank you," Kate said, turning to walk across the lobby to the elevator. She stepped inside one of the elevators and pressed # 6. In a few seconds, it reached the sixth floor and Kate stepped out and walked toward room 647. Nice place, she thought, as she walked down the hallway. Once inside her room, Kate freshened up and walked over to the telephone on the nightstand. Sitting down on the bed, she picked up the phone up and dialed 0.

"Front Desk," a voice answered.

"Brittany Beardsley's room," Kate said.

"Yes ma'am," the clerk replied. "She heard the phone ring immediately.

"Hello, Kate," a voice answered. "It's about time you got here."

"Bebe," Kate said, as memories flooded into her mind.

"I'm in room, 649," Bebe said. "I asked for adjoining rooms. Unlock the door between our rooms."

Without saying "goodbye," Kate dropped the phone and quickly walked over to the door connecting the two rooms and unlocked it. As Kate pulled the door open, Bebe rushed through and they immediately embraced. Both of them were laughing and crying at the same time.

"Kate, I can't believe it's you," said Bebe. "They said you would be here but I couldn't believe it. But, here you are. There was so much I couldn't remember but seeing you brings the memories back to me."

"I can't believe it either," said Kate excitedly. "I'm so happy we're together again, but it seems like we're back where started, being forced to risk our lives on some kind of crazy suicide mission. I don't want to die, Bebe. I want to be with you."

"I feel the same way," Bebe said, pulling Kate closer. "I don't want to die either, but you're right. They've got us right back where they want us and can force us to do whatever they wish."

"Let's order a bottle of wine from room service so we can catch up and sort this all out, Kate replied."

"Okay," Bebe said. "I'll get us a bottle of red wine. They say that's good for the memory," she laughed.

"Is that what they say?" asked Kate laughing as she hugged Bebe again. Then she added, "Before we have too much wine, we have to compare notes on what they told us. Bebe, did they tell you what they want with us?"

"No, not really," answered Bebe. "But, it's like you said. They want us to do some kind of mission for them but Evelyn Rankow wouldn't say what."

"That's all they told me too," said Kate. "They said something about atom bombs and the Lorgenberg facility, but that's all. You know, we were killed on that mission. I was just in Germany and went to the funeral home that handled our bodies. That was really a bizarre experience," Kate added shivering.

"Like you said, Kate, it's deja vu. The only difference is we're in a different time seventy years later. We know OSTRO will send us on a mission on which we stand a good chance of being killed. Otherwise, why would they bring us here?"

Kate put her finger over her mouth, signaling Bebe to not say anything else. She picked up the note pad by the phone on the nightstand and wrote, "The room may be bugged. They could be listening to us."

Bebe nodded that she understood. "Why don't we go down to the bar for a nightcap instead of ordering room service," she said.

They left the room and walked down the hall to the elevator and took it to the first floor. They easily found a secluded table in the hotel bar and sat down next to each other in order not to be overheard by the few guests around them. "Bebe," Kate said, "do you remember the plan you had for us to escape from OSTRO?"

"Yeah, I do," Bebe replied. "We were going to complete the mission over Lorgenberg and on the way back we would fake a problem with the airplane and have the crew bail out once we got into friendly territory. Then we would bail out and disappear. It would look like we got killed and we'd be free."

"It was a good plan, Bebe. We need to make it work this time. Bebe. Our boss in OSTRO is named Jack Farley. He's going to ask us about the 1942 mission tomorrow morning. Something apparently went wrong because he said there was a big problem for the country today which is related to our 1942 mission. I have no idea what the problem could be, but we need to try and remember every detail so we'll be ready for his questions."

"You mean up to the time our B-17 crashed in the German forest and we got killed," replied Bebe, an expression of irony on her face. But her tone quickly became serious. "You know, Kate, what happened to us is so crazy. If someone else told me this happened to them, I wouldn't believe it. It's even harder to realize how ruthless OSTRO is. They're really terrible people."

"I know, Bebe," replied Kate. "Jack Farley threatened to kill my parents and my friend if I didn't cooperate this time. They staged my death in a car accident in St. Louis a week ago. My parents think I was killed."

"That's horrible," Bebe said.

"Yeah," said Kate. "But, getting back to the mission, do you remember anything unusual happening?"

"There was a lot of anti-aircraft fire just after we crossed the English Channel. It continued through most of the flight," Bebe replied. "And, we had German aircraft chasing us just before we crashed."

"Bebe," Kate said, I remember a few minutes before we crashed our navigator Captain Max Brumfeld bailed out. You told me to go down to the nose cone to check on the bombardier Naston Geyerson. I did. His throat had been cut."

"You're right," Bebe replied. "Why did Brumfeld kill him?"

"I guess he did it to cover his escape," Kate said. Maybe Brumfeld bailed because he was afraid we were going to crash, but that doesn't explain why he killed Nasty Geyerson."

"We did crash," said Bebe. "We probably should have bailed out with Captain Brumfeld," she replied sarcastically. "But, seriously, I wonder why Captain Brumfeld killed Lieutenant Geyerson and bailed out. We were deep into enemy territory. Besides, the German pilots probably killed him as he parachuted to the ground."

"But, Brumfeld must have had some other reason to bail out," Kate said. The chances of survival are always better staying with the airplane."

"If it doesn't crash and kill everyone, Bebe countered. "Do you remember anything else happening?"

"In the final minutes before our plane crashed, our tail gunner Johnny Bradford was still alive, but only you and I were still functional. Geyerson was dead, Brumfeld had bailed and Johnny was hurt too badly to use his parachute. That's all I remember. Bebe, are you ready for tomorrow?"

"Yeah, but we'll both have headaches. Let's get some sleep. It's going to be a rough day."

"There's one last thing," said Kate. "What about that etching in the stone at the site of the plane crash? What did it mean?"

"Kate O K, B B, you mean?"

"Yes," said Kate.

"I was trying to tell you not to worry. Somehow I knew we'd get back together."

"You were right," Kate replied.

Bebe and Kate had talked late into the night, finishing one bottle of wine and half of another. Neither of them was looking forward to the following morning meeting at OSTRO headquarters.

# 28

September 25, Present Time     Washington D.C.

The next morning Kate and Bebe woke up early and had a quick breakfast. At eight o'clock a car arrived to take them the short distance to OSTRO headquarters. In less than ten minutes, the driver pulled the car into the underground garage at the OSTRO facility. They were met at the door by a young woman, who escorted them to Dan Scoggins' office. As they followed the woman through the door, Kate saw Dan Scoggins and Jack Farley sitting at the desk having coffee.

"Hello Kate," Scoggins said "and you are Brittany Beardsley, I take it. "I'm Dan Scoggins and this is Jack Farley."

Bebe nodded, and with as much sincerity as she could manage, said "Hello, Mr. Scoggins. It's nice to meet you."

"Yes, I'll just bet it is, Miss Beardsley," Scoggins answered. "It's nice to have you with us this morning, ladies. Please, sit down," he said, gesturing toward two chairs in front of his desk.

Kate and Bebe sat down directly across the desk from Dan Scoggins. Jack Farley sat on Scoggins' left. When everyone was seated, the young woman who brought them to the office walked out, closing the door behind her.

"Would you ladies like some coffee?" Jack Farley asked.

"No thanks," said Bebe. Kate nodded that she would like a cup and Farley got up and walked to the coffee pot. "Black," Kate said.

"What is it you want with us?" asked Bebe, as Jack Farley handed Kate the cup of coffee.

Dan Scoggins, who preferred to control conversations, was put off by Bebe's question and he avoided giving her a direct answer. "Miss Beardsley, do you and Miss Darron ever wonder how you have been able to bounce around through time as you have been doing?" Before Bebe could answer, Scoggins continued. "The facts of the situation are these. As you know, both of you would have been killed in accidents long ago if it weren't for this agency. Miss Beardsley, I know you are unhappy about your fiancée's untimely death. That was unfortunate, to be sure, but such is life.

"OSTRO could have saved him too, Scoggins!" exclaimed Bebe, an unhappy expression on her face. "Don't tell me about life after everything that Kate and I have been through."

Ignoring Bebe's comment, Scoggins continued. "You, Miss Darron, were chosen for similar reasons."

"We both know all of that, Mr. Scoggins," said Kate abruptly. "Will you get to the point of why we are here now?"

Now ignoring Kate's remark, he continued. "By virtue of a teleporter gadget we possess, we have been able to keep you both alive by transporting you from the time you were in to the time we needed you in. Do you understand?" Scoggins stated sarcastically. The cold expression on his face made it clear he considered the two women expendable commodities. It was obvious his only concern was what OSTRO wanted done and that he would use Kate and Bebe to get the mission accomplished.

"We understand. Cut to the chase, Mr. Scoggins," said Kate. "You want us to undertake a suicidal mission."

"Of course, you're correct, Miss Darron," replied Scoggins. "I know you two would like to be on your merry way and leave all this behind, but you owe OSTRO a big debt, namely your lives. However, the world is such an evil place and there are so many unpleasant people who must be dealt with. Now this agency took the trouble to go into time and save both of your lives. In return we asked you to perform a certain mission for us back in 1942. However, you botched that mission and inconveniently died in the process. Like I said, the bottom line is you owe us and I intend to collect that debt," Scoggins said with a smirk on his face.

Kate felt the blood rushing to her neck. "Just a minute, Scoggins," she said. "As I see it, the mission was successful. We destroyed the assigned target."

"I don't give a damn how you see it, Miss Darron," Scoggins replied curtly. "There are complications related to that mission. And you will call me Mr. Scoggins."

"You go to hell," Bebe said.

"Just a second," Jack Farley interrupted. "We all need to calm down here. Dan, Kate is right. They destroyed the assigned target. That was the objective of the mission and they accomplished it. We have to remember the purpose of this meeting today is to find out what happened on that mission.

"Kate," Farley continued, "it is true the Lorgenberg complex was destroyed, however, the nuclear weapons were removed from the facility before you and Bebe dropped your bombs. Somebody tipped off the Germans but we don't know who."

"That's not our problem," Kate countered, still furious with Scoggins."

"Well, it really is," Farley responded. "We think those nukes ended up at another location in our present time. That location is now the target of the mission you and Beardsley must undertake."

"I know who tipped them off," Bebe said angrily. "Our navigator Captain Max Brumfeld killed our bombardier Lieutenant Naston Geyerson, smashed the Norden bombsight and bailed out."

"Hold on, Miss Beardsley," Farley said, "that's quite an accusation. After I got back from my trip to Bad Steffen, Germany the other day, I researched Captain Brumfeld's file and his record is exemplary. There are no indications he would ever do something like that. Let's move into the conference room, I have a screen set up so we can all be looking at the same facts while we talk."

Kate and Bebe got up from their chairs and followed Farley and Scoggins into the spacious meeting room. Kate and Bebe sat down on the left side of the large table directly across from Dan Scoggins and Jack Farley. "Alright, this is better isn't it?" Farley said. "We're going to look at all three of your crew members. We'll discuss each man in detail. Okay."

"You headquarters types are unbelievable," snapped Bebe. "You just can't listen, can you? Kate and I discussed the mission in detail last night. There was no one else on the aircraft that could have tipped off the Germans. I didn't trust Brumfeld from the start. He was a rat."

"Your 1940's expressions are charming Miss Beardsley, but I

need facts." Jack Farley clicked a key on the computer and a picture of tail gunner Johnny Bradford appeared on the screen. "What about Johnny Bradford?" Farley asked. "Could he possibly have told the Germans about the bombing mission?"

"Of course not," Bebe answered. "Johnny was a good kid." She lifted her left hand to wipe a tear from her cheek. "We'd suffered heavy damage from ground fire and German fighter planes. Our B-17 was so shot up I was having trouble holding altitude. Johnny was badly wounded. He probably died in the airplane before we crashed. If he had told the Germans, he would have bailed out long before we got to the target area."

"So you don't think he could have been involved in warning the Germans?" asked Scoggins.

Bebe rolled her eyes in frustration. "Absolutely not. I told you Captain Brumfeld was the rat in the attic. I reported my suspicions to Colonel McKilleps the night of the mission. Like you, he wouldn't listen to what I was telling him."

Jack Farley clicked his computer. "What about Naston Geyerson, the bombardier?" he asked, as Nasty Guy's picture flashed before them.

"Not a chance," answered Kate. "He was a good man just like Johnny. Captain Brumfeld cut Lt. Geyerson's throat before he bailed out of the airplane several minutes before we reached the target."

Farley and Scoggins looked at each other as if they didn't like what they were hearing. "We didn't know Lt. Geyerson's throat had been cut," Farley said.

"Didn't you look at the pictures of the crew in the files at the funeral home?" Kate asked.

"I have those files," Farley said. "I took them with me when I left Bad Steffen."

"You mean after you killed that nice old man," added Kate.

"Now we'll talk about your navigator, Captain Max Brumfeld?" Farley said, ignoring Kate's comment. The third photograph blinked on the screen.

Kate and Bebe stared at the picture of Captain Brumfeld magnified on the screen. Then they looked at each other. "Wait a minute," Kate said. "That's not Captain Brumfeld."

"What do you mean it's not Captain Brumfeld?" a surprised Jack Farley replied. That most certainly is Captain Max Brumfeld. I verified all of these pictures using three different sources."

"You may have verified the photos, Mr. Farley," Bebe said. "But, Kate's right. That is definitely not Captain Max Brumfeld."

A visibly shocked Jack Farley looked at Dan Scoggins who also appeared surprised.

"Jack, are you sure that photo is Captain Max Brumfeld," Scoggins asked. "Could there be someone else with the same name?"

"Dan, that picture on the screen matches military and personal pictures of Brumfeld. That man is absolutely Captain Max Brumfeld."

Kate and Bebe looked at each other, then at Scoggins and Farley.

"You guys really are screwed up," Bebe said. "We've never seen that man before today. He doesn't look anything like Captain Max Brumfeld."

"What's his date of death, Jack?" asked Scoggins.

"The file shows he died on the date of the mission, March 6, 1942," Farley replied.

"That's not Captain Max Brumfeld," Kate said. "That picture's not even close."

As Kate spoke, Bebe sat back in her chair, momentarily closing her eyes and wishing they could be anywhere else but in this room talking to these two men. As she opened her eyes, Dan Scoggins was still discussing the validity of Brumfeld's picture with Jack Farley.

As disinterested people often do, Bebe let her eyes wander. There was nothing of particular interest in the room, not even windows. There was a credenza to hold meeting materials and coffee pots. There was also a podium for speakers to the left of the screen at the front of the long conference room.

Then she gazed toward the door they had entered at the rear of the conference room. She wished she could run through it and instantly be at Ebbers Field where she first met Kate in 1939. They would climb into that little Jenny and fly far away. It seemed like so long ago, she pondered. Then she noticed half a dozen photos of men hanging on the wall to the right of the door. "Leaders of OSTRO" a sign above the photos read.

Scoggins and Farley were still arguing about Brumfeld's picture while Bebe struggled to see the pictures from where she and the others sat near the front of the room. It was easy to recognize the man in the first photo. It was Dr. Elbert Beale, the founder of OSTRO. Even with his smiling face, he looked like a dangerous man. He was an S.O.B, she reflected. She strained her eyes to see the face of the man in the next photo. He looked familiar, but she couldn't see his features clearly. "I know him," she mumbled to herself, as she gazed at the photo.

"Miss Beardsley," Dan Scoggins said, "are we boring you?"

With her eyes focused on the second picture, Bebe got up from her chair and slowly walked toward the back of the room.

"Miss Beardsley," Scoggins said more firmly, "where are you going?" She was ten feet from the wall with the pictures when she stopped and turned around and looked at Scoggins and Farley.

"Yeah, you are boring me, Scoggins. The two of you aren't smart enough to find your hands in a barrel of flour. There's Captain Max Brumfeld!" she exclaimed, pointing at the second picture on the wall.

"What are you talking about," Scoggins cried in disbelief. "Are you crazy?" he said in a rising voice. He climbed out of his chair to walk toward the wall near the doorway.

"That's Captain Max Brumfeld right there," Bebe repeated angrily, pointing at the second picture from the door.

Kate walked across the room and stood near Bebe. She too became angry as she looked at the picture. The little bronze plaque at the bottom of the picture read Dr. Horst Lange. "That's the Captain Max Brumfeld that was on our B-17," Kate said.

"There's no doubt about it," Bebe added. "It was OSTRO that screwed the mission up, Scoggins. Your own man told the Germans we were coming. I remember he also broke radio silence to warn them we were approaching the target. Then he bailed out, probably to meet his comrades on the ground and steal the atom bombs they had already moved out of the facility."

Scoggins glared at Bebe and Kate, furious and embarrassed that an OSTRO man, especially a high ranking one, would betray the country and the agency.

Dan Scoggins and Jack Farley looked at each other. "I don't believe it," Scoggins said.

Before Kate or Bebe could speak, Jack Farley replied. "Dan, I've got a real bad feeling about this whole thing."

"What do you mean?" asked Scoggins. "It happened seventy

years ago. It doesn't make any difference now."

"It does to us, Scoggins," shouted Bebe angrily. "Because your man tipped off the Germans, there was no reason to go on that mission. The nukes had already been moved out of the facility. Your man also helped get us killed. Of course, you don't care about that."

Farley spoke, once again trying to calm things down. "You're right, Miss Beardsley. What you don't know is that Dr. Horst Lange was the man who decoded the Boethian Wheel. He obviously travelled into time and impersonated Captain Brumfeld. "Dan," he said, directing his words at Scoggins, "it had to be Dr. Lange who warned the Germans."

"I agree," said Scoggins, a deep frown on his face.

"Alright, we've solved your puzzle," said Kate. "Are we free to go now?"

"No, Miss Darron," Scoggins replied. "In fact, this revelation brings us to the exact reason we brought you here."

"And what reason is that?" asked Bebe.

"Yes, Mr. Scoggins," added Kate, "please tell us why we're here. It's really not our mess to straighten out."

"Like I said, those ten nuclear weapons that disappeared from Lorgenberg have recently resurfaced," said Scoggins. "Some very bad people have come into possession of the Lorgenberg nukes. We need you to finish the job you should have completed in 1942."

"Are you blaming us, Scoggins?" asked Bebe angrily.

"I told you, it's Mr. Scoggins," he replied authoritatively.

Kate put her hand on Bebe's left arm, signaling her to be calm.

"Why doesn't the government just take out the bad guys?" asked Kate. "They have the technology to do it. Why do you need us?"

"You're right, in a way, Miss Darron. It would be very easy to take out these guys using any number of devices. However, if we used a high tech method, satellites would identify the source of a missile or airplane and the United States would be blamed. We need to make it appear that it couldn't possibly have been the United States that destroyed the facility we are targeting.

You might say we are disguising the mission to make it appear a Third World country carried it out. That way, the United States won't be blamed. You see, the problem is that if it appears the United States did this bombing, there would be severe political repercussions, which might lead to a serious military conflict. The country where this particular group is located is already a tinderbox just waiting to erupt in war.

So you see Miss Darron, to make it look like a Third World country executed this mission, we are going to have to do things the old fashioned way. We are using old-fashioned airplanes such as the B-17 bomber and old-fashioned people such as yourself and Miss Beardsley. "

Kate looked at Bebe, then back at Dan Scoggins and Jack Farley.

"We need you to perform that mission for us," Scoggins said. Once you complete the mission you and Miss Beardsley are free to be on your way. You will never have to see OSTRO or be involved in this nasty business again. Does that sound like a good plan ladies?"

"That depends on exactly what you want us to do," replied Kate.

"Good answer, Miss Darron," replied Scoggins.

"Alright, I'll lay it out for you," he continued. "The man you knew as Captain Max Brumfeld and who we now know is also Dr. Horst Lange has yet another name. He is now known as Patrice Betaine. This is the same man who decoded the Boethian Wheel, warned the Germans and parachuted out of your airplane. He also has control of the Lorgenberg nuclear weapons. He's using the Nazi nukes as models to build updated atom bombs, to use your parlance, Miss Beardsley.

We need to have him and his group eliminated and the facility with their cache of nukes destroyed. One accurately dropped bomb will handle this assignment. That's all we're asking of you two," Scoggins said.

"When do we leave?" asked Bebe.

We will provide you with more information as soon as intelligence confirms the exact date these people will visit the target facility. It's actually pretty simple, don't you think," Scoggins said.

"It always seems simple for you headquarters types," Bebe replied scornfully. "But in reality, it never is. Things happen in the field which you people never anticipate," she added, "and suddenly, things aren't so simple."

"Jack," Scoggins said, "tell them about the facility." He purposely didn't address Bebe's point.

"The site we want destroyed is called the Ronganai Depot. It is located approximately one hundred miles northeast of Hoginpuu, the capital city of Nomgai, which is in North Africa. It's called a depot because it has long functioned as a weapons clearinghouse for arms dealers and Third World countries. They have the Lorgenberg nukes there. That creates a very bad situation for the United States. The people who run this facility sell nukes to the highest bidders. The man in charge of this place is none other than Patrice Betaine, a.k.a. Dr. Horst Lange, a.k.a. Captain Max Brumfeld."

"So that's the bottom line, as you call it," Bebe said, "except we know it won't be as easy as you say or you would have handled the problem already."

"That's a good observation, Miss Beardsley," replied Scoggins, and also why we need you and Miss Darron to handle this particular assignment. You and your girlfriend Miss Darron are the best B-17 pilots still alive and able to fly the damned things."

Kate had been waiting to speak. "Are you crazy? A B-17 would be shot out of the air before it got ten feet off the runway. The high tech weapons they have today make us sitting ducks. We might as well shoot at these guys with a BB gun, no offense meant, Bebe."

Bebe laughed, but again became serious. "Kate is right, Mr. Scoggins."

"Not really," replied Scoggins. "You will execute a low altitude night raid traveling no more than two hundred miles one way. There are no ground defenses along the route. The target group will not expect an attack because of their Nomgai location. They assume they're safe because no country would conduct a raid such as this because it violates the sovereignty of Nomgai. They think they're beyond reach. As I said, they also think no one will attack them because of the political fallout and potential military conflict which would follow."

Scoggins continued. "By using an old B-17, even if your aircraft is detected it will be assumed it's not a military plane because it will be traveling so slowly. No one will pay any attention to you."

Kate and Bebe frowned, not believing Dan Scoggins. That was the reasoning of a headquarters type they thought. However, they had no choice but to listen.

"What do you think, Bebe?" asked Kate.

"Alright, Mr. Scoggins," replied Bebe. "We'll do this if you guarantee that if we are successful, you will never bother us again."

"You have my word on that, Miss Beardsley," replied a smiling

Dan Scoggins.

"There are two other small items, Mr. Scoggins," added Bebe.

"And what are those?" asked a smiling Dan Scoggins.

"You will need to deposit five million dollars in a Swiss bank account today," she said. "I will have a bank account number for you in a couple of hours. You said you would release Kate and me from any further obligation to your agency once we accomplish the mission. We'll also need that in writing before we leave town."

Dan Scoggins looked at Bebe. His smile faded and he paused before he spoke. "And what if I say no to your proposition?" he replied.

"You won't, Mr. Scoggins," Bebe answered confidently. "You don't have anyone else as experienced with a B-17 as Kate and me. Besides, there's no one foolish enough to take on such a high risk mission. We're only doing it because we have no choice but, I can guarantee the chances of success are far better when you deposit our five million in the account. I mean, it would be a real shame if we missed the target when we dropped the bomb. I'd feel so bad about disappointing you and Mr. Farley. With the five million in the account, my aim will be much better. And, if we miss, we'll give you your money back. Besides, you know very well the odds of our getting back alive are poor to none. The more I think about it," Bebe added, "maybe five million isn't enough."

"Alright, Miss Beardsley, you have a deal," replied Scoggins, scowling because he came out in second place.

Kate was surprised that Bebe came up with the money idea. That was a good move, she thought.

Bebe and Kate left the office to go to the hotel. Scoggins told them to be at his office the day after tomorrow for a briefing on the mission. They could have the rest of the day and tomorrow off to enjoy themselves. While both women were concerned about the coming mission, they were happy they were together once again.

Their taxi reached the hotel in less than ten minutes. As they walked through the lobby Kate mentioned that she was tired because of jet lag.

"What's jet lag?" Bebe asked.

Kate laughed, remembering Bebe had never flown across the ocean in an airplane with a jet engine and rapidly changing time zones. "Let's take a quick nap and I'll tell you later."

Bebe looked at her and smiled. "I'm from 1947, Kate. I don't know about these things."

Kate laughed as the elevator doors opened and the two women stepped inside. She touched the panel lighting the # 6 button and the elevator began its ascent to the sixth floor. "Do you ever think about Ebbers Field where we first met?" asked Bebe.

"All the time," Kate answered.

# 29

Present Time    Hoginpuu, Nomgai (North Africa)

The two free days went by quickly for Bebe and Kate. They walked into OSTRO headquarters at eight a.m. on the third day to meet with Dan Scoggins and Jack Farley on the mission they were to undertake.

"Good morning, ladies," Scoggins greeted them. "I hope you enjoyed the interesting sights of our wonderful city in the last two days."

Bebe and Kate stared at Scoggins without answering. Get on with it, they were thinking, and tell us what we need to do.

"Jack will conduct the briefing," Scoggins added, handing the conversation off to Jack Farley.

Farley, who was sitting to Scoggins left, rose and walked over to a map hanging on the wall. "The first thing you'll need to do is go out to a little town in Kansas for two weeks of re-training on flying the B-17. I doubt you need it but we'll put you through the drill just the same. The mission is too important to chance any mistakes.

From there, you will fly to Nomgai, a small country in North Africa," he said, pointing to its location on the map. "Once there, you'll be joining an archaeological expedition which is excavating a site approximately two hundred miles from the target point. That is your cover.

There is a small airport approximately ten miles from this site. The owner of the airport, a man named Manus Tsugano, has rebuilt a B-17 that he normally uses to haul passengers and cargo. We have paid Mr. Tsugano to allow us to re-construct the airplane specifically for this mission. The bomb bay has been completely re-configured to carry one large bomb. This almost sounds like the mission you were on seventy years ago, doesn't it?"

"It sounds a lot like it," replied Bebe. "Let's hope it doesn't end the same way."

"Anyway," Farley said, deflecting Bebe's comment, "you will base yourselves with the archaeological team. There will be an old truck there you can use to travel to the airport the night of the mission. You will not meet Manus Tsugano until then. We'll give you a photograph and description of him so there will be no mistakes. The one bomb your airplane will carry will be smuggled into the country. We will take care of that and also make sure the bomb is installed in the bomb bay and the aircraft is mission ready. As we said at our meeting two days ago, the mission target where the Lorgenberg nukes are stored is called the Ronganai Depot."

"Mr. Farley, are you positive the nukes are there this time?" Kate asked cynically.

"They are there, Miss Darron," Dan Scoggins replied.

Farley handed Bebe a manila envelope. "These are your travel documents and tickets and twenty thousand dollars in cash. The archaeology team leader, a man named Bill O'Hanlon, will meet you at the airport when you arrive in Hoginpuu, the capital city of Nomgai.

You will get the coordinates of the target the night of the mission. On that night, you will drive to the airport and secure the B-17 in Manus Tsugano's hangar and fly to the target and drop the bomb. When you return, Manus Tsugano will put the plane into his hanger and pull the wheels off so it will appear that it was not recently flown. Also, Tsugano will disassemble the special fixture holding the bomb in the bomb bay. That way there is no way to link the bomb to him. Are there any questions?"

"What happens if we are captured, Mr. Farley?" asked Kate.

"Unfortunately, you're on your own. We will disavow any knowledge of the plot, the target site or yourselves. Nomgai is at war with the neighboring country of Goriana. It will appear that you're operating independently and you're mercenaries for Goriana. You'll probably be executed as spies. So don't get caught. By the way, Tsugano will have some side arms for you, just in case."

Bebe and Kate looked at each other. It was a given the mission was dangerous, however the planning was badly flawed. "This whole thing stinks," Bebe interjected. There are too many loose ends and opportunities for surprises."

"Jack Farley, not used to having his mission planning expertise challenged, was visibly shocked. "What are you talking about, Miss Beardsley?" he said, making no attempt to hide his irritation.

"Manus Tsugano is item number one. Who is he? How do we know he can be trusted? What kind of condition is the B-17 in? All we know for sure about the airplane is that it's seventy years old and sitting in the middle of the desert in some Third World country. If the airplane hasn't been maintained, and I'm betting it hasn't, it will fall apart on us."

"I assure you we've checked all that out, Miss Beardsley," Farley shot back.

"The hell you did," replied Bebe. Things in the field are never the way headquarters thinks."

"I wouldn't worry about it if I were you," Farley replied.

"You wouldn't worry about it because it's Kate and I, not you, who have our lives on the line."

"I told you we've been very careful about checking out Manus Tsugano and the airplane. Everything will run smoothly if you two don't screw things up," Farley said.

"We need to have our own guns, Mr. Farley," said Kate. "We're not going to rely on Manus Tsugano to give guns to us. I agree with Bebe. The planning on this mission stinks."

Dan Scoggins could see that Jack Farley was becoming increasingly upset. "Alright, ladies," he said, "the discussion is over. We'll double check on this guy Manus Tsugano. He will give you your guns, period, end of report. Anything else you're concerned about?"

"I want my own guns, Mr. Scoggins," Kate protested.

"No way," he said. "Guns might tip off the wrong people. We'll make sure Manus Tsugano gives you plenty of firepower. Next question." Kate didn't like Scoggins' answer, nor did she like Scoggins.

"What about positioning a second airplane at the archaeological dig site?" Bebe asked. That way, if things go bad, we've got a way to escape."

"There's no way we can do that," Farley said. "The government of Nomgai would never allow that. They've had a great deal of theft at their archeological sites and they would view an airplane as a way to carry stolen artifacts out of the country. You're going to have to go with what we've given you," he added.

Two weeks later they had finished their B-17 re-orientation training and flew back to Washington. After a final briefing at Dan Scoggins' office, Kate and Bebe boarded a plane at Dulles Airport to start the first leg of their long trip to Nomgai. The trip took two full days. There were no direct flights to Nomgai or anyplace close to it. They had to switch airplanes seven times before finally arriving at Nomgai's only major airport which was located in Hoginpuu.

As their plane taxied toward the passenger terminal, Kate and Bebe peered through the round window to see the airport. There wasn't much to look at. The airport consisted of a small main building and several hangars. Two small aircraft were parked on the ramp. One of them was missing a propeller. There was only one passenger aircraft in sight, an ancient DC-3, the two-engine plane first built in the 1930's.

"How many of those have we flown, Kate?" asked Bebe.

"Lots," Kate replied. "What a great airplane."

Their flight was unremarkable other than the fact the rickety two-engine propeller driven craft had actually managed to stay in the air for the two and a half hour trip. "That was fun," Bebe said mockingly, as they got up from their seats and walked toward the exit at the front of the airplane.

Kate and Bebe stepped out of the aircraft into a wall of suffocating heat. The still air offered no hint of movement and the stench of humanity and diesel fumes made breathing a sickening chore. As they walked down the portable steps they could see heat waves rising from the scorched concrete ramp. When they stepped onto it, Kate could feel its heat through the soles of her shoes.

They made their way to the terminal building and walked through a wide door above which hung a huge, faded blue sign proclaiming "Welcome to Hoginpuu, Nomgai." As they walked under the sign, Kate kept her eye on it, certain it would fall off the building at any moment.

A small sign inside the building pointed the way to customs where a very black man with a perpetual smile searched through their bags. He seemed to take extra time inspecting the area around their underwear. Then he checked their passports and asked the reason for their visit to Nomgai. Satisfied with their answer, he wished them a "very nice day."

As they walked from the customs section they saw a thin, middle-aged man in a khaki outfit waving excitedly as he hurried toward them. He was tall, gangly and his arms were flapping about.

"Welcome to Hoginpuu, Nomgai!" he exclaimed as he walked up to the two women. He reached out to shake hands and said, "I'm Bill O'Hanlon, the team leader. No, I'm not Irish, in case you were wondering."

Neither Kate nor Bebe cared whether he was Irish. They shook hands with O'Hanlon and said they were pleased to meet him, but neither really was. The man was loudmouthed and a bore, the kind of personality always accompanied by trouble.

"Everyone always asks me if I'm Irish. I wonder why," he laughed, prolonging his tedious attempt to be humorous. Kate and Bebe smiled, but each had formed an instant dislike of their host.

"It's a long ride to the site, nearly sixty miles west," O'Hanlon told them. "We can grab some lunch before we go. I have a favorite cafe." They walked out the front door of the small terminal building toward a battered maroon SUV freckled with two feet wide spots bleached white by the sun. "Sorry about all the junk in the back seat," O'Hanlon said, as they climbed into the rickety vehicle. "We'll all have to sit in front." They climbed in, Kate sitting between O'Hanlon and Bebe, and they were soon driving toward the downtown area.

Hoginpuu was barren and depressing. That most of the heavily travelled roads were unpaved resulted in every vehicle raising clouds of dust as it travelled through town. In turn, a ghostly, tan haze hovered over the dilapidated buildings and shops of the city.

There was an overabundance of bars, strip joints and ramshackle car repair shops, but little else. Motorcycles and bicycles were the preferred transportation, greatly outnumbering the few worn out cars and trucks spewing black smoke as they rumbled through the streets. The majority of people were walking, too poor to afford any other form of transportation. There were also numerous wagons pulled by mules.

Finally they arrived at the small cafe O'Hanlon swore was the best one in town. He said it was the only place in town where a person could eat and not have severe intestinal issues the next day. As they walked through the door, they noticed only one of the eight tables in the place was occupied. Two men sat at that table. Bebe saw one of them making a call on his cell phone as they sat down at a table next to the south wall. The cafe was small and had what looked like a dark colored concrete floor, but wasn't. O'Hanlon noticed Kate was staring at its deep red color.

"It's actually a dirt floor," Kate," he said. "They get that red color by mixing cow's blood with the dirt. The blood makes the dirt floor hard. Not very appetizing for a restaurant, is it?

By the way, don't drink the water," O'Hanlon warned. "The water will play hell with your innards. Have a beer, instead."

Bebe and Kate agreed that was good advice. "Three Langa," O'Hanlon called to the waitress. "Langa is the local brew," he said. "It tastes like formaldehyde, but if there's any bugs in the bottle you can be sure they're dead," he laughed. "Just spit it out if you happen to find one in your mouth after you take a swig." He laughed at his own joke. Bebe looked at Kate and laughed. What was funny was that O'Hanlon thought he was funny. He wasn't.

The waitress, whose name was Beija, was dressed in a long, bright blue, flowered skirt and white top. She smiled as she set the three beers and an opener on the table. Obviously, she was familiar with O'Hanlon's eccentricities. He wanted to open the beers himself to make sure they weren't somehow contaminated. He must be a frequent visitor, Kate and Bebe concluded.

They also noticed Beija was quite friendly with O'Hanlon. "Looks like you and the waitress are buddies," Bebe remarked. Kate smiled, knowing Bebe suspected the two were more than buddies.

"You could say that," said O'Hanlon. "I stay at her house whenever I come to the city." Kate looked toward Bebe and smiled, raising her eyebrows to acknowledge she had guessed it right.

"She's your mistress?" asked Kate. "Yeah," laughed O'Hanlon, "in a way she is. She's my mistress who charges twenty-five dollars a night. She shares her charms with others. I'm hardly the only one."

Two men walked in the door and joined the two already sitting at the table across the room. O'Hanlon opened the beers and Bebe reached for the bottle nearest her. It was warm.

"Refrigeration isn't the best in this country," O'Hanlon said. "Every once in a while we get cold beer but today isn't one of those times. The electricity isn't reliable in the dry season. Come to think of it, it's not reliable in the wet season either. Mainly because there isn't a wet season," he laughed.

Two of the men from the other table got up and walked toward Kate, Bebe and O'Hanlon. The waitress rushed across the small room and yelled something at them. The taller of the two men pushed her out of the way and she fell over a chair onto the floor. O'Hanlon, seeing what was coming, jumped to his feet and charged the two men. He threw one to the floor but the other man grabbed O'Hanlon by the neck and had a headlock on him. He proceeded to punch O'Hanlon's face repeatedly.

Bebe took a drink of her beer as she watched O'Hanlon getting pummeled. Kate was thinking about helping O'Hanlon, but the beer, even though it was warm, seemed more appealing than O'Hanlons plight.

The second man got off the floor and joined in punching O'Hanlon. The waitress ran back toward the three struggling men and plunged a knife into the neck of the man with the headlock on O'Hanlon. He fell to the floor screaming as blood gushed from his carotid artery. Bebe and Kate knew he would be dead in less than a minute. The other three men ran out the front door, leaving the waitress, Kate, Bebe and O'Hanlon to face the police.

"Damn," said Bebe, "we haven't been in town fifteen minutes and our cover is already blown." She took another drink of the ghastly hot beer.

The man lying on the floor writhed wildly for a few seconds, but soon became still, his face twisted in an agonized grimace. He emitted a final gasp and died in a pool of his own blood which was visibly shrinking as it soaked into the dirt floor.

The police soon arrived and interviewed O'Hanlon and Beija the waitress. The police chief then questioned Bebe and Kate. He wanted to know what they were doing in the country. Kate thought the chief was suspicious of them. He stared at them continuously and asked more questions than Kate and Bebe thought necessary. While the police were finishing up their investigation, the waitress cleaned up O'Hanlon's battered face. Bebe and Kate had several more beers. Food didn't seem like an appetizing option.

Finally, they were in O'Hanlon's rattletrap SUV heading west through the desert toward the dig site. The dry, ragged country had long since been stripped of its trees. There were no streams or rivers along the way, only dried up traces in the mud where water had once run. The country had been in a drought for the last three years and it showed in the parched, cracked landscape.

As they drove, O'Hanlon briefed them on the excavation. They were unearthing buildings of an ancient civilization known for their written language, very unusual for this part of Africa, he said. The dig would take a long time.

"I understand you'll only be with us for a short while," O'Hanlon said abruptly.

"Yes, that's true," Kate replied. "We're just here to observe for a few days and then we'll be leaving. We'll make sure we stay out of your way."

"Don't worry about it," replied O'Hanlon. "We just dig and sift dirt. It's a pretty routine operation. It will get a lot more interesting after you leave, I'm afraid. We'll start running into some walls and structures in a few weeks."

"Is there a small airport near the dig site?" asked Kate.

"Yes, there is," O'Hanlon replied. "It's about eight or ten miles from the site. We can go by it if you like. It's pretty much on the way, maybe a mile off the main road."

"Let's do that," replied Bebe. "That sounds interesting."

Neither Bebe nor Kate thought they were fooling O'Hanlon. They assumed he knew they weren't there to observe his routine excavation. They also figured that O'Hanlon was aware of the sensitive political climate in the country. Bebe thought he must know they were with the United States government and on some secret operation. Unfortunately, he was right. However, Kate and Bebe also thought O'Hanlon's attitude was that, whatever their true intentions, he wanted to focus on his dig and not get involved in anything else. Smart man, they concluded, but he's still boring as hell.

In an hour and a half they reached the turn-off for the small airport and O'Hanlon steered the SUV into a right turn and drove onto the dirt road. They followed the road across the rugged terrain.

Shriveled bushes dotted the desolate landscape. Thick tufts of wind-whipped brown grass were the only other vegetation. O'Hanlon stopped the truck on a small ridge several hundred yards from the airport.

Bebe and Kate looked toward the primitive hangar. O'Hanlon could have been excavating the hangar, thought Kate. It's old enough. Both women studied the airport closely. There was a dirt runway running east to west. The hangar door was partially opened and they could see the B-17's left wing. A second building, an office, was situated fifty yards west of the hangar. There were two old pickup trucks parked near the building but nothing else. There were no other airplanes. Neither Bebe nor Kate cared for the layout. They both had a bad feeling about the place.

"Seen enough?" O'Hanlon asked.

"Yes, thanks for stopping," replied Bebe.

O'Hanlon swung his old SUV around on the dirt road, stirring up a large cloud of dust. In another twenty minutes they arrived at the dig site. O'Hanlon introduced them to his crew. There were six Americans, four men and two women, and ten local men who helped dig out the dirt and perform other chores. Everyone seemed cordial enough, however Bebe and Kate would avoid making friends. They were focused on getting the mission over with as quickly as possible.

Dan Scoggins had given Kate a cell phone. He would call her to let her know when to begin the mission and tell her the target coordinates at the same time. That seemed almost preposterous, she thought. There should be a more sophisticated, secure way to contact them.

I don't like any part of this operation, Kate thought. She looked at Bebe and she glanced back. Kate could tell the operation didn't set well with her either.

# 30

Present Time    Hoginpuu, Nomgai (North Africa)

Bebe and Kate had spent two nights with the team waiting for Scoggins' call to begin their assignment. So far, there had been nothing from Scoggins. Other than watch the archaeology team digging in their respective grids, there had been little to do. The work was tedious and slow. The team had set up tent-like canvas canopies overhead to shelter them from the punishing sun. As O'Hanlon told them, the work amounted to dumping shovelfuls of dry dirt through screens in order to locate small pieces of pottery or other objects the ancient civilization had used in their daily lives. As Bebe and Kate sat down with the team for dinner the evening of the third day, Kate's phone rang. It was Dan Scoggins.

"How's the excavation going, Kate?" he asked. Scoggins had told her that when he contacted her he would talk as if he were calling about the excavation, a thinly veiled artifice to throw off anyone who might be listening in. Kate thought it was silly. If someone were listening in, they couldn't be that dumb.

"It's going very well," she said. "We're making a great progress. We've found a lot of small pieces, but nothing big yet. The best is yet to come. It will probably take a couple more weeks."

"That sounds good," replied Scoggins. Kate quickly wrote down the coordinates of the target location as Scoggins read them to her, after saying they were reference numbers of paragraphs in some archaeological journal. "Good luck with everything," he said, and hung up. She shook her head. There was nothing she liked about that guy.

They had gotten the signal to begin the mission. Bebe and Kate had made it a point to be prepared so they could leave immediately when the call came. As they rose from the dinner table set up under one of the canvas canopies, Bebe apologized that they had to skip dinner. They couldn't tell their hosts the real reason they had to leave; they merely said they would be away for the night. It was a weak explanation because there was no place to be away to. There was nothing between the dig site and Hoginpuu except the small airport and a tiny, squalid village. Certainly their hosts would have questions, however, they didn't know Bebe and Kate well enough to ask them. They were left wondering where the two mysterious women were really going and what they were up to.

Bebe and Kate slowly walked over to the truck Manus Tsugano had left at the dig site. "I'll drive," said Kate, climbing into the driver's seat of the ancient vehicle. As Kate pulled the truck away from the dig site and turned east on the main road, the sun was moving low in the sky behind them. As Kate drove, Bebe read aloud the physical description of Manus Tsugano. They needed to make sure they correctly identified the man.

Kate drove faster than O'Hanlon had on the trip from Hoginpuu. Maybe it was the tension, hanging thick in the claustrophobic cab of the speeding pickup. Or perhaps it was a mutual foreboding, the feeling she and Bebe had that something just wasn't right. That neither of them trusted Scoggins or Farley added to their anxiety. In the distance, Kate saw the dirt road leading to the small airport. It was on the left or north side of the road. The short trip had taken only ten minutes. As she slowed the truck to turn left, she turned off the truck's lights. Then she looked at Bebe. "Here we go," she said.

Bebe winked. "It will all be over soon, Kate," she said. Kate smiled as the truck headed up the slight incline to the ridge. She stopped the truck at the same spot as O'Hanlon had the day they arrived in Nomgai, parking the vehicle facing to the northeast at a forty-five degree angle to the dirt runway and the two buildings sitting parallel to it. The driver's side of the old truck faced to the southwest.

Kate and Bebe sat in the truck looking down the slope at the airport less than a half mile away in the valley below. The airport's only buildings were the shabby, unpainted office and dilapidated metal hangar sitting fifty yards to its east. The large doors on the hangar were closed. They hoped the B-17 was inside and ready to go.

"This entire country is covered with dust," Bebe said, as she looked down the north slope of the ridge and the airport below them. Dusk had slowly spread across the valley and the sun's last rays pierced the hovering cloud of tan dust illuminating it with an otherworldly orange glow. The airport's office and hangar took on an eerie luminescence in the setting sun, casting elongated El Greco shadows across the desert floor. There were no airplanes or vehicles and no sign of activity. Other than a dim light in the small office, the airport appeared deserted.

"I don't like it," Bebe said. "It's too quiet and looks spooky as hell."

"I'm not crazy about it either," replied Kate. "It doesn't look right does it?"

"It doesn't feel right either," Bebe replied, turning around and looking through the truck's rear window."

"What," Kate said.

Bebe was staring at the bed of the thirty-year old vehicle. It was beaten up, dented and had no tailgate.

"Kate, how about you get in the back of the truck and stay hidden. I'll drive up to the small office and park west of it, but facing the hangar. You can slip out the back of the truck bed and move along the wall to the back door of the office. I'll go inside and tell them I came alone. If anything goes wrong, it's up to you to get us out of it. Besides, you're better with a gun than I am," Bebe added.

"Yeah," said Kate, "except I don't have a gun."

"I know," laughed Bebe. "Improvise."

"Funny," replied Kate, as she yanked the plastic cover off the truck's dome light and popped out the bulb. "Here I go," she said, opening the driver's door and sliding off the seat to the ground. Crouching low, she moved around the side of the truck and climbed into the bed through the tailgate opening. Keeping her head down, she slid forward on her stomach. Bebe moved across the seat and behind the steering wheel. She put the old truck in first gear and started driving down the ridge toward the airport.

Bebe drove the truck to the edge of the dirt runway, crossed over it, and headed to the west side of the small office. She turned the truck to face east as she pulled up to the tiny wooden building, parking the truck in a spot where the inside of the bed could not be seen from the office windows. Kate lay prone in the truck bed waiting to make her move when Bebe knocked on the office door.

Bebe climbed out of the truck and slowly walked toward the door of the office. She knocked once. The door was opened by a Middle Eastern looking man with a long beard and dressed in dark clothing and a white turban.

"Come in," he smiled, "we have been waiting for you."

Bebe hesitated. "May I ask who you are?"

"Yes Madam," the man smiled. "I am Manus Tsugano."

The description of Manus Tsugano did not include a long beard. This was clearly not him.

"I see," replied Bebe, not moving as she tried to look past the man into the office. However, the bearded man was now pointing a gun at her stomach.

"You will please come in, madam," ordered the man. "Where is your friend?"

"I had to come alone," Bebe answered. "She became ill." Bebe wasn't sure the man believed her.

As Bebe walked into the building, three other men emerged from the back room of the small office. One of them was the police chief they met after O'Hanlon's cafe brawl in Hoginpuu on the day they arrived. Bebe had worried about him, knowing he was suspicious of her and Kate. She remembered he had asked them a lot of questions. Bebe figured they would run into him again, and here he was, holding a pistol pointed at her.

The second man was Manus Tsugano and he had a large stack of American dollars in his hand. Manus Tsugano, OSTRO's trusted agent, had sold them out. Bebe wasn't really surprised. She had a bad feeling something like this might happen. That was why she told Kate to hide in the truck bed and come in the back door. Kate's not having a gun was going to be a real problem, she thought.

"You Americans bring very good money," Manus Tsugano laughed. "I get money from the Americans to help them and I get money from the Nomgai Rebels when I sell them the Americans. Life is good!"

Great, thought Bebe.

As Kate slipped out of the back of the truck, two loud gunshots boomed inside the office. She moved over near the office window to look inside. A man lay on the floor with a large quantity of American dollars scattered near his body. From the photograph and description she had studied, it had to be Manus Tsugano. He had landed on his back and Kate could see an oozing, reddish hole in his forehead and a bloody wound in his midsection. His eyes stared blankly at the ceiling. Then Kate saw the man who shot him, the police chief from the cafe. He was laughing as he gestured with his gun.

Two other men stood near Bebe, one pointing a gun at her. As the police chief stooped to pick up the money, the other two men walked toward the front door with Bebe.

Kate quickly ran around to the back door, slowly opening it and sticking her head inside to listen. She heard a door slam in the next room and figured the police chief had finished gathering the money and left to join the other men on the front porch.

Kate slowly stepped inside the small, dark room. The only illumination was faint light from the main office seeping underneath the door. As her eyes adjusted, she saw a large metal desk directly in front of her. It was the only piece of furniture in the room and it sat at an angle, almost as if someone had tossed it aside to get it out of the way. She must find a weapon, anything, she thought, as she quietly pulled open the desk drawers one by one. There was nothing.

She crept over to the door leading into the main office, quietly opened it a crack, and peeked in. The office was dimly lighted and sparsely furnished. A worn out wooden desk piled high with papers sat to her left. There were three equally decrepit wood chairs, one without a back, scattered about the room. An antiquated refrigerator painted dark green stood against the west wall on her right. There was nothing else in the room except Manus Tsugano's bloodied body.

Kate lay down on her stomach and quietly pulled herself toward the dead man. As she expected, the money, which had been scattered on the floor, was gone. As she moved to the right side of Tsugano's body, she had some luck. There was a pistol in Manus Tsugano's belt. Kate grasped the gun and pulled it from the dead man's belt. She checked to make sure it was loaded. It was.

Still on her stomach, she stealthily moved across the floor to the office's front wall then momentarily paused to look at the window above her. The porch light was on and she could see men's shadows on the thin curtain. Their voices were loud and their laughter was celebratory. They had come here with money to buy the American women. They had only one woman, but all of their money, plus the additional money OSTRO agents had given Manus Tsugano.

Kate cautiously rose from the floor, taking care to stay to the right of the window so the men on the front porch would not see her shadow on the curtain. Putting her right index finger on the curtain's edge, she pushed it back a tiny crack. She squinted to see through the sliver of an opening between the curtain's cloth and the wall.

The bearded man had his gun pointed at Bebe and the police chief was holding a black leather bag. He's the money guy, Kate thought. Both men had their backs to the window. The police chief's gun was in his holster. The third man had apparently gone to the hangar, probably to get a vehicle hidden there.

The hoarse rumble of a truck engine grew increasingly louder and Kate peeked through the window. The truck was approaching from the direction of the hangar and Kate knew she would have to make her move. She quietly stepped toward the front door, waiting for the truck to pull up and stop in front of the two men and Bebe. The squeaking of dusty brakes signaled the truck was slowing as it neared the porch. Kate kicked open the office door, the crashing sound of her boot signaling Bebe to instantly throw herself to the porch floor even before Kate yelled, "Duck!"

"Kate pulled the trigger and shot the bearded man twice in the back of his head. The police chief dropped the black bag and was turning to confront Kate when she shot him once in his left temple. Blood gushed from the bullet hole and splashed down on Bebe as the mortally wounded man fell away to his right. Kate turned her gun toward the truck and fired three times, the shots smashing through the truck's windshield. Two of the bullets struck the driver's face before he could aim the gun he'd pulled from his belt.

Warily, Bebe raised her head and looked around, then slowly rose from the porch. "That was good shooting," she said, surveying the two bodies lying on the porch and the third man slumped behind the bullet-pocked windshield. She raised her hand to wipe the police chief's blood from her face and looked at Kate. Bebe's shocked expression reflected her awe at Kate's coolness and killing efficiency.

But Kate was trembling. She had never killed anyone before. No, that wasn't true. There was the Lorgenberg bombing. She and Bebe had killed hundreds when they dropped their bombs on the Nazi facility. But the victims at Lorgenberg were anonymous. She had never seen them nor would she ever see them. It was different, she thought, but then shook her head.

But killing these men today, was not the same. It was not as impersonal as Lorgenberg. She could see the injuries of the men that lay before her. She had inflicted those fatal wounds. It was she who put the bullets into their bodies. The bearded man's body momentarily quivered. For a brief moment she thought, even hoped, that he might be alive. But he was not. She had taken his life and the other men's lives. She remembered the deer her father made her kill and again looked at the three bodies before her. It was not so easy to kill. Kate walked past Bebe and around the corner of the building and threw up.

Several minutes later Kate walked around the building's corner onto the front porch. Bebe had gone inside to clean up and Kate walked to the front door and looked in. Manus Tsugano's body lay on the dusty floor in the center of the small office. Bebe stood at a dirty sink in the corner wiping her face with a blood splotched white towel. "You think those guys are part of the Ronganai Depot group?" Bebe asked.

"That's the way I have it figured," Kate answered.

During his briefing, Jack Farley mentioned the Ronganai group was actually part of the government of Nomgai which the United Nations labeled one of the most brutal and dangerous dictatorships. Ronganai not only sold nukes, but other powerful weapons as well. The weapons trade was a huge revenue producer for the Nomgai government.

"There is a civil war raging in Nomgai," Farley said, "and a large rebel group is trying to overthrow the Nomgai government. They are led by a man named Tarsus Mudja who is just as cold-blooded as the Ronganai group. Stay out of the local politics," Farley warned. "And don't get caught. Either group would love to take two American women hostage."

"Tsugano must be the one who tipped those guys off," Kate said.

Bebe, looking at Kate in the cracked hazy mirror above the sink, nodded in agreement. "It had to be him," she replied, "but it doesn't much matter at this point. What matters now is that get out of here. This place gives me the creeps."

Kate and Bebe moved quickly now. They took five guns from the dead men, two Glocks, a 38 caliber six shot revolver and two smaller pistols the men had in their boots. Bebe grabbed the black leather bag holding Manus Tsugano's money plus the money the men brought to pay Manus Tsugano for betraying the two American women. "One of them mentioned there was two hundred and fifty thousand dollars in this bag," said Bebe. "That might come in handy."

The mission was not beginning as planned and probably wouldn't end as planned. They would have to come up with a different exit strategy. There was no way they could come back to this place. "Yeah," Bebe said, "that two hundred and fifty thousand will definitely come in handy."

Bebe and Kate held their guns ready, carefully watching for any sign of movement as they walked toward the dilapidated hangar. It was difficult to see as there were no outside lights and daylight was nearly gone. They reached the building, pausing momentarily before quietly inching through a small doorway. Inside the building it was pitch black and visibility was zero. They crept along the back wall for several feet groping for a light switch. "Get down," Bebe whispered. They crouched down ready to fire their guns when Bebe flipped the switch. The weak lighting improved the visibility, but not greatly. The big B-17 sat in the middle of the hangar occupying most of its space.

Kate saw a second light switch on the south wall. Scanning for trouble in the hangar's dark corners, and with her gun still drawn, Kate ran across the hard dirt floor of the hangar and flipped the light switch. The large room was now brightly lit by the large ceiling lights. The B-17's faded tan camouflage paint didn't diminish its ominous appearance. Regardless of what it had been used for in its recent past, the airplane had been built seventy years earlier for two reasons only-destruction and death. That's what it would be used for tonight.

There were two small planes near the back of the hangar. One plane's engine had been for removed for maintenance and was hanging on nearby chains. The other plane must have been stored inside for Manus Tsugano's own use.

"What do you think, Bebe?" Kate asked.

"Let's take a look."

Still holding their pistols, the two women walked to the side exit door behind the right wing of the B-17. They didn't know if anyone else was lurking about, perhaps even inside the airplane. Bebe pulled the metal door open, carefully looked inside then stepped into the plane and crept toward the cockpit. As she walked past the bomb bay she saw the menacing appearing bomb they were to deliver to the target two hundred miles away. Kate was outside the airplane, checking it over to make sure it was ready to fly. Everything looked okay.

Bebe climbed back out the side exit door and walked over to where Kate stood. She put her hand on Kate's. "We'll make it this time," she said. "Find a backpack for this bag of money so it will be easier to carry. Oh yeah, and see if Manus Tsugano has any desert survival kits stashed around the hangar. I didn't see any in the airplane."

Kate quickly searched the hangar and came up with a worn out backpack a mechanic had been using to hold his tools. There were no survival kits, however. She walked over to Bebe and opened the backpack and they stuffed the money inside.

The two women assumed that if there were other bad guys outside the hangar they would have shown themselves by now. Everything appeared quiet. They decided that Kate would push the hangar's big doors open while Bebe started the airplane's engines.

The hangar doors rested on small metal wheels which allowed the doors to be rolled to an open or closed position. The massive doors were heavy, and even though they moved on rollers and a steel track, Kate wondered if she was strong enough to push them completely open. As she struggled with the doors, Bebe got engine numbers one and two running. Engine number three's propeller was slowly beginning to turn and suddenly started up with a burst of black smoke. Number four propeller was turning and quickly caught.

Kate wished the hangar doors were powered, but she managed to wrestle them open after what seemed like a long time. She ran through the hangar which had filled with smoke and exhaust from the B-17's engines. Reaching the side exit door of the airplane, she jumped in and pulled the door shut behind her. Kate quickly made her way to the cockpit and touched Bebe on her shoulder.

Bebe pushed the throttles and the airplane slowly rolled forward. As the B-17 moved out of the hangar, Bebe steered into a rolling right turn to the west and the light breeze blowing toward the airplane. She and Kate wanted to get airborne fast, concerned that they might encounter other hostiles.

Bebe eased the throttles forward and the airplane lumbered down the dirt runway gradually picking up speed. They soon felt the tail lift and moments later the plane slowly lifted off the dirt strip into the air. As soon as they reached one thousand feet, Bebe turned the plane left for a one hundred and eighty degree turn.

Part of their training in Kansas had been on learning to operate a state of the art autopilot bomb-targeting device. Neither Kate nor Bebe understood it completely, but they didn't care. Their job was to fly the airplane to within a few minutes of the target, flip the switch and the device would fly the airplane to the target coordinates and automatically release the single bomb. It was a lot simpler than the ancient Norden bomb-sight which had required a bombardier. My god, that was seventy years ago, Kate thought.

Bebe and Kate wondered why they were even needed to fly this mission. Anyone could get the B-17 in the air and turn it over to the autopilot-targeting device. That it specifically had to be them flying the airplane didn't make any sense. But they remembered OSTRO had reasons for everything it did. And that's what worried them.

It would take nearly an hour to reach the target. Bebe and Kate agreed they would not return to Manus Tsugano's airport where they took off. Kate checked the map and the two women decided that once the bomb was dropped, they would fly on to Tumburu, a large city in the neighboring country of Goriana. Tumburu was fifty-three miles on the other side of the Nomgai-Goriana border.

Kate grabbed the flashlight and walked back into the B-17's fuselage. Since getting into the airplane, she had an uneasy feeling but didn't know why. She moved past the bomb bay and its lethal cargo and walked further back past the waist gunner's section. The ball turret below and to the rear of the wings had long ago been removed, as had the tower turret. Everything seemed to be in order.

As she walked back through the bomb bay to return to the cockpit, her flashlight's beam glanced what she thought was a small black box. She turned the light back, focusing on a twelve-inch square black box attached to the wall above the large bomb. She moved closer, shining her light above and below the box.

At first, she thought it was a self-contained unit, but then she saw a tiny black wire running from the bottom of the box down to the corner of the bomb bay. She shined her light to her left and looked more closely. The wire was attached to a second much smaller black box. What was this thing, she wondered.

Kate, like Bebe, knew every inch of the B-17. She had never seen anything like these black boxes before. A dark thought crept into her mind. What if this is a bomb triggered to explode after the main bomb is dropped? That would destroy the airplane and eliminate any connection the United States might have to the attack. Maybe Bebe and I are only along for the ride so when the bomber crashes there will be two unidentifiable bodies in the wreckage.

It was a terrible thought, but OSTRO was a terrible group of people. Murdering Kate and Bebe would be of no consequence to them. They had already tried to do it once. Dan Scoggins and Jack Farley had made it very clear they considered the two women expendable.

Kate quickly moved forward through the airplane and climbed into the co-pilot's chair beside Bebe. "I think we've been set up," she said. "I think there's a second bomb attached to the wall above the bomb bay which will blow up the airplane after we drop the main bomb. I'll take over and you go look at it?"

Bebe climbed out of the pilot's seat, grabbed Kate's flashlight and hurried toward the bomb bay of the airplane. She flashed the light on the bomb bay wall and saw the black box. She immediately knew it had no function with regard to the airplane. It had to be a bomb.

Bebe returned to the cockpit. "It's a bomb," she said. "Once we drop the big one, it will detonate and blow us out of the sky."

"We're twenty minutes from the target," replied Kate. "Do you think we can trust those parachutes hanging in back?"

"We have no choice," said Bebe. "We have to gamble the chutes are okay. I'll flip the switch for the auto-pilot bomb targeting device," she said. "We'll bail out now. The bomb will destroy the target, the plane will blow up and they'll think we're dead. I hope."

"It's just like the escape plan we set up on our mission in 1942," Kate said. "Of course, we might end up dead anyway. Who knows what we'll be parachuting into?"

"Let's get those parachutes on," said Bebe, sticking the map into her shirt.

Bebe slung the backpack holding the money over her chest and followed Kate to the back of the airplane. They selected two parachutes from the four that were hanging on the side of the fuselage and helped each other strap them on.

Bebe and Kate looked at each other, both aware it would be a dangerous jump. They were less than eight minutes from the target as Kate pulled the handle on the exit door. "Are you ready to go?" she asked.

"Almost," said Bebe, and she put her hand on the back of Kate's head. "Good luck Kate," she said.

"Is that all you can say?" Kate asked, leaning forward to kiss Bebe on the cheek.

Bebe smiled. "Like I said, we'll make it this time."

Kate put her hand on Bebe's left cheek, then turned and stepped through the door into the blackness. Bebe quickly followed Kate through the door into the night sky and fell toward the dark earth.

The moon was bright and the two women watched each other's parachutes float slowly downward. A slight breeze from the west was carrying them eastward, but as Kate descended to one hundred feet, the ground appeared to be racing sideways as if she was driving over it in a fast moving car. The breeze was light, but gusting dangerously, at least fifteen or twenty miles per hour, she guessed.

"Damn, it'll be a hard landing!" She quickly looked up at Bebe's chute then downward at the dark earth rapidly closing on her. She braced herself, her knees not locked, positioned so the balls of her feet would strike the ground first and she could fall sideways to distribute the shock of the landing along her body. But it was too dark to see and she slammed onto the rocky desert floor.

# 31

Present Time     Nomgai Desert (North Africa)

Bebe dangled from her parachute as the ground drew nearer. In the bright moonlight, she had watched Kate land to the southwest, which she now faced. The breeze was pushing her eastward and she would come down about a quarter mile or more from Kate's touchdown point. She thought she could see lights, fires, perhaps ten miles to the south.

Bebe braced for the landing, intent on rolling into a controlled fall to absorb the shock of colliding with the earth. But, like Kate, she couldn't see the ground, only an opaque immensity of moonlit twisted profiles of the desert's trees.

Suddenly she rammed into the hard earth; her legs instantly buckling as she crashed onto her back. There was a harsh crack as her helmet struck. So much for the controlled landing, Bebe thought. She lay dazed, wondering if she was injured.

She moved her arms, then her legs. There was a slight pain in her right knee, but nothing else hurt except her head. However, it was throbbing painfully. Her ears were ringing. Slowly, she sat up and bent her head forward. "Oh," she moaned, as she took off her helmet. She reached back with her hand and felt a large bump and wetness. She pulled her hand back; her fingers were covered with blood.

Feeling dizzy, Bebe sat for another minute or so. She was thinking about standing up when she heard a loud rumble in the distance. The bomb, she thought, as the sound echoed in the black mountains north of her. Moments later, there was a second explosion, this one smaller. "The airplane, she mumbled. "Mission accomplished." She put her hands on the dusty earth and pushed, rising to stand.

Bebe needed water and she needed to find Kate. When they parachuted into the Nomgai wilderness, the only equipment they had were their guns and two bottles of water Kate brought from the archaeological dig site. She figured Kate brought the water when they bailed out. She probably had the flashlight too. "I wish I had it," Bebe thought.

Woozy from the pain and fighting to keep her balance, Bebe rolled up the parachute, tying it into a backpack so it could be more easily carried. She looked toward the south, the general direction of where she thought Kate might be. "Kate," she yelled abruptly, chancing Kate might hear. There was no response.

She looked at her watch and started walking. It should take about ten minutes to reach Kate, she thought. Using her watch was the only way Bebe could keep track of how far she'd gone. She didn't want to wander aimlessly and become separated from Kate or lost.

Actually, she was already lost, she thought, but if she found Kate, she wouldn't be. They would both be lost together at that point, but that was different than being lost-lost, she laughed. "I feel like I'm drunk. I'm dizzy, confused.... I think I've got a concussion."

She would walk ten minutes, find a high spot and try to spot Kate's collapsed parachute in the moonlight. Although the moonlight was helpful, it was hardly sufficient but Bebe still hoped she could find Kate tonight. Maybe Kate was injured when she landed. "Kate," she yelled. "Kate." Again, there was no answer.

Though she was light-headed, Bebe kept walking. She checked her watch. Seven minutes had passed. She bumped against plants she couldn't see and thorns from unfriendly bushes poked through her jeans. There were random clear areas completely devoid of vegetation. That was easy walking, or would have been, if she weren't so dizzy. She stopped for a moment, afraid she would fall on her face. She took a deep breath and walked on.

She remembered she had seen what she thought were fires in the south. When she found Kate, they would head in that direction. "Kate," she yelled. "Kate."

Although days in the desert are unbearably hot, nights are bitterly cold. Bebe was wearing a jacket, but the evening's rapidly cooling air was penetrating her clothes. She thought about Kate. If she was injured, she could use her parachute to keep warm. But what if she wasn't conscious? She could freeze if she wasn't covered up. Bebe looked at her watch. Eleven minutes had passed.

Bebe had to remain calm and stick to her plan. Her concussion was sparking wild ideas in her brain, tempting her to venture further into the desert to find Kate. "No," she said firmly, "I've got to stay in one place. If I go wandering, I won't know where the hell I am. I'll never find Kate if I go stumbling around out there. We'll both die."

"Kate," she screamed. "Kate. Kate, answer me. Kate. Damn it, Kate. Answer me."

Bebe was becoming worried. She knew Kate had to be close, probably within a few hundred yards. Why won't she answer?

"Kate. Kate, where are you?" Bebe yelled.

She suddenly collapsed, landing in a sitting position. She struggled to get up, but instead, slumped backwards to the ground. She was breathing rapidly and her head was pounding. "God, that hurts," she gasped. She lay unable to move, staring through the blackness at the stars. She stared for a long while. The sky had cleared, and without the light pollution of a nearby city, she could see the entire universe, she thought, or at least the Milky Way.

"The ancients were right," she babbled. "There is a big black curtain above the earth. And the planet is flat, not round. Screw Columbus. He got it all wrong," she screamed. "The earth is flat and it has a big black ceiling to protect us from the light of the universe which is heaven and where God is. Those things we call stars are holes in the ceiling and the light of heaven shines through them. I'd like to go there," she murmured. "Yeah, I want to go there with Kate. I love Kate."

"Kate," she called. "Kate. Answer me."

Bebe held her fists against her eyes, but the pain wouldn't go away. "Water," she called out. "I need water."

"Wait a minute," she splutterd in amazement, her eyes focused on the bright moon. "Look at that hole in the ceiling. That's a big, big hole." She was slurring her words and drifting toward unconsciousness. "I think I'm drunk. I gotta go home now. Who's gonna drive? I can't drive. No, I can drive. I'll drive. I feel better now, No, I can't drive. Kate. Kate. Get the car. Get the car. I'll get us home. Don't worry. Kate," she yelled weakly. "Kate," she sighed, and closed her eyes.

Kate lay on the ground stunned. She had been trained in parachute jumps and bailed out once before when a P-36 fighter plane she was flying lost its engine over Lake Michigan. Splashing into the cold water wasn't fun, but there was little wind that day and it was an easy jump. But this jump was a tough one. A night jump meant limited visibility and a vigorous crosswind assured a tricky touchdown.

However, touchdowns are always a bit tricky. In the ideal landing, the jumper's legs are bent and she braces herself, but at the same time, stays loose so as not to break a leg. Kate had these things in mind as she drifted downward, but with the nasty conditions, her landing became an uncontrollable crash.

She knew she came in hard and bounced a couple of times, but the details escaped her. The pain did not. Her body ached all over, but luckily, she had no serious injuries. She would be hurting for days, she decided.

She pulled herself to a sitting position then stood up. She unstrapped the parachute harness and rolled it into a rectangular backpack shape. It would keep her warm at night and shelter her from the sun during the day. She pondered whether she should try to find Bebe or stay put.

Because of the wind's direction, she knew Bebe landed northeast of her. Although they hadn't really discussed it, she reasoned that they would have to go south to Hoginpuu to find a way out of the country. There was nothing to the north, and even if there was, they were ill equipped to take a long desert hike. Hoginpuu, approximately fifty miles to the south, would itself be plenty difficult. Since they were going to travel south, Kate figured she should stay where she was and wait for Bebe to come to her. Kate checked her watch. She would give Bebe twenty or thirty minutes to find her. If Bebe didn't show up, she'd go looking for her.

Kate suddenly remembered she had a flashlight. She took it out and shined it toward the northeast where Bebe had come down.

"Bebe," she yelled. "Bebe." She listened for a moment; there was no answer. She called Bebe's name several more times, but got no response. She knelt to sit down, the sharp pain in her back reminding her that when one performs a parachute landing, she is supposed to roll on the ground, not bounce on it. She leaned to her right and lay down, putting her head on the rolled up parachute. Every move was accompanied by pain.

She looked at her watch. Only four minutes had passed. She lay there a while longer then sat up. She checked her watch. Six minutes had passed. She slowly rose to her feet. It was then she heard the faint sound of Bebe calling her name. She wasn't far away.

Kate looked into the darkness toward the northeast. Shining the flashlight northeast, "Bebe," she yelled back. "Bebe, where are you?" There was no answer. She called out another half dozen times, but Bebe didn't respond. She flashed the light skyward. She must be able to see the light, Kate thought. Why can't she hear me? Maybe she's behind a ridge or a stand of trees. Fighting an urge to walk toward the direction of Bebe's call, Kate decided she should wait.

A short time later, she heard Bebe calling to her again. She was much closer now. Kate immediately turned on the flashlight and waved it in the direction from which Bebe's voice had come. "Bebe," she shouted. "Bebe." She called several more times, but Bebe didn't acknowledge Kate's yells. However, Kate could hear Bebe's voice. Strangely, she was talking in a normal tone, making no effort to get Kate's attention.

Kate began walking toward the sound of Bebe's voice. She couldn't be more than twenty-five yards away, thought Kate. As she walked to the northeast, the sound of Bebe's voice grew stronger. Ahead, Kate saw a large tree silhouetted in the moonlight. She could hear Bebe's voice plainly now and moved quickly toward the tree with her flashlight beamed directly at it. Can't she see the light, Kate wondered, but Bebe's voice had become silent. She finally reached the small clearing near the tree and Bebe appeared in the flashlight's faint ray. She lay unconscious.

Bebe groaned, putting her hand on the back of her head. "Oh, that hurts," she sighed. She opened her eyes but couldn't see because of a damp cloth covering her face. She reached and pulled it off and looked around the small room where she lay in a single bed. Where am I, she wondered. There was noise outside, the sound of laughter and children playing. People were talking excitedly, but in a language she couldn't understand. She raised her head, then moved higher and rested on her elbows.

But, she crumpled back on the pillow. The effort had been too much. She stared at the ceiling pondering where she was and how she'd gotten here. A smiling black woman in a brightly colored sarong-style skirt entered the room. "How you feel, missy?" she asked.

"I'm okay," Bebe replied. "Where am I?"

"You here in Kitremi with me," she said. "This my house."

"And who are you?"

"I Mama Paloo and I fix you up. You got big bump on head."

"Are you a doctor?" Bebe asked.

"No doctor," Mama Paloo laughed, "just fix people."

"How long have I been here?" Bebe asked.

"You sleep three days. We wake you up to feed you. Head hurt now?"

"Yeah," Bebe said. "It hurts now."

Mama Paloo laughed. "You be back number one in few days."

"Is Kate here?" Bebe asked.

"Yeah she here in Kitremi right now." You eat this," Mama Paloo said, handing Bebe a bowl of a gray, mush-like concoction.

"What is it?" Bebe asked as she looked into the wooden bowl.

Mama Paloo smiled. "No tell you." Then she turned and walked out. The gray mush didn't look appealing, but Bebe was starved and gulped it down. It tasted pretty good. She went back to sleep.

It seemed like she'd only been sleeping five minutes when she was awakened by the sound of screaming outside Mama Paloo's little house. Mama Paloo suddenly burst through the doorway. "You must hide," she whispered loudly. "Government soldiers come to village. You hide."

Though drowsy, Bebe immediately understood. "Where do I hide?" she said.

"Go into pantry," Mama Paloo whispered, pointing to the tiny closet across the room. "Close door."

"The pantry?" Bebe asked, startled. "I'm sure they'll never look there," she said facetiously. But she didn't argue as she struggled to climb out of the bed and stand. The sound of gunshots outside helped clear her head. As she scurried across the room toward the pantry, she felt the Glock still stuck in the left side of her belt.

She ducked inside the tight enclosure and pulled the flimsy door closed just as three soldiers with rifles burst into the room. "You get out my house," Mama Paloo screamed.

Bebe watched through the slats of the pantry door as one of the soldiers pushed Mama Paloo backwards and pulled a machete from his belt. The other two soldiers grabbed her arms and threw her onto the kitchen table facedown. As they held her firmly, the soldier raised the machete and said, "We know who you are," just as gunshots blasted from the pantry. Bebe's two bullets tore through his chest and he lurched backwards and fell to the floor.

Two more shots boomed and a second soldier staggered, his lifeless body falling near the other man. The third soldier had run to the front door. As he pulled it open, Bebe fired twice as two other shots cracked from the outside. The soldier was killed instantly in the deadly crossfire and slumped in the doorway.

"You okay in there?" a voice called. It was Kate.

"Yeah, I'm as good as new," Bebe answered.

"I okay too," Mama Paloo said.

Bebe rested on the bed listening to Kate talk. There had been seven soldiers in all. Of the other four, Kate had shot two of them, and two others had been killed by men from the village. As the men carried the dead soldiers from Mama Paloo's house, Kate brought Bebe up to date about how she found her in the desert and managed to bring her to Kitremi.

"I heard you call to me a couple of times," Kate said. "I kept calling you back, but you never answered. But I could hear your voice. You were rambling on about something and I just followed the sound. When I got to where you were, I could see you had a concussion so I decided we better stay put until morning. At the first sight of daylight, I put together a litter out of some tree branches and one of the parachutes.

I dragged the litter for nearly four hours when I came across a dirt

244

road. I was exhausted and we were out of water so I stopped to rest in the shade of a small tree. You were still unconscious. The sun was high and the heat was unbearable. I left you for a few minutes and tried to find some food. When I got back, I saw Mama Paloo kneeling next to you and giving you water. She was an angel from heaven. She was travelling to Kitremi with her mule and little wagon.

Although I never saw anyone else, Mama Paloo told me the road was heavily travelled and lots of government soldiers used it. She brought us here and you know the rest. When Mama Paloo came across us, we were about eight miles from Kitremi. It would have taken me two days to get us here, and with no food and water, I don't know if we would have made it."

Mama Paloo, who had been outside, walked into the room and asked Bebe how she felt. "I'm okay," Bebe said.

"You get plenty rest," Mama Paloo said. "You be fine."

"What about the dead soldiers and their truck?" Kate asked. "Our people take them far away. Make it look like they get killed by rebels."

"Mama Paloo, is there anyone who could take us to Hoginpuu?"

"I tell Nee take you there," she replied. "But, you should not go there. It bad place. You die there."

Kate already knew it was a bad place to go, but there was no other city for hundreds of miles. While she was pulling Bebe on the litter, Kate had made a plan. They would travel to Hoginpuu and stay under cover until dark. Then they would go to the airport, steal an airplane, and fly out of the country. "Simple enough," she had said to herself, knowing it really wouldn't be.

She knew it was a gamble there would actually be a plane at the airport. There were only a few there when they landed one week earlier, but there was no other choice. If there was no airplane, they'd steal a car. Hoginpuu was their only option, but it was a dangerous one.

The police would be looking for the killers of the police chief and the three other men. And they needed to change their names and travel under the radar. She didn't want OSTRO to find out they were alive.

"I must leave village now," Mama Paloo said abruptly. "You go too. Soldiers come back. Always come back. You go Nee." Mama

Paloo walked out the front door and climbed into her little wagon.

"Bebe, are you okay to travel? We have to leave here today."

"Yeah, I'm okay, Kate. Let's get out of here while we still can. I've got some real bad vibes."

"Bad vibes about Kitremi?"

"Bad vibes about everything," Bebe answered.

"You rest while I go see Nee," Kate said.

Nee's bleached wood shack was located at the edge of the village. Kate knocked on the door, but there was no answer. She knocked again and a skinny, rough looking man pulled the door open. Kate smiled, but before she could speak, the man said, "Mama Paloo say you go Hoginpuu with me. We go one hour." Then he closed the door.

Kate returned to Mama Paloo's house and woke Bebe. "We're leaving in an hour," Kate said. "Let's see if we can find some canteens. We'll need to carry plenty of water."

They would travel light so it didn't take them long to pack. The most important items were the backpack with the two hundred and fifty thousand dollars, their guns, and food and water. Once everything was ready, they walked to Nee's house.

Nee was standing next to a mule-drawn wagon, similar to the one owned by Mama Paloo. He waved when he saw them coming. "We go now," he said, as they walked up to him. Kate nodded her head in agreement and asked if Bebe could lie in the back of the cart. Bebe climbed in and lay down, putting the backpack full of money under her head. "Expensive pillow," she smiled.

The man steered the donkey south and they began to walk. "We go through desert," Nee said. That was obvious, Kate thought. I wonder why he would say that. She soon found out. They were not going to take the main road to Hoginpuu. "Too many soldiers," Nee told them. "Trail is safe. We take it."

What Nee called a trail was little more than a trace that often disappeared completely as it meandered across the monotonous flat expanse. There was the occasional ridge, and the little mule labored as it pulled the wagon up the rise.

Nee and Kate walked ahead of the mule and Bebe slept in the

wagon covered with a light blanket to shield her from the sun. Nee told Kate that Hoginpuu was thirty miles south of Kitremi and they would travel half way today and spend the night in the desert. They would arrive in Hoginpuu early tomorrow afternoon.

Kate gazed at the trail winding aimlessly across the heated desert, wondering why it didn't follow a straight line. That's the shortest distance between two points, she pondered. She would ask Nee about that at the next stop.

The temperature was approaching one hundred degrees and Kate was getting concerned. Nee must have felt the heat too because he stopped to rest at every stand of trees they came across. "Trail follow trees," he said. That answered Kate's question as to why the trail randomly veered off into wide turns. Walking in the desert's heat required frequent stops in shaded spots.

"No water here now," Nee said during one stop. Apparently the stop was once an oasis, but the drought took away the water.

Kate was hoping to see Hoginpuu in the distance, but it was still twenty miles further. There was nothing ahead but the desert, its stunted trees and dwarf-like bushes stretching into the far horizon. Other than the heat, it was good terrain for hiking. Kate figured they were walking at about three miles per hour, but they were resting often. They were averaging much less than that.

Dusk was upon them and Nee pointed to a stand of trees a half-mile ahead and said they would spend the night there. It sounded good to Kate. She was looking forward to food and sleep. She had checked with Bebe throughout the day and made sure she had plenty of water and food. Bebe said she was getting stronger, but slept the entire afternoon.

Mid-afternoon the following day they reached the outskirts of Hoginpuu and were within sight of the airport. They told Nee he was no longer needed and Kate offered to pay him, but he refused. "Mama Paloo say no charge," he said. Kate insisted he take one hundred dollars. Smiling, he reached for the money, turned his mule and cart around and headed back north. Kate and Bebe hid in the desert and waited for darkness. Bebe continued to sleep. Several hours later, they walked a quarter mile to a street and waved down a taxi.

"Take us to the airport," Bebe said.

# 32

Present Time     Hoginpuu, Nomgai (North Africa)

Several small buildings similar to the rundown office at Manus Tsugano's airfield lined the cracked taxiway. Bebe remembered when they flew in a week earlier Kate had remarked that it looked like a giant spider had built a web in the taxiway's concrete. "There's not an airplane in sight," Bebe said in disgust. "This is the first airport I've ever been that doesn't have any airplanes."

They walked past the shabby buildings, not sure what they expected to find. A heavyset white man was working inside one of them. He was the only white man they'd seen other than those on the archaeological team.

"What do you think, Kate?" Bebe asked.

"It's worth a try," she answered.

The two women walked up to the small building, a tiny wooden structure with faded green paint and dirty windows, and knocked on the door. Through the dusty window they saw the man walk to the door. When he pulled it opened, he was plainly startled that two attractive white women were standing before him. Bebe and Kate were equally taken aback by the man's appearance.

To call him disheveled would have been a compliment. His greasy black hair was in disarray and he badly needed a shave. An oversize black belt, its worn tip flopping below his waist, held up stained khaki pants. The man's gray shirt may have been white at one time and his tan leather shoes were torn and scuffed. Although of average height, he was overweight and a ponderous beer belly hung over his belt. His hands were thick and there was enough dirt under his fingernails to plant potatoes. He didn't appear to be a man who could be trusted.

He looked closely at Kate and Bebe, wondering why they'd come to his office. He fumbled to recover his composure and assume a business-like demeanor. "Come in, ladies. Please, come in."

Bebe and Kate followed the man into the run down structure and he asked them to have a seat on a tattered sofa in front of his desk. He went behind the desk and sat down in a worn, high-back leather chair.

"My name is Hendrik Lutjens. My nationality is Dutch. And who might you ladies be, if I may ask?"

"My name is Lana," Bebe told him. "This is my friend Ann."

"Of course you are," the man smiled knowingly. He was used to people lying about their names and circumstances. "And you are American, I presume."

"No," Bebe said, aware the man didn't believe her.

"I see," Lutjens replied, smiling cynically. "Well, I've never been particular about details. How may I be of service to you beautiful women?"

"That depends," replied Bebe. "What services do you offer?"

"I have a rather uncommon profession," Lutjens said, his smile exposing tobacco stained teeth. "I provide certain hard to get items for visitors to our fine country."

"What can you provide us?" asked Bebe.

Lutjens hesitated before he spoke, studying the two women closely. "I find it quite odd that two attractive women should suddenly appear at my establishment in the middle of the night. That is every man's dream, but I highly doubt you are here to fulfill my dreams. No, I would guess that you came to the airport tonight seeking a flight out of the country. Would that be correct?"

Bebe stared at him icily, "Perhaps.".

"Alas, there are no airplanes, as you must have observed. Even worse, none are scheduled to fly in here for at least three days. So I would guess you need help in the transportation department. Would I be correct in that assumption?" asked Lutjens.

"Perhaps," said Bebe. "What else do you offer?"

"Let us stop these foolish games," Lutjens said sharply. "I know very well who you are. Every policeman and soldier in the country is looking for you. You killed our police chief and three of his associates, but that is the least of your crimes. You blew up the Ronganai Depot and killed one hundred and sixty-two of our leading citizens. The government is quite unhappy about that."

"Suppose we are who you say, Lutjens. Are you going to help us or not?" Kate held her right hand near the Glock in her belt, anticipating trouble.

Lutjens thought for a moment. "I can get you and your girlfriend out of the country and I can give you passports under your phony names. That is what you want, is it not?"

"How do we know we can trust you?" asked Kate.

"You have no choice, Miss Ann, or whatever you call yourself. But you may be confident I don't want to sully my good name by betraying you. That is all the assurance I can offer. But there is no one else who can provide you with what I just offered."

"We need an airplane to fly us out of here fast," said Bebe. "And we need the passports. How much will that cost us?"

"Normally," Lutjens said, "I would charge ten thousand dollars each. Unfortunately, you have created quite a mess for yourselves. The roads are heavily patrolled. The airport is locked down. Of course, that hardly matters because there are no planes on the ground," he laughed. "And they're scouring the countryside looking for you everywhere. I'm afraid your particular case is especially difficult and brings with it a great deal of risk."

"We know that, Lutjens," Bebe said. "Just tell us what it will cost."

Lutjens lowered his eyes and scribbled on a sheet of torn paper on his desk. He thought for a moment then scribbled some more. He looked at Bebe and Kate. "It will cost you fifty thousand dollars," he said. "Each."

"You're crazy," replied Bebe.

"Take it or leave it," Lutjens said. "And I need it in advance."

Bebe and Kate knew they had no choice but to take a chance on Hendrik Lutjens.

"Do you really think that we're stupid enough to walk around with one hundred thousand dollars in our pockets?" replied Bebe.

"How much do you have?" asked Lutjens.

"I brought five thousand with me tonight. The rest of the money is hidden in the desert," Bebe replied, although she was actually carrying it in her backpack.

"I'm sorry, madam, but five thousand dollars is not enough."

"Alright, Mr. Lutjens," Bebe said as she stood up, "we'll see if we can find someone else to help us. Come on, Ann. Let's go." Kate got up and the two women walked to the door.

"No, wait," Lutjens said. "Five thousand dollars will be fine. But, I must have the other ninety-five thousand dollars in cash tomorrow."

"You'll get it when we board the airplane," Bebe replied. "How soon can we leave?"

"You can leave tomorrow. We must wait until dark. Come here at nine p.m. tomorrow night. Write down the names and addresses you want on the passports," he said, handing Kate a sheet of paper.

Bebe pulled five thousand dollars from her right pocket and handed it to Lutjens. "If you double cross us, you'll never see the rest of the money," Kate said.

"Do you have a place to stay tonight?" Lutjens asked.

"What do you recommend?" asked Kate.

"There's only one decent hotel in town. It's near the center of the city. I'll drive you there and get you a room in my name. You can come into the hotel by the back entrance. Obviously, you must stay under cover."

"You're very kind," said Kate, though she didn't trust Lutjens.

"No, I'm really not madam. I just wish to protect my investment. If you're caught, it will cost me the remaining ninety-five thousand dollars you are going to pay me."

# 33

Present Time   Hoginpuu, Nomgai (North Africa)

Because Hoginpuu wasn't a large city it took only ten minutes for Lutjens to drive Kate and Bebe to the hotel. They waited in Lutjens' car parked behind the hotel while he went inside and registered. He returned shortly and led them up the back stairway to their room on the second floor. "I took the liberty of ordering a hot meal and some wine for you," he said. "I'll wait in the room until they bring your dinner and I can answer the door while you stay out of sight."

As they waited for the food to arrive, Lutjens told them that getting the passports would be easy. And he always had a small four seat airplane on standby in a small village to the south, although he wouldn't say which one. "There would be no problems," he said. "Trust me." Kate and Bebe didn't.

There was a knock on the door and Kate instantly reached for the gun in her belt, but didn't pull it out. Lutjens smiled. "Relax, the food has arrived. Hide in there," he said pointing to the bathroom. The women walked into the bathroom and Kate pulled the door nearly closed, but left a small crack she could peek through and keep an eye on Lutjens.

Bebe and Kate listened closely, their pistols in hand and ready to fire. They heard the room door close as the waiter thanked Lutjens and walked out. Lutjens came to the bathroom door and whispered the all clear. "You can come out now."

Still holding their guns, Kate and Bebe walked out of the bathroom. Lutjens, startled the women were holding pistols, stepped back.

"What's wrong, Mr. Lutjens?" Kate asked. "You look a little pale."

"No, madam, I'm fine," he said. "I was surprised by your guns. That's all."

"We don't like surprises either, Mr. Lutjens," Kate replied, sticking the pistol under her belt. She kept the pistol on her left side so it was within easy reach of her right hand.

"No, I suppose not," he said in a shaky voice. "Anyway, I must be on my way to arrange for the passports and procure the airplane. You will please excuse me, ladies."

"Just a moment, Mr. Lutjens," Kate countered. "Bebe and I appreciate your providing a nice meal and the wine to go with it. Certainly, you will join us for a glass before you leave."

Bebe, like Kate, noticed the wine had been poured into the glasses. She understood Kate's suspicions. Although their acquaintance with Lujens was brief, their distrust of him had grown.

"Thank you, but I'm afraid I must go," Lutjens said.

"But, I insist, Mr. Lutjens," Kate replied. "You must have a glass of wine with us. It's not often two lonely women have the good fortune to be alone in a bedroom with an attractive man like you."

"Oh thank you, madam," Lutjens said, "but I'm in quite a rush to make sure everything is taken care of for you ladies. These things take time, you know."

"You seem nervous, Mr. Lutjens," Kate said.

"Perhaps I'm a bit out of sorts, madam. It is my role to worry until you have escaped and are safe."

"Oh never mind that, Mr. Lutjens," Kate replied. "Now that we're in your capable hands I'm confident we are no longer in any danger. I insist you have a glass of wine."

"No, madam," Lutjens answered. "I appreciate your offer but I really must be on my way."

He turned to leave but Kate moved in front of him and blocked the doorway.

"What are you doing, madam?" Lutjens asked, an anxious expression on his face. He felt a poke in his midsection and looked down to see Kate's Glock sticking in his stomach.

"Give our friend a glass of wine, Bebe," Kate said.

"No," Lutjens said fearfully. "I will not drink the wine."

"You'll drink it or you'll be dead in two seconds," Kate replied angrily.

Bebe handed Kate the full glass of wine. "Drink it now," she ordered, offering the glass to Lutjens.

"Please, madam, he pleaded, refusing to take the glass, "do not make me drink that wine."

"Drink it," Kate demanded.

"Madam, please," Lutjens cried, dropping to his knees. "Please."

"Why won't you drink the wine, Mr. Lutjens?" Kate demanded. "Is it poisoned?"

"No, madam. It is drugged. The police are on their way now. I'm sorry. I have deceived you."

"We're getting used to being deceived since we came to this godforsaken country," Bebe said. "How long do we have before the police arrive?"

Suddenly, they heard the sound of car doors closing in the street immediately below their room. Bebe went over to the window and pulled the curtain back to peek out. "There are six men, Kate," she said.

"Come here, Bebe," Kate said. Bebe walked across the room and Kate handed her Lutjens' glass of wine. "Put it on desk," she said.

Lutjens was still on his knees and Kate placed the barrel of her gun on his forehead. "What do we do, Mr. Lutjens?" she asked.

Panic stricken, he replied, "I don't know. They have come sooner than I thought."

"Get up, you idiot," she ordered. Lutjens quickly rose to his feet. "Bebe, pour most of the wine out of our glasses and put them on the desk near Lutjens' so all three glasses are in view. We need to make them think we drank the wine."

Bebe moved quickly into the bathroom, dumping nearly all the wine out of the two glasses and then placing them on the desk.

"Mr. Lutjens, step into the closet," Kate ordered, gesturing to her right.

Lutjens walked to the mirrored door and slid it back. Kate slammed the handle of her gun on Lutjens' head and he fell forward into the closet. She moved his legs inside the door and closed it. Then she fastened the small security chain on the room door so it would only open a crack when she answered it.

"Bebe, lie down on the bed and face the wall. Have your gun ready. We'll pretend we drank the wine and you've passed out and

I'm drunk."

There was a loud knock on the door. Kate, who was standing by the door, paused. With her gun now stuck in her belt behind her, she yelled, "Whash!" purposely slurring her words.

"This is the police. Open the door," said the man.

"Awright," Kate replied, again slurring her words and pretending to be drunk. She grasped the handle and pulled the door toward her, but the chain prevented it from opening more than three inches.

Feigning an intoxicated expression, Kate looked through the door's three inch opening and said, "Whash do you want? I gotta' go to bed."

"Let us in, madam," the leader demanded.

Kate could see two men standing directly in front of the door. There appeared to be two other men in the hallway standing to the right of the door, but she couldn't see them. Although they said they were the police, they were not wearing uniforms. Bebe had said there were six men in the street. The other two men must be posted downstairs, Kate figured.

"Unlock the chain and open the door," the leader smiled.

Kate slid down to the floor and knelt on her left knee. "Oh my goodness," she slurred, "I think I a little drunk."

The four men were laughing now, believing they were dealing with an intoxicated woman. "Madam," the leader repeated, "open the door."

"Awright," Kate replied, reaching upward for the chain. Still kneeling, she fumbled with the chain, acting like she was having trouble unlocking it. "Jush a minute. I gosh ta shut the door and unhook it," she slurred, gently easing the door closed.

She stood up, unhooked the chain and slowly opened the door. She moved aside, her back slumped against the wall as the first two men entered the room. The other two men stopped at the doorway, one of them using his left foot to hold the door partially open. The half closed door blocked both men from Kate's view.

The two men inside the room were checking it out before the next two entered. The lead man went over to the bed where Bebe lay on her left side facing the wall. She had positioned herself almost completely on her stomach, her right hand clutching a pistol under her chest. "Hey you," the man said, shaking her right shoulder. "Huh," she said, not moving. "Go away." The man laughed and sat down on the bed, his back to Bebe.

The second man sat down at the desk looking at the two nearly empty glasses of wine and the full glass. He smiled. "Hendrik did it again," he laughed, gesturing to the two men in the hallway that it was safe to come in.

The man with his foot against the door pushed it open wider. It's okay, sir," he said, moving aside so the other man, obviously the leader, could walk through the doorway.

"Thank you, Muka," the leader said, walking toward the doorway.

Kate bristled at the sound of this all too familiar voice, instantly reaching for the pistol stuck in the back of her pants as the man walked into the door.

"Darron!" he screamed, lunging for Kate as she brought the pistol around her right side. He grabbed her right arm, attempting to wrest the Glock away from her, but Kate's grip was firm. Though he managed to push her arm slightly downward, Kate pulled the trigger twice. Two shots exploded through the room and the man fell away to the floor. Kate settled for a gut shot, leaving two large holes in his midsection beneath his belt.

The man holding the door had reacted quickly and pulled his gun but Kate had already spun her right arm toward him and fired twice, hitting him in the face and neck, throwing him backward across the hallway.

Bebe, too, had recognized the voice and immediately reacted, pointing her pistol at the man sitting on the bed. She shot him once in the back of his head and he slumped forward, his lifeless body falling to the floor. She pulled the trigger two more times, instantly killing the man sitting at the desk. He had just pulled his gun from its holster when her first bullet went through his right eye socket, knocking him backwards in his chair, his eyeball hanging on his cheek. The second bullet had entered his heart, "for insurance," Bebe later said.

Bebe jumped from the bed and reached underneath to grab the backpack with the money. Kate quickly pulled open the closet door and searched Lutjens' pants pocket for his car keys. "Got 'em," she said. They walked over to the leader lying near the door.

"You gut-shot me, you bitch," he gasped. "The hospitals here are crap. I'll die."

Kate and Bebe looked down at the bloody holes in the man's

pants. There was a noticeable lump underneath his belt. "Your guts are spilling out through the bullet holes," Kate said. "That's the trouble with a gut shot, Captain Max Brumfeld." Or is it Dr. Horst Lange? Or is it Patrice Betaine?"

"I should have killed you both when I had the chance," he blurted, his mouth twisting in pain.

"We'd love to stay and chat, Captain Brumfeld, but we really must go," Kate replied, aiming her gun at his forehead.

"Go ahead," he said weakly. "Pull the trigger."

"Kate, hurry up. We gotta go," Bebe said anxiously.

Brumfeld smiled. "See you another time."

"I don't think so" Kate replied bitterly.

"I know a secret about the wheel," he gasped.

"What wheel?" Kate asked.

"Kate!" Bebe exclaimed. "We gotta' go."

Brumfeld grimaced. "You don't know, do you?"

"Kate!" Bebe yelled firmly.

Kate looked toward Bebe then back at Brumfeld. She squeezed the trigger and the gunshot boomed in the small room, leaving a pencil-sized red hole in the middle of Brumfeld's forehead. Kate fired two more bullets into his heart to make sure he was dead. His body momentarily convulsed then stopped, his lifeless eyes frozen in a hollow stare.

The two women ran out the door, pulling it shut behind them. They reached the back stairs and had started down when a man rushed through the back door and began running up the steps. Kate shot him through the chest and he slumped, tumbling backwards down the four steps he just climbed. Kate and Bebe ran through the back door to Lutjens' car.

Bebe opened the driver side door and Kate jumped in on the passenger side. She would cover their escape. As Bebe drove the car through the hotel parking lot to the main street, Kate told her to turn right. "We're going west?" Bebe asked, pulling onto the road.

"There's no use going to the airport," Kate said.

"I know," Bebe replied. "Where do you think we should head?"

They travelled several blocks and passed three policemen on motorcycles racing to the hotel. Kate had ducked down so it appeared only one person was in the car.

"How much gas do we have?" Kate aksed.

"It has about a quarter of a tank. It won't get us far," Bebe answered.

"Keep going west. Let's see if we can find some gas," Kate said.

Luckily, the traffic wasn't heavy and they didn't see any other policemen as Bebe drove the car down the main road.

"They'll be looking for us all over town," Bebe said.

She didn't speed, keeping the car at thirty-five miles per hour to avoid suspicion. As they drove further on the main road, there were fewer houses and lights. Soon there were none. They were in open country now and Bebe accelerated to fifty miles per hour. The dirt road had so many potholes she didn't dare go faster to avoid breaking an axle or wrecking the car. Unfortunately, they hadn't seen any place to buy gas. Bebe figured they could get fifty miles at most.

"Bebe, this road will take us to the archeological dig site or Tsugano's airport. That small plane stored inside the hangar looked like it was operable. If we can make it to the airport, we might be able to get that plane in the air."

"It's our best shot," said Bebe.

"It's our only shot," replied Kate.

Bebe kept the car's speed at fifty miles per hour. She wanted to conserve all the fuel she could, however she didn't want to travel too slowly in case the police were chasing them. If she saw lights coming behind them she would have to speed up.

An hour passed and the car had been running on empty for the last fifteen minutes. "Look," Bebe said, "it's the turn-off for the airport." Bebe turned right onto the dirt road. As the car passed over the top of the ridge, the engine began missing and the car started to lurch, indicating it was out of gas. The car was traveling down the small slope from the ridge to the airport when the engine died. Bebe quickly shifted into neutral and the car continued to coast for a few hundred feet then slowly rolled to a stop.

Bebe switched off the car lights and the women got out and began running toward the airport buildings. Without the car lights, they could barely see the ground on which they ran. The office porch light was on, but the area around the hangar area was completely dark.

They stopped two hundred yards from the runway to check things out. There was no sign of anyone near the office. Looking toward the hangar, they strained their eyes to see through the darkness, but all they could make out was that the big doors were closed. They ran toward the office in a wide circle, ending up near the window on the east side of the small building. They listened, but heard nothing. Kate whispered to Bebe to cover the front door, but to stay out of the light. Kate walked silently around to the back. She listened at the back door, but there was no sound. She kicked the back door open and moved aside in case gunfire came from the building. There was nothing.

Then Kate heard a commotion at the front door. She kicked open the office door and ran into the building. The light was on and Bebe was pointing her gun at a soldier who had been left to guard the place. He'd been sleeping inside the office. Apparently, he was the only one there. He couldn't speak English and they couldn't understand anything he said, but he gestured that he was alone. They tied the soldier up and headed for the hangar.

They cautiously walked to the hangar, crept inside, and turned on the lights at the west end, pointedly not switching on the big overhead lights. They were alone. They ran across the hangar to the small airplane still parked near the back wall at its northeast corner. She climbed into the plane and turned the switch. The plane was full of gas and ready to go. As they figured, it must have been Manus Tsugano's personal airplane.

"Kate," Bebe said, jumping out of the plane and slipping off the backpack. She quickly took a small stack of money out of the backpack and gave it to Kate. "You go over to the hangar doors and push them open and I'll hide the backpack in the back of the plane."

Bebe pulled open the airplane's luggage compartment behind the second row of seats. Using a screwdriver from a nearby mechanic's bench, she removed the back interior panel of the luggage compartment and stuffed the backpack with the money into the opening. She quickly replaced the panel and climbed back into the cockpit. Customs might have a problem with a quarter million dollars in cash, she figured.

Bebe started the engine and released the brakes, then carefully steered the airplane across the hangar floor. Kate had only opened one of the hangar's doors because of the plane's small size. As Bebe carefully moved the airplane forward, Kate waved to guide her as the airplane rolled from the hangar to the outside ramp. Kate ran around the right wing and climbed into the cockpit.

"We're on our way," Bebe smiled, as she slowly pushed the throttle forward. Kate was smiling too. "I wasn't sure we'd make it," she said, as Bebe turned the plane to line up with the runway.

Suddenly, they were blinded by bright spotlights shining directly at them from fifty yards up the runway. A second set of spotlights appeared on their left. They could see the lights of half a dozen vehicles moving down the ridge. Two helicopters swooped in from the north and were hovering above them, the circles of their spotlights moving back and forth across the ground.

# 34

Present Time     Nomgai (North Africa)

Bebe and Kate cupped their hands over their eyes trying to see outside the cockpit. A dozen uniformed men with rifles were walking toward their airplane. An officer holding a pistol was gesturing to shut off the airplane's engine. Bebe turned the engine switch and the propeller spun to a stop.

"Get out with your hands up," the officer called. "Do exactly as you are told or we will fire."

Bebe and Kate looked at each other then turned and got out their respective doors. Two soldiers, their rifles leveled and ready to fire, cautiously approached each of the women. The other eight soldiers stood next to the officer, their rifles aimed directly at Kate and Bebe.

The soldiers took the women's Glocks and searched them for other weapons. Kate and Bebe each had a smaller gun strapped to their ankles underneath their jeans. They were easy to find. The soldiers told the women to put their hands behind them and slipped handcuffs on their wrists. They ordered Kate and Bebe to walk toward the officer and the other eight soldiers.

"You have caused us a great deal of trouble," the officer said. "We shall repay you accordingly." A windowless white van drove up and stopped nearby. The driver got out and opened the vehicle's back doors. The officer, who hadn't given his name, nodded to the four soldiers guarding Kate and Bebe. They pushed the women toward the van, and when they reached it, gestured for them to step inside. The four soldiers then climbed in.

There were two benches, each running parallel to a side-wall of the van and facing each other. Kate sat one of the benches and Bebe the other. Both of them had a soldier sitting on each side. It was dark inside the vehicle and the women couldn't see anything. Bebe started to say something, but a soldier yelled at her to be quiet. The van was speeding to somewhere and they weren't anxious to arrive.

Bebe wondered if Kate was thinking about what was going to happen to them. There wasn't going to be any escape from this one. At best, they'd be held for ransom, which the United States would never pay, because no one other than OSTRO knew who they were. Their most likely fate was to be tortured and killed. Maybe they'd be put on public trial and then executed. Whatever their fate, the future was looking grim.

Kate was also thinking about their situation. The best time to escape is immediately after capture. She learned that in OSTRO's training program. That was great strategy, except she and Bebe were both handcuffed and sitting between two guards, both much bigger and stronger than either of them.

Kate figured they were being taken to Hoginpuu to be held in some maximum-security prison. The odds of escaping from that didn't look too promising either. Once they reached their destination, they would no doubt be separated so they wouldn't be able to communicate

For a moment, Bebe thought she could slip her right hand out of the handcuff. She twisted her arm and turned her wrist, but it was no use. The handcuffs were too tight. Kate, too, tried to squeeze her hand out of the cuffs, but her luck was no better than Bebe's.

Suddenly, the van screeched to a stop as gunfire broke out. The driver slammed the van into reverse, frantically backing away to turn the vehicle around. Bebe and Kate felt the back of the vehicle drop as the van backed into the steep ditch on the side of the road. The engine raced loudly as the wheels spun, but the vehicle couldn't move. "Get down," Bebe screamed, and she and Kate threw themselves to the floor.

The gunfire had quickly become heavier and explosions burst on every side, one rocking the van. A soldier opened the van's rear doors and three of them jumped out, leaving one man to guard Kate and Bebe. They didn't shut the van doors but a nearby blast slammed one the doors so hard that it hit the door frame with a metallic boom and bounced back, ripping from its hinges.

"Get out," Bebe yelled to the soldier. "We gotta' get out of this thing. They're gonna' blow it up you idiot."

"You stay," he said, pointing his rifle at the women.

"If we don't get out of this van, we're gonna' die, Bebe said to Kate.

"You be quiet," the soldier yelled, shaking his rifle to underscore his point. Kate noticed he was shaking.

Bebe and Kate could see little of what was happening outside. In the random flashes of gunfire and explosions they could see men running, but they could make no sense of it. Suddenly, the soldier jumped from the van and began to run. He got only a few steps when he screamed and fell to the ground.

"Now's our chance," said Bebe. "He's got the keys to the handcuffs. She struggled, quickly rising to stand. Kate got up and the two women moved to the back of the van. Knowing the van had backed into the ditch, they wanted to see where they would land when they jumped. The explosions, mortar fire they figured, had died down. They were waiting for a flash and one finally came as a mortar round exploded nearby.

"You see it, Kate," Bebe whispered.

"Go for it," Kate said, and they both jumped. The ditch was narrow and its far side was only a foot away from the van's bumper. It was an easy jump and the women landed on their feet, but immediately dove to the ground. The gunfire had lessened, but was still heavy.

They crawled on their stomachs to the dead soldier's body and Bebe backed against it, straining in the handcuffs to stick her hand into his pants pocket. Several seconds passed as she searched each of his pockets. "Got it," she gasped, finally locating the key in his back pocket.

Bebe rolled over on the dusty ground and moved against Kate, passing the handcuff keys to her. "Unlock my cuffs, Kate; then I'll unlock yours. And snatch the soldier's pistol."

Moments later they were crawling on their stomachs, moving as quickly as they could to leave the gunfire behind. They had gotten several hundred yards when they decided it was safe to stand up and run. They crouched low, running as quickly as possible through the darkness. Finally, with the sound of the battle far behind, they sat down on a rock to rest. "We got lucky," Bebe said panting. "I thought we bought the farm."

"Huh," Kate said. Bebe laughed.

"I mean I thought it was all over for us. It's an old expression," Bebe said.

"You need to learn some new ones if you're going to live in modern times," Kate replied laughing.

"Bebe shrugged. "We'll see."

There was a rustle of bushes behind them. Kate spun and dropped to her right knee, holding the soldier's pistol in front of her.

"Put your gun on the ground," a voice ordered. "You are surrounded."

Bebe desperately peered into the darkness, looking for a place to duck into or run, but she could see nothing. "Put down your gun," the voice again ordered. Bebe and Kate could hear other men moving in the brush. They were surrounded. Kate dropped the gun on the ground and men moved through the darkness toward where they crouched.


Six heavily armed black men stood around Kate and Bebe. In the moon's dim light, the women could see the men weren't wearing uniforms and their clothes were worn and dirty. Obviously, they weren't military. Though rough looking and crude, they appeared to be seasoned fighters. They must be part of the group that attacked the military convoy carrying Kate and Bebe to Hoginpuu. And they must have won.

One of the men checked Kate and Bebe for weapons, and none too gently, tied their hands behind their backs. They put cloth covers over the women's faces. As they began to walk, men on each side of the women grasped their arms to lead them through the desert.

They were walking for approximately ten minutes and stopped. Bebe and Kate heard the sound of an animal snorting and suddenly felt themselves being lifted onto the backs of horses. They felt the animals move forward in an evenly paced but rapid walk. They were moving quickly, probably to avoid military reinforcements and helicopters.

It seemed as if they travelled several hours, but it was hard to tell how far they'd gone. They felt the animals moving up and down uneven ground and sometimes stumbling. The ride was uncomfortable and the smelly cloth masks over their heads made it even more unpleasant. Suddenly they stopped and men lifted them down from the horses.

Men grasped Bebe and Kate's arms and led them up a rocky path. They could now hear other men talking and laughing. One of the men holding Bebe's arm knocked on a wooden door. The women could hear it open and sensed they were being led inside. The men pulled the masks from the women's heads, inadvertently yanking Kate's hair in the process. It hurt, but she made no sound.

Kate and Bebe struggled to adjust their eyes to the light. Once they did, they saw they were in a room with approximately twenty men sitting around a large U-shaped table. They were led to the center of the main table, and with tables full of men on each side, stood facing the apparent leader of the group. It was an intimidating situation. Bebe and Kate had concluded the men who captured them were rebels. Jack Farley had warned that the rebels were even more brutal than the regime's military. It appeared they jumped from the frying pan into the fire.

Kate and Bebe watched the leader closely as he looked them over. "Who are you?" he asked.

"My name is Lana and she is Ann," Bebe replied, using the names on their passports.

"They are liars," a voice shouted from the corner of the room in back of the center table. "They are Americans and they blew up the Ronganai Depot."

Kate and Bebe recognized the voice. It was Hendrik Lutjens. We really have jumped into the fire, Kate thought, as Hendrik Lutjens walked from the shadows to where the leader sat.

"The Americans will pay good money to get them back," Lutjens smiled. "The Nomgai government will also pay good money for them."

Kate and Bebe hadn't thought about it, but now realized it had to be Lutjens that sent the Nomgai military to Tsugano's airport to catch them. He knew they needed a plane and the only one in the vicinity was Tsugano's personal plane.

"You double-crossing SOB, Kate yelled. That's twice you sold us out."

Lutjens laughed. "I actually sold you out three times, ladies. I told our friends here where to find you. Like I told you, I'm in a rather curious profession.

Kate and Bebe glared at Lutjens.

"I am Tarsus Mudja," the leader of the group said abruptly. "I don't really care about your names, however, I am greatly indebted to you." He signaled to a nearby female attendant and whispered in her ear and she hurried away.

Kate and Bebe looked at each other puzzled, wondering what this man was talking about. They looked at Lutjens. He suddenly looked worried.

"Hey ladies," sounded an immediately recognizable female voice. The female attendant had returned with someone they knew well. It was Mama Paloo!

Kate and Bebe stared as Mama Paloo walked to the center table to join her son, Tarsus Mudja. "Mama said you saved her life. I cannot thank you enough," he said. Bebe smiled, remembering she shot the three soldiers who had come to the village to kill Mama Paloo.

"We will eat," Tarsus Mudja said. "Then we will shoot Hendrik Lutjens."

"Oh no, sir, please," Lutjens screamed. "Please do not kill me."

Tarsus Mudja waved his arm and two of his men hauled Hendrik Lutjens from the room. "Sit down," he said. "After we eat I will have my men take you back to Tsugano's airport and you can get his airplane. My men are attacking an outpost near Hoginpuu so the military will be too busy to bother you again. I will have plenty of my men with you as a precaution however."

Bebe and Kate sat down across the table from Tarsus Mudja and Mama Paloo. "Are you really you really going to kill Hendrik Lutjens?" Kate asked.

Tarsus Mudja looked at Kate and Bebe. "He tried to get you killed three times. Is shooting him not the just thing to do?"

"Would you do us a favor?' asked Kate."

"Of course," Mudja answered. "What would you like?"

"Just give Lutjens a very bad scare and let him go."

Tarsus Mudja laughed. "Alright, if that's what you want."

"How you feel?" Mama Paloo asked Bebe.

# 35

Present Time     Tumburu, Goriana  (North Africa)

Dinner with Tarsus Mudja and Mama Paloo lasted into the early morning hours. It was too late to travel and Tarsus Mudja had Bebe and Kate stay overnight. It was dusk the following day when they started the three-hour trip to Tsugano's airport. Bebe and Kate had been anxious to get started, but they had become attached to Mama Paloo. It was tough saying goodbye to her.

As Tarsus Mudja promised, fifty of his men accompanied Kate and Bebe to the airport. They travelled by horseback.

The fifty mounted warriors watched as Bebe started the airplane's single engine and slowly taxied it to the front of the hangar and through the open door. Kate jumped in and Bebe rolled the plane to the dirt strip and stopped.

They waved a final goodbye to the men and Bebe pushed the throttle forward to begin their takeoff. The plane quickly picked up speed and lifted off in a few seconds. They had climbed to one thousand feet and Bebe turned the airplane to fly northeast. The plane was flying at one hundred miles per hour and they would reach Tumburu in less than three hours.

Bebe told Kate she had moved the five million dollars from the original Swiss account to a different one so that Scoggins couldn't trace it. Once they got to a safe haven they should be able to live comfortably.

Everything seemed to be going nicely however both women had the feeling that all was not well.  Bebe was the first to mention it.

"Kate, I just can't get rid of this foreboding that we don't have everything covered. Dan Scoggins and Jack Farley are smart guys. You know they must have backup plans for everything they do. I just have a bad feeling."

"What do you mean?" asked Kate. She knew Bebe had a sixth sense about impending danger but Kate, too, was unsettled.

"We think we've fooled them but I wonder if we really have," Bebe replied. "I mean that bomb to blow up our airplane was in plain sight. They must have figured we would see it and figure out what it was. They also might have figured we would set the target sighting device so we could bail out. I mean they gave us the information on how to do that exact thing. I just don't know if we've fooled them or ourselves."

"Bebe, I wish you wouldn't over-think things so much, but it's a good thing that you do. I have the same thoughts as you. I can't get rid of the feeling that OSTRO has something more in store for us. I don't think they even know we're still alive, but there is a way for them to track us."

"How could they do that?" asked Bebe. Coming from the 1940's, Bebe hadn't yet gotten up to date on current high tech gadgets.

"They could have a GPS device somewhere in our belongings or even inside of our bodies. It's the same as the targeting equipment they put in the B-17. It's a device that tells you and others where you're located. They could track us that way." Bebe was shocked, having never heard of such a thing.

Both women thought for a moment. They had left all their belongings at the archaeological dig site, assuming they would return. But Kate still had the cell phone. She pulled off the back of the phone and took out the battery, then tossed all three pieces out the airplane's window. They would check their clothes and shoes when they landed to see if they could find anything that would indicate OSTRO was tracking them. If they're tracking us through GPS, they already know we're alive and where we are," said Kate.

The flight to Tumburu, Goriana was fast and smooth. They arrived at three a.m. When they landed, they taxied their small plane up to the operations office and went inside. The people were especially friendly, and since Goriana was in a state of war with Nomgai, there was no danger of their being sent back from where they had just come. The agents at the operations office quickly checked the passports provided by Lutjens and told Kate and Bebe to have a nice visit. They had decided to use the phony passports in order to stay under the radar and, hopefully, not be detected by OSTRO.

Tumburu, unlike Hoginpuu, was a friendly place, the women happily discovered. However, Kate and Bebe were keenly aware that, as two American white women, they had been very conspicuous in the small city of Hoginpuu which had a nearly one hundred percent black population. And they would be conspicuous here too. Also, and even more alarming, their shooting of the four men at the hotel in Hoginpuu was surely picked up by Washington. OSTRO would have to be blind to not immediately connect the dots and conclude Bebe and Kate were still alive. They could only keep their fingers crossed and hope luck was on their side.

Kate and Bebe took a taxi to the Tumburu Palace, the nicest hotel in the city. It turned out to be luxurious for this part of the world. Bebe and Kate registered under their assumed names, hoping the deception they pulled off was successful and they had tricked OSTRO.

They were pleasantly surprised when they opened the door to their room. It was even more luxurious than the lobby of the hotel. They were exhausted and the two huge beds were inviting. There was a bottle of wine on the dresser, but they were also starved. Although reluctant to leave the extravagantly appointed room, they decided to have breakfast. Besides, the dining room was also gorgeous. They went downstairs to see if they could get something to eat this early in the morning.

"You know, Kate, maybe we should stay here for a while," suggested Bebe.

"I think that's a very good idea," replied Kate.

As Kate and Bebe enjoyed their early breakfast they reflected on their situation. They had two hundred and fifty thousand dollars in cash from Manus Tsugano and five million dollars in a Swiss bank. They should be able to relax for quite awhile.

"I do like this place," Bebe remarked smiling.

"You said that already," replied Kate.

"But, I really like it. I'd like to stay for a long time," Bebe laughed.

The two women finished breakfast and slowly walked upstairs to their room.

"I think I'll sleep for twenty-four hours," said Kate.

"That sounds good to me."

At one p.m. the next day Kate was the first to wake. She sat up and looked over at Bebe still asleep in the other bed. Her head lay on the pillow, her un-brushed blond hair, making her look like a Greek goddess. What a beautiful woman, Kate thought.

"You're a beautiful woman," she whispered to the sleeping Bebe.

"So are you," Bebe replied, as she rolled over on her back.

"So get up and let's do something," Kate laughed.

"Let's sleep one more hour," answered Bebe.

"Okay," Kate agreed.

They awoke two hours later at three p.m. "Good morning, once again," Kate said.

"Good morning," replied Bebe. "I'm starved. Do you feel like eating?"

Bebe and Kate jumped out of their beds to get ready for the day, but it was four p.m. before they were ready to leave the room. The day was nearly over so they headed for the bar to have a drink, which they felt they richly deserved. Kate went through her laborious martini building process while Bebe ordered a Glenlivet Scotch. Their drinks came quickly and the two women toasted each other and smiled happily. They lingered with the drinks for a while and then ordered a second round.

"I could get used to this life," said Kate.

"I'm already used to it," replied Bebe.

Bebe looked at Kate who was staring at her drink. "Something has been bothering you, Kate. What's wrong?"

Kate looked up, a distressed expression on her face. "Bebe, we were killed when our B-17 crashed in 1942." We were dead, Bebe. Dead. So how can we be alive now? My god, you must have thought about that."

"I did, Kate. I've thought about it often. I don't know the answer to your question. Thinking about it scares me. I'm just glad that we are alive."

"Bebe, I keep remembering what Captain Brumfeld said just

before I shot him. Did you hear him?"

"I was standing in the hallway watching for his friends and I couldn't hear you two talking. What did he say?"

"Bebe, he told me he would see me another time. I was about to put a bullet in his head and he told me he would see me another time. That's crazy."

Bebe laughed. "Come on, Kate. I saw you put three bullets into him. He was dead, period and end of report, as they say."

"Is that what's bothering you?" Bebe asked.

"That's part of it. He also said he knew a secret about a wheel. Does that make any sense to you?"

"I have no idea what he was talking about."

The head waiter walked up to where they sat. "Your table is ready, mesdames," he said.

They walked into the dining room and the headwaiter led them to their table. They had asked for the quiet one in the corner and soon were sitting across from each other enjoying themselves. There was absolutely nothing to complain about. The food was wonderful and the service was great.

"I hope it can be like this forever, Kate," smiled Bebe.

"Don't worry, it will be," said Kate, as she lifted her martini glass.

"To us," Bebe toasted.

"To us," smiled Kate. "Here's hoping we have them fooled."

As they set their drinks down, the headwaiter approached their table.

"Madame Ann, please," he whispered, looking directly at Kate.

"Yes, I'm Ann Haskins," Kate replied, responding to the fictitious name on her passport. "What is it?"

"The front desk received a fax for you, Miss Haskins."

"What's a fax?" asked Bebe.

"I'll explain in a moment," said Kate apprehensively. "Damn, they've found us," she whispered to Bebe.

The headwaiter handed the fax message to Kate. She unfolded it and held it so Bebe could also read the message.

"Good job, girls!" it said. "It was a little messy because you screwed things up and survived and caused me to lose my one hundred dollar bet with Jack Farley. He told me you would find the bomb we planted on the airplane. I bet that you wouldn't and that it would kill you, but you girls are really good. I'm mad at you for costing me one hundred dollars though. Just kidding. Sorry about the bomb. It was just another little test.

Welcome back to the team. Enjoy yourselves for a few weeks. By the way, we've got a little problem in the South Pacific, but it's an easy job. I'll need you in my office in exactly thirty days. Signed, Dan Scoggins."

Bebe and Kate looked at each other and shook their heads in disgust.

"They bet one hundred dollars on our lives," said Kate. "The whole thing is a game to them."

Bebe looked at the glass of Glenlivet Scotch in her left hand, momentarily pondering their situation. Lifting her glass, she smiled. Kate raised her glass and touched it to Bebe's.

"I know what you're thinking," Kate grinned.

Bebe took a sip of her drink. "We can play the game too."

*About the Author*

James Wharton's books include:

*Detour*
*The Destiny Project*
*The Jaguar Queen*
*Deluxe UFO Tour Company*
*Voyeurs*
*Ghost Pets*
*Strange Breakfast & Other Humorous Morsels*
*Ghosts of the Grand Canyon Country*
*Ghosts of Arizona's Tonto National Forest*
*Invasion of the Moon Women*

**www.jameswharton.net**

I highly value my reader's satisfaction and would be most appreciative if you could take the time to write a few comments and let me know your opinion.

It's a very simple process:
Go to Amazon.com

1. Type in The Destiny Project
2. Click on the picture of the book
3. Click on Customer Reviews
4. Click on Create your own review

**The Destiny Project II is coming in late 2013!**

Made in the USA
San Bernardino, CA
26 February 2014